Eight At The Lake

Books by J.L. and Lin Stepp

The Afternoon Hiker
Discovering Tennessee State Parks
Exploring South Carolina State Parks
Coming next – Visiting North Carolina State Parks
Traveling Georgia State Parks

Books by Lin Stepp

The Smoky Mountain Series

The Foster Girls *Tell Me About Orchard Hollow*
For Six Good Reasons *Delia's Place*
Second Hand Rose *Down by the River*
Makin' Miracles *Saving Laurel Springs*
Welcome Back *Daddy's Girl*
Lost Inheritance *The Interlude*

The Mountain Home Books
Happy Valley
Downsizing
Eight at the Lake
Coming next – Seeking Ayita
Shop on the Corner

Christmas Novella
A Smoky Mountain Gift
In *When the Snow Falls*

The Edisto Trilogy
Claire at Edisto
Return to Edisto
Edisto Song

The Lighthouse Sisters Series
Light the Way
Coming next –
Lighten My Heart
Light in the Dark
The Light Continues

Eight At The Lake

A MOUNTAIN HOME NOVEL

LIN STEPP

Cover design: Katherine E. Stepp
Interior design: J. L. Stepp, Mountain Hill Press
Editor: Elizabeth S. James
Cover photo and map design: Lin M. Stepp

Library of Congress Cataloging-in-Publication Data

Stepp, Lin
Eight At The Lake: A Mountain Home novel / Lin Stepp
         p. cm – (The Smoky Mountain series)

ISBN: 979-8-9853681-0-9
First Mountain Hill Press Trade Paperback Printing: April 2022

eISBN: 979-8-9853681-1-6
First Mountain Hill Press Electronic Edition: April 2022

1. Women—Southern States—Fiction   2. Mountain life—Great Smoky Mountains Region (NC and TN)—Fiction. 3. Contemporary Romance—Inspirational—Fiction. I. Title

Library of Congress Control Number: 2022900702

DEDICATION

This book is dedicated to all our fans who live in or near Dandridge, Tennessee … and to all our readers who kept saying, "Lin, write another book with a whole lot of kids in it, like your book *For Six Good Reasons!*" I listened!

ACKNOWLEDGEMENTS

"Don't let the sun go down without saying Thank You to someone." – Stephen King

Gratitude and thanks to everyone in Dandridge, Tennessee, who helped and encouraged us with this book, sharing area history and personal stories to give me ways to make this book as special as this charming small town.

Special thanks to The Dandridge Visitors Center and the Dandridge Memorial Public Library where I collected helpful literature and brochures, a walking tour guide, books, and personal tips and information when visiting the city.

Thanks especially to all the individuals we met downtown while exploring the city who made us feel welcome and shared stories and area information with us, like at: Dandridge Mercantile, Tinsley Bible Drug Company, The Shoppes at Roper Mansion, Shepard Inn, Appalachian Yarn Company, Hynds House or Maxwell House, and many others.

Gratitude also to A. J. Bush & Company, its Visitor Center and General Store, that we enjoyed visiting in Dandridge and to all the friendly staff we met on our tour and trip to this well-known local industry.

Final thanks to nearby spots that found their way into the book … Cosby Campground and the Elkmont Campground in the Great Smoky Mountains and Douglas Lake and Douglas Dam. A little tribute, also, to all the quaint historic bed and breakfasts and wonderful resorts we've visited around Tennessee that inspired Aunt Dixie's downtown Dandridge Inn and the charming Sycamore Lake Resort belonging to Ford's family.

Acknowledgements to all those who helped with this book:
- Elizabeth S. James, copyeditor and editorial advisor
- J.L. Stepp, production design and proofing
- Pat Werths, final proof reader
- Katherine Stepp, cover design and graphics
- And ongoing gratitude to the Lord, who helps me in all my books.

Sycamore Lake Resort Map
WOODS
COVE LOOP
RIDGE TRAIL
The Cove
WOODS
COVE BOAT DOCK
COVE CABINS
shed
Cove Point
GARDEN
BARN
DOCK ROAD
COVE LOOP
McDANIEL FARMHOUSE
RUSTIC GAZEBO
POOL
McDANIEL LODGE
FIELD
SYCAMORE LAKE ROAD
WOODS
FENCE
HIGHWAY

HIGHPOINT TRAIL

OVERLOOK

WOODS

Park area

Chapel

Pavilion

SYCAMORE Point Event Lodge

Sycamore Point

DOCK

Sycamore Lake

Sycamore Lake Trail

COVE PAVILION

SWIM BEACH

Raft

WOODS

Walk Bridge

BEACH POINT

Pavilion

PLAYGROUND

BIKES

BEACH POINT LANE

WILLOW Point

HOUSE at WILLOW POINT

Store Trail

VET'S OFFICE

CHAPTER 1

Samantha, wired and ready for the next broadcast update, walked from under the concrete building where she and her crew stayed into the howling wind and sheeting rain of the incoming hurricane. She ducked chunks of flying debris as she made her way across the road, now ankle deep in water. With the storm strengthening rapidly by the minute, this would probably be the last broadcast from outside. They'd shoot the rest of their coverage from a covered balcony in the hotel where she'd step out to give her report from relative safety.

Hoisting herself onto the low seawall between the road and the beach behind it, Samantha spread her legs to steady herself, keeping her eyes on her camera crew for their signal. The roaring of the wind drowned out all other noise and the incoming rain, blowing horizontally off the ocean now, beat against her back. The storm had strengthened in intensity and Samantha's ears popped with the dropping air pressure. Hearing her lead-in on her headset to begin, her heartbeat quickened and she felt the familiar adrenalin rush that always accompanied her job.

"This is Samantha King with Weather First at Mexico Beach, Florida, where Hurricane Michael is moving in to make landfall," she said, raising her voice to be heard above the wind. "The storm has now become a dangerous Category 5 hurricane, stronger than initially expected, and this small coastal town is battling for its life as this powerful storm moves in."

She paused as a rolling gust of wind smacked her full force and a blast of sea spray doused her from behind as a wave crashed on the beach. "As you can see, debris is flying in the air now, flooding is beginning, and there are already power outages in most all coastal areas with lines down and the ferocity of the wind breaking out windows and ripping off roofs."

As she spoke, the roof of a beach home across the street was jerked from the house and tossed into the air, the entire house then ripped off its pilings, tumbling apart before her eyes with a thunderous crash. The camera panned to catch the sight, giving Samantha a moment to wipe the rain from her face and spread her legs further apart to brace herself in the gale.

"With Hurricane Michael intensifying and the storm winds now over 155 MPH, this will be our last broadcast outdoors," she continued, listening to instructions on her headset as the camera returned to her. "If you are in this vicinity please take cover immediately."

A telephone pole crashed to the ground to her right and Samantha turned to describe the scene, watching a towering sea wave wash over a parked car down the street, flipping it on its side. As she shifted back to face her camera crew, a loose street sign, flying wildly in the wind, slammed into her left side, tearing into her arm and leg, and smacking her off the wall.

She flew into the air to fall and hit the rocks and sand below, struggling as she landed to roll over and regain her footing. A monster wave battered into her from behind as she tried to stand, tossing her in its hold and slinging her into the sea wall.

Over the sound of the wind, and hardly able to move now, she heard the crew scrambling over the wall, coming for her and calling. She clutched the edge of a rock beside her, trying to hold on until they could reach her.

"Jackie. Arnie. Over here," she yelled, knowing they could hardly see her in the driving rain with the surf swirling and pummeling around her.

And then she felt hands and heard a voice.

"Wake up, Samantha. You're dreaming."

Gulping in breaths of air, heart racing, Samantha opened her eyes to see her Aunt Dixie patting her face, speaking soothing words.

"You're okay, dear." Her aunt smiled. "Safe and well in the same little bed you grew up in. You were only having a bad dream."

It took a minute for Samantha to shift from the dream's hold and then she sighed and closed her eyes for a moment. "I was back in the storm, covering the hurricane at Mexico Beach, reliving that fall," she explained.

"Well, you survived that fall and all the recovery that followed, and now you're fine and nearly back to yourself."

"*Nearly* is the appropriate word." Samantha made a face. "I still have some pretty bad dreams sometimes."

"Who wouldn't? I saw that coverage if you remember." Dixie frowned at the memory. "I think I aged five years watching you tumble over that sea wall."

Samantha groaned. "The whole world got to witness that humiliating scene, watched me blow off that sea wall like a piece of flying storm debris."

Aunt Dixie sat down on the side of Samantha's bed. "Be assured no one felt anything but sympathy for you. Everyone sat watching with growing horror the ferocity of that storm—tearing up houses all around you, crashing down telephone poles, and throwing cars around like tinker toys." She shook her head. "They never should have let you out in that."

"The hurricane escalated in force. We were getting ready to pull in. I wouldn't have gone into the storm again except on a balcony and maybe not at all. That hurricane literally destroyed that beach town, Aunt Dixie. I couldn't believe the coverage I saw of Mexico Beach after. It looked like a war zone—buildings and homes totally annihilated and demolished. Nothing but rubble and massive piles of debris for miles. Many people lost absolutely everything. That town still hasn't recovered."

"Nature can be a cruel thing." Aunt Dixie smoothed back Samantha's hair in the familiar way she'd always done to comfort her since Samantha was a little girl. "Do you want me to go get you a glass of milk?"

"No, I'm good now. Sorry I woke you."

"Not a problem. Sometimes the bad times of our lives revisit us, perhaps to remind us we survived them, that we're tough and still here."

"That's a good thought. You always have a way of making me feel better about things."

She patted Samantha's shoulder. "Then I'm glad you're here with me for a while until you're ready to go back to work."

Samantha scowled. "The network doesn't want me back until fall, even though I feel great now. It will be nearly a year by then since the hurricane."

"The work you do as a storm chaser is highly physical and mentally challenging. You know you need to be in top form to do the job."

"Yes, but I'm totally fine now." She gave her aunt a mulish look.

Aunt Dixie raised her eyebrows. "Hmmm. Let's see. Fourteen days in the hospital, almost two months in that rehab center, then ongoing outpatient rehabilitation this winter and spring. And now suddenly you're quibbling over a little designated time to strengthen and fully get your health back." Dixie paused. "Samantha, be honest with yourself. You know all this hospital and rehabilitation time took a lot out of you."

"I know." Samantha frowned. "I'm simply impatient. I miss my work; I miss my life. I hate this waiting period."

"I know, but quit worrying about it." Dixie straightened Samantha's covers. "The station assured you they would take you back. You're too good for them not to want you back. You've built a name nationally."

"I hope that's true and that Weather First won't stick me back in the studio doing daily forecasts when I go back."

Dixie smiled. "I remember when you loved those at one time."

Samantha glanced at the clock, not answering. "You need to go back to bed, Aunt Dixie. You have guests at the inn and you need to get up early to do breakfast."

She waved a hand dismissively. "I put two breakfast casseroles together before I went to bed, cut up some fruit, and made cinnamon rolls. I only need to pop everything into the oven in the morning."

"You make it sound easy but I know it's work."

"It's work I enjoy though. You should know well enough I've always loved running my inn." She leaned over to give Samantha a kiss on the forehead as she stood up. "If you can't get back to sleep, go in the kitchen and get yourself a glass of milk—and maybe a Lorna Doone cookie or two. I bought some since I remembered you and Andrea always liked them."

Samantha glanced across at the other twin bed where her younger sister always slept. "I miss Andrea."

"So do I, dear. So do I, but it's good to have you here for a time." She started out of the room and then paused at the door, looking back. "I remember I experienced a few bad dreams of my own after we lost Andrea and Adam. I'd wake, thinking I heard the sound of the car wreck, the sound of Andrea crying out for me."

Tears swam in Samantha's eyes. "You weren't even there when their car wrecked, Aunt Dixie."

"I know, but dreams are full of imaginings. It seemed like I was there."

Samantha couldn't think what to say.

Dixie gave her a thoughtful look. "You'll have time to enjoy Andrea and Adam's children while you're here. That will be nice. They are your nieces and nephews, you know." She blew Samantha a kiss and slipped out of the room, leaving her with a nagging guilt that she'd seen far too little of Andrea's children over the years.

"It isn't as if I ever have free time to spend with them," she said aloud to no one. "Always traveling, always working."

She got up and walked over to the window to look out into the darkness. Her bedroom, once the old carriage house behind the historic Dandridge Inn, offered a fine view across Douglas Lake in the daytime, although only a ribbon of moonlight across the water was visible now.

Restless, Samantha walked around the room, wondering how she'd spend her days here until she could go back to Atlanta to her job. She was used to working, used to being busy, and this time of recovery had been trying. She'd wished a million times the accident never happened, crashing her life to a painful standstill. Aunt Dixie had been good to her through it all, taking time from work so many times to come to see her, to be there for her. Surely she could spend the summer here, giving back a little while she finished healing. Tired now, Samantha climbed back into her bed and, after tossing and turning for a time, drifted off to sleep.

The muted sounds of conversation and laughter woke her the next morning, along with the wafting aroma of coffee and Aunt Dixie's cinnamon rolls. Samantha took a quick shower, dressed, and made her bed—a given at Aunt Dixie's—before heading to the sunny kitchen of her aunt's home.

She found Aunt Dixie standing by the counter in the kitchen, talking to her guests gathered around two comfortable round tables in the breakfast room. On the sun porch, opening off the breakfast room, Samantha could see more guests at one of the cozy tables there.

"You have a full house," Samantha said to her, pouring herself a cup of coffee before perching on a stool at the kitchen counter.

Dixie pointed to the tables in the breakfast room. "The Gardners, the Howells, and the Winters are traveling together. They are all packed and leaving right after breakfast this morning. The other couple Leland and Dottie Hartman, sitting on the porch, are staying with me for the week. They're escaping renovations and painting going on in their house, all the smells, noise, and disarray."

Dixie cut a square of breakfast casserole from a dish, scooped out a mound of mixed fruit to put beside it on a colorful plate, and dropped a gooey cinnamon roll beside it before pushing the plate across the counter to Samantha. "Do you want juice, too?" she asked.

"No, and this looks incredible."

She smiled at Samantha. "You grew up here and should know it's nothing fancy."

"Stop diminishing your gifts. I seem to remember hearing those words often enough from you growing up."

Dixie chuckled. "One of the unfortunate things about raising smart children is that they parrot your own wisdom back to you."

Samantha laughed, digging into her breakfast.

While she ate she watched her aunt interact with the out of town guests, taking seconds around to them on her old teacart, chatting with them about Dandridge history and things to do and see around the area.

Her warm laugh and affectionate sprinkling of Southern phrases drifted across to Samantha, bringing back a wealth of rich memories. Samantha had learned hospitality and the art of getting along with a wide array of people from an early age living here at the Dandridge Inn with Dixie.

"How long have you owned this lovely inn?" one of the guests asked.

"My husband Jackson and I bought the inn not long after we married. Francis Dean, one of my husband's early ancestors and the founder of Dandridge, once owned much of the land downtown, including the property this house sits on. The original house, once a gracious residence complete with carriage house, later got renovated into an inn for travelers. Papers show the home belonged to some of the Dean family descendants at one time, drawing our interest to the inn when Jackson and I relocated here." She hesitated. "We were always happy here. Jackson was a practicing attorney in Dandridge until his early death."

"Oh, I'm so sorry," one of the ladies said.

Dixie smiled. "It was a long time ago, and I always ran the inn while Jackson attended to his business anyway, so the transition to continue after his passing wasn't as difficult." She changed the subject. "I'm sure you noticed Francis Dean's portrait in the front parlor as you came in and Martha Dandridge Washington's lovely oval portrait in the dining room across the hall. You might remember reading that the town of Dandridge was named for

Washington's wife."

"Did she ever live here?" one of the men asked.

"No, but Lady Washington was greatly admired all over the country. A college in Virginia, a warship, and an ocean liner were named for her. Her image was also used on a postage stamp and later on gold and bronze coins. You can see some replicas of those and a fine painting of Mt. Vernon, George and Martha Washington's home, in the front dining room. I've always felt proud Dandridge chose to honor Martha's memory by naming their town after her. She was a great lady."

"I love all the mementos to her I saw around the house," one of the women said.

Samantha jumped into the conversation. "I'm fond of those, too," she added. "You'll also find porcelain figurines of George and Martha Washington in a curio cabinet in the dining room. Aunt Dixie has quite a collection of them, and many are rare and valuable."

Her aunt preened. "My husband Jackson started that little collection for me. I do cherish it."

She introduced Samantha then. "This is my niece, Samantha King, visiting me from Atlanta. She and her sister grew up here. I feel blessed my brother Robert brought them to me after he lost his wife. My husband Jackson and I couldn't have children and it was a joy to raise Samantha and Andrea."

Shifting the subject, one of the women asked, "What can you tell us about that interesting old letter from a Civil War soldier that's framed in the parlor?"

Dixie smiled. "That is a copy of an old letter from one of my relatives, Sam Houston Hynd, to his mother. Sam was in the 3rd Calvary in the Civil War. Near the bottom it reads: Give my love to all the girls who sing and shout Dixie." She laughed then. "That's where my name Dixie came from. I've always been rather proud of that little story. My mother's name was Martha Jane Hynds King and my family roots, like my husband's, go back to an early Dandridge settler, Judge Robert Hynds. My brother Robert is named after the judge. My family history ties in deeply to the Hynds family of Dandridge and to the King family of Sevierville, the town where I grew up."

More questions followed and Dixie answered each one skillfully and well with her usual grace and charm. Samantha thought back over her aunt's earlier words. She'd been kind to not mention that Samantha and Andrea's mother deserted them as preschoolers, although their mother Colleen did die later on. She didn't mention either that their father, Dixie's brother Robert, made little place for them in his life.

Samantha smiled. She'd always admired Dixie's artful tact in skirting around personal questions her guests asked.

"We have little enough privacy running a public inn," she said to Samantha and Andrea once when they'd chattered away a little too freely about a private family issue to their guests. "Always remember, girls, our personal business is our own personal business and no one else's business." She'd drilled those words into Samantha again and again over the years, teaching an often impulsive and outspoken young girl valuable lessons in prudence and tact.

Out of the corner of her eye Samantha watched her aunt now. As a full-figured woman, she favored long shirts over loose capris or slacks, paired with comfortable shoes she could slide her feet in and out of easily. Dixie's short hair was doctored now with a little blond coloring and if she carried one indulgence, in relation to her wardrobe, it was jewelry. Today she wore an array of lavish rings and a beaded multi-layered, turquoise choker, pretty against her dark teal shirt. Despite her weight, which often worried Samantha, Dixie always dressed stylishly.

After breakfast, she helped Dixie clean up the kitchen and then as Aunt Dixie checked out her guests, Samantha headed upstairs to clean the guest rooms, a familiar routine for her, easy to fall back into.

The Dandridge Inn was laid out in the traditional pattern of an old Georgian house. The covered front porch of the white brick home led into a wide entry, flanked by a front parlor filled with antiques on the right and a large formal dining room to the left. On the back left side of the house were a kitchen and sunny breakfast room, and behind it a pantry and laundry area, leading to the garage. To the right, down a private hallway, lay Aunt Dixie's bedroom and sitting room. From behind her personal suite a glassed in sun-porch led to the bedroom and small sitting room created for Andrea and Samantha from the old carriage house.

Nestled in the middle of the inn was a comfortable den-like room called the Drawing Room with a glass-enclosed sun-porch behind it. The wide porch connected to the breakfast room and an outdoor garden area, both looking across a green lawn and an expansive view of Douglas Lake.

Upstairs, where Samantha worked now, were four large guestrooms, each with a small sitting area and private bath. A paneled library also sat tucked at the top of the stairs, a quiet place where guests could rest and read. The guestrooms displayed color names: the blue room, red room, green room, and white room. The Hartmans had chosen to stay in the green room this week, so Samantha attacked the other three bedrooms, now vacated, changing the sheets and towels, cleaning the bathrooms, dusting the furniture, and running the vacuum to finish.

She came downstairs afterward to find Aunt Dixie sitting on the sun porch in a wicker settee with her feet up on a stool.

"I feel like the Queen of England with you doing all my work." Dixie waved a hand in an airy way. "Perhaps you wouldn't mind bringing me a little glass of sweet tea from the refrigerator before you sit down. Get some for yourself, too. You'll find a pot of fresh lemon mint outside the back door near the garage if you want to add a sprig to each of our glasses."

Before Samantha turned to leave, Dixie added, "Heat those two cinnamon rolls the guests didn't finish, too, would you? They're under the glass cake stand on the kitchen counter."

Samantha came back a few minutes later bringing the tea glasses and cinnamon rolls on an antique vintage tray with a floral picture of fruit painted in the middle of it. She'd poured unsweetened tea for herself but sweet tea for Aunt Dixie.

"I love this old tray, " Samantha said, sitting it on a side table.

"It's one of my favorites, too." Dixie glanced toward Samantha's glass of tea as she sat down. "I assume you poured your tea from that pitcher of unsweetened tea." At Samantha's nod, she shook her head. "You just don't know what you're missing not drinking real Southern sweet tea."

"You know being on camera as much as I am means I have to watch what I eat and drink. Cameras really can add as much as ten pounds to your weight. It's called the Hitchcock Zoom effect, although there are ways a camera can actually make you appear thinner."

"Well, I'm for that. Life's too short to watch every bite you eat. What's the fun in that?"

Samantha lifted an eyebrow. "How's your blood pressure?" she queried.

"I suppose I asked for that, criticizing you for watching what you eat so much." Dixie wrinkled her nose. "My blood pressure and my cholesterol are too high, but Dr. Trumbley adjusted my medicine. He fussed at me, says its hard on my joints carrying so much weight but he says my activity level running the inn is good for me. So don't fret at me too much."

She smiled at her aunt. "I just love you and want you to stay strong and healthy."

Dixie watched Samantha nibble on a cinnamon roll. "Those rolls are really good aren't they? I got the recipe for them from one of Ree Drummond's cookbooks. She's that pioneer woman who started a blog and then wrote a bunch of cookbooks. I love her cooking show on the Food Network."

"No one is a better cook than you, Aunt Dixie."

"Well, no matter what you do well in life, you always need to keep learning and improving." She pulled a cookbook out from under a side table beside her. "Here's Ree Drummond on the cover of one of her cookbooks. She's a redhead like you."

Samantha picked up the book to study the woman's picture. "I've seen her on television."

"I bought her memoir book *Black Heels to Tractor Wheels*. I'll loan it to you to read. It will make you laugh, reading about a corporate city girl falling in love with a rancher on a remote ranch out in Oklahoma. Despite how she met her husband, Ree shuffles a diverse life now, with kids, a busy ranch life, and celebrity status."

"I'll be looking for books to read to help pass the time this summer." Samantha looked out the windows to the blue sky over the lake with its puffy while cumulus clouds.

Her aunt followed her glance. "It's a beautiful day, and cumulus clouds mean fair weather. I learned that from you."

"Yes, they do mean fair weather until they begin to stack vertically, which can mean a severe storm is coming. Even tornadoes. I've certainly seen enough of those."

Dixie laughed. "I often feel like a tornado has blown through my house when I invite all of Andrea's children over here. That Madison is so much like you and the spitting image of you at about the same age, except for your green eyes. You know, all four of Andrea's children inherited the red hair from your mother's side of the family, like you and Andrea, but they all got Andrea's pretty chocolate brown eyes and not your mother's green ones as you did. Adam had similar coloring to Andrea, reddish brown hair and dark eyes. Andrew makes me think of his father in looks."

Samantha looked away. "I haven't seen the kids in a long time. They probably don't even remember me."

"I show them pictures and tell them about you." Dixie grinned. "And they watch you on television. They like bragging about their famous aunt."

She winced. "Doesn't it hurt seeing them since Andrea died?"

"What?" Dixie look horrified. "Is it their fault they lost both their parents tragically? Should I avoid those sweet children because they make me think of Andrea? How could you even say something like that?"

Samantha fidgeted with her hands.

Dixie gave her a steely look. "Those children are our blood

family." She pointed at a scrapbook on the coffee table. "Get me that book. I want you to see some pictures of them."

Samantha got up to retrieve the book and then sat down by Dixie on the settee in the spot she indicated. Dixie spread open the book. "Here are all the children in a photo taken at Madison's birthday in April. She's holding that cell phone you sent her." Dixie laughed. "Ford was sure mad about that. He'd told both the girls they couldn't have one until they turned thirteen. But I talked him out of taking it away from Madison, and of course then Ford had to break down and buy Natalie one, too. He's encountered a few upsets with those girls about phone usage, but he's managing."

Dixie's voice softened. "He's had a lot to manage, having all those children."

Samantha mentally counted. "Eight children. How in the world does he manage, Aunt Dixie? I couldn't believe it when he and his wife Laura took in Andrea and Adam's four when they already had four children of their own."

"The two families were close, and you know Andrea and Laura had been best friends since they were little girls, like you and Lucy."

"How is Lucy?"

"Good and looking forward to seeing you. Maybe tomorrow you can walk downtown to her store and spend some time with her. On a weekday in May she won't be overly busy in the bookstore or the coffee shop."

"I'll text her to see if that would be okay."

Dixie returned to topic. "Ford and Laura McDaniel told Andrea and Adam they'd take their kids in if anything happened to them. Adam was raised an orphan, and you know your father Robert wouldn't be taking in four children at his age when he wouldn't even take in you and Andrea so long ago. A music and booking agent like he is travels all the time. His life still isn't one a child could fit into, much less four. I could hardly take them in, either, with my health touchy and the inn to run, so I was grateful Ford and Laura stepped up."

She traced a hand over the photo book while talking. "I took in you and Andrea back when I was younger, but I don't have the stamina and strength to run herd on four children now. Besides, they were all so little when Andrea and Adam got killed—Tamela still in diapers, Wesley only two, running all over creation, Andrew four and Madison barely six. Those children were devastated and confused, too."

"You know I couldn't consider it, either, with my work and travel."

"No. Neither of us were right for the job." Dixie nodded, remembering. "Laura and Ford McDaniel *were* right, though, with their own children nearly the same ages. I remember Andrea's children spent so much time with the McDaniel family. The children already knew and loved Laura and Ford and their children as well. Laura did a remarkable job handling that rough time of transition, with her nursing background and her sunny, competent disposition."

Dixie paused. "I helped as much as I could, of course. I always have and I still do in my own ways."

"I'm sure you do," Samantha said.

"Sadly, after the children were all resettled, thriving, and doing well, Laura died, too."

"When did that happen, Aunt Dixie? Three years ago?"

"Yes, three years ago. As I said, Ford hasn't had an easy time of it." She stroked her chin thoughtfully. "I really worried about him for a while, grieving and angry, so overwhelmed carrying the load of parenting all those children alone with his veterinary practice. Thankfully Juanita Helton stepped in to help him. You'll meet her when you go over to the house. Juanita's daughter works for Ford in the veterinary office and she knew what a time Ford was having. I heard she simply showed up one day and said, 'I know about large families; I can cook and I can clean. I can help you.' The woman basically runs the home now while Ford works. She's been a godsend to him."

Samantha felt relieved to know someone was helping Ford. She still remembered when Dixie called to tell her that his wife had died unexpectedly.

"Didn't you tell me Laura died from a heart attack?'

"Actually it was cardiac arrest from an undetected heart abnormality. She simply dropped dead while running one morning. So tragic and just another blow for Andrea's children. Laura had become like a mother to them by that time, and they had to transition all over again to death, change, and sorrow."

She patted Samantha's leg. "I want you to go out to the house to see those children and spend time with them while you're here. You won't be sorry for it. You used to counsel at that summer camp every year. I remember you loved working with the kids. This won't be very different, and you know Ford lives in the old lodge at Sycamore Lake Resort his family owns."

"Do his parents help with the kids?"

"As much as they can. His mother is in a wheel chair. Had polio as a girl, before that nasty disease got erased for children. It came back on her as an adult. It can do that, you know. So she isn't strong, but she's a loving, valiant lady. I'm very fond of Coralee, and she and Burl give a lot of time to those children and love them all fiercely. I'm grateful to them for that. They stepped up to be grandparents in a fine way."

Samantha looked down at the photo again of all the children and then turned the pages to see more.

Dixie looked over her shoulder, making remarks about the different photos, telling her about the children. "Madison is twelve now, finishing sixth grade at Maury Middle, red-haired like you, with a pixie face. Andrew will be ten in September, starting fifth, already so handsome. A smart boy, he likes to work with his hands. He can fix almost anything and wants to be an engineer like his father Adam was." She smiled pointing to a smaller boy, red-haired with a smattering of freckles. "Little Wesley will be eight in July, beginning third grade in the fall, a lovable boy, full of fun. Adores the outdoors. And the baby Tamela—who doesn't like me to call her a baby anymore—with that sweet face, just turned six in

February and will start first grade this fall. She makes me think so much of Andrea."

"They surely have grown fast."

"They have," Aunt Dixie smiled at her and then turned back to point to an earlier picture again. "These are Ford's children, all with dark brunette hair and brown eyes like their father's. Natalie, the oldest, and also twelve like Madison, is sensible and mature, a sweet girl and loves to read. Clay, ten, looks and acts like his dad, and has Ford's gift with animals." She laughed. "And, oh gracious me, this is Gareth. Enterprising but a handful. You never know what that boy will come up with next. While little Rebecca simply steals your heart away. Loving and tender-hearted."

"I wish I could tell you I'll remember all Ford's children after this talk, but I know your words will come back to me as I meet them later." She studied the photo of all eight children again. "How did Andrea and Adam become such good friends with Ford and his wife? I'm trying to remember."

"You might not recall," Dixie said, "but Andrea married Adam about the same time Ford and Laura got married. Andrea and Laura birthed their first babies, both girls, only a month apart. Andrea said they planned after that to have children close in age so they could play together."

"I guess that created built in playmates when the families merged," Samantha commented while looking at another photo of all eight children sitting in a row on the side of a boat dock, bare feet hanging over the water, grinning and happy.

Dixie pulled the photo Samantha was admiring out of her book. "Here, you take this photo with you to keep all these kids straight. I have another exactly like it in a drawer in my bedroom. I wrote the children's names on the back of this one, too. They're sitting oldest to youngest, which will make it easier for you to remember them— the oldest girls, Natalie, Madison, then the boys, Clay, Andrew, Gareth, Wesley, and last, the little girls Rebecca and Tamela." She pointed to each as she named them again.

Samantha glanced out the window at the sunny day. "Maybe I'll run over to see them this afternoon when they get home from school. Take some cookies or something. Break the ice." She always liked to get difficult tasks done quickly, to stop dreading them. Procrastination seldom helped any situation.

"What a wonderful idea." Her aunt Dixie stood up, laying the photo album back on the coffee table. "Let's go make some cookies you can take with you. It's always smart to show up to see kids with gifts. I bought them a new game last week that you can take over for me, too. It's an eight-player Chinese Checkers game, not easy to find, and a hand-carved wooden one, too. I thought it would be fun for the children to have a game they could all play at once if they wanted to. A local man in Dandridge makes them."

Samantha grinned. "I'm sure it will push me to the top of the popularity list to show up with cookies and a new game."

Dixie turned to smile at her. "I know you're a little nervous about seeing the children again, but you'll be fine. And keep in mind they're Andrea's and all we have left of her besides our memories."

CHAPTER 2

Dwayne leaned his head into the examination room where Ford checked out a male kitten he'd neutered early that morning. "Ms. Greeley is here to pick up her kitten," he said. "Are you ready to see her or do you want me to talk with her?"

Mondays, always busy at the Lakeside Veterinary Clinic, kept Ford and his vet tech Dwayne Coleman busy all day.

"We're about finished for the day," Ford answered. "I'll talk to Ms. Greeley for a minute. Send her back."

"Will do, and I'll go finish that dental cleaning on the Anderson's Siamese."

A few minutes later, Maria Rodriguez, Ford's office manager—and veterinary assistant—brought Ms. Greeley back.

"Oh, there's my little Sylvester," Ms. Greeley said, moving into the exam room to pet and cuddle the black and white kitten on the table. She looked up at Ford. "Is he doing all right?"

"He's great," Ford said, glad to see the obvious affection between owner and pet. "Neutering a male cat is a straightforward procedure. He did fine but he'll need to stay indoors and rest for about a week before he's fully back to his old self."

Ms. Greeley raised her eyebrows. "As we know well, he'll never be quite back to his old self. But that is the point of this, of course." She smiled as she watched Ford pick up the little tomcat, giving him an affectionate snuggle before putting him into Ms. Greeley's carrier. "I love how sweet you are to the animals you work with Dr. McDaniel. It's a welcome change from the vet where we lived before. He was competent, of course, or we'd never have gone to him with our pets, but he lacked the warmth you always show."

"Thank you Ms. Greeley. I'm glad to see how loving you are with your pets, too." He closed the pet carrier and handed Ms. Greeley a sheet of paper. "Here are some post-op instructions. Sylvester's anesthetic from this morning has pretty much worn off, although he may still be a little groggy tonight. A male cat doesn't get sutures with neutering like a female cat but Sylvester will be a little sore until he heals and there are some instructions on this sheet you should follow. Contact us at the office if you see any of the problems mentioned, which isn't likely."

"I'll do that." She picked up the carrier.

"Maria will check you out at the desk," he said, opening the examination room door for her. "It was nice to see you again, Ms. Greeley."

"And you, Doctor."

Dwayne stuck his head in the door as she left. "Ford, could you come back here and look at the dog brought in earlier that got hit by that car? I don't think the poor guy's going to make it."

"Yeah, I worried about that when I saw the extent of the injuries." He followed Dwayne into the hall and then into the other exam room next door.

"We'd better call the Fosters," Ford said a short time later, coming out of the room with Dwayne. "We need to see what they want to do about Riley. I hate calling them. They really loved that little dog."

"Yeah. It's hard." Dwayne nodded. "I'll call them." He glanced at his watch. "It's time for Maria to leave and for us to close. If you want to head home, I'll wait for the Fosters to come get the dog if they want to bury him. I seem to remember they bury any animals they lose out at the farm rather than having us take care of them."

"Thanks. I'll take this paperwork to Maria and lock up."

After seeing Maria out and looking over his schedule of appointments and surgeries for the next day, Ford moved around the office in a familiar pattern checking rooms, locking doors. The

Fosters would call Dwayne on his cell when they arrived to pick up Riley. The little dog had simply sustained too many injuries to make it. They'd tried, of course, even knowing the odds were slim that the small terrier could recover.

He was locking the last door when a red-haired woman bounded up the steps to try the door he'd just locked. She peered in the window and then pounded on the door.

Ford unlocked the door and cracked it open a little. "I'm sorry, we're closed," he said. "Do you have an emergency?" He looked for a car in the front parking lot but didn't see one.

"Are you Ford McDaniel?" she asked in a brisk, annoyed voice.

He studied her angry face. "Yes. Is there a problem?"

"I was just at your house." She gestured to the side road by the office leading to the lodge and his home in the resort. "Your housekeeper refused to let me in, basically insulted me, and got your children upset as well."

He knew his mouth dropped open. "That doesn't sound like Juanita. Could you tell me why you came to our home?"

She put her hands on her hips. "Don't you recognize me?"

He let his eyes rove over her, a beautiful redhead, hair waving around her shoulders, with green eyes and a perfect figure, dressed in a skirt he thought a little short, but showing off long well-shaped legs.

"When you finish checking me out, I'll introduce myself," she snapped.

Ford knew he blushed then.

"I'm Samantha King, Andrea Bradley's sister."

He looked back to her face then. "I'm sorry I didn't recognize you. It has been a while." That was an understatement, he thought. The last time he'd seen the woman had been at Andrea and Adam's funeral six years ago. He knew the kids had seen her a time or two at Dixie's since, when she'd buzzed in for a quick holiday visit, but he'd been working then.

She lifted her chin. "Your housekeeper told me quite plainly that since I'd had so little involvement with the children over the years that I'd need to get your permission to see them. Her attitude about that was quite obvious."

Ford rubbed his neck, uncomfortable. "Juanita is very protective of the children and she can be somewhat outspoken about her views on some subjects. I'm sorry if she offended you." He paused. "In her defense, we do have some house rules about admitting visitors when I'm gone."

She gave him a steely look. "I'm hardly a visitor."

He decided not to argue with that. "Listen. If you'll come in for a minute while I finish closing up the clinic, I'll walk back to the lodge with you." Ford glanced out to the parking lot again. "I don't see a car so I assumed you walked down here."

"I did." She stepped inside. "I'm going to be here in Dandridge for the summer while I complete recovery from an accident, so I hope to have some time with the children while here. I know I've spent little time with them in past. My work, as you know, is highly demanding. It's rare I get time for vacations."

Ford decided not to answer that. "I saw that fall you took in Florida during Hurricane Michael."

"I count it a lucky day when I meet anyone who hasn't seen that fall."

She paused inside the door, glancing around.

He looked her over again as she did. "I'm glad to see you've made such a good recovery. I remember Dixie saying you went through a difficult time."

"Yes." She pointed to a group of pictures on the wall. "I see only cat paintings in here. No dogs."

He grinned. "This is the Cat Lobby. The Dog Lobby is on the other side of the office." He gestured. "I like separating the two when the dogs and cats come in to be seen."

"Sensible," she said, studying more of the photos, cat magazines and books around the lobby. "It's amazing all vets don't do that."

Dwayne opened the door to the lobby, hearing their voices. "I thought you were closing," he said.

"I am. This is Samantha King, the Bradley children's aunt. She's in town and stopped by to see the kids."

Dwayne smiled broadly, reaching out to shake her hand. "The storm chaser with the Weather First channel. I haven't seen you on air since that fall but I read you'll be going back." He glanced over her, like Ford had done. "Man alive, you're prettier in person than on television, but don't tell my wife Bonita that."

A handsome black man, Dwayne and his wife Bonita hadn't been married long. Ford still counted his blessings every day that he'd met Dwayne at a veterinary conference in Chattanooga and lured him to move to Dandridge to be his vet tech.

A car pulled up outside the clinic, interrupting their conversation.

"That will be the Fosters to get Riley," Dwayne said. "I'll go out and direct them around to the back door. I've got Riley ready." He left them to walk outside.

"We lost a dog this afternoon," Ford explained. "Hit by a car. A beloved family pet. They've come to get the body to bury it on their farm property."

"Oh, I'm sorry." She looked out the window sympathetically.

"Let me hang my lab coat in my office and we'll head to the house. I don't want to hold Juanita up. She has family of her own to get home to."

A short time later, after Ford took a minute to offer sympathy to the Fosters, he and Samantha walked up Sycamore Lake Road and into the resort belonging to his family for three generations.

"This old resort has been here a long time," Samantha commented. "I remember coming to the swim beach as a girl. Is it still on the lake?"

"Yes," he answered, moving into an easy stride beside her up the road. "Why didn't you drive down to the clinic?"

"I'm trying to walk and move as much as possible now to build strength." She sent him a steely look. "And I needed to walk off a little steam."

He winced, avoiding comment.

"When did you move into the old lodge?" she asked. "I thought I remembered you owned a house behind the vets' office at Willow

Point. Andrea used to talk about it. Said it was a pretty place."

"It is a pretty place. But when Laura and I took in Andrea and Adam's children, it proved a little small for such a big family." He paused. "We renovated, and moved into, the lodge house then. Over time, people had stopped coming to stay there on a regular basis. Times change. We were only using the lodge occasionally for events at that point, so Dad and Mom suggested we make it into a home. It was a good decision. We still have the Sycamore Point Event Lodge on the backside of the lake and the chapel and pavilion there for events. The cabins nearby are available for groups who want to stay over for retreats or week long events, too, and there's a campground in The Cove."

She glanced around as they walked. "This has always been a pretty place. Andrea and I often thought it would have been fun to grow up here as you did."

"I somewhat envied you growing up at Aunt Dixie's inn," he replied. "She's a fabulous cook, and Andrea used to tell us wonderful stories about the guests who stayed there over the years. Some really funny ones about odd characters Dixie entertained." He felt glad to see her smile at that comment. Her anger earlier had been a force to reckon with.

Ford started to ask her about the extent of her injuries, but then thought better of it. She seemed sensitive about the subject. Instead they chatted about the resort and mundane topics until they arrived at the house.

Natalie's voice met him as soon as he walked in the back door of the kitchen. "Daddy, you didn't answer my text," she complained.

"Or mine and Juanita was rude to my aunt," Madison added in an emotional voice before he could reply. Ford noted the remnants of tears still on her face.

The kitchen, partly filled with several children helping Juanita with dinner, grew eerily silent as they all saw Samantha behind him.

Juanita glared at Samantha before turning back to the stove. "I told her she'd need to check with you about seeing the children. I mind your rules Dr. McDaniel even if folks get upset over them."

Even though Juanita was a short Hispanic woman, there was nothing short about her personality. Her plucky spirit and strength of character had served her well dealing with eight children these last three years and, although she could be somewhat outspoken on occasion, Ford felt grateful every day for her help. She'd mothered his eight kids like they were her own since Laura died— amid arguments, sickness, childish pranks, tender moments and occasional tragedies.

Tamela, the smallest of the Bradley children, broke the silence. "Can Samantha stay for dinner with us Daddy Ford? We hardly ever get to see her and we've got lots tonight with baked spaghetti."

"Oh, can she?" Madison sent him a beseeching look. "Please?"

Ford sent Samantha a sideways glance. "Would you like to stay to dinner with this crazy clan? Juanita does make good baked spaghetti and I see she's made salad, bread, and cake, too. We have plenty to share."

Samantha hesitated, but when Juanita turned to glare at her again, Ford watched her lift her chin and reply with a touch of smug satisfaction. "I'd be delighted to stay. Thank you for the invitation. Let me go out to the car to get my purse and cell phone so I can call Aunt Dixie. I'm sure she won't mind."

When she left, Ford glanced at the girls gathered around in the kitchen. "I'll expect everyone to be on their best behavior tonight with company here." He looked around. "Where are the boys?"

"They had outside chores today after school and they're over at Granddaddy Burl's now helping him fix a fence somebody ran into," Natalie answered. "Granddaddy said whoever hit it just drove off and left it knocked down and two of his cows got out in the road."

He glanced at the two youngest girls, perched on stools at the counter, putting colored sprinkles around the sides and top of the cake. He frowned at the candy-coated cake. "What is that?"

Juanita answered. "It's a Funfetti Cake. Natalie found the recipe on one of those Internet sites and asked if she and Madison could make it. The cake might be a little sweet for your taste but the children will love it. There's vanilla ice cream in the freezer if you'd prefer that yourself."

"Tamela and Rebecca, why don't you two run over to tell the boys to come wash up for supper," Ford said. "It looks like everything is ready here and we need to let Juanita start home."

He heard Madison mumble as Juanita walked into the dining area to check the table, "Hurrah for that."

Ford frowned at her. "I don't think you want to sit alone in my office to eat dinner tonight, do you Madison?"

Her eyes flew wide. "No sir."

"Well then, why don't you and Natalie offer to clean up the kitchen for Juanita so she can go on home?"

"Yes, sir." They all but raced into the dining area to make their offer as Samantha came back in the side door.

"Dixie was delighted I planned to stay over for dinner." She sat two boxes on the counter. "This is a game Dixie picked up for the children and asked me to bring over, and the tin in the other box is filled with cookies she and I made before I came."

Ford opened the lid of the tin. "Ummm. Peanut butter cookies, one of my favorites."

He saw Samantha smirk. "Aunt Dixie said you were fond of them."

Ford snagged a broken piece of cookie to pop in his mouth. "I am fond of them, and I'll enjoy these much more with coffee after dinner than Funfetti Cake." He eyed the cake, thick with multi-colored candy sprinkles. "Although I'll need to try the cake since Natalie and Madison made it."

The girls came back in the room, excited over the game and cookies Dixie sent, and Ford took a minute to walk Juanita out the back door.

"Listen," he said to her, out of hearing of the others. "Samantha King is spending the summer here, from what she tells me, recovering from an injury on the job. She says she wants to spend time with the children while here."

"Is that right? About time I'd say," Juanita replied in a sarcastic tone, frowning with disapproval.

Ford kept his voice calm. "I would appreciate you being polite to her despite your feelings, Juanita. She is the Bradley children's only aunt, even if she hasn't been around much."

"You know how I feel about that, Dr. McDaniel. Family is our greatest gift. And neglect of those who need you is selfish." She scowled. "Where was she when Laura died, leaving you with all these kids to raise on your own? She didn't even come to Laura's funeral and she barely made her own sister's funeral. She took off right after it, too, with the body barely cold."

"That's harsh, Juanita. Samantha holds a demanding job. She can't always take off when she wants to when on location."

"Well, you tell her to check with you to set up her visits, and frankly I'd prefer it if she scheduled her visits on the weekends or after I've left for the evening. I've answered one too many questions from those sweet nieces and nephews of hers about why she never comes to see them—despite the gifts and money she sends on occasions. Gifts don't make up for love and affection, which is what those children really needed from her." She glanced back toward the house. "I will admit I'm bitter she didn't do better by them, her own family."

Ford sighed. "I've found bitterness seldom helps any situation."

Juanita looked contrite at his words. "You're right and I'll start praying about it. *Mea culpa.* I am sorry." She crossed herself. "I'll pray the Father will help me with my attitude."

Ford went back into the house to wash up and soon joined all the children and Samantha in the dining room off the kitchen, with its long table looking out over the lake through wide picture windows. The boys sat along one side of the table and the girls on the other. When extra children stayed for a meal, they added chairs on either side, but Ford noticed for tonight that Madison and Natalie had set the extra place for Samantha at the opposite end of the table from his, in Laura's old spot.

It shouldn't have bothered him; it was probably the appropriate and honorable thing to do. But it hurt Ford to see her in Laura's place. He had to admit, too, that many of Juanita's bitter feelings spoken out loud echoed thoughts of his own. There were nights he'd spent with sick children throwing up and crying, himself tired and worn out from lack of sleep and long days at work, when he'd resented the pretty, carefree meteorologist traveling about the country reporting on the nation's storms. He'd felt angry himself many times, like Juanita, that she seemed to experience no remorse leaving him to raise her sister's children.

Over dinner, the children pummeled Samantha with questions about her job, the places she'd visited, the things she'd seen. She answered patiently in that deep, compelling voice of hers—one of her trademarks with Weather First, like her bright red hair. Irish hair. He knew her mother had been an Irish singer, who came to America on tour, married her manager Robert King, and then left him with two small children to return home. Andrea had talked about it to them, and he'd heard the wistfulness in her tone when she did. She'd missed growing up in a warm family unit, as much as both girls loved their Aunt Dixie. The experience made Andrea yearn for a rich family life later while, from what he'd heard, Samantha always wanted adventure and couldn't wait to leave Dandridge for a larger life.

"Dad, can we go outside and play for a while after dinner?" his oldest son Clay asked. "We don't have much homework with school almost out now."

"Only one more week!" Gareth added, pumping a hand in the air.

Ford smiled. He'd been eager, too, as a boy for summer vacation to come. He doubted Juanita as eager as the children to shuffle them all underfoot again every day, but his mom and dad would help out. They'd manage. They always did, and it was easier now with the children older.

After sampling the Funfetti Cake, not as bad as Ford imagined, he invited Samantha to join him out on the porch where he could keep an eye on the kids playing in the yard down by the lake. The older boys had scraped plates and loaded the dishwasher, since it was their night for it, but were soon outside with the others.

Ford's favorite place to relax after dinner in good weather was on a covered terrace on the back of the house. It gave him the perfect vantage point across the broad back yard behind the lodge, to the playground area to the right, the old gazebo and wooden dock by the lake, and even to the long wooden walk-bridge leading across a narrow neck of Sycamore Lake.

"I'd never tire of this view across the lake," Samantha said, propping her feet on a rail of the porch. "The kids are growing up in a beautiful place, and I love how much the lodge feels like a family home now."

"It's hard for a place with eight kids not to feel like a family home."

"I don't know," she replied. "In my travels I've seen some pretty opulent places, often with multiple children, that held no sense of home about them."

He leaned back, relaxing, not responding. Tired.

"It must be a hard day for you when you lose a pet like you did at the clinic today. I saw that family crying before you left."

"Death is a part of life with animals, but those are the days you don't like much. Not being able to save someone's pet. Wishing the day had a different ending, a happier one."

"Yes, I know that feeling."

Ford knew she was thinking of her accident. "I don't see any noticeable signs of the injuries Dixie said you suffered now. You must be doing much better."

"I am," she said. "I tore a tendon, dislocated my shoulder, suffered a concussion, broke a few ribs, sprained an ankle and a wrist, sported a fine array of cuts and bruises, plus more. It took a toll. Now I'm mostly working to get my stamina back, to strengthen. This summer I want to run, swim, hike, walk, and bike a lot to get ready to work again. I spotted a gym I can join but outdoor exercise would be better in my case."

Ford grinned at her. "Feel free to come over to the resort anytime. You'll find walking and hiking trails, side roads to bike on, a lake to swim in and a pool." He gestured to the left where a glimpse of the pool could be seen behind some trees and fencing.

"Thanks. Maybe I can sub for Juanita occasionally, keep an eye on the kids while they swim or boat. I used to counsel at camp every summer. I always had more kids to be responsible for than eight, too."

"That's a kind offer. I'll keep it in mind and tell Juanita about it. She might want to give you a jingle some day this summer when she has a lot to do around the house or needs to take off a couple of hours for errands," Ford replied. However, he doubted Juanita would be eager to have Samantha around much when she was at the house.

He considered how to field that problem. "Juanita is a little structured in how she does things around here. You might want to give me a call before you drop by, let me check with her to schedule a good time for you to come."

"Meaning she doesn't like me." Samantha laughed that rich, deep throaty laugh of hers. "You don't need to tiptoe around that, Ford. I may be popular with the children around here but I'm well aware the adults don't see things in the same way."

Ford crossed his legs, thinking how to answer.

"I'll call or text you first before I come," she said after a moment. "Maybe in time Juanita—and possibly you—will decide I'm not such an ogre after all."

He started to object, but she interrupted. "Don't knock yourself out being nice, Ford. I know I haven't been a support for you with Andrea's children. I had choices to make when she and Adam died. I could have come back to raise them but it would have meant giving up my life, my career. It didn't feel like the right thing then. You may think I made the wrong choice, perhaps a heartless choice, but I made what I felt was the right choice at the time—and not only for me."

"I think I'll get some more coffee," he said, deciding not to respond. "And perhaps a couple of those peanut butter cookies. Want a few?"

She smiled at him. "No, I think I'll walk down in the yard and talk to the kids a little more before I head home. I know they'll need to come in to do homework and baths soon. They have school tomorrow and I also want to spend time with Aunt Dixie. I only got here Sunday. I'll check with you later in the week about a time to visit with the children again. Maybe the weekend?"

"That would be good," he said, probably too quickly. "Maybe Saturday. It's warm enough to swim now. We'll probably spend most of the day at the swim beach and on the lake. You can hang out with us."

She hid a grin as if reading his mind. "Juanita is off on Saturday, isn't she? I think Madison told me that."

He nodded. "And the kids are out of school. They'll have more free time."

She picked up her purse to drape it over her shoulder. "Let's just say I'll come around mid morning. I'll text you before I head over." She started down the stairs from the porch. "And thanks for dinner, Ford."

"Sure. You're welcome," he answered. "You'll need to stop to open the gate and close it before you leave." He told her the code. "We close the road into the resort at night for safety for anyone staying here."

"I'll do that, and I'll see you Saturday."

He stood for a moment, watching her walk through the yard. As Dwayne had said, she was a beautiful woman. She'd handled herself with the children in an easy, gracious way, too, giving each of them her attention, asking them questions, laughing at their silly comments and jokes. He admitted he was surprised at her ease with the kids, at her general ease with herself and life, except for her annoyance about being sidelined and injured.

Maybe things would work out okay having her around for a time. He hoped so. And he'd work on Juanita to be a little more accommodating.

CHAPTER 3

On Tuesday, after helping Dixie tidy up the kitchen after breakfast, Samantha headed out the door of the Dandridge Inn to walk downtown to see her friend Lucy. The route was familiar, following Circle Drive past the library to the main road leading into town, called Gay Street—a popular name for downtown U.S. streets in the 1800s.

Dandridge, a small, historic town, still had many of its picturesque buildings including the courthouse, notable homes, a jail, coach house, an old bank, taverns now converted to businesses, and more. The town, proud of its heritage, took care of its city and had retained much of its early charm. Samantha knew from Aunt Dixie's talks at the Inn that Dandridge had been recognized by the National Trust for Historic Preservation and received several other awards of distinction. Although small, Dandridge got its share of visitors, being right on Douglas Lake and only a hop, skip, and jump from the nearby Smoky Mountains.

A short distance past Tinsley Bible Drug store, one of Samantha and Andrea's favorite girlhood spots for ice cream and milkshakes, she spotted Lucy's family store, Newberry Books and Coffee, on the left. She opened one of the aged double doors to step inside and was immediately swept into a huge hug by Lucy, who all but danced across the room to greet her.

"I can't believe you're here," Lucy exclaimed. "You look fabulous, my famous friend."

Samantha hugged her back. "My famous label is a little frayed right now."

"Well, you keep in mind I loved you when you were only Samantha King, girl sleuth in Dandridge, working alongside her trusty sidekick Lucy Newberry, now Lucy Howard."

"We did have some adventures." Samantha laughed as she followed Lucy to a small table at the window, one of several nestled amid shelves of books reaching to the ceiling.

Samantha looked around at the cute store filled with bookshelves, cozy sitting areas, a small coffee and pastry counter, along with an array of round tables tucked in a cluster near the front of the store. "I still can't believe you did all this, converted your Aunt Clarice's old general store and bakery shop into this wonderful book store and coffee shop."

"You know I always envisioned the old store could have new life if it just changed character a little. Everyone loves a coffee shop today and this is the only bookstore in the area. Because I keep the whole back of the store stocked with used books, too, I stay busy—and in the black financially. I'm pleased with the business and so is Aunt Clarice. She still makes her baked goods for the store. They sell great with the coffee, and her homemade sweets already carried a name and following."

A large white cat with dark tabby markings came over to rub against Samantha's legs.

"Vincent remembers you."

Samantha leaned down to rub the cat's back. "I remember when we found him down by the lake when I came home for Christmas about seven years ago, the year before Andrea died."

"Yes, poor little kitten—mewing and hungry, obviously dropped off by someone. He was sure glad to come home with us that day."

"I'm glad you took him in. You know I couldn't." She reached down to pet the cat again, hearing him purr. "I remember when we were trying to think of a name for him that we decided to name him after Bert Vincent, the journalist and author that lived in Dandridge in the latter part of his life."

"Bert married Ellen Hynds and lived in the old Hynds ancestral home right across the street. It's the Maxwell House boutique now—nice place to browse and shop if you haven't been there recently."

"I want to explore old places downtown one day, remember good times," Samantha said.

"Well, we've snatched a lot of good memories and times together when we could through the years and kept in touch emailing and texting, too."

"We have. Maybe you can wander around with me one day when you have a day off from the store, catch me up on everything."

"I'd love that."

They watched Vincent leap up into a wide sunny window to settle down for a nap.

"How long can you stay this time?" Lucy asked.

"Probably long enough for you to get sick of me. Weather First doesn't want me to come back until fall. They know I've basically recovered from my injuries but they want me to strengthen a few months longer before they put me back in the trenches. It's tough out there. They want to be sure I'm totally back to myself." Samantha glanced down at her lap. "Frankly, I probably need a little more time. My stamina is off and I still get occasional headaches, a little dizziness, and bad dreams from that concussion shake up."

"Dixie said you were on paid leave, though. I know that helps. I'm sure big networks like Weather First, that send their meteorologists out into inclement and dangerous weather, are forced to carry great insurance, disability, and benefit packages."

"Well, it does help."

"How long have you been with Weather First now? I was trying to remember this morning."

"I went on scholarship to Mississippi State after high school, spent almost six years there getting my degree and masters in meteorology, and then because of that great break when I interned at Weather First, I got hired as a morning forecaster right out of school at twenty-three. Then they moved me out in the field later when broadcasting storms live on television began to become popular. I've been at Weather First now for almost fourteen years. I'll be thirty-seven soon. Hard to believe."

Lucy giggled. "I remember that break you snagged as an intern at Weather First. The main forecaster got sick and, with everyone else working out in the field, they put you on. You were so great they told you they'd give you a job when you graduated."

"I was scared, too, but I knew it a big opportunity, kind of like when an actress's understudy gets that unexpected chance to go on stage."

Samantha looked around as several women came into the store. "Do you work the store by yourself?"

"Sometimes, but Aunt Clarice still works part-time hours with me and Melanie Hynds works almost full-time." A sweet-faced, short-haired girl came out from behind some book shelves in the back to talk to the customers, waving at Lucy and Samantha. "Melanie will take care of those women, but let me go say hello. They're regulars who come in about once a week after a civic meeting."

Samantha watched her old friend walk across the store, her dark, almost black hair still hanging past her shoulders, her long bangs brushing her eyebrows. Shorter than Samantha, Lucy had a slightly fuller figure, a round face with dancing brown eyes, and a great laugh. The two had been best friends since kindergarten. They met the first week Samantha and Andrea came to stay with Aunt Dixie. Lucy had been visiting practically next door with her Aunt Clarice that day, and she didn't live far away with her family, either, over on Church Street near the park.

While Samantha had yearned for adventure outside of Dandridge, Lucy had always wanted to stay in Dandridge. She loved helping in her Aunt Clarice's store and dreamed of taking it over one day, knowing Clarice and her Uncle Mack had no children to inherit.

"What were you thinking about looking out the window all dreamy eyed?" Lucy said coming back with two bottles of cold water.

"I was thinking how we both got our dreams in life. I wanted to be a forecaster and meteorologist and you wanted to run your aunt and uncle's store and change it into a bookstore and coffee shop."

"Well, I didn't get the latter idea until I was older and saw the old store losing business with the times." She grinned. "You forget I always wanted to marry Vance Howard, too, and I did. I sometimes think that proved more challenging than the store."

Samantha laughed. "How is Vance?"

"Fine and thrilled he made the good decision to marry me. He still thinks it was all his idea and I plan to go on letting him think that, too, so don't tell him different." She paused. "Vance and I, and the children Claudia and Mackie, moved in with Aunt Clarice this year. Did Dixie tell you?"

"No." Samantha knew her mouth dropped open. "You're practically right next door to the inn now. How did I not hear about that?"

"We haven't been there long. Aunt Clarice was thinking about selling the house. You know it's large, and she's older now. I couldn't stand the idea of it going out of the family, so Vance and I talked about it and decided to buy it. You know the old place has that guest wing in back, so we asked Aunt Clarice if she might like to stay on there. She loved the idea and our little family has always spent so much time at her house anyway that it already felt like home. The little house we rented had grown too small for us, and we were trying to decide where to buy. The older houses near downtown go fast and are pricey so this was a great opportunity for us, and it put me in walking distance of the store. The kids can run down after school or stay with Clarice until I close. It's worked out perfect."

"I've always loved Clarice, and I'm tickled to know I can simply run across the street to visit with you now. That's great news." She took a few sips of water. "I'm sure Aunt Dixie is pleased, too. She and Clarice have been friends for a long time. Dixie would miss her if she moved."

"Life has a sweet way of working out to the good."

"You've always believed that."

"Of course. Don't you? I can't seem to remember you being the negative, pessimistic type."

"No, but this year has tossed me for a loop. It gave me some big wakeup calls, too. I guess I thought I was pretty invincible."

"Life has some tough moments now and then. I resented it for a time when my parents decided to sell their home on Church Street in Dandridge and move to Florida near my brother Reese. It's so far and it sort of hurt my heart when they made the decision. But they're happy, and Aunt Clarice really stepped in to fill the role of family for us. Of course, we have Vance's parents here, too, and his brothers and their families, so we're not left alone. I just like keeping people close. It hurts when those you love are far away, when you hardly ever see them."

"You still carry that big sentimental streak, don't you?"

"I do, I guess. You've always been so independent, but I like having everyone I love close around me."

Samantha stayed for an hour, talking and catching up on all their news. She told Lucy about her reception from Juanita at Ford's home.

"I'm not surprised. The Heltons are Hispanic, originally from Mexico, and they still hold tight to many of their old cultural ways. You might not know it but Juanita, her husband, her daughter Maria—who works at Ford's office—Maria's husband and their two children, and Juanita's parents, all live together. They used to live crammed into an old house in a pretty rough area of town, but after Juanita went to work for Ford, he moved them all into the house behind the vet's office at Willow Point where he and Laura once lived."

"He didn't mention that."

"Juanita is fiercely loyal to Ford for hiring Maria to work for him when she had a hard time getting work here because of her background. Small towns can be funny and a little clannish about hiring. You know that. When Ford realized their family situation, after Juanita started working with him, he offered them the house at Willow Point. You can imagine how wonderful that was for them to move into such a nice place. I think he gives them free rent for the work Juanita does for him. The man was stressed to the max and sinking in grief when she showed up offering to help him."

"You're kindly saying she probably resents me because I didn't come home and step up to take the children when Andrea and Adam were killed."

Lucy looked away. "I didn't say that."

"It's okay. Enough people have spoken up about it, directly or indirectly, that I know how the wind blows on that subject. It was a decision I wrestled with long and hard." She shook her head. "I never figured out any way for it to work with the life I lived. Two of Andrea's children were babies then; the other two not much older. They hardly knew me, either. They deserved better than being left alone most all the time with some nanny while I traveled. My only other option was to walk away from my job and come here, to raise four children alone with no income."

Lucy put a hand on hers. "I've never felt bad toward you for the decision you made."

"Thanks." She sighed. "Maybe over the summer I can work myself into a better relationship with Ford, the kids, and maybe even Juanita. I'd like to hold a part in the children's lives."

"Do you think you'll ever marry?"

She wrinkled her nose. "I've never met anyone I've wanted to marry and spend every day with yet. Oh, I thought I fell in love a few times, but the relationships soon seemed to crowd me. They pushed demands and expectations on me I didn't want. I think you need to be able to be yourself in a relationship and to feel encouraged to be who you are. Don't you?"

"I do." Lucy grinned. "Vance and I have that kind of relationship. It is possible, Samantha."

"Well, then you keep your eye out for another Vance for me. Marrying a man whose family owns a marina wasn't a bad idea either. You get lots of lake time."

"Dig out your bathing suit. Lake season is starting and we usually head out on the lake every weekend. Do you still remember how to ski?"

Samantha giggled. "I think it's like riding a bicycle. You may get a little rusty, but the old skill comes back quickly."

Lucy looked around. "Speaking of Ford," she said, lowering her voice. "I don't think either he or Juanita realize Madison and Natalie are getting close to those teenage years, especially Madison. Gosh, Samantha, she looks and acts so much like you. You know Aunt Dixie was quick to tell the facts of life to us and to give us a lot of practical wisdom about boy and girl issues."

"I well remember." Samantha rolled her eyes. "Whenever any of our friends wanted to know anything, they'd say, 'Go ask your Aunt Dixie, Samantha' because they knew Dixie would tell it to us straight every time."

"Yes, and it kept us out of trouble in a lot of ways. Your Aunt Dixie knew everybody in town and everything about them. Still does. She kept you, me, and Andrea out of difficult situations and relationships, many a time."

Samantha nodded. "Like the little Pomeroy boy Andrea got that big crush on."

"Yes." She agreed. "Dixie broke that up with some solid in-your-face facts Andrea could hardly dispute. Andrea did tend to be idealistic."

Lucy got up. "Wait here a minute. I want to show you something." She came back carrying an envelope and then looked around furtively before opening it to be sure none of her customers were close by. "I shouldn't show you this, but these are some photos a couple of the teenage girls brought in here one day giggling over them. I found them in the bathroom later; they must have accidently left them. One of the girls come back to look for them but I played innocent. I didn't think they needed to get them back."

After glancing around again, she passed the photos to Samantha and whispered. "They're pictures of Michael Denby with some girls. I learned later that one of the girls in the store, Jessica Martin, got dumped by Michael and was trying to get even with him by sneaking photos and sharing them around to show what a player he is. You can see one photo is a pretty passionate one, and in this one Michael has his hands up under the girl's shirt. Honestly, these teens today are much more adventurous than we were. This last one, the most innocent, is just a kissing picture, but the girl is Madison Bradley, your niece. I've been trying to decide if I should show it to Aunt Dixie. Madison is only twelve. Michael Denby is fifteen."

She blew out a worried breath. "The kids love to come in here and hang around after school and on the weekends. I don't mind. They buy snacks, colas, and books. But they talk, too. I learn a lot of things without meaning to. Most of it I try not to pay attention to but this situation worried me."

Samantha frowned. "It worries me, too. Do you think I could take these pictures and talk to Aunt Dixie about them?" She paused. "Does Madison come in here often with Michael Denby?"

"No, she lives too far outside of town to come here, not driving or anything yet. I heard the girls say Michael meets a lot of his girlfriends at the Wells Branch General Store out on the highway, not far from his house on Smoky View. Some of the kids walk down to that store at night and hang around talking at the old picnic tables outside. You know the ones."

"That old store is only a block from the resort on the highway. It would be easy for Madison to walk down there. I wonder when she could get away to go though?"

"How did we used to do things, Samantha? At night after our parents were asleep. Check your memory."

Samantha tried not to grin. "We used to climb out the window. We only walked around or went to meet some friends down at the lake or something but it was still pretty daring."

"Then your Aunt Dixie caught us and that escapade ended."

Samantha laughed. "I remember."

Lucy tucked the photos back in the envelope. "These are only print-offs from photos the girls obviously snapped on their phones, but it could hurt Madison's reputation or bring teasing from her peers if word got around." She shook her head. "Think how humiliated these girls will be if they see these photos? Teenagers can be really ugly spreading things around on social media today. The other girls in the photos with Michael are older and more in his age group. It worries me that Madison is only twelve. She probably really thinks Michael likes her or something."

Samantha left Lucy later with this on her mind, wondering what to do about it. Starting up the hill, at the intersection of Main, a voice called out to her. "Samantha, wait up." She turned to see Paulette coming out of a shop on the corner.

"I thought that was you," Paulette said, catching up to her. "I haven't seen you in an age. What are you doing in town?"

"I'm visiting Aunt Dixie," Samantha answered, pleased to see Paulette again.

Paulette Everett, an event caterer with a small business in Dandridge, often helped Aunt Dixie with larger meetings and events at the Dandridge Inn. Her business, Everett's Events, catered a multitude of events around the area, business meetings, weddings, showers, receptions, special club meetings and more. When Samantha was a teenager, she often worked part-time helping Paulette with her events. Andrea did, too. They'd also helped in Paulette's shop making table and flower arrangements and occasionally helping to serve at events, always wearing neat black skirts and white blouses.

"Well, it's a treat to see you, Samantha. Are you staying long?"

"Probably most of the summer, if not all. I'm on leave from work, recovering after an accident."

This comment led to the usual remarks about Samantha's accident. It was rare she ever ran into anyone who hadn't seen that fall during the hurricane. She wondered if it was on some YouTube site for public viewing or something. You'd think most people would have forgotten about it by now.

"How's Jimmy?" Samantha asked, eager to change the subject. She remembered with fondness Paulette's smiling jovial husband, who always gave her and Andrea big hugs and told them they were the prettiest girls in town. They knew Jimmy was only joking around, but he was always a fun and loving man.

"We're divorced." Paulette's eyes looked down toward her shoes. "Only recently. You're old enough at your age now to understand he just cheated on me. About broke my heart. The other woman, who lives over in White Pine, later dumped him. Jimmy's wanting to get back with me now, but I'm too hurt to even think about considering it."

"Oh, Paulette, I'm sorry."

"Well, life happens. The good and the bad. I've kept the house. It's near town and my business. Jimmy moved to live on a houseboat belonging to a friend of his. He's thinking about buying it, I heard." She looked back at Samantha. "We got married right after high school when I was only nineteen. He wasn't but twenty. We've been married over thirty-six years, raised two boys. You simply don't expect someone to stray on you after you've lived all the good years we did. I'll be honest and say it's been hard."

Samantha tried to think of something to say.

Paulette smiled then. "I didn't mean to hit you with sad news here at our first hello, sweetheart." She looked Samantha over. "You sure have turned out fine and beautiful, prettier than that skinny young teenager who used to help me with my events. Real mature and glamorous now."

"Thanks. You look good, too. I like the short curly hair."

She patted her head. "I cut it off and got a little perm. I wanted a change and it's easier to care for." She shifted the subject. "You heading back to your Aunt Dixie's?"

Samantha nodded.

"Well, tell her I'll be giving her a call about setting up Renee Switzer's wedding at the Inn next month if that would work for her. With the weather nice, we can do a big tent in the back yard behind the outdoor garden. Ask Dixie if she wants to do any of the catering. Sometimes she likes to help with that, depending on how she feels. The extra money is nice for her. She and Clarice Newberry have been thinking about taking one of those cruises so I know she's trying to save up some extra cash. Maybe they can schedule that trip while you're here to watch out for things. It's hard for her to find someone reliable to cover the inn so she can get away. Sometimes I do it. I took care of things when she came down to stay with you a few times. My catering falls off in the winter and the extra money was nice for me then."

"I appreciate you covering for her."

"I was glad to. We're both sociable women and enjoy people." She glanced at her watch. "Hate to scoot, honey, but I have an appointment. I need to get back to the office."

Samantha waved her off and then continued her walk back home. Noticing the wind had whipped up slightly and that a layer of dull grayish stratus clouds stretched across the sky now, Samantha picked up her pace. It looked like a little storm was on the way.

CHAPTER 4

Over the next days, after Samantha King showed up at his clinic in a fury, Ford found his thoughts often drifting in her direction. He didn't like the direction of those thoughts either. Oh, he appreciated a pretty girl as well as any man, but inappropriate thoughts about Samantha King, the Bradley children's aunt no less, shouldn't find a way into even a small corner of his mind. First, he didn't really like her or know her. Second, it would prove difficult enough to negotiate the situation with her, wanting time with the children this summer, without his mind straying in awkward directions.

"That Samantha King sure is a beautiful woman," Dwayne said on Friday as they sat in the break room at the vet's office eating a sandwich for lunch between appointments.

"I think you mentioned that before," Ford answered, getting up to snag a bag of cookies from a shelf, hoping to change the subject. "Want a few of these cookies?"

Dwayne ignored the offer. "You've been distracted the last couple of days. Are you worried about that situation with Samantha? Maria said Samantha and her mother Juanita got into it at the house, that her mother isn't happy the Bradley kids' aunt is going to be hanging around this summer. She also mentioned you invited Samantha to stay for supper."

"Actually the kids invited her. It put me in a spot, so soon after Juanita refused to let Samantha in the house to see her own nieces and nephews."

"You see?" Dwayne lifted a brow. "You're still acting grumpy.

Most of the guys I know act like that when they have a burr up their butt about a woman."

Ford turned to glare at Dwayne. "The fact that Samantha King wants to spend time getting to know her sister Andrea's kids has nothing to do with me. Except that I'm forced to negotiate the animosity between her and Juanita and to try to make nice with the woman whenever she stops by."

"I'm sure that will be a real trial." Dwayne grinned. "I also hear you're going to be forced to make nice to her on Saturday when she comes over. Tough break."

"Why are you messing with me about this, Dwayne?"

"Because you've been alone and without a woman for three years now, and I haven't seen you give even an interested glance to anyone until Samantha King dropped by." Dwayne rubbed a hand over his head. "Having a woman in your life is nice, man. You've got great kids but it's not the same. So, yeah, if you're interested in her, I'd like to see you make something of it."

"Look." Ford came to sit down at the table again. "I appreciate your concern, but if I did want to make something of a relationship with a woman I find attractive, it wouldn't be Samantha King. She's the kind to flit in and out of your life like a pretty butterfly. Because of the kids I need to think differently. They come first with me. You may remember she didn't even stay a couple of weeks to help me out with those kids after their parents' funeral. Flew in, flew out the next day."

Dwayne considered this. "If I remember right she was covering those Washington state wildfires then. It was a mess out there. I saw her on television the next day, on the scene, reporting a new fire that started after she flew back. That fire burned up whole towns up there. It wasn't like she went home and sat by the swimming pool or something." He snagged one of Ford's cookies. "That's dangerous work; I wouldn't have wanted to be there. No way, man. I'd take a dog bite any day over that."

Ford chuckled over his last words. "You have a point, and I know a few dogs waiting to see you right now—that little bulldog we had to pull that infected tooth out of and the Pekinese with the urinary tract infection. Both should be okay to go home later today, and Mrs. Smith is bringing in her poodle with skin allergies again at about 1:30. That little dog has problems with allergies every spring about this time. Check the dog's file for the usual meds and advice we give. Let me know if you see anything more I should look at. I have a hip dysplasia surgery to do on an older retriever and then some new client visits for a couple of kittens and a pup. If we're lucky and no emergencies come in, we might be able to take off early."

Ford did get home a little earlier than usual but only to walk into a nest of problems with the kids.

"Gareth got in trouble on the bus," Rebecca tattled in a singsong voice as soon as he walked in the kitchen door.

"Snitch." Gareth stuck out his tongue at her.

"It was only a little stupid thing," Clay added in Gareth's defense.

Clay and Gareth had kitchen duty this afternoon helping Juanita with supper. It looked like Juanita had baked a pork roast and sweet potatoes, and she had the boys chopping up cabbage and carrots for slaw.

"I don't know anything about that bus business," Juanita told him. "This is the first I've heard of it, but Tamela fell out of the swing and bloodied her knee. I sent her up to the bathroom crying with Natalie and Madison to clean it and put some medicine on it. You might want to take a look. I don't think it's much but since you're here you can check it."

"Everything else okay?"

"Yes. I'll finish helping the boys get this slaw finished but then I need to head home. Maria and Carlos are going out to dinner with friends and I promised to mind the kids."

"Go on home," he replied. "I'll help the boys with the slaw and then go check on Tamela."

"Thank you." She took off the apron she wore and hung it on a hook by the pantry before retrieving her purse to head out the back door. Ford shut the door behind her as she left before turning back into the kitchen.

"Gareth, tell me what happened on the bus," he said to his son as he went to the sink to wash his hands.

"It was dumb, Dad. I had some extra Pokemon cards that some of the other boys on the bus didn't have so I sold them my extras."

Clay added to his story. "The bus driver saw Gareth taking money from a couple of boys when he stopped to let some kids off. He asked some questions, and then fussed at Gareth. It's against the bus rules to sell things on the bus."

"Did you know that Gareth?"

He shrugged. "There are so many rules. I didn't remember that one, but the bus driver said I had to be suspended from riding the bus until you and I talked to the principal on Monday."

"Looks like we'll all need to sit down and read over the bus rules more carefully." Ford got mayonnaise from the refrigerator to put in the slaw. "We'll need to talk about this more later, too. Gareth, I know you like to make money but sometimes you step a little too far over the line in ambition. I can remember a number of money-making schemes of yours we should have discussed before you took off with them."

Clay, older than his brother Gareth by two years, tried to smother a laugh. "Remember the time Gareth tried to sell river rocks to those kids staying over in the cabins? He told them they were lucky, magic rocks."

Gareth frowned. "Well, they might have been. Some people think rocks with shiny quartz in them are lucky."

Ford shook his head at Gareth. "There are ways to make money in an honorable way and ways to make money fraudulently or on the shady side. It's important to learn the difference, Gareth." He hesitated. "How much did you charge those kids for the Pokemon cards?"

He watched Gareth fidget and hesitate. "The cards were cool ones the guys really wanted."

"Meaning you overcharged them," Ford answered for him. "If some of the parents call the school to complain about that, we may also need to answer for that concern to the principal on Monday."

"They didn't have to buy them," Gareth defended.

"Like I said, we'll talk about this more later." He finished stirring the last of the mayonnaise into the slaw, adding a little vinegar, celery seeds, and a dab of sugar and salt to the mix.

"Who's setting the table?" he asked, looking around to see that every thing else was basically ready to serve.

"Natalie and Madison did it before Rebecca came in crying about her knee."

"Well, I'll go check on that and then round everybody up to eat. You guys put everything on the table for dinner, put ice in the glasses, and get that pitcher of tea out of the refrigerator."

Dinner moved along without any more problems after Ford checked on Rebecca. She mostly needed assurance and attention over the skinned knee. Of all the children Rebecca cried the most easily. Maybe because she was the youngest. He didn't really know.

Ford helped Wesley and Andrew clean up after dinner. It was their turn for it on the chart.

As he put the food away, Ford noted there was enough extra pork roast to chop up and put in Manwich pork sandwiches tomorrow night. Enough slaw left, too, for another meal. That would make dinner easier for him. Juanita probably planned it that way to help. Weekends he was on his own.

After dinner, with the weather beautiful outdoors, the older kids set up the croquet set for a game. Rebecca and Tamela opted to play dolls in the gazebo by the lake, which meant Ford could sit out on the terrace with a cup of coffee and the newspaper and relax from the day, keeping an eye on all the kids. On a Friday night like this, most of his single friends were out, and many of his married friends sat in their homes somewhere laughing and talking about their day. Sharing. He still missed that. Missed Laura.

Dwayne was right; he'd hardly looked at a woman with any interest since Laura died. He laughed at the thought. With eight kids and all he dealt with in his life every day, he seldom had time to notice women. Quite honestly, few women encouraged his interest after learning he had eight children. He could hardly blame them. Personally, he'd run hard and fast from any woman with that many kids.

Tamela and Rebecca wandered up on the porch to join him, followed by Frou Frou, a small, fluffy, white mixed breed dog, especially devoted to the girls. The other dogs, a shaggy brown mutt named Benji, and two Labrador retrievers Jefferson and Gracie, played in the yard with the kids. The family had four cats, too. It seemed to be a given as a vet that you ended up with animals. He'd drawn the line with Laura at eight children, and a year ago with Frou Frou, he'd drawn the line at eight pets.

"No more after this," he said when they begged him into taking Frou Frou, abandoned on the vet porch in a cardboard box. "Eight is enough." He'd pointed to a weathered board sign in their kitchen reading, *Limit: Eight at the Lake.* It referred to fishing limits, of course. Laura had found it at some antique mall and gave it to him as a gag gift in the past. With eight kids and now eight pets the sign had become somewhat of a family joke.

"I hope no kitties or dogs died today," Rebecca said, climbing up in the chair to scrunch in beside him. Ford and Laura's youngest, she looked so much like Laura with her dark hair and eyes. All his natural kids, Rebecca, Gareth, Clay, and Natalie, had his and Laura's dark brunette, almost black hair, and deep brown eyes. But having raised the four Bradley children, most since babies and toddlers, Ford didn't love them any less. They felt like his now.

Tamela, sitting cross-legged on the floor playing with her dolls, looked up at him. "I don't remember Aunt Samantha much. Madison does and she texts and writes to her sometimes, but Andrew and Wesley said they don't hardly remember her either."

"Andrew was only about seven the last time Samantha came to Dandridge, Wesley five, and you only about three. It's no surprise you don't remember her. Her work keeps her traveling." He tried to think what else to say on a positive note. "Samantha is looking forward to getting to know all of you while she's here this summer though."

"She's pretty. She looks kind of like Mommy did," Tamela said.

"Sisters often look alike."

Rebecca curled under his arm. "Natalie's old pictures look like me."

"Natalie did look a lot like you when she was five, Rebecca. Both of you are pretty girls and smart."

"Are the Larsens coming over tomorrow?" Tamela asked.

Ford almost groaned. He'd almost forgotten that. "I think they plan to come by. Their kids want to play at the swim beach with you and maybe at the pool."

Ben Larsen, a medical doctor in practice with his father in Dandridge, had been one of Ford's closest friends since school years. He and his wife Vickie, good friends of Andrea and Adam Bradley, too, had been a great support to him through these years of grief and adjustments.

"We like Emmylou," Rebecca said.

"She likes having you and Tamela to play with, too. I'm sure you'll have fun tomorrow."

The Larsens had three children, Courtney, eleven, almost Natalie and Madison's age, Jake, nine, right between his four boys, and Emmylou, six like Tamela. The families often got together on the weekends. He'd forgotten about them coming over when he invited Samantha to come. Oh, well. It would prove a good distraction.

"Look! Fireflies!" Tamela pointed out into the yard.

"Yes and it's getting dark and time for baths and bed."

"And time for bedtime stories." Rebecca looked up at him with bright eyes. "Will you read to us tonight?"

"Sure," he said. Sometimes when he had paperwork or chores to do, he let the older kids read to the younger ones, but tonight he decided he would read.

He stood up to call the other children in. "It's time to head in, guys. Put the game in the shed. Whoever's ahead wins this one."

Ford heard groans, but they stopped and began to pull the wickets up and put the croquet set away.

"Bring in all the animals, too," he said. "I'll get Rebecca and

Tamela started on baths. Call if you need me."

Ford hoped after baths and bedtime stories that he could snag an hour or two to himself. He seldom found time alone, and when he did he usually fell asleep over a good book.

CHAPTER 5

After a call to Ford, Samantha headed over to the resort on Saturday morning. She wore her swimsuit under her shorts and in a tote bag she carried a towel, sun lotion, and a few other items she'd need for a day in the sun. Stuffed in a second bag from the dollar store were squirt guns for the kids, a pack of bubble wands, and a jug of extra bubble solution.

Dixie smiled at her gift selection. "It's always smart to woo the favor of kids with gifts. The gifts don't need to be much, of course, but it tells children in a way they understand that you thought of them."

"Well, I need all the help I can get in that arena," Samantha said as she left Aunt Dixie visiting with her new guests at the inn.

The drive from Dandridge down Highway 139 to the entrance to the Sycamore Lake Resort took only about ten minutes but all evidence of town quickly disappeared as the highway followed through farmland and past the entrances to a few quiet subdivisions on the lake. Nearing the resort, Samantha passed the Goose Creek Farm Bed and Breakfast on a cove of Douglas Lake and not far after the rustic Wells Branch General Store at the corner of Green Hill Road. Painted a weathered red, the old store had stood along the highway for as long as Samantha could remember—one of those icons you smiled to see with its battered front porch and American Flag hanging from a porch post. The entrance to the McDaniel family's resort, beside Ford's clinic, lay only five minutes further down the road, making Samantha remember what she'd learned about Madison.

Samantha hadn't found time to talk with Dixie about this situation yet but she probably should in the next day or two. In all honesty, she hated the idea of sticking her oar into Ford's business right now when she was trying to win favor with him, and with Juanita and the kids.

A winding road led into the Sycamore Lake Resort, twining through a lush green property and then on to the lodge sprawled across a verdant expanse of lawn. A small pond lay tucked under willow trees across the street from the old lodge, and Samantha could see the glorious sweep of Sycamore Lake visible behind it, pretty and blue in the May sunshine today.

Samantha slowed her car studying the old lodge, the McDaniel's home now, a long, white two-storied building with a weathered slate grey roof above its gables. The middle portion of the building had a deep, inviting covered porch across its front with side additions tucked at angles off the main building's two ends in a pleasing way.

"People used to flock to that resort back in the 1940s and 1950s," Dixie told her that morning over breakfast. "The McDaniel family developed the resort from their vast tract of farmland around Sycamore Lake after tourists began to flock to the Great Smoky Mountains and Douglas Lake. I know you remember the lake was formed in the early 1940s when the dam was built. Lodges were popular then, before the days of so many motels. People preferred a quiet rural spot for vacations in those days with scenic beauty and a wide variety of outdoor activities."

"I'm glad to see the resort still thriving," Samantha said.

"Yes," Dixie agreed. "Ford's grandparents were smart to find new ways to keep the resort popular, especially building that event lodge on the back side of the lake, a chapel and an outdoor pavilion. A lot of weddings and business events use that site. The family modernized the cabins, too. People want that now—air-conditioning, microwaves, and such."

Samantha considered this. "It's sad so many old resorts, once so popular like Sycamore Lake, haven't survived, like Pressmen's

Home in Rogersville. I remember when we went there one summer for vacation. Do you?"

Dixie smiled. "I do indeed. You, Andrea, and I enjoyed a fine time in our week there. Jackson and I visited on a trip once before and I wanted to go again." She shook her head. "It's a sorrow how they let that old place run down, abandoned and neglected now. It was a pretty spot in its day."

Feeling happy Sycamore Lake Resort had not met the same fate, Samantha pulled her car into a spot by the lodge's garage. A note on the door told her she'd find everyone at the swim beach and she soon spotted the trail that followed along the lake to the beach, with rustic weathered guideposts tacked along the way. She could hear the kids whooping and playing as she grew closer.

Ford, probably watching for her, waved when he saw her. He sat with a man and woman Samantha didn't know, in weathered Adirondack chairs under a broad shady tree by the lake.

"Hey," he called out. "Glad you found us."

She smiled.

"This is Ben Larsen and his wife Vickie." He gestured to the man and woman. "Ben and I have been friends since school days. He practices with his father Dr. Hazen Larsen in the Dandridge Medical Clinic downtown. You've probably walked by it."

"I have, and I know Hazen Larsen." She reached out a hand to both Ben and Vickie. "Nice to meet you."

"You, too." Vickie smiled at her. "We knew your sister Andrea and her husband Adam well."

Great, Andrea thought, probably someone else who faulted her for not coming home to take care of Andrea's kids.

Vickie patted an empty chair beside her. "Sit down and make yourself comfortable. You can throw your things over on that table."

Samantha studied Vickie Larsen as she did. She was an attractive woman with dark eyes, dimples, a warm smile, and wavy brown hair tied up in a ponytail today. Her husband Ben, more rugged in appearance, with football player looks, had dark hair, beginning to bald on the top, and a fun-loving appearance. He laughed now at a comment of Ford's, and Samantha enjoyed seeing Ford laugh in return. She'd seen him laugh or smile very little since they met and she liked how he looked when he did.

Sitting in the chair Vickie indicated, Samantha let her eyes rove out over the broad lake scene before her. Sycamore Lake, although small compared with Douglas Lake, still covered a broad acreage with several scenic coves jutting off the main lake's body, good for fishing and small boating fun. It's banks were prettier in some ways than Douglas's shores since the Tennessee Valley Authority never lowered the levels of this natural lake, which had been here long before construction of the dam that created Douglas Lake.

The kids played, laughing and having fun in the water, reminding Samantha of scenes of her camp days. She noted the older children seemed congregated on a wooden swim raft about one hundred feet off shore. They dove off the sides of the raft, laughing, engaged in water fights, and then climbed back up to sit on the raft again. The younger ones played nearer to shore. The boys kicked along on paddleboards while the girls giggled and talked, sitting in a big float toy that looked like a giant turtle. She noticed the smaller girls wore swim bubbles around their waists, a good safety measure for their age if they weren't strong swimmers yet.

Seeing the younger children glance her way, Samantha waved at them and held up the sack she'd brought. They waved back and tumbled out of the water to come investigate. After exclamations, the three boys, Gareth, Wesley, and the Larsen's boy Jake, took off with the squirt guns to fill them at a water fountain by the pavilion's restroom on the hill.

"Use good sense with those and don't squirt anyone in the face or eyes," Ben cautioned as they raced off.

The girls, Tamela, Rebecca, and the Larsen's youngest Emmylou, were more interested in the bubble wands and were soon running along the bank, laughing and creating bubble magic with the wands.

"Well, you've won my children over quickly with those gifts." Vickie smiled at Samantha.

"I had fun in the toy section of the dollar store last night deciding what would be fun for them all to enjoy outside."

Ford frowned. "You don't need to bring gifts when you come to visit."

"I know, but a bag of squirt guns and a package of bubble wands didn't set me back much. And look how much fun they're having."

"That's one of the best joys of being around kids," Vickie smiled at her. "They remind you to enjoy life, to be more fun-loving and grateful."

Samantha smiled back at her. "I think I'm going to swim out to the raft," she said, standing to strip off her shorts and T-shirt down to her bathing suit underneath. As she leaned over to step out of the slip-on tennis shoes she wore, she caught Ford watching her out of the corner of her eye. Thinking she didn't notice, he continued to watch her while she wound her hair into a twist, securing it in place with a wide barrette she pulled out of her bag. When she glanced his way before heading out into the lake, he looked away, saying something to Ben.

Well, he might not like me much but he is noticing me, Samantha thought, as she waded out into the lake and then dove into the water to swim to the raft.

In the next hour she simply had fun, playing and diving with the kids from off the raft. She grabbed one of the paddleboards and swam out deeper into the lake and back with Madison and Natalie. Back at the raft again, she fielded a water fight with Clay and Andrew and impressed them afterward with her jackknife dive she'd always been proud of.

Resting on the raft a little later, she noticed a few other children playing across the lake near the cabins, two men fishing from a small jonboat, and a lot of cars parked near the Sycamore Point end of the lake, indicating an event going on today. She was glad to see the resort active and busy.

"Dad's waving at us," Madison said, interrupting her thoughts.

Samantha turned to look and saw Ford wave again and point toward the pavilion on the hill.

"He wants us to swim in for lunch." Natalie waved back. "We brought things down for a picnic and the Larsens brought stuff, too."

"Stay and eat with us," Ford offered when she got out of the water with the girls. "It's just a spread of sandwich makings, chips, and cookies. We eat light at the lake, but there's plenty."

"I don't need to stay for lunch," Samantha said, drying off.

"It's no problem, and it's a nice day." He actually smiled then. "You seem to be having a good time and you're getting some of that exercise you said you needed. I think the kids would like for you to stay, too."

"Please stay, Aunt Samantha," Madison added. "We're going to get the canoes out after lunch."

"Okay," she agreed. She pulled on her T-shirt over her swimsuit, slipped into her tennis shoes, and followed them up to the pavilion.

Eleven children sat around laughing and talking over lunch at the picnic tables in the big pavilion on top of the hill. The four adults sat at one table keeping an eye on the children at the other tables, breaking up small spats and once stopping a food fight from beginning with the older boys.

Samantha smiled. She could remember times here as a girl, when the pavilion used to serve concessions at one end.

"Penny for your thoughts," she heard Ben Larsen say.

She looked across at him, such an easy man to be around. "I was remembering coming here as a girl, getting a hot dog, sitting at the tables like all your children, laughing and enjoying a good time." She looked around. "I don't see the old jukebox anymore."

Ford smiled then. "We still have it. It's inside the concessions area. Sometimes we pull it out for an evening party or a rental event. Dad and I rent out the pavilion and swim beach for some parties, like we do the event lodge, chapel, and pavilion on the backside of the lake."

"I'll bet it doesn't have the same old songs in it."

He grinned. "You'd be wrong. It's still full of what my parents call oldies but goodies—songs from the fifties and sixties when the jukebox was made."

"Man, we need to get that out one evening," Ben said, laughing. "Show these kids how to shake a leg."

"Maybe we'll do that sometime," Ford said, before getting up to go speak to Wesley about shaking up his cola bottle to spew it out at Gareth.

The afternoon drifted by, a glorious day to Samantha, full of the outdoor fun she loved. They held canoe races across the lake, swam more, and played volleyball, a game Samantha could really hold her own in.

Toward the afternoon, she and Vickie sat again in the weathered Adirondack chairs in the shade, taking a break while Ben and Ford supervised the boys fishing off the walk-bridge.

"Will they catch anything?" Samantha said.

"Maybe," Vickie answered. "Ford and his dad Burl keep the lake stocked. They might catch a bluegill or a small bass. Maury Beck, who works the grounds here at the lake, used to work at one of the hatcheries. He's knowledgeable about keeping the lake exactly right for fish. Ford can explain more to you about that than I can."

"I'm pleased they kept the resort going."

"Burl loves the place. So does Ford." She smiled at Samantha. "So do Ben, the kids, and myself. We love to come over here and hang out."

"Do you live nearby?"

"We do. If you drive down the highway a few miles past the resort, swing left toward Douglas Lake, and head out Terry Point Road we live in a house on the end of a little peninsula at Goose Cove."

"So you live on the water, too."

"We do. Ford keeps his pontoon boat over at our place with our ski boat. We play on the water in different ways there, sit out on the dock on the lake, enjoy skiing and pulling the kids on tubes. Ford comes over to our place a lot. You should come, too."

Samantha glanced away. "Well, that's thoughtful of you, but I wouldn't want to intrude on your family times."

Vickie put a hand on her arm. "You are our family, too, Samantha. We loved Andrea and Adam; we love their children. You're their aunt, Andrea's sister."

"Thank you." Samantha almost felt like crying. "I thought of Andrea many times today playing here at the lake."

"You both grew up in Dandridge. It's natural you'd think of her more now that you're back." Vickie paused. "Andrea always talked about you with much affection."

"Thanks for telling me that."

"I can see the family resemblance between you and Andrea, but your hair is much redder. Andrea's hair was more reddish brown, like Andrew and Tamela's. She wasn't as tall as you are either and she wore her hair short." Vickie laughed. "Andrea would never have spent the day out on the lake swimming, getting into fierce water fights, racing the guys across the lake in a canoe, or jackknifing off the raft. I can tell you that."

Samantha grinned a little. "I was always the more adventurous one, Andrea quieter and more cautious."

"Yes, and Andrea was sweet and wonderfully good-hearted, too. We all miss her."

Hearing a shout, they looked across at the bridge to see one of the boys pull in a small fish.

"That's my Jake. He'll be proud about catching that fish tonight." Vickie watched the men and boys on the bridge for a few minutes.

"Ford told me he gave his heart to the Lord out there on that bridge."

Samantha knew her eyes widened at this turn in the conversation.

"He shared about it to Ben and me one night after Laura died. He said he didn't know how anyone got through death and grief and sorrow without a deep faith in God, and he cried after saying it. It was so hard on him losing Laura with them both so young and the children so small."

"They did have a large family."

Vickie crossed her leg. "Laura loved babies. I think she'd have begged Ford for more if they hadn't taken in Andrea's kids. I know

Ford held reservations about doing that, taking on such a huge responsibility, as much as he loved Andrea and Adam's children." She hesitated. "Taking in four children is massive for anyone."

Samantha didn't answer, thinking Vickie faulted her, like so many others, for not stepping forward to do just that.

"Ben and I didn't volunteer," she continued. "Frankly, I don't think I could have done it. I had three children then, Emmy just a baby. I don't know how Ford and Laura managed. But Laura had been a nurse. She worked for Ben and his dad at their medical practice. That's where she met Ford, you know." Vickie looked out over the lake thoughtfully. "Laura always wanted a big family. I think she got Andrea caught up in that wake with her. The two literally plotted having their children about the same time, one every two years after the first, like clockwork."

At Samantha's glance her way, Vickie smiled. "I don't mean that to sound negative. It's only that women are all different in what they want in life. I like kids, love mine, but I love my music, too."

Samantha couldn't conceal her surprise at that remark.

"You didn't know I was the pianist at the church where Ford and the children go? At Dandridge Community Church on Green Hill Road?"

"No, I didn't know that."

"Well, music is my passion—that and my love for the Lord. My father is the pastor at the church. I grew up in a strong faith-filled family. Did you?"

"Did I what?" Samantha tried to follow Vickie's train of thought.

She smiled. "Did you grow up in a strong faith-filled home?"

Samantha wasn't sure how to answer. "I grew up with Aunt Dixie. She belongs to an old Presbyterian church downtown that some of her ancestors helped to establish. Andrea and I went there with her whenever Dixie could get away from the inn. We went to Sunday School, Bible School, did all those things. You know."

Vickie studied her, making Samantha feel somewhat uncomfortable. "Going to church and knowing God in a personal way aren't the same thing. When did you come to know God for yourself, Samantha?"

She shrugged. "I suppose as a girl. I went through Communicants class with Andrea. Dixie saw to it we got there for all the classes. Andrea was nine; I was eleven, I think. You learn all about the Presbyterian faith and then join the church. Commit your faith and all that."

Vickie shook her head. "It was ritual for you, something adults wanted you to do."

"Well, yeah, I guess. Isn't it that way for everyone?"

"No, and I hope you've experienced something stronger since." Vickie leaned her head back against her chair. "I'll tell you my story. I'd always been a believer, too—you know, believed in God, went to church and all." She smiled. "But one summer I went to a church camp in the mountains. The leaders were so strong and sure in their faith, the singing so glorious. I kept feeling like God was pulling on me, wanting something from me that I didn't have."

She paused for a moment. "I started going off by myself, feeling odd, like I wanted to pray, get quiet and hear from God. Then one evening a visiting ministry leader came to talk with us. She was from Jamaica, and she told how she had gotten born again, how she'd come to know God and asked Jesus to come into her heart. This woman was so alive in the Lord and I knew I had not experienced what she talked about. I did not have the smile on my face talking about God she did, the joy she radiated. I sat there and began to cry, and when she asked if anyone wanted to come down front and pray to know Jesus, I went. Maybe the leaders were surprised to see a pastor's child come down, but when that Jamaican woman prayed with me, I gave my life totally over to God and I've never been the same again since."

She gave Samantha a sunny smile. "That's what I was talking about."

Samantha couldn't think of a single thing to say.

"My passion for music," Vickie continued, "simply exploded after that. I'd always taken piano lessons but after that I loved playing. I never wanted to be a concert pianist or anything, but I knew I wanted to study music and play in church. I wanted to teach piano, too. I do both now."

Again Samantha tried to think of an appropriate comment.

"You're a passionate woman Samantha, passionate about your life, passionate about your career. I've seen you on television braving a storm, standing strong with a tornado spinning in the sky behind you. If you don't have a faith that feels as passionate as those things to you, don't settle. Don't feel that just going to church and sitting on a pew and reciting some ritual words is all there is." She leaned toward Samantha. "Faith can be as exciting as chasing a storm. I just wanted you to know that if you don't."

"This is a really odd conversation to me," Samantha told Vickie after a moment. "I'll be honest in saying I have never experienced anything in faith like you're talking about."

"Then start seeking for yourself. Faith is real and personal. Don't let anyone fob you off telling you that you have all the faith you need when you know and feel you don't." She gave Samantha a wistful smile. "Remember that old Peggy Lee song 'Is That All There Is?' If that's what your faith feels like to you, then you don't give up until you find something better."

"How will I know if I find something better or if there is anything better? How do I know that what I've been raised in isn't all there is for me?"

"You'll know that you know," Vickie said with certainty. She stood, seeing Ben wave to her that they needed to pack up and go.

Vickie turned to her and gave her a hug. "I'm not sure why I shared these things with you today when we just met. But I felt I was supposed to. I hope I didn't offend you."

"No." Samantha began to gather up her things to leave, too. "I like honesty. And whatever our experiences are in anything in life, they are real for us. No one can take them away from us if they are real."

"There. I knew you'd understand." Vickie beamed. "I hope we'll be friends and that I'll see more of you while you're here. I'll get Ford to bring you over to the lake one weekend with him and the kids. I hope you'll come to my church one Sunday to visit, too."

Samantha grinned. "To hear you play the piano?"

"Yes, and maybe to learn more about God." She hesitated. "Just because I was slow in catching on doesn't mean my father isn't a good pastor. I figured that out later and Dad felt bad he hadn't helped me, or realized I wasn't in a sure, strong place with God. Sometimes churches assume too many things about the people who attend there."

Samantha said her goodbyes and went home to Aunt Dixie's with an odd mix of thoughts to think about, especially on the faith issues Vickie had thrown out at her. She'd always believed in God and sort of talked to Him now and again, like He heard her. Wasn't that what you were supposed to do?

She glanced out the window toward the moon as she got ready for bed. "Well, God, if I need a richer sort of faith of some kind, maybe You could help me with that," she said out loud. "While I'm working on getting things right with the kids and my health this summer, maybe I can get things more right with You, too, if it's needed." She grinned at the big moon out her window. "You know how much I always hate to be on the losing end of things. You let me know if I'm missing out on something I need."

She climbed into bed. *Well, at least this summer isn't turning out to be boring,* she thought. *I can definitely be thankful for that.*

CHAPTER 6

The next week proved busy for Ford, seeing the children through their last week of school and dealing, along with Milton Hornby, a vet in Morristown, with the painful situation of a puppy mill closed down by authorities. He and Dwayne volunteered with Dr. Hornby, to examine and treat many of the malnourished and neglected dogs removed from the rural site, their living conditions abominable. The dogs that survived had been sent on to the shelter in Morristown and into foster homes of volunteers willing to take on the task of nursing sick and abused dogs back to health.

Dealing with situations like this, and the inhumanity of people in relation to animals, always put Ford in a foul mood, and his mood wasn't helped when on Tuesday Maria came back to find him while he was treating a small Persian cat's ear infection.

It annoyed him that the cat's owner had waited so long to bring the little cat in. You'd think she'd have noticed the cat shaking her head and not hearing well even before discharge started from the ear. Didn't people realize an untreated ear infection could lead to permanent deafness and other health complications?

Ford glanced up from working on the cat to notice Maria's upset face.

"Is there an emergency?" he asked, knowing she usually didn't interrupt him in the exam room for other reasons.

"Ford, I'm sorry to interrupt, but my grandmother Ivanna has taken a fall. It's serious. My grandfather Esteban, not wanting to bother any of us at work, called 911 for help. An ambulance picked

Ivanna up. They think she may have broken her hip. Mother has gone to the hospital already but I think I should go, too." She wrung her hands as she talked. "Could you do without me this afternoon? Dwayne says he can cover the front office around his work to help."

"Of course. Go right away; we'll take care of things. I'm sorry to hear about Ivanna." He petted the little Persian idly while he talked. "Let us know how things go with your grandmother."

"Thank you, *gracias*." She paused at the door. "Juanita called your parents to cover at the house with the children. She didn't want to interrupt your work."

Ford groaned after she left. His mother wasn't strong enough to ride herd on the children anymore. Watching eight kids for more than a short time was too much for her and Burl to handle. Plus his father had his own work to do around the resort. With summer here, they entertained more visitors in the cabins, more people fishing and swimming on the lake, more campers in the little campground in the cove."

"Great," he said to the cat. "Just what I needed right now with the kids out of school."

He finished with the cat, calling in Mrs. Mincey to get her. "I've cleaned Cloris's ears out, given her a shot to ward off more infection, and I have some drops I want you to put in her ears over the next days."

He watched the older woman's eyes barely meet his. "I should have brought her before, Dr. McDaniel, but I live on a very limited income now since my husband passed. I was waiting for my social security to be deposited before I came so I could pay you."

Ford felt bad then for his critical thoughts toward her. "In the future, don't wait if you have problems with Cloris or your collie dog, either, Mrs. Mincey. We'll work something out, and as you leave, tell Dwayne you need to pay your bill in payments," he added, writing a note on the cat's chart.

A few minutes later, while he cleaned up the exam room, Dwayne leaned his head in the door. "I adjusted the bill for Mrs. Mincey according to your note." He smiled. "I also found her some samples in the back room for the medicine she needed for the cat so she wouldn't need to pay for it."

"Good." Ford looked at the clock. "Call Ivy Loman, that woman who volunteers at the shelter walking the dogs. See if she will come fill in at the front desk for us. Maria may need to take a day or two off, depending on how things go with her grandmother, and I may be in a mess at home with Juanita needing to tend to Ivanna. You know Estaban isn't strong enough to do anything to help with his health problems and needing a cane to get around and all. I see him out in the yard barely able to hobble around some days, and Juanita worries over his heart. He's had one heart attack."

He paused. "Do you think you can cover things later this afternoon if I leave early? I don't want to leave my mom and dad stuck with the kids for too long."

"No problem," Dwayne assured him. "Do you know anyone to call to look out for the kids for a few days if Juanita can't come?"

He frowned. "I guess Vickie might come to help or she might know someone in the church good with kids." He shook his head. "Things always happen at the dangdest times, don't they?"

"Yeah." Dwayne grinned. "But we always manage. I can cover here if you're out a day or two and when Maria comes back she has good vet tech skills, even if she isn't fully certified. We'll be all right. Don't worry. If we get an emergency we can't handle here at the clinic, you can run down from the house to help for a short time with your parents covering."

"You're right. We'll manage," Ford agreed, but he knew his mother needed help herself now. A home health aide came nearly every day to help her with dressing and basic needs that Burl found difficult to handle alone. The aide took care of their meals and the housework his mother could no longer do, as well. The polio weakened her more each year.

As he came up the driveway to his house later, the family labs Jefferson and Gracie greeted him with wagging tails, brightening his day. It was nice how dogs didn't worry and were always so glad to see you.

Ford pushed open the back door, glad to be home despite some new problems to deal with. For dinner, he could heat up frozen pizzas and toss together a salad if Juanita hadn't started anything before she left.

Laughter met his ears as he walked into the kitchen and he stopped in surprise to see Samantha King working with Madison and Natalie in the kitchen, obviously making dinner.

"Grandma got to feeling kind of bad so Madison texted Samantha to come and help," Natalie explained, looking at him with a smile. "We almost have dinner all ready. Juanita planned to fix chicken casseroles, rice, and peas and Madison and I know how to make those things."

"Juanita keeps all her recipes in that recipe box." Madison pointed to a long wooden box on the kitchen counter.

Ford glanced toward the box. It had been a lifesaver to him many times, packed with Laura's old recipes, recipes of his mom's, and now recipes Juanita had added. He was at a loss in the kitchen without a clear recipe to follow.

Samantha smiled at him, seeming to notice his silence. "It was no problem to run over to help and I enjoyed visiting with your mother and Burl for a while before they went back to the house. I told them I'd be glad to help until Juanita comes back."

Madison looked at Natalie and grinned. "Maybe Juanita's mother will need her to watch after her and stay with her for a long time."

Natalie, with only minimal remorse for Madison's comment, added, "Samantha is lots more fun than Juanita, Dad."

"Well, those are unkind thoughts to voice," Ford reprimanded. "You know Juanita must be very worried about her mother right now and your thoughts should be focused on praying her mother will get well soon."

"Sorry, Dad." Natalie wrinkled her nose. "You know we love Juanita and all her family."

Samantha had turned to pull casseroles out of the oven and to check on rice in a pot on the stove while he talked to the girls. "I think everything is ready for supper," she said.

"We aren't on the work chart for dinner," Madison put in. "But we changed out jobs with Andrew and Wesley so we could help Samantha. Granddad said it would be okay."

"Thanks for doing that," Ford said. "Where are the boys?"

"Doing house and yard chores, but they should be done. Rebecca and Tamela are working on a puzzle Samantha brought."

"I didn't buy it," Samantha said, seeming to read his mind about that. "Dixie keeps a stack of boxed puzzles at the Inn for the guests. I brought one over that isn't too complicated, and the girls and I started it before we came in the kitchen to begin dinner."

Not liking the way she seemed to follow his thoughts so easily, Ford said, "I'll go find all the kids if dinner is ready." He glanced at Samantha. "Thanks for helping out today."

"My pleasure. I hate being bored and I was running out of things to do at Aunt Dixie's." She hesitated. "I like being with the kids, too."

After dinner, Ford helped the younger girls clean up from dinner and then followed them outside to where the other children played in the backyard. The kids were playing a hide and seek game, Samantha joining in on the fun with them.

He flagged her to come and join him on the terrace.

"You don't need to stay longer," he told her as she walked up to sit in one of the wickers chairs across from him.

"I was having fun, and I knew you were helping with cleanup in the kitchen." She paused, studying his face. "How's Juanita's mother?"

He heaved a sigh. "Her hip is broken. A hip fracture is dangerous for an older person like Ivanna. Fortunately Juanita says the doctors say her bones are still pretty strong, so they think a hip replacement her best option for a full recovery. She's having the surgery tomorrow and then she's going to need a lot of recovery time. Full healing can take 10-12 weeks to months. A lot of complications can occur during the healing time. Juanita and the family are torn up about this. She'll need help at the rehab and then more at home."

"I can imagine. I well know how rough healing times are."

"The family is in for a difficult time. Ivanna has limited English and I know Juanita will want to do everything in her power to see her mother gets all the care she needs to recover her strength and mobility."

Samantha leaned forward. "Let me help, Ford. I can come stay with the children every day."

Ford closed his eyes and leaned his head back. "That's a huge job to take on Samantha. I know you mean well and I appreciate the offer…"

She interrupted. "Is it because you're still bitter toward me that you're saying no, because I didn't stay to help after Andrea and Adam died?" She rubbed her arm. "I know that was a hard time for you and I offered no help. Let me make up for that in a small way by helping now. Even though you and Juanita don't totally approve of me I can do kids. I worked as a counselor at camp many summers. I know how to keep kids entertained. I know first aid. I have good training."

She offered him a small smile. "Fortunately for you, too, I grew up at the Dandridge Inn. It was a given that Andrea and I learned how to clean house and to cook. I may not have used my domestic skills much in the last years, but they're latent skills I can draw on. Some things you don't forget, Ford."

Ford hesitated. Desperate times called for desperate measures. "I'd insist on paying you."

"I'd insist on declining that offer. I know part of your payment arrangements with Juanita include their house rent. I wouldn't want her to feel threatened about that. And she'll be coming back when her mother is better. Let this just be something I do to help you out." She sent him a saucy grin. "I know you hate to take favors from me but it won't kill you to do so, Ford."

He wracked his mind to think of another answer, but nothing came to mind quickly.

"Come on. Say yes. I'll come over to get started in the morning."

"I need to be at the clinic by nine at the latest every day. You'll need to get up early."

She laughed out loud. "You really don't know much about me to say that. When I first started with Weather First I did the morning forecasts. I got up at four every morning to come to the station to prepare. When I moved into the outdoor coverage team, I counted myself lucky to get a few hours of sleep half the time when a storm or dangerous weather conditions started moving in. You said you used to watch me on television. Did my job look so easy from your chair in front of the TV? I'll tell you for a certainty it wasn't."

Ford couldn't help grinning. "Dwayne said he'd rather get a dog bite any day than face some of the weather conditions he often saw you in."

Samantha's lips twitched. "Dixie said having the kids over was like facing a tornado. So you see? I'm well trained for the job."

"We'll try it out," he said with resignation after a few moments. "I'm too boxed into a corner right now to turn down the help." He ran a hand through his hair. "I've seen you're good with the kids and they like you."

"Well then." She looked satisfied. "I'll come around eight-thirty in the morning."

"I try to close the office at five every day, but sometimes emergencies hold me up. My dad can come over to fill in for times like that."

Her eyes softened. "Your dad has his hands full with your mother. She told me how the light case of polio she weathered as a girl came back on her. She never expected that."

"None of us did."

"I won't mind staying over when needed," she added. "Just get your work done at the clinic and come home when you can. I'll be fine."

He studied her for a minute, an idea forming in his mind. "What are you doing this weekend?"

Her eyes widened and Ford laughed at the thoughts he saw race across her face.

"The kids and I are going camping over at the Cosby Campground. I thought you might like to go with us, hang out, do a little hiking, play campfire girl." He paused. "I thought it might give us a chance, too, to talk out things about the kids, house rules we follow, things you probably should know. I want consistency with the children through this time. I've worked hard to get the kids into routines and systems that work for us."

She looked relieved and it tweaked Ford's pride a little to see it. He knew Samantha thought he was suggesting a date. Not that he would do that, of course, but he hated to see her so glad she'd been wrong. He could remember when women thought he was pretty good-looking, even chased after him. Was he getting too old to attract any attention now? He knew his fortieth birthday just around the corner.

Samantha snickered. "I thought you were asking me out," she said, always so direct.

Ford raised an eyebrow. "Just suggesting a camping trip," he replied, keeping his voice casual.

"Camping would be fun." She studied him for a minute. "Give me more details later in the week, and I'll help the kids get ready for it."

"I own an Airstream and a couple of tents, but the kids and I camp a lot. They know the drill, what to do to get ready, the rules when we camp."

"I was hoping for some time in the mountains while here." She nodded and stood up. "I think I'll head on home."

"Listen, if you change your mind after a week keeping up with all these kids, just let me know. I won't mention it to the kids before then in case you decide you want a break by then."

She grinned at him again. "Summer camp sessions followed consecutively all summer at Rock Brook Camp in Brevard—kayaking, swimming, rock climbing, horseback riding, archery, hiking, skits, arts and crafts, campfires, games. I think I can hold my own."

Ford's only question now, seeing the evening sun flashing over her red hair and trying not to let his eyes wander down to her long legs below her shorts, was how he'd hold up through the summer with her around every day. Maybe he'd simply get used to her over the days. After all, he didn't get much time around women, spending his days with cats, dogs, and kids. It would be odd for him not to notice a woman with Samantha's looks.

He kept telling himself that as he tossed and turned later trying to get to sleep. "Lord, I could use a little help here with my thoughts," he prayed. "Help me keep my mind on track. This woman is being kind enough to help me out with the kids here in this emergency. But You know, as I do, that we're only time fillers for Samantha King until she heads off in the fall again to chase weather around the U.S. Help a lonely man not to make a fool of himself."

CHAPTER 7

The next morning Samantha showed up promptly at Ford's for her first day with the kids. She'd talked to Aunt Dixie the night before about volunteering to watch the children for Ford.

"I'm proud of you for taking this on," Dixie said after Samantha explained the situation. "I know Ford is grateful and the opportunity will give you time to build strong ties with Andrea's children."

Samantha studied her aunt. "I worried you might be disappointed I wouldn't be helping you out more. You came to help me in Atlanta a couple of times and you left the Inn with Paulette or Clarice to do so. I planned to help you in return this summer. Maybe cover for you so you could take a trip."

She waved a hand. "I've been running this inn on my own for a long time, darlin.' I manage nicely. You know Irma and Eugene Rice come once a week to help me with all the major work around the place. Irma, half my age and as strong as a mule, cleans the house top to bottom and Eugene does all my yard work, mows, weeds, trims the shrubbery, cleans the gutters, power washes the walks when needed, and handles needed repairs or finds someone who can. I'm blessed to have their help."

"Don't they go to your church?"

"Yes, and that's how I met Eugene. He's the janitor at the church, very thorough, reliable, and as nice as can be. When I approached him about working for me he seemed pleased and he suggested his wife Irma could help me with cleaning. They've been with me ten years now." She reached over to pat Samantha's hand. "So don't you worry. I'll be fine. You'll carry the bigger job every day."

"I'll be okay." She shrugged. "I'm used to challenges and the unexpected. I'm sure I can handle whatever comes along with the kids until Juanita can come back to work." She hesitated. "Filling in to help Ford might go a long way, too, toward making up for past absences. You know my vacation time is scanty working with Weather First, usually only snagged in short spurts between crises."

Aunt Dixie raised an eyebrow. "I hope you didn't volunteer out of guilt."

"No." She shook her head. "I really like all the kids. I wanted to do it."

"Well, good. You go have fun. I've got a meeting with Paulette about that wedding she wants to host here."

Samantha found the McDaniel family still at breakfast in the big sunny dining area off the kitchen when she arrived. Ford encouraged her to pour herself a cup of coffee and sit down with them at the table.

"I've told the kids you're going to ride herd on them while Juanita is taking care of her mother. I also went to the hospital last night to see Ivanna and to talk to Juanita and the family. My folks came over to stay with the kids for a little while so I could go." He paused. "I let Juanita know you'd be covering for her at the house and to take all the time off she needed to care for her mother."

Samantha nodded, trying to keep a straight face. She'd loved to have been a fly on the wall for that conversation.

Ford glanced around the table at the children. "I talked with all the kids as well. They promised not to make your job harder." A smile flickered at the corner of his mouth.

"I'm sure we'll get along fine," Samantha assured him.

He looked around at the children again. "You guys go make your beds, clean up your rooms, and play upstairs for a little while on your own. I want to talk to Samantha before I leave for the clinic."

They all headed upstairs without opposition, obviously primed for Ford's announcement. Samantha sipped on her coffee, waiting.

After a few minutes Ford said, "I asked Maria to shuffle my

schedule this morning so I could stay and talk to you. There are some things I want you to know." He hesitated. "First, all eight children have chores in our home and everything runs on a schedule. Laura always used a looser system and somehow it worked for her but it didn't for me."

He took a minute to close his eyes. "I'll admit my life fell apart three years ago when Laura died. I was grieving, the kids were grieving, and nothing worked the same for me. Every day seemed full of upsets and arguments. The children, my parents, our friends, and everyone I knew offered advice and ideas and many came to help out, which I appreciated, but things kept getting worse."

Samantha waited, not commenting.

"I desperately needed to find something that worked for me," he said. "The clinic works on a schedule. Everybody knows their jobs, when and how to do them. I understand system and schedules so I sat down and worked out a system to run the house. After that I sat the kids down to candidly tell them I'd failed at running the household on my own and at parenting as well, and that I needed to try a system around the house that I could handle as the one in charge. I laid out everything I'd figured out, put up charts, and we took off with it. Amazingly, it worked – and better than anything I'd tried before. I found the kids could do more things than I imagined to help our home run well and that the responsibilities didn't need to fall too hard on the oldest, which was creating bitterness."

"How old were the kids then? I'm trying to remember."

"When Laura died the older girls, Natalie and Madison, were nine, Andrew and Clay about seven, Gareth and Wesley five, and the small girls three. There were things all of them could do … and learn to do if they didn't know how."

"I've seen while working at camp that kids are much more resourceful than adults imagine them to be."

"That's true, and I've learned little kids really care that things are fair. They don't understand grey, subjective reasoning yet. They understand black and white, right and wrong, good and bad. Kids relate to absolutes and they believe in them." He smiled. "We could learn from kids in that. When children see good, sensible reasons for doing things they cooperate better and especially if it seems fair to them."

"I've seen that."

He nodded. "Kids also understand the difference between being good and bad much more clearly than many people believe. They relate well to the concept that when they do well, follow the rules, and do their part … that's good. And when they don't do well, don't follow the rules, and don't do their part … that's bad. They soon see that when you do well and demonstrate good character that people like you and everything works better in your life. They also understand, better than adults sometimes, that when you don't do well, slack off, act like a jerk, and don't show good character that people don't like you, that things don't work out well in your life. I really think, especially in the world today, children understand being good citizens better than adults."

Samantha thought about his words. "I think you're probably right."

He seemed pleased she wasn't arguing with him and continued. "Children also relate well to consequences, especially when they know what negative consequences will come from breaking rules … and they like when those consequences are clear and understandable. In our rules system, when you fall out of line, you pay some consequences. I fit the consequence to the rule broken, like an eye for an eye. Oftentimes, I let the kids help me decide on the consequence. If the boys who were supposed to take the trash out forget, then they have to go back and do it, of course. If someone else had to do it for them they need to apologize, and they might need to add an extra duty to make up for skipping the assigned task. The point is they always know there will be some consequence and that it will be fair – or as fair as I can make it."

"That sounds sensible. Clarity and a clear protocol in anything make things run smoother. We receive employee handbooks at Weather First and other written guidelines and rules to follow for individual jobs."

Ford drummed his fingers on the table, perhaps a little restless with his new employee session. "I designed a handbook of our house rules," he added. "I wrote things down for myself to begin with, kept adding to it. When Juanita came to work with us, I printed it for her. My parents have a copy, too. Sometimes we do updates when new things come along, like when the kids get into new sports, involvements, or outside activities. Or when new situations arise, like when the girls got cell phones this spring."

Samantha rolled her eyes. "You don't need to give me the lecture on that. Dixie told me you didn't really want the girls to get cell phones before they turned thirteen. Madison wrote wishing for one near her birthday and I knew friends of mine whose kids had phones. It seemed like a good gift idea."

His eyes met hers across the table and she imagined that look alone quailed the kids. "It might be good if you check with me about gifts you send to the kids in future."

"I try to pick appropriate things and gifts they're wanting...." she began.

He interrupted. "You sent Andrew a dart gun for Christmas with a twenty round ammo belt."

She knew her face flamed. "It said ages eight and up and ..."

He interrupted. "One of our dogs Benji ran in front of a dart from the gun and almost lost his sight over it. I've treated dogs that lost an eye over toy guns. Ben, as an MD, treated a little boy this spring hit in the eye from a Nerf gun. The boy landed in the emergency room, with bleeding in the eye. Kids are not always responsible with toys."

"Ouch." She shook her head. "I'm sorry. Is Benji all right now?"

"Fortunately, yes. Andrew was torn up about it though. He totally stomped the gun afterward. Nothing personal, but he was upset."

She put a hand over her mouth. "I feel awful."

"You don't have kids, so you're not as used to the problems kids can get into. So please keep the rules around the house while you're sitting with the children. If you run into questions about anything, don't hesitate to call me. If I'm in surgery or something, I'll get right back. I want us to work together, not to push against each other. In parenting, one of the most important principles is that the two parents stay united in working with the children. You don't ever want to let kids play you one against the other because you're not in unity. That principle works with sitters, too."

She knew he was right. "I'm sorry if I worked against you with the children, Ford."

"Well, everyday is a new day to get it right. It's one of our favorite sayings around here." He grinned at her.

Glad to see his smile after such a serious talk, she grinned back. "I've seen some of those sayings on boards and signs around the house."

"Well, it's good to have words to live by, even in fun sometimes." He reached across the table to hand her a spiral bound booklet. "These are the House Rules. You might want to look them over. I'll be candid and say I want to see them kept if you plan to stay with the kids for a time."

She took the booklet. "I'll read through them when I get a chance."

"Daily chores are posted on a chart in the kitchen," he added. "All the chores rotate. Occasionally you might need to help one of the younger children with things, but now that Tamela is six and Rebecca heading that way, they can do most things they're assigned even if slower."

He glanced out the window. "It's a beautiful day outside. I think kids should spend a lot of time outdoors when they can. Knowing you, I think you'll encourage that. If they swim or boat or spend time around the lake, you'll need to play lifeguard. Until you learn all their ways, you may want to do group activities, not letting them go off in pairs too much where you can't keep an eye on them. I encourage the buddy system." He paused. "You can call my mom or dad anytime for advice. They've helped to raise the kids. They know them all well."

"Besides usual chores, do you have any other specific rules or expectations about summer I should know?"

He thought for a minute. "I like for them to each read a book every week. Obviously the younger girls need help with that, just beginning to know words and all. We talk about what they've read on the weekend. I'm a big believer in learning new things, so I often ask them about what they've been learning, too. It kind of encourages them to ask questions and look up things. You probably have some things you can teach them from your travels and areas of expertise. Feel free to jump in about anything like that."

"I'll do that." She waited.

Ford glanced at his watch. "I guess that's about it. The kids know about dinner tonight. We talked last night about what they could make easily with your help and about lunch. You said you thought you could still find your way around a kitchen. You will be sort of in charge with that; I am when I'm home. You'll find we don't have any gender-specific roles here."

She saw him glance at his watch again. "Go on to work, Ford. I'll manage all right and you won't be far away if I need help. Things might not go as smoothly with me here as with you or Juanita, but it will be all right."

"I really appreciate you doing this." He stood up. "I told the kids you'd call them and have a talk with them after I left."

"I'll do that. Don't worry." She grinned. "I plan to let them give me a tour around the resort this morning. I hope that's okay."

"They'll like that."

Samantha let out a sigh of relief when he left. It looked like she would not only be on counselor duty but also answering daily to the camp director this summer. Oh, well, he had a right.

After Ford left, she called the kids downstairs for a short talk and then they took off to explore the resort. The children had fun leading her around the resort's shady roads, pointing out their grandparents' house and farm, and stopping along the lakeside roads to tell her about spots of interest.

At the Cove Boat Dock, Samantha met Maury Beck, the resort's full-time caretaker and groundskeeper. With summer here, he was busy at the dock today renting out two paddleboats to guests staying in the nearby campground area. Further around Cove Loop road they passed the small campground and the row of charming, rustic cabins along the back of the lake.

On the backside of the resort where the road ended in a turnaround loop, they explored the event lodge, big pavilion, and the log chapel where many weddings were held. Trails jutted out at many spots along the road, stretching into the woodlands behind the main resort. Another trail looped the entire lake. When the road ended, they followed that trail from the event lodge down the east side of Sycamore Lake to a fishing dock at Willow Point. From the dock, Samantha could see Ford and Laura's gracious Cape Cod home where the Heltons now lived. A pretty place, set among willows and hardwoods. Rounding Willow Point took them within view of Ford's veterinary clinic and another side path to the small store on the highway.

"Can we walk down to the store?" Wesley asked. "Maybe we can get a candy?"

"We didn't bring any money," Natalie chided him.

"I did," said Gareth.

"You always have money," Clay said, grinning.

"It would be fun to walk to the store," Madison pressed, and Samantha noticed her looking longingly in that direction.

Samantha smiled. "I haven't been to that old store in a long time, and I have some money in my waist bag. I'll spring a dollar each so you can all get something—a candy bar, an ice cream snack, or a drink."

"Dad said we shouldn't hit you up for money," Natalie put in.

Samantha considered that remark. "Okay. In payment each of you can write a short report telling me about yourself when we get back. How's that?"

Wesley wrinkled his nose. "Can't we just tell you our report? I'm tired of school and papers."

"Aunt Samantha should be able to say what she wants us to do," Natalie argued in a prim tone.

Samantha tried not to laugh as they walked along the trail to the store. "I'll make it easy, Wesley. I'll get one of those "All About Me" fill-in sheets off the Internet so you only need to write in short answers."

Rebecca wrinkled her nose. "I can't write many words yet."

"I can't either, Aunt Samantha," Tamela added. "Will you help us?"

"Madison and I will help you both," Natalie jumped in.

It didn't take long to get to the old battered general store on the highway. They all tromped in, picked out treats, and then went outside to eat them on the shady picnic tables in back of the store.

Samantha, sipping on a flavored-water, watched Madison look around. She assumed this the place Lucy mentioned where the teens sometimes met in the evenings. She and her friends used to have a spot where they met on an old dock by the lake.

Back at the house again, the kids gave her a house tour. She'd only been in the old lodge a few times as a girl, so it was fun to see the layout. The former main lodge room in the middle of the house had a vaulted ceiling, high bookshelves filled with books, and a giant rock fireplace. Long windows offered views down to the lake and sliding doors led out to a wide covered terrace. The sofas and chairs in the comfortable room were deep brown leather, accented with pillows that blended nicely with a patterned rug spread over the weathered hardwood floors.

She'd seen the big dining area and the kitchen with its beamed ceiling, but the kids took her through that space now to the girls' bedrooms in a wing to the side. The rustic feel of the former lodge showed in the twin beds and pretty old furniture pieces in both the girls' rooms—Madison and Natalie's with deep pink and grey spreads and a big rag rug, the younger girls' room with girlish quilts and fanciful furnishings. The boys' rooms were upstairs, Clay and Andrew's room in blues with a nautical flair and Gareth and Wesley's in gold and red with a western motif. In all their rooms, Samantha could see evidence of the things they enjoyed.

In the wing on the western end of the lodge was Ford's study and office and his large master bedroom, with a beamed ceiling, rock fireplace, a sitting area, and a private outdoor porch. Upstairs were two guest bedrooms, still decorated like lodge rooms. In all, it was a sprawling home, reminiscent of its history and past as a popular resort, still carrying the flavor of the former era.

For lunch they packed bag lunches to take to the big pavilion at the swim beach and after lunch and a rest they swam and played at the lake. Following a romp and swim with the children, Samantha sat in one of the old Adirondack chairs to lifeguard.

The day passed easily and Samantha enjoyed getting to know the children through the day, only needing to intervene in an occasional quarrel. The dinner planned for the evening included two tuna casseroles, easy to put together, plus heat-and-serve yeast rolls, a big tossed salad, and ice cream for dessert. Clay and Andrew, on kitchen duty with her, helped put the meal together, bantering and entertaining her with stories while they worked.

"How did things go?" Ford asked, coming in the back door just before five.

"The kids made my first day an easy, fun one," she told him, putting a few items back in the refrigerator while she talked. "They gave me tours of the resort and the house, and we had a great time out at the lake swimming. My guess is they'll all sleep hard tonight."

"No problems?"

"No, but don't hold your breath. There's a long summer ahead or at least a number of weeks before I imagine Juanita can come back." She paused. "Have you heard any more about Juanita's mother?"

"The surgery went well," he said, perching on a stool at the counter. "Maria ran over to the hospital at lunch, said Ivanna was out of recovery, back in a room, in some pain but otherwise good. Usually patients only spend one night in hospital after hip surgery, but the doctors may keep Ivanna an extra night because of her age."

"That's good news."

"Juanita is trying to get the doctors to let her mother come back to the house to recover with outpatient physical therapy. I agree with Maria that might be best if they can arrange it. But Juanita is going to have her hands full for a time with her mother and her dad Esteban, who isn't strong. Ivanna handled most of Esteban's care, with Juanita working for me, and Ivanna kept Carlos and Maria's two children after school. With summer here, someone will need to watch Ana Sophia and Dylan every day and not just after school. Juanita's sister has kept them during this crisis period but once Juanita gets her mother home and settled Juanita will need to keep up with the kids, too."

Samantha smiled. "If she's watched these eight children every day and run your household, I'm sure she'll manage even that difficult situation."

"Knowing Juanita, I imagine you're right," he said with a grin.

"Dinner is ready." She pulled the two casseroles and bread out of the oven. "I think you and the kids can take it from here. I'm going to head home. Aunt Dixie just called to tell me she has our dinner about ready."

"Drive safe and thanks for everything." He reached down to pet a black and white cat curling around his leg.

"That's Oscar," Samantha said, watching him. "I'm getting acquainted with the dogs and cats, too. Also please know I personally apologized to Benji today for the dart gun incident and I gave him a dog biscuit when the other dogs weren't watching."

Ford laughed over those words. "I'm sure you're well forgiven."

As Samantha drove home to Dixie's, she decided she'd try to make Ford laugh and smile more often. He needed it. He was entirely too serious. But who could blame him with all his responsibilities? When he wasn't scowling, though, he was really quite handsome. Tall, dark haired with those fine brown eyes, a good square chin, and that touch of a beard he kept. The man had possibilities for being likable.

CHAPTER 8

After dinner, Ford was surprised to see the children settle around one of the big tables on the outside porch to finish filling out some sort of handout.

"Playing a game?" he asked.

"No, we're finishing the sheets Samantha printed for us on your office copier," Natalie told him, helping Rebecca write in her answers.

Madison looked up. "Granddaddy Burl stopped by and said it was okay for her to use the copier," she added. "We talked Samantha into walking over to the Wells Branch store with us. She bought us a treat but said we had to earn it by filling out a sheet telling about ourselves in payment."

Wesley grinned. "First she said she wanted us to write a report." He emphasized the last words and groaned. "But I told her we'd had enough school this year. So she found a sheet for us to fill out on the Internet instead."

Ford looked over Wesley's shoulder at the handout titled "All About Me." It asked for name, age, and favorites in categories like colors, foods, movies, and books, along with fill-in-the-blank options. Ford spotted fill-ins for what each child wanted to be when they grew up, hobbies, things that made them laugh, and more.

"Looks like these will help Samantha know more about each of you," he commented.

"That's what she said." Madison smiled. "Aunt Samantha is really great, Daddy Ford. She's smart and she's fun."

"She can swim really good, too," Andrew said. "She's teaching me how to do back stroke the right way."

"Yeah, she can swim super good," Clay added. "She can even do butterfly, and it's hard."

Gareth looked up from his paper. "She taught swimming at her camp. She was a camper and then she got to be a counselor for lots of summers. She taught cool stuff like zip-line, rock-climbing, archery, and kayaking."

Clay, his oldest, gave him a wistful look. "I wish we could go to a cool camp like that, Dad. It's in the mountains of North Carolina and it sounded really fun."

He glanced around the table, at his four dark-haired children and the four chestnut-haired Bradleys. "I'd like that, too," he admitted. "But camp for eight children isn't something I can afford."

"Does it cost a lot?" Tamela asked.

"Yes," Natalie answered. "I looked it up, and the average cost of about two weeks of overnight camp is way over a thousand dollars each."

Tamela's eyes widened. "That's a lot!"

"That's why Daddy bought a camper and tents, and why we all go camping together instead, isn't it, Dad?" Natalie asked.

He smiled at her. She was such a smart and sensible child. "Camping is fun, too, don't you think?"

"Yes," Gareth agreed enthusiastically. "Are we still going this weekend?"

"We are." Ford felt glad to offer this good news after the discussion of summer camp. Sending eight children to camp had never been an option for him. "I made reservations over at the Cosby Campground. When I can plan a longer weekend we'll go to a state park or on a trip further from home."

"Oh, boy." Gareth punched a fist in the air.

"Cosby Campground is an awesome campground," Andrew put in, "and we can play in the streams and hike."

"Maybe Aunt Samantha would like to come?" Madison asked.

Ford hesitated for a minute, but after seeing the eager faces around the table, decided to be honest. "I invited her, but she might be sick of us by the weekend. She's used to being a freewheeling independent woman."

Madison lifted her chin. "I bet she'll come."

"Maybe she will." Ford stopped to run a hand over Madison's red hair, a lot like Samantha's. He'd noticed, too, she'd started growing her hair out and wearing it in a style like her aunt's. She obviously admired her.

Ford walked over to look out the window toward the lake. To the west, he could see the sun starting to set behind the back ridgelines of their land. He hoped he hadn't made a mistake letting Samantha stay with the kids. They obviously liked her, and it seemed inevitable they'd grow attached to her over the weeks to come, causing more hurt when she left again. He hated they'd known so much hurt and loss already in their young lives.

A pounding on the door diverted his attention. Starting into the kitchen and seeing his dad there, he walked to unlock the back door.

"We've got a situation," Burl announced when Ford opened the door to him. "Maury was checking some of the back cabins and found the body of a dead woman in one. He just called me. I notified the police but I think we both need to get over there."

He gestured toward his car in the driveway. "I brought your mother to stay with the kids." He lowered his voice. "I didn't really want to leave her alone over at our place with a possible murderer around either. Maury said the woman was strangled with a wire."

Ford didn't comment for a moment, shocked into silence.

"Come help me get your mother and her chair in," Burl said, heading out the door.

Ford followed him. "I'll need to speak to the children about this before we go. I don't want them hearing about this through a random news report or someone calling."

"Yeah, I guess that's wise, but be quick about it. Coralee can talk to them more after we leave."

Less than twenty minutes later, Ford and his dad pulled up at one of the cabins on the backside of the resort. Maury stood outside talking to the Police Chief, Ben Barclay, and another officer from the Dandridge Police Department.

"Well, this is a first at your resort," Chief Barclay said, reaching out to shake hands with both Ford and Burl. "I've got an extra officer keeping interested campers away from the site. Especially the kids. We don't need them tracking around here, damaging any evidence we might find."

"Exactly what happened?" Ford asked.

"Best we can figure from talking to Maury, and checking out the scene, is that someone brought the woman to the cabin, probably already dead. We'd see more blood if she'd been killed here." He glanced toward the rustic log cabin, the last in a row of similar cabins along the back of the lake. "I'm sure this cabin, separated from the others, made it a good target spot. Along with the fact it was empty and not rented."

Ben looked around and called out a word to one of his other officers before turning back to them. "We've secured the scene and started searching the area. It seems evident this murder happened some time ago, probably last night. It also seems likely any possible suspect or suspects are long gone." Ben hesitated. "I think it might be good if you see the victim and where we found her before medical personnel come. It might help you to help us, and you might know the woman's identity. We don't. Are you up to that? It ain't pretty but it could be worse."

"We'll help," Burl answered, following the police chief up the cabin steps, Ford behind him.

"We'll stand here at the door," Ben told them, pushing it partially open. "Forensics and an investigative team is on the way and I want to keep this area as clean as possible so as not to contaminate any evidence we might find."

Ford glanced into the cabin. The woman was clearly visible, tied to a chair in the room, head leaned back, the sight grisly.

"That's Norma Doyle," Ford said, wincing. "She works at that gas station and pick-up store up Green Hill Road past the freeway near Highway 70. Now and again when a dog or cat is dropped off at her place, she would bring it to me to check. She often kept the animal afterward until she could trace an owner or find someone to take it in. Good-hearted woman."

"I remember meeting her now, too," Burl added. "I used to stop in the store coming off Highway 70 on my way home to the resort. Norma and her husband Earl ran a little deli in that store. I'd stop and get a bite to eat there sometime." He paused. "Didn't I hear that couple split up?"

"Yes, I heard that, too," Ford answered. "She and Earl separated not long ago. I'm not sure why. I remember Maria mentioning it the last time Norma stopped by the clinic."

The police chief sighed. "Well, I reckon I'll know who to talk to first. Her husband Earl is in Rotary with me. I'll break the news to him after we leave here, see what more I can find out. Then I'll go to the store."

"I think the store is called Cross Corner Market, if that helps," Burl added. He paused to sigh and shake his head. "I can't imagine why anyone would want to kill a nice woman like Norma."

"Murder never does make sense about half the time," Ben added, ushering them out of the cabin.

"Chief," one of the deputies called out. "Medical is here."

Ford saw the unit pull up.

Ben Barclay spoke to them and then turned back to Ford and Burl. "We'll need to interview everyone staying here at the resort, everyone working here, too. I hope you understand that. We need to determine if they saw anything, heard anything. I've got some men canvassing the area now, looking for any clues or information they might find." He glanced down. "With the ground dry and so many car tracks around the area, we probably won't find anything on possible car or truck tracks."

He paused, looking toward the back of the cabin. "One of the men found a window jimmied open in back, some footprints, although not clear ones. It seems likely the window was the route of entry. Maury told us the cabins are kept locked when no one is staying in them, and he said this cabin had been empty all week."

Burl heaved another sigh. "You know Ford and I will be glad to do anything we can to help with this. Talk to anyone you need to. Maury experienced a shock finding the woman as he did, but he'll help you in any way you need him to. He'll also lock the cabin up again when you tell him it's all right to do so."

Chief Barclay nodded. "We'll need to cordon the cabin area off as a crime scene until we finish our investigation." He pointed to yellow crime tape already in place. "I'll be bringing one of my homicide detectives in, too. He should be on his way now. His name's Jim Culver. Good man. If you two want to go on home, I'll send him there to talk to you after we finish here."

"Can we leave now?" Burl asked.

"Yes and thanks for your help."

"Will you stop by the lodge or call if you learn more?" Ford asked. "You know we'll probably be hit with a lot of questions."

"Yeah, and the media will probably stop by." He made a face. "Tell them I told you not to talk to them, to call me for ongoing information. No sense in that bunch stirring everyone up or bothering folks around the resort."

Ford paused as he and Burl turned to head back to his dad's minivan. "Why do you think someone brought that woman's body here to our resort after murdering her?"

"I don't know," Ben replied. "The killer might know the resort, know your cabins aren't always full this time of year and thought it a good place to stash a body. I can't say. A lot depends on how premeditated the murder was. We'll be looking for all the reasons for that while we look for the murderer."

As they drove back to the house, Ford's dad said, "I sure feel sorry for Earl to learn his wife was killed like this."

"Do you think he might have killed her?" Ford asked. "They were separated. Maybe they had problems we don't know about."

"Earl struck me as a congenial, easy-going type—maybe too easy-going, somewhat lazy and not very ambitious by nature. It wouldn't surprise me to learn Norma was the one who asked for the divorce. She always carried more of the weight of running that store than Earl. Her son helps now and he's done a lot with the place. Calvin is more like Norma. A good worker." Burl slowed to take a turn in the road.

"Well, I guess the police will find who did it in time." Ford glanced at his watch, noting the time. "In the meantime, this will negatively impact business at the resort. I wouldn't be surprised if some of our campers check out."

"A few folks traveling in might cancel, too, if they hear about this," Burl said as he pulled up in Ford's driveway. "But it will blow over. Things do."

He stopped the van and turned to Ford. "You'll need to talk to the kids, though. They need to be more cautious around the resort until this person is caught." He ran a hand around his neck. "I may get Maury to hire a little extra security, too. He brings in boys to mow and do work now and then. It wouldn't hurt to have a few extra staff around for a time. We can find tasks for extra workers to do, painting, staining decks, clearing out brush or weeds, that sort of thing. It would give more eyes around the place."

"I agree, Dad. Maury knows several retiree friends and a few boys out of school for the summer he can call that like to make extra money." He paused, thinking. "They can check all our property fencing, too, and we'd better secure our main entry gate at night better."

"These are good plans, but it's getting late now." Burl glanced at his watch. "I'd better get Coralee home and I know you need to talk to the children and get them settled in for the night."

Ford reached for the door handle and then paused as a new thought hit him. "I'll need to talk to Samantha, too. Do you think this will upset her?"

His dad laughed out loud. "I guess you've forgotten what that girl faces every day on her job. She's plucky. You don't need to worry about her. She can hold her own in any crisis." He paused. "You know, your mother and I carried some resentment and hard feelings toward her, not taking on the kids or seeming to care more about their welfare, but we both admitted since she's been here we might have misjudged her. She's good with the kids and they really like her. She jumped in to help you without a thought and wouldn't let you pay her, worrying how that might impact Juanita."

"Well, I worry the kids might get too attached to her," Ford added. "She's fun-loving in a way Juanita isn't and the kids do like her—maybe too much."

Burl raised an eyebrow. "She isn't bad to look at either, is she?"

Ford looked away.

"It's healthy for a man to notice a good-looking woman when his wife's been gone as long as yours, son. No need to feel bad for it."

"Samantha King isn't the sort of woman for a man like me to think about, with eight kids to put first, Dad. She's only here recuperating and then she'll head on back to her job and travel."

"Well, it sounds to me like you're telling yourself that news more so than me." Burl patted him on the arm. "Come on, we've got more to worry about than Samantha King tonight. Let's get on in the house."

CHAPTER 9

After Samantha came home, she and Dixie shared dinner and then had a surprise visit from Lucy and her Aunt Clarice. The four visited over dessert and then Samantha and Lucy went outside to sit and talk in the little gazebo sitting near the back of the inn's property looking out over the lake.

"Gosh, we spent many happy days playing here as girls," Lucy said, settling into a wicker chair and propping her feet up on a low table. "A lot of imaginative games and deep confessions happened here."

"You first told me about your crush on Vance and that you wanted to marry him here when we were only twelve."

Lucy laughed. "I'd forgotten that. I met him at his family's marina one sunny June day, a lot like today. Of course, he didn't notice me, being so much older, but I certainly noticed him."

"Where did you say Vance took the kids tonight?"

"To a soccer game. Mackie is playing and Claudia is spending the night with her friend Alisa. When I told Aunt Clarice I thought I'd walk over to visit with you, she wanted to come spend time with Dixie."

"Clarice looks good. She still has that sweet smile and her hair has turned such a beautiful silvery white." Samantha looked across at her friend. "I'll bet your dark hair will turn a gorgeous white like that, too."

Lucy swatted at her. "Well, I'm not ready to think about that yet." She changed the subject. "Tell me about your day and the kids."

"I think I've finally learned all the kids' names and a little about them—a challenge with eight of them. It makes it easier to remember which are McDaniels and which are Bradleys by their hair. All Ford's children have his dark almost black hair, like yours, and big brown eyes. Andrea's children are mostly red-headed in varying shades."

"That helps all of us at church keep them classified, too."

Samantha looked at her in surprise. "Do you go to the same church with Ford? I thought your family went to the little church over on Church Street near your parents' old house."

"We did, but Vance's family, the Howards, go to the Dandridge Community Church so we've started going there, too." She wrinkled her nose. "I like it better. Come visit and you'll see why."

"How is it different?" Samantha probed.

Lucy looked away and then back at Samantha more directly. "You can feel more of God's presence there. Does that sound hokey?"

"No. Did you think I wouldn't understand that?"

Lucy looked uncomfortable. "Well, the two of us got to a point where we didn't think much of church, thought it a little boring and dull, wished we didn't have to go. You remember."

"I do." Samantha looked out over the lake remembering her discussion with Vickie Larsen. "I spent some time getting to know Vickie Larsen out at the lake with her family this weekend. She plays piano at that church."

Lucy's face brightened. "The Larsens and our family are friends. We hang out a lot with them on the lake and at church. Ford boats, too, so a lot of times there are a big crowd of us either playing together out on the lake or around the marina, or just hanging out at the Larsens' boat dock. Have you been there?"

"No, but Vickie invited me to come over."

"They have a beautiful home on the lake and a great dock."

Samantha tried to think how to redirect the conversation. "Vickie told me how she came to know the Lord in a deeper way."

"Oh?" Lucy looked uncomfortable.

"Why are you acting weird about this, Lucy? We've always been totally honest with each other about everything."

She sighed. "I just felt uncomfortable sharing that I've come into a deeper place in my faith."

Samantha crossed her arms, annoyed. "Well, don't. It's not like I'm an atheist or anything."

Lucy leaned forward. "There's so much more than what we knew or were taught growing up."

Samantha's cell phone, lying on the table, rang before she could probe Lucy more. "Samantha here," she said answering the phone.

"This is Ford. We've had a situation here I thought you should know about before tomorrow. Maury Beck found a body in one of the cabins on the back of the resort. The police have been here investigating."

"Are you saying someone was murdered at the resort?" She put her phone on speaker knowing Lucy would want to listen in.

"Actually, the murder apparently happened elsewhere but someone brought the body to the resort, broke into an empty cabin and left it there."

"Has that person been caught?'

"No, the police are looking into it, interviewing everyone staying at or working at the resort. They have the cabin area cordoned off for now. It's been a pretty eventful evening."

"I imagine so. How awful. I am so sorry to hear this, Ford. Did you know the person killed?"

"Only as a client at the clinic. The woman ran a gas station and a small store on Green Hill Road near the highway." He paused. "Listen, I needed you to know about the murder but that isn't the only reason why I called."

Before Samantha could respond, he said, "I wanted to ask if Madison was with you or if she'd called you."

"No, she isn't here and she hasn't called. Oh, my goodness, Ford. Is she missing in the midst of all this other situation?" Samantha knew her mouth dropped open and she saw Lucy put a hand over her mouth in shock.

"I went in to check on her and Natalie about fifteen minutes ago.

Natalie was asleep, but I thought it odd how covered up Madison was in the bed." He paused and she heard the break in his voice as he continued. "Turns out she wasn't in her bed. Natalie didn't even know Madison was gone and swears she doesn't know where she is. I searched the house and the grounds nearby but I haven't found her. Natalie said Madison was really upset about something before they went to bed. She wouldn't say what, but she suggested that maybe Madison might have called you."

Lucy mouthed some words to Samantha reminding her of the photos of Samantha with Michael Denby and their conversation earlier in the week.

"Listen," Samantha said, trying to keep her own voice calm and rational. "I think I have an idea where Madison might be. I'll stop by there to check on my way over to the resort. If she's not there, I'll stay with the kids so you can search more without worrying about leaving the children by themselves. With this murder happening, it would scare them to wake up and find you gone or to learn Madison is missing."

She hesitated. "You and Natalie didn't tell the other kids, did you?"

"No. We are keeping this as quiet as possible for now." He heaved a sigh. "Natalie said that sometimes Madison goes for a walk at night to think."

Lucy rolled her eyes.

"Well, that's probably what she did, upset over this murder and everything," Samantha said, trying to ease Ford's worry. "I'm sure she'll turn up soon. Keep your phone on in case she tries to call or text you. I'll be there as soon as I can."

"Bless his heart," Lucy said as soon as Samantha hung up. "He must be worried sick, especially after an evening of finding a murder victim at the resort. Poor man."

They both stood and started back toward the house.

"I assume you're going by the store on the highway to check to see if Madison is there."

"Yes. It won't take me ten minutes to get there."

Lucy caught her arm to stop her. "I know someone who will have the Denby's phone number. If you don't find Madison at the store, you might want to call the Denby's house, to see if Michael is there or not. You can try to find out if they know somewhere he might be."

Samantha scowled. "We don't know she's with Michael Denby."

Lucy shook her head. "I know Michael Denby better than you. And I saw that smitten expression on Madison's face in the picture. I imagine he's enjoying leading her on. He's like that, Samantha."

Samantha looked out over the lake for a minute. "If I find them together at the store should I take Michael home and talk to his parents?"

Lucy smiled. "Maybe, but I'd let Ford do that. You're putting your oar in deep enough if you find the two of them and take Madison home. Ford will push to know why you didn't talk to him about what you knew before. You'd better come up with an answer."

Samantha grimaced. "I hadn't thought of that."

"You could simply go to the house and send Ford to the store, tell him your hunch. Let him handle it."

"No. He's so upset right now. And I think Madison would be more receptive to me about this than her dad."

"You're right." Lucy said as they headed in the back door of the inn.

Samantha turned to her. "Go tell Aunt Dixie and your aunt about the murder if you would. Tell them I've gone over to talk to Ford about it for a little while. They don't need to know about the other issue."

"Good plan, but call or text me to keep me informed." Lucy turned to start toward the kitchen where they'd left the two older women visiting. "I'll pray, too. A murderer is on the loose out there somewhere. That's scary to think about."

Samantha offered up some prayers of her own as she headed down the highway toward the resort. She slowed as she neared the Wells Branch store, pulling into the dim parking area.

Slipping out of her car, she walked around back of the store into the shadowy picnic area, not lit at night. At an old table in the dimmest area, she spotted Madison with a boy.

Samantha watched Madison's eyes widen as she came closer to the table. "What are you doing here, Aunt Samantha?"

"I came to get you." She slid onto the bench across the table from them and then addressing the boy, said, "I assume you're Michael Denby."

His eyes jerked wide and he pulled away from the close position beside Madison. "How do you know who I am?"

Samantha ignored him for a minute, turning to Madison instead. "Your dad knows you are gone. He checked your room. He's upset as you can imagine, especially after this murder business tonight."

Madison looked down at the table. "I promised Michael to meet him. We were only talking, Aunt Samantha. I was going to walk home soon."

Samantha addressed Michael then. "You are fifteen years old, Michael. Madison is only twelve. At your ages, that is a huge difference. Being older, you should well know asking a girl Madison's age to sneak out of her house to meet you is wrong."

She watched Madison's chin come up. "He didn't make me come, Aunt Samantha."

Looking from Madison's defiant face to Michael's angry one, she decided she'd have to use another approach. From her purse, she took out an envelope and laid out the four pictures in it across the table. "Michael, I imagine that Madison doesn't know you like to play around with a lot of girls. She probably thinks you see her as special and I'm sure you've told her exactly that."

Madison's shocked face told Samantha all she needed to know.

"Here's the situation, Michael. I don't care much for liars and cheaters. I've met my fair share of them along life's way. And I don't like you playing games with my niece and making her think she's special when you obviously play around with a lot of girls—and most closer to your own age."

"Where'd you get those pictures?" Michael tried to make a swipe toward the photos, but Samantha was faster, slapping his hand away and picking them up.

"It doesn't matter where I got these pictures, but you're aware now that I have them. That means you won't be seeing Madison anymore, texting or calling her. Hopefully, she sees why she wouldn't want you to now, either."

Madison began to fight tears, moving further away from Michael and giving him a mixed hurt and angry look.

Michael stood up. "I don't have to hang around and listen to this."

"No, you don't," Samantha agreed. "But hear me well. If I learn that you call or text Madison again or if I hear that you spread any gossip or talk about her to any of your friends, your mother and the principal at your school will get these pictures. Do you understand me, Michael?"

He clenched a fist. "You're threatening me."

"I am. I imagine you'd do the same thing if you caught your little sister Susie in the same situation."

Samantha saw him consider this. "She's only ten!"

"Not much younger than Madison, so I hope you can see my point."

He frowned. "I was only having a little fun that's all."

Madison's tears started then. "I thought you really liked me."

"Ah, come on, Madison. You aren't that dumb. You're a sixth grade kid in middle school and I'm fifteen, almost sixteen. I'm in high school. I just thought it was cute you had a crush on me."

He glared at Samantha. "That's what I'd tell my mom, too."

Samantha stood up to look at him directly. "Well, I hope that you or I won't need to discuss this with your mom."

He stalked off, tossing out a couple of expletives.

After he rounded the corner, Madison burst into tears.

"Have your cry and then I need to take you home. I told your dad I might have an idea where you'd be when he called."

"How did you know?" Madison asked, sniffing and trying to dry her eyes on her arm.

Samantha sat back down, deciding to be honest. "A lot of the teenagers like to hang out at my friend Lucy's bookstore and shop downtown. Lucy found the pictures. She was worried for you and gave them to me. I was trying to decide what to do about them, or if I should do anything with them, when your dad called. Lucy and I were sitting out in the gazebo talking when the call came. Both of us thought there was a good chance you'd be here. She'd heard the girls say Michael often met his girlfriends here since he doesn't live very far from here himself."

A horrified expression crossed Madison's face then. "Are you going to tell Dad?"

Samantha gave her a steady look. "No, you are. You're growing up and you need to learn how to own up to your dad when you do something you shouldn't. He told me he always talks out with all of you what consequences there will be when you break house rules and do things that aren't right."

She sniffed again. "You mean do things that are stupid."

"Life is full of times when we do stupid things. Everyone, at one time or another, is deceived by someone in business, school, everyday life, or in love. We want to believe people are sincere, that they mean what they say, are good people and not liars. It hurts when we learn differently."

Madison heaved a sigh. "I feel so dumb. He was older and so cute and I swear, Aunt Samantha, he said he really liked me."

"I'm sure he did." She smiled. "In adolescence boys have a tendency to say a lot of things they don't mean to girls. All those movies and books you've watched on those themes were accurate. It's something you and your dad can talk about."

She winced. "I can't talk about stuff like that with dad."

"Why? He was a boy once. He's not stupid and he's a doctor. He can give you a guy's view." She paused. "I always wished I'd had a dad I could talk to about things when I was growing up, like some of my friends did. I had Aunt Dixie but it wasn't the same."

Madison hugged herself. "But this is personal." Her eyes widened then. "Are you going to show dad the photos you have?"

"Yes, but not until you talk to your dad yourself. I won't keep things from your father, not now, not ever. If Michael does something vengeful it will be your dad that goes to see his parents, not me." She paused. "Ford loves you, Madison, as much as if he was your natural father. I heard that in his voice when he found you gone. You can hear love and concern. And you can feel it from another person. He was scared for you, worried and upset."

"I wasn't thinking about that much."

"You only wanted to see Michael. But you're growing up and you're going to have to think more about the decisions you make. Realize more that all the decisions you make impact other people." She reached a hand across the table to put it over Madison's. "You're a smart, pretty, caring, and fun girl. Life is going to hold a lot of wonderful opportunities for you. But more and more now, as you leave childhood behind, you're going to have to think before you act. Think carefully and try to get all the facts before you do things."

Madison closed her eyes and learned her head back. "Will you tell Lucy and Aunt Dixie about this?"

"I'll tell Lucy unless you want to. It's thanks to her I had the pictures so you could know the truth about Michael and that I knew where to find you tonight. You might want to thank her for that." She hesitated. "As for Aunt Dixie, you can decide if you want to tell her about this and what you want to tell her. Not a lot of people need to know about this, Madison, and I hope Michael doesn't spread any gossip."

Madison wrapped her arms around herself again. "Oh, my gosh, these pictures were from someone's cell phone. Other kids saw them!"

"I'd say the other photos drew more attention than yours. But if someone says something to you about it, don't lie. Just stick your chin up and say you got a crush on him until you found out what a creep he was."

"What will I tell Dad?" She gave Samantha an anguished look.

"The same thing. Be truthful. Your dad will listen if you don't try to lie or act sassy and justify what you did."

Madison glanced toward the road obviously thinking about the encounter ahead. "Will you stay while I talk with dad?"

"If you want me to, but I won't do your talking for you." She frowned at a thought. "I may be in trouble myself with your dad when he learns I had those pictures and didn't come to him with them right away."

"Maybe you can tell him you just got them tonight," Madison suggested.

She shook her head. "No, that would be lying. I'll tell him the truth. The truth is always best."

Madison considered that. "Dad said it's sometimes best not to tell the truth, like telling someone you don't like them, that their dress is ugly, or that they have B.O."

Samantha crossed her arms. "There are always exceptions. You're smart enough to know when exceptions are needed."

"I don't want you to get in trouble with Dad, though," Madison explained. "I'm so glad you're staying with us, that we're getting to know you."

Samantha smiled as she stood up. "I don't think Ford is going to fire me over this, Madison. So don't worry. But I need to get you home. He's worried and more so because there may be a murderer out there."

"Oh my gosh, I didn't even think about that!"

Heading up to the resort, Samantha tried to stay light and positive, but inside she felt as worried as Madison.

CHAPTER 10

Ford thought he'd looked at his watch every five minutes since talking with Samantha. What was taking her so long?

He jumped up from his chair in the living room as soon as he heard her car pull in the drive. So did Natalie. He could hardly have expected her to fall back to sleep with Madison missing, and it was Natalie who flew across the kitchen to throw her arms around Madison when she walked in the door.

"Oh, Madison," she exclaimed, hugging her. "Where have you been? Daddy and I were so worried!"

Ford saw Madison looking over Natalie's shoulder at him. "I'm sorry, Dad," she said, extracting herself from Natalie to come and hug him.

Despite how upset he felt, Ford hugged her tight to him, so relieved she was safe. Kissing her forehead, he told her, "You know we need to talk about this, but I'm glad you're okay. Natalie and I love you. Don't do this to us again. Knowing there might be a murderer around the resort, who slit a good woman's throat with a wire, didn't do anything to my nerves while you were missing."

He glanced up to see Samantha. "Thanks for bringing Madison home. I'm glad you remembered something she said to alert you to where she might be."

He turned toward the living area. "Let's go sit down, so you can both fill us in on this situation."

Ford watched Madison clench her hands and glance at Samantha after they sat down on the grouping of sofas and chairs around the big rock fireplace. And he saw Samantha nod to Madison.

"I got a stupid crush on this boy who doesn't live far from here," Madison said in a rush. "I walked down to meet him at the Wells Branch store. It was dumb, I know, and wrong for me to sneak out. But he was older and really cute and he said he really liked me. I didn't think you'd let me go meet him at night." She paused to take a breath. "I'm really sorry."

"I see," he said, trying to digest that his little girl would have a crush on a boy. Good grief, she was only twelve!

"Was it Michael Denby?" Natalie asked.

Madison glared at her. "It doesn't matter who it was."

"Doesn't it?" Samantha asked and Ford watched her give Madison another of those looks.

Madison sent her an anxious look. "Do I have to tell this part?

"One of us does," Samantha said, sitting back on the couch and crossing her leg. "I thought we agreed it would be you."

Ford watched Madison take a deep breath.

"Samantha's friend Lucy Howard found some photos of Michael with some different girls." Madison winced. "The girls were high school girls, Michael's age, and the photos weren't very nice." She paused, seeming to gather her courage, and then looked up at him. "One was of me and Michael kissing."

Stunned, Ford started to react, but then caught a cautionary glance from Samantha.

"You kissed Michael Denby!" Natalie exclaimed in the silence. "He's fifteen, Madison!"

"Will you just let me tell this, Natalie?" Madison snapped at her. "Don't make it worse."

Madison took a deep breath and continued. "Like I said earlier, I thought he really liked me. He acted like he did and he said nice things to me…" Her voice trailed off. "I didn't know he was only one of those kinds of boys that acts like that with all the girls. Maybe I should have but I didn't." She glanced at Samantha then. "Dad, when you called Samantha, she remembered Lucy also said the girls in the store giggled that Michael often met girls he liked at the Wells Branch store."

Ford looked at Samantha and frowned.

"Samantha thought I might have gone there to meet Michael," Madison said in a rush. "So she came by to see and she found me there."

"With Michael?" Ford asked, trying to check his anger.

"Yeah, we were just sitting and talking, Dad. That's all. And I was getting ready to walk back home. Honest."

Ford struggled to stay calm. "I think I may need to take those pictures and talk to Michael Denby's parents. I know them. They live on Smoky Drive not far up the highway. I've treated their cocker spaniel at the clinic."

Madison leaned forward, eyes large. "You don't need to do that, Dad. Samantha talked to him. He won't be calling me anymore and I won't be seeing him, either. Samantha threatened him and told him she'd talk to his parents and to his school principal and show them the pictures if he tried to spread any gossip about me or anything."

Ford couldn't find words for a minute.

"The girls who took the photos had been passing them around to each other on their phones," Samantha put in. "I don't think it's gone further than that. Lucy said it was a part of a retaliation ploy by one of the girls Michael dumped to get even with him, to let other girls know he was a player."

"And you were planning to tell me about all this when?" he asked, unable to hide the annoyance in his voice.

"I'd been trying to decide if I should tell you and when," Samantha answered, lifting her chin and making him think so much of Madison in that moment. "I didn't want to seem like a person trying to tattle on your kids and tell you what to do about them. Especially in my position."

"I see," he said again. "I thought we talked about staying unified about issues with the children."

"We did." Samantha shifted in her seat. "But that talk was after Lucy gave me the photos. It wasn't a current issue."

Madison leaned forward. "Samantha said I had to tell you, Dad, or that she would. She said we needed to be truthful about everything. She gave me a big talk about needing to act more grown up and smarter in future, too."

His mouth twitched in a grin. "That sounds like good advice." He glanced at the clock on the mantel. "I think it would be good if you and Natalie both went on to bed now. It's late. We can talk more about this tomorrow."

Ford looked directly at Madison as she got up to leave. "I want you to think about all the things you did wrong, the family rules you broke, and the ways you handled this situation poorly. Then think about what consequences would be fair in this. I'll have some ideas, too. This is a little more serious than playing catch in the house and knocking over a vase and breaking it." He paused. "It looks like we need to talk about some boy-girl issues, too—you, me and Natalie. I hadn't realized you girls were growing up so quickly, getting interested in boys now."

"Natalie has a crush on Ricky Pence," Madison put in with a toss of her head in Natalie's direction.

"Madison!" Natalie's mouth flew open, obviously upset.

Ford wondered how many more shocks he'd get before this night was over. "At least Ricky Pence is twelve and not fifteen," he said, remembering the blond, friendly little boy who went to their church.

"I can't believe you told that," Natalie fussed as they left the room.

"Well, you told on me," Madison replied, unrepentant.

She stopped before leaving the room. "Thanks for coming to get me, Aunt Samantha. And I hope Dad doesn't fire you."

Ford's eyes flew to Samantha's, wondering about that comment.

Samantha grinned at him. "I'll see if I can talk him out of it, Madison. You girls sleep well. I'll see you in the morning."

When they left, Ford leaned his head back against the sofa and let out a long breath. "This has been one heck of a day."

"Yeah, it has. You got any ice cream?" she asked, surprising him.

"What?" he opened his eyes to look across at her.

"I always like ice cream after a stressful day."

He smiled despite himself. "Let's go check the freezer. I wouldn't mind some myself. We can go sit out on the terrace to eat it."

After discovering two kinds of ice cream in the freezer, they scooped out dishes of Rocky Road and Vanilla and carried them out to the terrace.

"Don't turn on the lights," Samantha said. "I want to see the moon over the water and the stars in the sky."

They sat in the dark and ate ice cream, neither talking for a time.

"I can't decide what to say about tonight," Ford said at last.

"Like covering a big storm, it takes time to come down after a stressful sweep of events like we experienced today. You've dealt with more than me with the murder here, too. Tell me about that."

He did, filling her in on the facts. "I know these things happen, but we've never had anything like this happen at the resort."

"Have you talked to the kids about it?"

"I did. They asked a lot of questions. I tried to answer them as honestly as I could."

"You're good at that," she said. "Not blowing off and overreacting like I've seen so many parents do. You stop and think. And you bite your tongue sometimes." She grinned at him.

"I did a lot of that tonight." He placed his empty ice cream dish on the table beside him. "How can my little girls be interested in boys already?"

"The scary news today, Ford, is that many girls in middle school are already sexually active. It's time for you to have a good long talk with both Madison and Natalie."

"That's so hard to wrap my mind around."

"Lucy said the other day how glad she was that Aunt Dixie always candidly told us about everything as we grew up."

"I think it will be easier for me talking to the boys."

"Probably, but when you talk to the girls, be honest. Tell them how boys think in adolescence. Don't sugarcoat things. Encourage the girls and your boys to come to talk to you about anything, too.

Don't ever let them think any issue is taboo to discuss."

He grinned at her. "How'd you get to be so smart about kids not having any?"

"By being a somewhat wild and unruly child myself. Like the old saying goes, 'it takes one to know one.' Lucy and I used to climb out the window at night to go down to an old dock to meet boys."

"Really?" He was surprised she'd tell him this.

"Don't tell me you never broke any rules and did things you shouldn't have in adolescence. As good looking as you are I imagine a lot of little girls swarmed after you."

Ford smiled over the compliment. "Well, I don't think we need to reminisce about the wayward acts of our youth."

"No, but don't forget them. And don't let your kids ever think you were always some goody-two-shoes that never broke the rules, got in trouble, or did anything wrong. Or chased after girls and probably lied to a few and broke their hearts."

"You think I might have done that?" he asked in surprise.

"I'm sure you did, even if you didn't realize it. We all have a string of memories of being hurt and of hurting someone in the romance category."

"I suppose." He resisted the urge to ask her about her own hurts. At her age and with her looks and personality, he felt sure she had a long, rich string of romance memories.

"Are you going to fire me?" she asked after a space of silence.

He shook his head at her direct manner again. "Well, you did jump in ahead of me to find and confront both Madison and the Denby boy. I might have enjoyed my own chance at that arrogant, two-timing boy leading my little girl on."

She laughed. "Probably better it was me then."

"You don't think I should talk to his parents? I know them."

"If you do that we'll lose our edge over Michael not to retaliate and spread gossip about Madison. He could do that, you know. Kids can be ugly. And today they have their cell phones to broadcast information out. They can be hateful in that way."

"I admit I wouldn't have thought of that."

"Lucy actually suggested I let you handle going to talk to Michael and his parents later. But when I saw Michael's no-care, smart-ass attitude, I realized a little blackmail would work with his type better."

"Are you going to let me see the pictures?"

"If you want to." She took an envelope out of her purse and passed it to him.

Ford got up and walked to where the light streamed in from the doorway to study them. "These are pretty graphic. I guess I can be glad we discovered Madison's involvement with this boy before it went further."

"Yeah, me too." She stretched, yawned, and stood up. "It's after midnight. I need to head home, and you need to get some sleep yourself."

"You can stay over if you want." He watched her eyes widen.

Her lips twitched then. "Where would you expect me to sleep?"

He felt himself blush. "The lodge has two guest bedrooms." He tried to sound matter-of-fact. "I thought you might not want to drive back home with it so late."

"It's only about ten minutes to Aunt Dixie's. I'll be fine. You don't need to make chivalrous offers to me, Ford. I'm a pretty tough and independent girl."

"Maybe every girl needs to feel a little protected sometimes. A little cherished."

"Cherished?" Her voice softened.

"I meant cared for. You know."

She walked over to take the photos from him, tucked them into her purse, and then draped her purse over her shoulder.

Ford was very aware of her standing close in the dark. He could hear her breath wafting softly in and out and he caught the smell of some earthy, fresh, minty scent in the air around her. A light, outdoorsy smell that felt a good match for her; he'd noticed it before.

A little frisson of tension gathered in the air and neither of them moved for a moment.

Then Samantha smiled and raised her eyes to his. "The guest bedrooms in your house are over your bedroom in the west wing, far away from the children. I imagine I'd lie in my bed there and think about this moment if I stayed over and that you might do the same. Neither of us would get a good's night sleep."

He started to protest, to say something to make light of the unexpected awareness that had popped up between them, but Samantha put a hand over his mouth.

"Don't say anything and spoil it. It's a nice moment. And I'm glad to see you don't hate me anymore." She backed away a step from him. "Even if you don't believe it, I faced my own times of grief and sorrow when Andrea died. She was my only sister. Our mother neglected us to a great extent when we were small; my father, too. We bonded tighter due to that. It was scary for us when our mother deserted us to go back to Ireland. Dad brought us to Aunt Dixie then. His work world and his own issues and sorrows allowed no place for us."

She looked away from him. "I knew what a painful, shattering time it was for Andrea's children. It had to be when she and Adam were killed. But what could I do? My work sent me traveling all over the country, into dangerous situations, with no time to nurture family. I'd seen so many of my colleagues divorce over it. I only had two options, to take the kids—two babies, the other two small—who didn't know me and then to hire a nanny to care for them, hardly ever seeing them. That sounded so cruel. My other choice was to give up my life completely, my career, all I'd worked for, what I loved passionately, to come back to Dandridge to try to raise them as a single mother with no job."

"You'd have been miserable and ill-equipped," Ford said softly, seeing the situation through her eyes for the first time.

"Believe it or not, I thought either option not a happy one for the children. I knew you and Laura loved the kids, that they knew you. Andrea told me she asked you and Laura to be guardians to the children if anything happened to them. She didn't want me to feel hurt about it, she said, but she knew my life. I paid little attention to her words at the time, but I saw the wisdom of her choice as I weighed my options later."

"Why are you telling me this?"

"I do care about the children and it's troubled me that you and Laura didn't understand. I could feel your resentment at the funeral."

"So you avoided coming around at all?"

"My work life is crazy, but I probably did. When I did come home, I let Dixie bring the children to the inn."

"To avoid us."

"Since it seems a time for honesty, I guess that's true. I'm not sure I fully realized it before."

"And now?"

"Now I'm glad, in a small way, that events have opened an opportunity for me to develop a relationship with the children." She turned to look at him again. "I want you to know I really love them, and I admire so much how you and your wife took them in. How you loved them, gave them family. Even on your own, it's obvious how much you love not only your own children but my sister's children. Thank you."

"I'm not sure what to say."

Her eyes met his. "Just say you don't hate me anymore."

Ford shook his head. "I don't think I ever hated you, Samantha. I didn't know you much before and I didn't always understand your choices, but I never hated you."

"That's good." She smiled at him, and then glanced beside him to a weathered sign on the wall. "I love all your wonderful signs around this house, many also tacked to trees around the property in different places."

He turned to glance at the sign on the wall, one of many lake signs that had hung in the lodge since he was a kid or that he'd picked up over the years.

"Is that sign true?" she asked, reading it. "That what happens at the lake stays at the lake?"

"I guess," he said, confused at her question.

"I'm glad to hear it." She put a hand on his cheek and then leaned in to kiss him, long and well. "You are a good man, Ford McDaniel, and work so hard raising all these children. I thought it would be sweet for you to know you're also an attractive and sexy man, too. I loved that little moment earlier. I know you'd never have acted on it but I wanted to."

Leaving him slightly stunned, she walked across the terrace to start down the back steps and then paused looking back, the moonlight shining on her red hair. "And don't forget that what happens at the lake stays at the lake. This little moment tonight was just for the two of us, a special moment of peace between us."

Ford watched her leave knowing full well that no simple, flippant little words she threw out in parting would change this new awareness of her she'd fired in him. He felt as stirred up as those adolescent pictures she'd shown him. And he had no idea what he was going to do with all these new feelings.

CHAPTER 11

On Thursday, Ford all but ignored her, not surprising Samantha much. Friday began in much the same way except that Ford came home early from the clinic to finish packing the camper for their camping trip. He'd done much of it with the kids already on Thursday night after she left.

"You still planning to go?" he asked nonchalantly when he walked in the kitchen not long after lunch.

"Yes, and my gear's in the car. I went by the list you posted."

"Good, you can help us load. I packed most everything last night." He moved into action, issuing orders and answering questions from the kids.

Since there would be two adults on the trip, Ford loaded their camping equipment not only into the big maroon van all the kids could fit into for trips, but into his own white SUV.

"Two Nissan vehicles?" Samantha asked as she helped to carry groceries, boxes, and camping supplies out to the cars.

"I take care of the Nissan dealership owner's hunting dogs. He gives me a good discount on vehicles."

"Ah, the barter system."

"Not totally, but it helps." He glanced over at her after throwing another duffle bag into the back of the van. "Are you sure you don't mind driving the SUV over to the campground? It gives me more space without putting the camp top on the van. I'll pull the camper behind the van and you can follow us in the SUV. Natalie and Madison said they'd ride with you to show you the way in case we get separated."

She grinned at him. "I know how to get to the Cosby Campground from Dandridge, Ford. Remember I grew up here. Aunt Dixie took us for picnics there when Andrea and I were small and I camped with friends when I got older. It's only a thirty to forty-five minute drive."

He made no comment but continued in what was an obviously familiar system of loading coolers, lawn chairs, and other gear needed for a weekend camping trip.

Now at four in the afternoon the family was settled into their campsite near the back end of the Cosby Campground. After arriving, Samantha kicked in with the kids to set up three outdoor sleeping tents, two for the boys and one for the girls. She also helped Ford set up a canopy tent to cover the two picnic tables they planned to eat their meals on.

"I'm putting you in the Airstream with the little girls," Ford told her as they were setting everything up. "You'll be more comfortable."

She started to argue, but then thought better of it. Madison had already told her Ford usually slept inside with Tamela and Rebecca. Knowing him, she thought it pointless to suggest she sleep outside while he slept inside.

"Do you always reserve two sites?" she asked as they settled down in a couple of camp chairs to rest.

He smiled at her, the first she'd seen all day. "The campground limit at any one site is six people. We have ten."

She passed him a cold drink from the cooler. "Well, these are nice sites." She looked around her now with all the work done.

"I always try to get these two sites when we come here." He gestured toward a building across the small paved road. "The restroom is right on that hill there, nice when you're camping with a bunch of kids—and when you're dry camping like we are in this campground with no electric or water hookups. Even with the solar panels on the Airstream and our batteries, we try to conserve water and electric as much as we can."

"The kids seem to be having fun," she said, watching them explore nearby, playing around the campsite area or by a small stream, while staying in sight and minding Ford's buddy system.

"We like this campground and it's clean and safe for the family." He crossed one ankle over his knee, relaxing.

"Tell me what's been going on with the police investigation, Ford. Your dad stopped by earlier yesterday and said little progress had been made."

"Everyone they've followed up on had alibis and no motive to want to harm Norma that the investigative team can find." He sat his cola in the holder of his lawn chair. "Wednesday, the day Maury found Norma at one of our cabins, was Norma's day off from the store, so Earl and Calvin didn't expect her at work or realize anything might be wrong. Norma often went shopping or did chores at home. There was no reason to call her or for her to stop by the store that day. Earl and Calvin knew she'd be in the store the next morning. A couple of neighbors even saw her at her house on Tuesday evening watering her flowers. However, the police found blood traces in her house showing it was evident she was killed there and then moved after."

"That's so sad. Where did Norma live?"

"Off Green Hill Road, not too far from the store. People drive past the driveway into her house all the time. No one saw anything suspicious, nothing unusual, but it's obvious someone killed Norma at the house and then transported her to the resort." Ford frowned. "No one at the resort saw anything suspicious either. But the police hope they will find a lead if they keep looking."

"I guess it takes time." She smiled at him. "I didn't mean to bring up an unpleasant subject on your weekend off."

"It's okay. I meant to update you about that anyway." He stopped to answer a question one of the boys called out to him and then continued. "I went by to visit Juanita yesterday, too. Ivanna is having a rough time, as you might imagine. And Juanita has her hands full."

Again, Samantha wondered what Juanita had to say about her.

She doubted the woman felt happy to know Samantha carried her duties for her, working in what she probably thought of by now as her kitchen.

"Aunt Samantha!" Madison called, running up with Natalie. "Come take a walk with us. We want to walk down to the amphitheater and the picnic area."

She glanced at Ford. "Do I have time before we start dinner?"

"Sure. We do things simple when camping. Go ahead. I'm grilling hamburgers tonight and heating two cans of pork-n-beans on the side. I'll get the charcoal started in a little while. Go walk around with the girls."

Seeing them leave, Tamela and Rebecca begged to go, too. Samantha saw both older girls give each other a look, but then they turned and smiled at their sisters, giving their okay. Samantha saw their father smile and wink at them, his way of giving them praise and recognition for being kind. She liked those little gestures of his she noticed so often.

"The boys are catching bugs," Tamela told her as they walked down the quiet road. Samantha could see campers on some of the other camp roads but even in June the campground wasn't that busy. "Grandaddy Burl helped them make bug boxes so they could catch insects and caterpillars and other bugs. "

"Me and Tamela have bug jars," Rebecca told her, skipping along beside her. "We made them in Bible School last summer."

"We helped with that," Natalie added. "They're cute with ladybugs painted on the sides of the jars and jar tops with holes in them."

"I like to catch lightning bugs in mine," Tamela put in.

The girls chattered away to her as they walked, pointing out sights along the way, telling her about past camping trips here, things they'd seen or done, people they'd met.

"Sometimes rangers give talks in the amphitheater and one summer some people sang." Natalie looked toward the covered amphitheater as they passed by it. "That was neat."

"Aunt Samantha brought a guitar," Madison added.

"Do you play, Aunt Samantha?" Natalie asked, her eyes growing wide at Madison's words.

"A little," she said. "I used to play and sing at summer camp with all the girls in my unit, but it's been a long time now."

"It would be fun if you sang and played your guitar when we sit around the fire later." Madison grinned at her. "Daddy Ford usually makes a big fire pit at night. We roast marshmallows over it and then tell stories or sing songs."

"I like the 'Froggie Went A'Courtin' song," Tamela told her.

"Maybe I'll see if I can remember that one," Samantha said, looking down into her niece's eyes. She looked so much like Andrea had at the same age with that sweet little smile.

After returning, Samantha pitched in with Ford and the kids to make dinner. He'd preplanned all their weekend camp meals, making a chart for them Samantha had studied at the house. Aunt Dixie, knowing their plans, sent a box of her mini cupcakes for them to enjoy, and Coralee made a big pan of fudge for them and a tin of chocolate chip cookies. They certainly wouldn't hurt for sweets.

The kids each had a duffle bag packed with extra clothes, a swimsuit, and other essentials, plus a small plastic toiletries bag with a toothbrush, toothpaste, a hairbrush, soap in a plastic dish, a washrag and a small towel that Samantha learned they took to the restroom with them every day.

"There's a shower in the camper but water is too much at a premium when we camp to use it much," Ford told her. "Cosby doesn't have showers in the restrooms but the kids can wash up at the sinks. It serves for a short weekend—that and dunks in the creek. Other campgrounds we go to for longer weekends or vacations offer shower facilities. I told you we'd be roughing it, but you can take a short shower in the camper if you need to."

"You always forget the outdoor life that I live much of the time, often in inclement weather with power outages and water mainlines breaking. I'm not used to a soft life, Ford."

He winked at her. "Then you'll fit right in."

The family laughed and talked around the picnic tables over

dinner, happy to be out-of-doors and enjoying a relaxing time together. It felt good to be with them, a good change for Samantha after the wearisome months of trying to recover and get her health back.

Watching her rub her knee a little when they finished cleaning up after dinner, Ford asked, "Does your knee still give you trouble from the spot where you had a torn ligament?"

She glanced up at him, unaware she'd been rubbing her knee. "Occasionally, after a lot of activity it sometimes still bothers me but not often anymore."

"I keep meds in the camper if you need anything."

"No." She looked away. "I think sometimes I simply rub it from old habit, from those months when it did hurt."

"I've seen few obvious signs that you were injured at all now. You've made a good recovery."

"Yes, I was lucky." Disliking the conversation and the old memories it brought back she got up to go help the kids roast marshmallows for s'mores over the hot coals still left in the grill.

After eating gooey s'mores, the boys brought their bug-houses to show Samantha their finds.

"She may not want to see your icky bugs," Natalie told them, moving a distance away from the boys.

"I like bugs." Samantha smiled. "Let's see what you've got."

The boys each had a small bug container with wooden ends and screened sides. They'd put leaves and twigs inside them with their catches.

"We found a grasshopper, a caterpillar, a beetle, and a spider," Andrew said as he and Clay pushed their bug boxes closer for her to see.

"You boys are not supposed to get spiders," Ford said from his chair nearby. "Many species are dangerous and it's hard to tell the difference. You know we talked about that."

"But this is a daddy longlegs spider," Clay replied. "We knew what it was."

"There are good reasons for the rules we have. If you collect spiders, some of the other children might, too, and that could cause a problem."

"Yeah, you could pick up a brown recluse or a black widow, Clay," Natalie cautioned.

"I'll let it go with the other bugs after a while, Daddy," Clay said.

"And we won't get any more spiders," Andrew added. "We do see some really cool ones sometimes though."

"So look and don't touch," Rebecca parroted.

"That's good advice, Rebecca," Ford said, picking up the newspaper he'd brought to read while he still had some light.

"Do you know what this caterpillar is, Aunt Samantha?"

"That's a tent caterpillar," she answered. "When you found this caterpillar did you notice a wedge of white in a crook of the tree nearby that looked sort of like a tent?"

"I did," Clay said.

"If you'd gotten closer you'd have seen clusters of tent caterpillars in that white wedge. They live communally in nests in trees and feed on the leaves in the tree. They can be pretty destructive."

"Like *The Very Hungry Caterpillar* in our book," Tamela put in, coming closer to look.

"Granddaddy Burl puts chemicals around the base of some trees at the resort to keep those caterpillars away," Wesley said.

"He does do that," Ford said. "That was keen of you to remember that, Wesley."

"Do you know this beetle?" Clay asked Samantha, shifting the subject. "It's fat and green and it can fly. I almost didn't catch it."

Samantha studied it, almost hidden under a green leaf. "It's a green June beetle or what you may know better as a June bug. But it isn't really a bug, it's a beetle in the scarab family. It can fly and it makes a flying sound when it does. The ancient Egyptians revered them and carved figures of them into the stones of their jewelry. They were supposed to bring good luck."

"I have a scarab bracelet," Madison put in. "It was my mother's."

Samantha smiled at her. "I have one, too. Aunt Dixie gave Andrea and me both one for Christmas one year."

"It has different colored stones. It's real pretty."

"How do you know all that stuff about bugs, Aunt Samantha?" Andrew asked.

"I've always liked science," she answered.

"Look at ours, too, Aunt Samantha," Wesley said, pushing his and Gareth's bug box closer. "We have a grasshopper, too, and a cricket and a ladybug, and another kind of caterpillar. Do you know what this one is?"

She peered into his box, quickly spotting the pretty yellow, black and white striped caterpillar. "Ah, this beautiful lady is a monarch caterpillar. She'll later wrap herself up in a cocoon and then emerge into a lovely monarch butterfly in about the same colors."

"Oh, I've seen those pretty yellow and black butterflies," Madison said, coming to look closer.

"If we keep this caterpillar, can we watch that happen?" Wesley asked.

"No, it would probably just die," Ford answered. "You know we like to look at our catches and then let them go."

"How do you know this caterpillar is a girl?" Gareth asked.

Samantha heard Ford chuckle as she answered. "I just guessed," she told Gareth. "But once Monarch caterpillars become butterflies there is a way to tell the gender by their markings."

"Your bugs are making noises," Rebecca said, leaning closer to the boys' bug box.

"Yes." Samantha smiled, leaning over to listen, too. "Your field cricket is chirping and your grasshopper is clicking."

"How do they do that?" Tamela asked.

"The grasshopper rubs his legs against his wings to create that clicking noise you hear." She grinned at the younger girls. "Their ears are on their bellies, too. Did you know that?"

"No way," Gareth said.

"Gareth." Ford said his name in caution.

"It does sound odd, Gareth, but it's true. And a katydid's ears are on its leg. A katydid is green, sort of like your grasshopper. You can tell them from grasshoppers though because they have big long antenna and they make a buzzing sound by rubbing their wings together."

"You're smart," Andrew said.

"If you listen right now, you can hear the cicadas," Ford put in. "Do they rub their legs together, too, to make that sound?" he asked.

She laughed. "No, that loud drone-like buzzing is made from special organs in their abdomen called tymbals."

"You are smart." He grinned at her and then looked around at the kids. "All these bugs we've been talking about are insects, except the spider. How do you know the spider isn't an insect?"

"I know," Clay said. "Because insects all have six legs but the spider has eight. He's a something with an A."

"Arachnid," Ford answered. "And you guys need to go let all those bugs go over in the edge of the woods before it gets dark."

"And not near our tents," Natalie cautioned, making a face.

"Tell me another cool thing about bugs before we let ours go, Aunt Samantha," Andrew said.

She thought for a minute, looking at their collection. "Only the male field cricket can chirp and he chirps to call to the girls. The chirp is a mating call and the females decide which male to like according to which one has the best and probably the loudest chirp."

Natalie and Madison giggled, and Ford chuckled.

"Crickets will chirp, too, with a warning chirp if a predator is nearby and they also chirp more by night than by day most of the time."

"I never thought bugs would be fun to know about," Natalie said as the boys got up to head over to the woods to release their catches.

"Everything in nature is interesting," Ford put in. "Especially with a smart teacher." He smiled at Samantha.

With dark falling, they began to clean up and secure their campsite so as not to encourage visits by raccoons, bears, or other creatures while they slept. While everyone cleaned up, Ford made a bonfire in the fire pit, and then they sat around the fire and talked as darkness fell.

The girls switched on a portable LED camping lantern to sit on one of the picnic tables nearby, and Samantha knew the children all had similar lanterns in their tents plus flashlights.

She watched Natalie and Madison switch one of their lanterns on to take Rebecca and Tamela to the bathroom across the road.

As if noticing her watching them, Ford sat down near her by the fire. "Rebecca and Tamela, being the youngest, are allowed to use the bathroom in the camper at night, but the older children walk over to the restrooms if they need to go. Usually they sleep through the night, but sometimes one of them needs to get up. My rule, probably like you remember from counseling at camp, is that they have to go with their buddy if they need to go to the bathroom."

"That makes good sense. The camp bathrooms sometimes harbor a spider in them and one time I remember running into a snake."

"Shhh," he cautioned, grinning at her. "Don't even suggest that idea here. So far we've never seen more than a bug or two in any of the bathrooms. And not many of those."

As the fire began to grow dimmer and Ford ran out of stories to tell, Madison begged Samantha to get her guitar out of the camper to play for them. Samantha had found it in her closet back at Dixie's house, tuned it, and practiced last night to see if she still could play a little, and decided to bring it along. The girls at camp had always loved singing a few songs to close out the day. It was a good memory.

Coming back to the fire, she chose to sit a little distance from Ford. Being near him in the dark reminded her of that time in the dark the other night. She smiled to herself remembering that impulsive kiss. It had been good, better than she expected, and he'd been too shocked to really kiss her back. She wondered what it would be like if he did? It had been a long time since she'd felt passion and interest like that flash in the air with a man.

CHAPTER 12

Somehow Ford got through the afternoon setting up camp with Samantha and the evening hours to follow. God have mercy, he couldn't recall a time in his life when he'd been so aware of a woman. Hadn't he known his share of girlfriends in the past? Hadn't he been happily married to Laura for years, a beautiful and wonderful woman, full of life and vibrancy? What in the world was wrong with him?

Every time he got close to Samantha King, he found himself catching the scent of her, that earthy smell with a subtle hint of mint or lemon. Working around the veterinary clinic, he thought his sense of smell had dulled by necessity but she seemed to have revived it. Her deep voice played along his nerves, too, tantalizing him, and he found himself often fighting the urge to move closer to her, to find an excuse to touch her, even on her arm or shoulder, or to put his hands in her hair. She was making him crazy, and then when she started to sing he almost lost it and groaned out loud. What other seductive talents did this woman hold up her sleeve? And who knew she could sing like that? He didn't remember Andrea or Adam ever mentioning it.

She'd started her first song to please Tamela singing "Froggie Went A Courtin" and soon encouraged the children to sing along with her. He watched her lure them into joining her with warmth, fun, and a pied piper magic, playing and singing other songs they asked for like "The Bear Went Over the Mountain," "The Ants Go Marching One by One," and "My Bonnie Lies Over the Ocean," teaching the kids hand motions to that one. Dad blast it, how would the kids settle back in to the rest of the summer with the practical, matter-of-fact, and authoritarian Juanita after this? Samantha was so different than what they were used to, and he knew only the oldest children remembered Laura and Andrea's more warm, affectionate, and fun-loving ways. To the kids, Samantha was like a breath of fresh air in their lives. And who would have guessed it while watching her chase storms on television?

As a deeper darkness fell and the fire began to die down, Samantha began to switch to folk songs, "If I Had A Hammer" and "This Land Is Your Land," drawing the children into singing along with her on the verses they knew. That rich, deep voice of hers sounded like Anne Murray or Carole King's, especially when she sang "You've Got a Friend." The lyrics and the painful draw of that song made him get up and walk away into the darkness just to get away from the siren words. Fortunately, when he returned, she'd put the guitar away and had the children involved in a fireside game whispering words around the circle to see if they ended as they began.

"You kids need to get ready for bed now," he announced after looking at the time. "It's late."

"Doesn't Samantha sing good?" Madison asked, obviously enraptured with this new side of her aunt.

"Yes, she does." He began to work to put out the fire.

"Who taught you to play?" Natalie asked her.

She smiled a little wistfully. "My father. He plays guitar and sings a little. It's why he enjoys working with bands and singers as an agent and manager." She hesitated. "My mother sang, too, with a voice much like mine from what Aunt Dixie tells me. I only carry a few memories of hearing her sing, but I've heard some of her old recordings."

"You never wanted to be a singer?" Madison asked.

"No," she answered quickly and Ford watched the unhappy memories chase across her face, visible even in the darkness.

She smiled at Madison then. "I wanted to be a weather forecaster as soon as I learned what they did when a television forecaster visited our school and gave a talk."

"I think that would be a fun job, too," Madison added.

"Well, it's a hard job but a rewarding one." She smiled at her niece. "I'll tell you more about it someday."

After everyone settled down with only night creatures and the wind rustling through the trees for sound, Ford tried to decide how he was going to handle this situation with Samantha. As a widowed man with responsibilities and with Samantha the Bradley children's aunt, he couldn't cultivate any kind of relationship with her. Even if she flirted with him and even if the air was sometimes thick with attraction between them, she was wrong for him.

He sighed, tossing in his sleeping bag. Maybe he'd go get some counseling from his minister. He probably needed it. And maybe like Dwayne said, he'd just been too long without a woman in his life. It was sure a confusing and frustrating situation.

Somehow Ford got through the night, finally, and the next morning, with the sun shining and the day fair, he decided to push his personal feelings aside to enjoy this weekend with his kids. After their tense week, with the murder investigation going on and the problem with Madison, they all needed a break.

When Samantha came out to help him with breakfast, Ford felt more like his old self, his emotions in check.

"What are you cooking and what can I do to help?" she asked.

"I'm making French toast this morning. I already heated a batch of pre-cooked link sausages. As you can see, I like using our two-burner propane stove for breakfast rather than starting a fire in the outdoor grill again."

He cut thick slices of French bread to dip into an egg and milk mixture before turning to Samantha again. "If you would cut up some of those oranges in the camper to go along with breakfast and make a pot of coffee, that would be great. I could use coffee this morning." Actually, he desperately needed coffee after his nearly sleepless night.

She watched him for a minute and then said, "I'll get right after that. I could use coffee, too."

They were soon sitting down to eat and planning their day.

"I want to take a hike," Andrew said with enthusiasm. "The little girls are old enough to walk further this summer."

"Me and Rebecca aren't wimpy. We can hike." Tamela scowled at him.

Ford grinned. "I think we can all hike a portion of the Lower Mount Cammerer Trail this morning. We'll hike up to Sutton Ridge, that's only three miles roundtrip, and after we get back you guys can put your swimsuits on and play in Cosby Creek behind the picnic area."

"Oh, boy," Wesley and Gareth said at the same time.

Ford hadn't hiked the Lower Mount Cammerer Trail for a while and he enjoyed the roadbed trail ascending gradually through the lowlands of Mount Cammerer toward the ridge top. The trail wound through hardwoods and hemlocks in the first half-mile before coming to an open turnaround. He'd listened to Samantha talk about some of the plants and mushrooms they saw along the way, and now he stopped the group for a moment.

"As we walk on, see if you can spot remnants of an old stone wall beside the trail. Many settlers used to live in this area. You know we've seen old pictures of their cabins, schools, and churches."

"And old cemeteries," Clay added.

"That, too."

They talked about the early history of the mountains then as they walked on. But the kids got diverted rock-hopping as soon as they arrived at Toms Creek and then enjoyed scampering over a long wooden foot bridge a little further along the trail.

Ford looked around. "This is a nice place for a rest before the upcoming steeper climb to the Sutton's Ridge. After we walk out to see the views off the ridge, we'll head back."

He sat down on an old log by the trail for a minute and Samantha joined him, turning to ask him, "Do you hike a lot with the children?"

"We're beginning to do more hiking now that the younger ones are older. Before that they tired quickly or lost interest before we walked very far. They're doing better now." His eyes moved to where Rebecca and Tamela played by the stream. "Often small kids would rather play than hike."

"Yeah, I can see that." She grinned, watching Gareth and Wesley turn over rocks looking for salamanders.

After moving on to climb the ridge, they took a short side trail out to an overlook on Sutton Ridge, which offered some nice views across the ridgelines and the valley. Although he was sure Samantha would enjoy walking further, the short hike was enough hiking entertainment for the children, especially the younger ones, eager to get back to camp for lunch and a swim.

In swimsuits after lunch, the children headed to one of their favorite spots at the nearby mountain stream. Ford took two lawn chairs and a small cooler with them and located a good spot for a streamside camp. It was a site the children had enjoyed before with mountain rocks to jump on and a waist deep pool to play in below a rushing cascade.

Samantha peeled out of her shorts and T-shirt, layered over her swimsuit, to play in the water with the kids, while Ford sat in one of the chairs he'd brought to keep watch. He'd wade and cool off in the cold mountain water later, but for now he was content to rest and keep an eye on the children. And to watch Samantha in her snug, formfitting swimsuit from over the top of his paperback book.

After a time, she came to join him, dropping into the chair beside him and digging into the cooler to get a bottle of cold water to drink.

"The kids are having a good time," she said.

"They like it here," he answered. Searching for a topic of conversation, he asked her, "What did you learn about the kids with those fill-in sheets you had them do?"

She smiled at him. "More than I imagined. Besides fun things like their favorite colors, foods, and such, I learned what they wanted to be when they grow up." She looked thoughtful. "I've read that sometimes those young wishes are good indications of a child's true and best vocation. Some books suggest adults should try to look back and remember those earlier wishes if they feel somewhat unfulfilled in life."

"Maybe. I think I always knew as a kid I wanted to do something with animals. Dad saw that interest and he dropped me off to spend a day with our vet, to shadow him I guess you'd say." He grinned. "It's probably an illegal thing for a child to do but this is a small town and it was a long time ago."

"Well, you heard me say it was a visiting forecaster, coming to our school and talking about his job, that made me know what I wanted to do when I grew up." She paused, looking thoughtful again. "Would you mind if I load the kids up and take them on a field trip to the University of Tennessee one day? I thought I might take them around to some of the university departments related to their interests, let them talk to people and pick up brochures. It would help them see how important their school work is toward seeing any of their career dreams come true."

He laughed. "Maybe it would get Madison and Natalie's mind off boys."

Her mouth twitched in a smile. "I doubt a field trip could totally divert that rising interest but it might give them something else to focus on as well."

He considered her idea. "I think the older children would enjoy the trip but I think Rebecca and Tamela would prefer having one of their tea parties with Coralee that day. She hosts little teas on a pretty table on her big screened-porch sometimes for the girls. Madison and Natalie are losing interest in them but Rebecca and Tamela still love them, dressing up, wearing hats, drinking out of pretty tea cups and eating little teacakes Mother makes."

Samantha thought about this. "That might be best. Rebecca said she wanted to be a nurse like her mother and Tamela followed suit to say she wanted to be a teacher like Andrea was."

"I doubt Tamela remembers Andrea in any strong way and both were only three when Laura died." His eyes moved to hers. "I hope you see they're bonding to you, holding your hand, sitting close to you whenever they can. They haven't really known a mother like some of the older children."

"I've seen that. Aunt Dixie filled that role for me. I hope I can fill it a little for Tamela and even Rebecca."

"I hope that means you might drop by every now and then after you go back to work this fall. The children are going to miss you."

"I'm aware of that, and we talked about this before."

He heard her voice grow snappish.

She made a face. "It's hard with my job to arrange vacation times but I'm going to push for more leave when I get back. When I can get off, even if unexpectedly between weather events, I plan to fly back."

"That's good," he said, not wanting to annoy her further. "What did the older children say they wanted to be when they grow up?" he asked after a moment to change the subject.

"Madison says she wants to be a weather forecaster at a television station, probably from spending time with me—but the desire could last, and Natalie wants to be a librarian, not a surprise as much as she loves to read." She glanced out at the boys, climbing on the rocks and sliding down them into the cold water. "Clay wants to be a vet like you."

"I knew that; he comes and helps me in his spare time already. The other kids enjoy the animals but he loves working with them, helping at chores with Dwayne."

"Andrew wants to be an engineer, like his father Adam was. He's been asking me a lot of questions about kinds of engineers, what engineers do."

Ford nodded. "I could help to introduce him to a few friends, maybe take him to see where his father used to work at Douglas Dam."

Samantha grinned at him. "Gareth wants to be a businessman and make a lot of money—his words, not mine."

Ford laughed out loud. "No surprise there. He's an enterprising kid."

"And Wesley said he wants to be a park or forest ranger."

Ford considered that. "From how much he loves the outdoors, the resort, and everything related to it, that doesn't surprise me much. When we camp, he loves any chance he can find to talk to one of the rangers. I could see that working for him."

"I thought I'd make a few calls to the university departments related to their interests to see if we could visit, pick up some materials, and if I could show them around in general."

"I think they'd like that. There's a nice botanical garden near the veterinary and agricultural college you could visit while on campus, and you could make a side trip to the park along the Tennessee River. I'd be happy for you to take the kids on any type of trip you think might be a benefit to them—or simply fun for them during the summer months. You'd need to drive the big van and keep up with them all though."

She shrugged. "I've driven trucks for Weather First and in horrible weather, like in mud, snow, and ice. I'll be fine."

"I imagine you will." He gave her a candid look. "I rather think you could do about anything you set your mind to. If I haven't said it before, I think you're a rather remarkable young woman, and you certainly carry talent in spades."

"Thanks." She gave him a warm look that began to stir the air with more of that uncomfortable tension.

He rubbed his neck, looking away. "I think I'll go get wet and play with the kids a little." He stood up and made his way toward the stream, eager to get out of the net of allure she created.

They made hot dogs, chili, and slaw for Saturday night's dinner and delved into the cupcakes, cookies, and fudge that Dixie and Coralee had sent. After dinner, Ford set up a volleyball net and the older children played, joined by several other kids camping nearby. Samantha took the little girls on a walk and then played cards with them on the picnic table. Later when dark fell and the kids begged Samantha to sing with them again, Ford slipped away and went for a walk.

In the morning after breakfast, they would pack up and head

back to the house. Although Ford usually enjoyed their camping weekends, this one proved more stressful than relaxing for him, and for once he looked forward to heading back to the resort.

At two in the morning, restless, Ford woke up and hauled out of his tent to walk across the road to the restroom on the hillside. With a little moonlight to guide him, he didn't take his flashlight, the route a familiar one. Rounding the back of the restroom, he almost ran into Samantha. She wore one of his old shirts, probably to cover a nightshirt.

She put a hand to her heart. "You startled me."

"It's dark; that can happen. I see you didn't bring a light either."

"No, and I decided to come here so I wouldn't wake the girls up."

"Having trouble sleeping?" he asked.

"Maybe." She lifted her chin. "You can walk on back, Ford. I'll be fine."

She started around to the girls' side of the restroom. Ford watched her for a moment and then followed to stand near the door she'd slipped into.

"You didn't need to wait for me." She frowned, coming out a short time later.

"I thought I'd walk you back."

"Why?" she asked, walking closer to him in the dark to look into his face with a defiant look. "You've practically avoided me all weekend. Keeping your distance, staying busy with anything to keep from talking to me except when you had to."

He looked away, not wanting to answer her.

"Look, I'm sorry if I upset you by kissing you impulsively the other night." She lifted her chin. "But I'm not sorry I did it. It's sweet when feelings get stirred up between a man and a woman—crackling like lightning. Exciting like a storm coming in. Maybe that happens often for you but it doesn't for me. I liked how it felt; I wanted to feel more of it. Get closer to the storm. I don't try to hide from life or my feelings, Ford."

"And you think I do?" He snapped the words back.

"Yes. Some people are scared of storms. They miss a lot being like that, always running into the house, shutting all the doors. Hiding. There are so many things in life that are exciting if you don't run away."

Angry, he moved toward her, only to be hit with the force of her nearness, kicking up his heartbeat, whipping up his senses.

She closed her eyes. "Ah, there it is again. It's so strong." She opened her eyes after a moment, her eyes meeting his in the moonlight. "Can't you feel that?" She made a small crooning sound. "I've been wondering ever since the other night what it would be like if you kissed me back. You didn't, you know."

Later, Ford would remember the exact moment he lost it, grabbed her, pushing her against the rock wall of the building to lose himself in kissing her. Wrapping his arms around her, pulling her warmth against him, feeling her heart thudding against his chest.

"You have no idea what you do to me," he muttered against her neck. "Every second I'm near you, I want to touch you, get closer to you." He let his hands slide into her hair as he'd dreamed of doing, moved his mouth back to hers to explore more deeply.

She kissed him back, pushing close to him. "I thought it was only me," she whispered.

"I don't know what this is between us, but I've felt it pulling at me from the first," he told her between kisses. "I don't understand it. It doesn't make sense, and it doesn't work for either of our lives."

"Why is that?" she said, putting a hand on his cheek. "I think this is lovely, better than the rush of standing in a hurricane moving in." She smiled at him over the last words.

He backed away a little. "The problem is I'm a possessive man. I don't want to stand in a storm, feel its passion and glory, and then watch it move on. I want to keep it. I'm that sort of man, not an adventurer, moving on to the next thrill. I'm the type who wants permanence. That's the way I'm made."

She traced a hand down his chest but her eyes didn't meet his.

"I'm your storm today, Samantha, and the turbulence between

us may whip up again. I've already seen that happen. But come fall, you'll move on to the next adventure. And I'll stay here. The children will stay here. You and I have to find a way not to make this harder for them than it will be."

She looked at him then. "I don't always think far ahead. My work often means I live in the moment."

"With eight children that perspective changes." He glanced back toward their campsites. "If any of them saw us like this, it would cause them to entertain unrealistic hopes. You do see that don't you?"

She hugged herself and nodded.

He put a hand on her face. "Then know that I need to be careful and watchful to keep any feelings I have for you to myself. And know that I'll try to avoid moments like these whenever I can because they are a torment to me."

Her eyes widened. "A torment?"

"Yes, because I want more. Anytime you feel this storm stir up between us, whether I act on it or not, you'll know I want more. So don't think I don't feel anything." He looked away and rubbed a hand through his hair. "You've torn my world apart, made me feel again and feel more passionately than I ever remember feeling before. I don't know how I'm going to get through the months to come or how I'm going to manage after you go away."

"Do you love me?" she whispered.

"If I let myself love you I'd have to have you. I couldn't let you go. So don't ask me that. To me, love is forever, not a fleeting emotion, even if the emotions are powerful." He looked back toward the campsite again. "As good as this is, Samantha, and I admit it's sweeter and better than I have words for, don't make this harder for us."

"Okay." She started down the steps back toward their campsite, but then turned to give him a saucy grin. "But I can't promise anything, Ford. I am a storm chaser after all. And that's a part of who I am."

As she walked away, Ford shook his head in wonder at her.

And he couldn't decide whether to dread his next encounter with Samantha King in the storm or to look forward to it.

CHAPTER 13

In the next weeks, Ford stayed true to his promises and avoided any more intimate moments with her, although some of his looks her way told her clearly he hadn't forgotten their time at the campground any more than she had. Samantha, admittedly, flirted with him a few times, testing his resolve. But he held firm.

Today on a Monday in July, it was pouring rain and Samantha found Ford on her mind as she tried to find ways to entertain the children indoors.

Gareth, giggling with Wesley in one corner with a book, looked across the room to Samantha. "What happens when you illegally park your frog?" Waiting only a moment, he answered, "It gets toad away!" Then he and Gareth punched each other and hooted with laughter.

Madison looked up from the book she was reading. "Honestly, Gareth. If you or Wesley tell one more of those stupid jokes I think I'm going to scream."

Thus challenged, Gareth immediately opened his mouth to tell another, but Samantha shook her head at him and then at Madison.

"I wish it would quit raining." Andrew glanced out the window with a sigh. "What causes it to rain, Aunt Samantha?" he asked.

She looked up from the emails she was answering on her laptop. Picking up an apple from the fruit basket on the table, she held it up. "We live on the crust of the earth, like the skin of an apple. The earth's atmosphere is like a blanket of air that covers the planet; it stretches about six hundred miles above us. High in the atmosphere the outer layer is made of gasses that keep us from freezing at night and burning to death during the day. Most of the atmosphere is calm, except for the six miles right above us, like the air directly above this apple." She traced her hand around it, noticing most of the children had looked up from what they were doing to listen.

"Most of the atmosphere above the earth is calm," she continued, "but that six miles right above us is not calm and is always changing, producing our weather. So storms, tornadoes, or bright clear sunny days or other weather patterns are the activity right in the close atmosphere above us that goes on every day."

"That's cool." Andrew said. "But how does that make rain happen?"

She smiled at him. "The way the air is circulating in that six miles above the earth creates patterns of wind movements. It's really winds that control the temperature and winds that cause precipitation—rain, snow, hail, or sleet. So it's changing wind patterns that cause rain. Warm air collects moisture while it crosses large bodies of water, like oceans, and then the moisture cools as it moves across the land. With enough moisture in the air and clouds—and with other factors—it storms and rains. It's simple but complicated, too."

"They teach you in school how to know what kind of weather will happen, don't they?" Clay asked. "That's what the man said in the College of Communication and Information where we visited at the University of Tennessee last month."

Samantha had taken the older children to the college to visit departments of interest the week after talking to Ford about it.

"Aunt Samantha, what was that man's name that worked in the broadcasting department who used to work with you at Weather First?" Madison asked.

"His name is Matt Glenn. He worked as a forecaster with Weather First." She smiled. "It was fun to run into him at the college. He teaches courses there now in electronic news gathering and field production, broadcast news operations, and radio and TV news."

Madison leaned forward, putting her book down. "He said you could teach there if you wanted to, that the department would be glad to have someone with your expertise."

"Could you do that?" Tamela's eyes widened. "And stay here and not go back to Atlanta?"

Samantha looked away for a minute, trying to decide what to say. "I hold the credentials to teach at the university with my masters degree, but that isn't what I trained to do. I studied to be a meteorologist and a forecaster."

Natalie studied her thoughtfully. "People do a lot of things in their lives. Sometimes they change jobs."

Samantha put the apple back in the basket on the table. "Yes, they do. I first worked as a morning weather forecaster, giving the weather forecast every morning, like Matt did; then I began to work in the field as national television began to cover intense weather situations and storms more closely."

She glanced out the window. "The rain is moving out now. Why don't we go fix lunch so we can go outside? It's going to be hot today. It might be muddy down at the lake, but if you want we can spend the afternoon at the pool."

"Yeah!" Gareth hollered, always the more restless of them all.

The family Labradors looked toward the terrace eagerly as the sound of the rain tapered off, going to the door, wanting to go out. Of all the family animals, they loved being outside the most. Jefferson was a black lab and Gracie a white one. The family had raised them from pups and Samantha often noticed how protective both dogs were about the children.

She'd come to know not only the children in these weeks but the family's pets. The two smaller dogs Benji and Frou Frou loved to tag along with the children and romp in their games. The cats, however, watched from a distance or went about their own business, more independent. Samantha thought Willowdeen the sweetest of the cats with her deep purr and long silvery, gray fur. Ford told her Willowdeen was a Maine Coon. Eudora, a long-haired mix, white with yellow markings, had developed a special fancy to

Samantha over the summer and was the most likely to come to find her to jump on her lap. Oscar, still young, was the most playful. Marmalade, a big yellow tabby male, proved the more stand-offish and independent of the cats, probably, as Ford mentioned, because of his troubled kitten years that left him less trusting of humans, even those he loved.

Everyday lunches were usually an informal affair in summer. Samantha and the children put out assorted lunch meats, cheeses, peanut butter, jelly, and bread and let everyone fix their own sandwiches. With this they ate fruit, chips, and later cookies.

After all was cleaned up, the children put on swimsuits, found towels, and headed for the resort swimming pool. The sun had popped out and with the July humidity at a high today all the kids were glad to hit the water.

Samantha, in a simple black one-piece suit, slathered lotion on and then settled into a lounge chair where she could keep an eye on the children. A pool and water on a hot day always made for a good time for kids. She'd given swim lessons since early June and all the children were better swimmers now.

She'd learned Ford worked with them in the pool and at the lake, but that Juanita did not. In fact, from what the children told her Juanita didn't swim and feared the water, disliking even spending time outside by the pool or lake. It had been Burl, the children's grandfather, who lifeguarded their times at the water in past, and he'd expressed his gratitude for time off this summer.

The long pool, with its typical deep and shallow ends, had a big rustic fence around it and broad concrete patios as well. As a lodge pool in past, it had restrooms, a storage room for chairs and pool equipment, and two covered pavilions for those who wanted to pull their chairs out of the direct sun. Maury and Ford kept the pool clean and maintained in summer and Samantha had enjoyed many fun days here with the kids.

Knowing Vickie Larsen's children enjoyed time with them at the pool on sunny days, Samantha gave her a call before they started lunch to invite them over, too, with the rains moving out. She saw Vickie coming through the gate now with her three children, Courtney, Jake, and Emmylou. The children called out greetings and wasted no time dropping their towels in chairs and hitting the water.

"Thanks for the call." Vickie spread a towel over the lounge chair by Samantha's before sitting down. "My kids were getting antsy after all the rain yesterday, last night, and this morning."

"My tribe, too." Samantha grinned at her. "How have you been?"

"Good. And thanks for kicking in to help with Bible School."

"It was fun. I'm sorry I couldn't help all week. I used the chance while the kids were busy most of the day to drive back to Atlanta for meetings."

"How did that go? Is everything on schedule for you to return this fall?"

"Yes, and they've scheduled me back sooner since my recovery has progressed so well." She spread more lotion over her legs. "Ford says Juanita can start coming back part-time in August when the children go back to school. She can pick up most of her duties then and make dinner before going home, like she always does when the kids are in school. Without them to watch during the day, she can run back home when needed to help her parents."

Vickie turned to look at Samantha. "You know the children are really going to miss you when you go back." She paused. "So will I. We've become good friends."

Samantha smiled at Vickie. "Lucy gave me the same talk last night. I promised I'd try to come back more often." She paused to call out to Wesley and Gareth to stop splashing the girls. "It's been fun having times with Lucy's and your family, and all of this tribe this summer. Our Fourth of July day on the lake at your place was especially fun, with the fireworks and celebrating Wesley's birthday. It's been a big change for me after a rough winter, but a good, memorable one."

Vickie grew quiet for a few moments. "It isn't only the kids who are going to miss you, Samantha. It's Ford too. We'd all need to be blind not to pick up on the fact that there's a simmering attraction between you two."

She shrugged. "He does seem to dislike me less than when I first arrived."

Vickie flipped her with a hand towel. "Don't make light of it. Ben and I haven't seen Ford show any interest in another woman since Laura tragically died until you came."

Samantha sighed. "What is your point Vickie?"

"Has Ford talked to you about staying? We all see how wonderful you are with the children and you seem to be happy here. Is it not even a possibility you'd entertain?"

Samantha rubbed her arm. "I don't think I'm the permanent family type. My mother wasn't; my dad isn't. Other places, other things, the passion of their work called to them more than making a home for Andrea and me. I think I carry that same restlessness in my blood." She bit her lip. "I would always need something more than just taking care of kids in my life. Even you shared with me your love of the piano. I've heard you play at the church now and with such skill. Watched and seen how you love it, enjoy what you do. You were able to combine family and your work passion. There is no opportunity for a meteorologist here in Dandridge, Vicki—not even a television station for a local forecast. No bigger opportunities, no challenges."

Vickie fell quiet for a time thinking about this. "Have you prayed long and hard over this, Samantha? God often has answers we don't."

Samantha shifted in her seat, a little uncomfortable. "I have prayed, and I am getting into a deeper place in my faith now. I admit my faith was shallow. My earlier conversion experience, if you want to call it that, was pretty meaningless, too. I've dealt with that."

"Have you?" Vickie's eyes widened.

"After reading some of those books you gave me, I went out to the gazebo behind the inn one night and prayed that prayer and got that all straightened out. Like you said, I knew things were different then."

Vicki all but clapped her hands. "You got born again!"

Samantha rolled her eyes. "The terminology doesn't matter as much as the experience. But I know change happened. I'm grateful to you and to Lucy for pushing on me and for sharing with me to make me want more."

"The terminology born again is in the Bible, Samantha."

"I know," she answered, annoyed. "Don't get all teachery on me. I've read that story about Nicodemus. I noticed Jesus didn't say 'verily, verily, it might be a good idea if you get born again.' It did say 'must.' I got that."

Vickie tried not to laugh. "I can't believe you're not more excited about this."

Samantha looked away. "Maybe I am but I'm just not sure how to talk about it much yet. I'm working on it; give me some time."

"Well, I'm thrilled you shared this with me. It's made my day."

Samantha wrinkled her nose. "I hate to be slow in anything, to be one of the last people to catch on to something important. When I talked to Dixie about this, she seemed shocked that my supposed conversion experience when I went through Communicants class at church had skipped over all the most important parts. We've talked a lot about that since." She hesitated. "Dixie had no idea my faith wasn't where it should be. I guess she assumed since she took me to church and all that I was all right."

"Have you shared this with Ford?"

"No!" She knew she looked shocked.

Vickie laughed. "It's not something awful or embarrassing to share, Samantha. I told you Ford had his own experience outside, too, on the bridge across the lake. He called it a bridging change."

Samantha couldn't help grinning at that. "Well maybe I had a gazebo change."

"Did you know the word gazebo comes from Latin terms that mean 'I shall look, I shall see'? That's rather spiritual if you think about it. And the Egyptians believed their gardens and gazebos would follow them to heaven."

"I like that idea. Thanks for sharing that."

While eating dinner with Aunt Dixie later out on the porch, where they could see the gazebo at the end of the garden, Samantha told her about Vickie's words.

"Well, that's a nice concept and I like the idea of our old gazebo being the spot where you found the Lord in a richer way. It is vitally important, the foundation for the Christian faith, and I regret I was lax in that aspect of your upbringing."

"Don't blame yourself. You can't see another person's heart inside and you thought you'd introduced me to everything." She shook her head. "You know I was always a stubborn, independent little thing, too."

Dixie finished off the last of a piece of pecan pie. "I'm glad Vickie talked to you about the possibility of staying on in Dandridge. I didn't want to mention the idea but you know I would be happy if you did. You could help me here at the inn."

Samantha grinned. "As if you need any help."

"Well, we could figure out something." She put a hand on Samantha's. "The times I've been around you and Ford I can see how it is with the two of you. Think carefully before tossing away love if that's what you two are feeling. It doesn't come along often."

"Well, whatever it is, it's confusing and disruptive to my life." She closed her eyes and leaned her head back. "I think I'm too much like my dad, and possibly my mother, to be a family person."

Hearing a hello from the back door and a tread of footsteps, the two were surprised when Robert King walked through the side door and out to the porch to join them. Talk about an eerie coincidence, Samantha thought, glancing up at her father.

"Robert, what in the world are you doing here?" Aunt Dixie pushed up from her chair and wrapped her brother in a warm hug.

He hugged her back and kissed her on the cheek. He came over and leaned down to give Samantha a kiss on her cheek next. "I hoped you might still be here," he said to her. "Dixie wrote that you were staying here for a while this summer until you could get back to work."

"Have you eaten supper?" Dixie asked him.

"No. I've been over at Myrtle Beach with the band for a concert booking and decided on the spur to rent a car and take an extra day to stop and see you two on my way back."

"Well, sit down and talk to Samantha," Dixie said. "I'll go fix you a plate. I cooked a nice chicken casserole for dinner with fresh home-cooked green beans and garden tomatoes."

"And pecan pie." He glanced at Samantha's uneaten piece. "I can always count on great food whenever I stop by."

"Here, you can have my piece after Dixie brings your dinner." Samantha pushed her plate over toward her father as he sat down at the table. "I'm up a few pounds and need to cut back. Especially since I'm heading back to work soon."

He studied her. "You look good. Healthy and tanned. Are you all recovered now?"

Samantha fought back a sarcastic comment. He hadn't visited her once after she got hurt. "Yes, I'm doing well," she said instead. "Thank you for asking."

"I meant to get down." He looked away. "But the band was abroad then, doing a European tour." He picked at a piece of lint on his slacks. "Did you get the flowers I sent to the hospital?"

"I did."

A little silence fell but then Dixie bustled back in the room with a dinner plate for him and a glass of tea. Dixie chattered away after that while her father ate, giving Samantha time to study him.

Unlike her and Andrea, Robert King was dark headed with attractive streaks of silver beginning to thread through his hair. His eyes were brown, as Andrea's had been. Only she'd gotten her mother's Irish green eyes and her mother's singing voice.

Affable and friendly, her father talked easily to Dixie, telling her about the band and recent travels, talking about a new talent he'd started to work with. They seemed comfortable and easy together where Samantha always felt awkward around her father and he with her.

Dixie turned to Samantha. "Your father stops by more often to visit with me these days. I think he comes for my cooking." She laughed. "He usually stays in the carriage house. I only use it for family. But with you here I'll put him in the blue room tonight. I don't have other guests here at mid week so the three of us can enjoy a good visit and share breakfast together in the morning before you go to Ford's and before Robert needs to head back to Nashville."

Samantha nodded, finding it hard to get into the cozy family scene concept.

Watching her father out of the corner of her eye, she noticed he'd become a little heavier with the years, not as much so as Dixie, but stockier than before, and she saw more wrinkles now in his face and the telltale blotches of age on his arms and hands. Since she was in her upper thirties now, he must be well into his sixties.

As her father finished his dinner and reached for Samantha's piece of pie, Dixie stood up to take his plate. "I'm going to take this plate back to the kitchen and wash things up."

She stopped and looked pointedly at Robert. "I want you to talk to Samantha about Colleen. I think her lack of understanding about her mother and about your marriage is getting in the way of her concepts about marital relationships. She shouldn't need to think she will be like her mother." She paused. "Or even like you as a parent if she should ever decide to marry."

"Aunt Dixie I don't really think …"

Dixie interrupted. "This talk is past due, Samantha. Let your dad talk to you and you ask him the questions you want to. I'd like the two of you to build a better relationship."

Her dad looked out over the back garden and toward the lake after Dixie left. "Whatever happened with your mother and me had nothing to do with you and Andrea. Colleen came to the states on tour with her family group the Dublin Hannigans. I booked their schedule here in the states and I fell for Colleen hard. Frankly, she'd have left me, I'm sure, to go back home, if she hadn't gotten pregnant with you. She tried to be happy afterward and to be happy with me."

He paused, wincing. "I helped to promote her as a single in the

U.S. She was so talented but still not happy. Then she had Andrea. We tried to make it work, but I traveled a lot, and she missed her home and family in Ireland. We quarreled all too often although we tried to hide that from you and Andrea."

"I don't remember any of that really. But I remember her singing with us, laughing and playing with us. The feel and memory of her."

"She was a sweet mother to you two girls, even if she grew more and more unhappy." He hesitated, finishing off his pie. "One day she just left. We had a woman we used as a sitter sometimes; she stayed over when we had shows. She called me to say Colleen hadn't come home."

"She just left?"

He nodded. "I had to leave a band on tour and fly home. I found a note then. It said she felt depressed, homesick, and needed some time back in Ireland, that she hoped I could understand. When I called she wouldn't talk to me. Her family said to give her time. I tried to." He ran a hand through his hair. "I brought you and Andrea to Dixie. I thought it would be temporary. I threw myself back into work, kept trying to call and talk to her."

"Did she never talk to you again? Didn't she call to ask about us?"

"Eventually she did. She called to say she wasn't coming back, that she was singing with her family group again and happy. Then the story came out, also, that she'd re-linked with her old beau from the past and wanted a divorce. Deserting you two and leaving the country, she knew she wouldn't get any rights with you. But she said later, when you both grew older, she hoped I'd let you come to stay with her for a while, to meet your Hannigan relatives."

"She never came back to the states to see us?"

He sighed. "I think she meant to, but she was working. She remarried. Time slipped away, and then she got ill and hospitalized and died of a sepsis inflammation that settled in. I never even got to see her again myself."

"I'm sorry Dad." Samantha had listened to his voice as he talked.

"I think you loved her a lot."

"I did. I can admit that more easily now and also admit how it embittered me after. I hardened my heart, locked it off, to protect myself." He sent her an anguished look. "I was a cruel father, seeing you and Andrea so little, but you both looked so much like her. You had her voice, her hair, her eyes and Andrea her smile, her sweet ways. Because it hurt to see you, I stayed away. It was wrong. I'm sorry."

He spread his hands. "I chose a career life that didn't leave much time for home and family. I travel. I work with bands. The life isn't one you want to take little girls into. I couldn't have you with me. I knew Dixie didn't have family and that she'd lost Jackson. She quickly fell in love with both of you and said she'd raise you. It seemed best."

"That explains a little but not all."

He studied her expression, obviously trying to think of what else to say. "I thought you might understand more, grown as you are now, with a demanding career of your own." He paused. "But I think if you ever choose to have a family, you'll be more like Dixie, not me. You may look like your mother, but in life you're always who you choose to be. Remember that. Make the choices that are right for you. Don't let old hurts and misunderstandings stand in your way, like I did. And don't stay bitter toward your mother that her heart called her home to her own country and her own people. I knew she never wanted to be here, even to be with me. But I didn't want to let her go."

Dixie came back into the room. "I knew from the first day I met Colleen Hannigan that her heart was in Ireland. If Colleen hadn't gotten pregnant with you, Samantha, she'd have gone home with her family after their tour in America ended."

"Is this all supposed to make me feel better, this talk?" She knew she sounded sarcastic but she didn't care.

"Yes, actually it should," Dixie said, ignoring her tone and sitting down with them. "It's only when things get bottled up that they grow nasty and misunderstood. In his way Robert loves you and he loved Andrea. He always sent financial support, paid for your school and clothes. He paid to renovate the carriage house into a nice suite with a big bedroom, sitting room and a bath, connecting to my room so you girls would have your own space here at the inn. Robert and I always kept in touch about you. He often gave me advice when I needed it."

She hesitated. "I know it was your father's presence, and his love, you really wanted and he held that back. But I also know, from talking to him more in recent years, that he regrets that. I wanted him to have a chance to tell you that. People change, Samantha. We all deserve second chances at things in life, things we've gotten wrong and want to get right. Things we might want to do differently. You and I were talking about God earlier. God is always a God of second chances. A God who will forgive and let us start over and do things in a new way."

Robert smiled at Dixie. "I've been working on making things right with Dixie, too. I've also neglected her. I try to stop through more often now. And I expect I'll come back here when I'm ready to hang up my work. We only have each other except for you two girls."

Samantha scowled at him. "You also have Andrea's children. Have you even gotten to know them?"

He lifted an eyebrow. "Seems to me that just because you've made a recent turnaround in that direction by necessity doesn't give you the right to beat me up over it."

Samantha felt herself flush at his words.

Dixie chuckled. "You did rather ask for that one, Samantha." She turned to Robert. "Samantha has really formed an affection for the children while here. It's the one good thing that came out of her injury."

"I'm glad to hear that," her father said.

Dixie didn't add more but Samantha saw the added smirk sent her way that meant Dixie was also thinking of Ford. She'd always been able to tell when Samantha cared for someone, even when she'd been a girl.

Not wanting to talk more, Samantha stood up. "I think I'll go for a walk, maybe go over to Lucy's for a little while. Let the two of you visit if it's okay."

"That would be fine," Dixie said. "With all we've aired out, you need some time to think things through. Come on back when you want."

Her father reached out to catch her hand. "No matter what's happened in the past, I want you to be happy, Samantha. I hope you know that. And if anything I did or your mother did hurt you, I want you to shake it off and move on. Our mistakes don't have to be yours. Or to keep hurting you. I'm sorry for how I didn't meet your needs well emotionally." He grinned. "I think I must be softening up in my old age. Family is starting to matter more to me. I haven't valued that as much as I should in past."

Samantha left then. She did go walking, but not to Lucy's. She just walked down the quiet dark streets of Dandridge. Thinking. Her life, her understandings about it, always seemed so clear and defined before. Now so many changes had hit her, and she struggled to feel as certain and focused as she always had before.

CHAPTER 14

In the clinic the next day, the lightning and sounds of an approaching storm reminded Ford of Samantha. Frankly, it took little to remind him of her. She filled so much of his life these days. He said goodbye to her every morning as he left for work and found her working in the kitchen getting dinner or laughing with the kids every evening when he came home. She shared many of their weekends now at the lake with the Larsens and the Howards. They'd all settled into a happy threesome of families.

He stopped to lean his head against the wall outside the exam room he'd just come out of. How was he going to manage when she left? Juanita would be back at the house to clean and keep up the schedule at his home, to supervise the kids after school, help with dinner and meals. She was an efficient helper, a good person, but she wasn't Samantha.

A crash of lightning and a flickering of the lights interrupted his thoughts. He walked around the hallway to Maria's desk.

"Looks like another big storm is moving in," he said, stopping to put some paperwork on the counter.

"Yes," she answered. "There's a severe wind and weather warning out for the area and several of our afternoon appointments called to cancel." She glanced toward the window. "It looks bad out. You can't blame them."

"No." He looked at the changes in the schedule.

"My grandmother is beginning to do much better," Maria said. "She is moving around more, able to do more for herself finally.

She hasn't been an easy patient."

"I expect not, knowing your grandmother." He glanced at Maria, a pretty, dark-haired Hispanic woman. "Your mother's had a rough time with this, but we'll be glad to get her back at our home, too."

Maria filed the chart he'd dropped off and then turned back to him. "I've enjoyed my talks with Samantha when she's stopped by. The children obviously like her and Mother says she is keeping the house nice."

Ford lifted an eyebrow at that, wondering how Juanita could know that. "Samantha hasn't mentioned her stopping by."

Maria laughed. "Mother has often stopped to check on things when she knew Samantha and the children would be gone for the day. She never stops by for long, of course, only to check on things. She loves her work there and feels possessive about the house and the family, as you might imagine."

He smiled. "I will never stop being grateful to your mother for stepping in to help me when she did after Laura died. She really saved my life."

"Many blessings came to our family, too, from her coming to help you." She paused. "Our family is truly grateful to you for allowing us to live in the home at Willow Point. I hope you know I am grateful for my job here, also."

Ford smiled. "I was lucky to get you here at the clinic, Maria. You keep my business as ordered as your mother does my home. And Juanita's husband Leon and your husband Carlos keep the Willow Point home and property up beautifully, even while running their restaurant outside Dandridge."

"You should bring the children over for a Mexican dinner one night. You know Dad and Carlos would be happy to feed you."

"I hate doing that because your dad won't let me pay."

She waved a hand. "It is his pleasure and a way to give his thanks."

"I'll try to plan a night to take the kids soon." Ford drummed a hand on the counter, wanting to talk to Maria about another matter. "When Juanita comes back next month, I still want Samantha to come over freely after the children get home from school to enjoy time with them until she leaves. She has done a very good job helping with the kids this summer. I know your mother resents her lack of help in the past but do you think she might have revised her opinion a little by now? It would make things easier."

Maria sighed and looked away. "Mother goes to visit often with Coralee, your mother. It has kept her in touch with the situation."

"Well, that's good. I know Mom and Dad have revised their opinion about Samantha. They're very fond of her now."

Maria shuffled some papers on her desk.

"What are you not telling me?"

"Mother is now upset that Samantha has merged into the children's lives, made them grow fond of her, only to plan to waltz out on them again." She looked away. "And to waltz out on you."

A bolt of lightning nearby rattled the windows and blipped their power, giving Ford a minute to digest these words.

"Maria, the children and I know Samantha is only here for the summer, that she's returning to work soon. She never promised anything different." He knew his tone sounded a little testy.

"I am not blind … *Yo no soy siego*, Ford," Maria said quietly. "I have seen how you look at her. "*Tu corazon esta ocupado*. Your heart is engaged. Surely you cannot deny it."

He scowled. "And you've told your mother your thoughts on this? That doesn't help things, Maria."

"I have not talked to her, but your mother has. She is concerned."

"Great." Ford rolled his eyes. "I was hoping for some peace between Juanita and Samantha, not continued animosity. You know your mother can be rather outspoken."

"Yes, because she loves fiercely—*ferozmente*. You know that is how she is and like an old mother hen, she will fight anyone she thinks will hurt her chicks. She is that way."

He sighed. "Fine. I will try to talk to her."

Another heavy crack of lightning interrupted them, blinking the power again.

Dwayne came out of his office. "Dang, that sounded close, like it hit something nearby." He looked out the window. "This storm is really bad."

Ford's cell phone rang and he pulled it out of his back pocket. Seeing his parents' number, he answered.

"I'm worried about your father," his mother said in a rush. "I think a tree fell on our back property by the old barn and I can't get your father to answer his phone. He was out there in this storm checking on things. You know how he is." She paused. "I called Samantha first to see if he might have gone over there, concerned about them, too." She hesitated. "I think Samantha might have gone out in this storm to look for him."

His mind didn't like to picture that idea. "I'll head home right now and I'll go look for Dad. Try not to worry." He hung up and turned toward Dwayne and Maria. "I've got to go up to the house. Mother's worried Dad is out in the storm and he's not answering his cell phone."

"Well, put that heavy rain slicker in your closet on," Maria said. "It's bad out there."

"We'll cover for you here," Dwayne added.

Ford headed out the door a few minutes later. With rain in the forecast he'd driven his SUV to the clinic today, so he made quick time getting back to the house.

Heading inside after stopping to shed his slicker in the back entry, he walked into the big lodge living room to find all the children huddled there around the rock fireplace. He looked around. "Where's Samantha?"

"She went to check on Granddaddy," Natalie answered. "Grandma was worried about him. We're all staying right here in one room together like she told us until she gets back."

He frowned.

"Don't be mad at her," Clay said. "She knows about storms. She wasn't scared, and Grandma can't get out to see about Granddaddy. You know that."

Ford didn't like the situation or leaving the children alone, but he said, "I need to go look for Granddad, too. Like Samantha told you, stay here together. Don't any of you come after us or go outside." He looked around, seeing the animals settled here and there. "Are all the animals inside?"

"Yes," Clay answered. "I got them in when it started to storm bad."

"Good." He nodded. "I'll be back soon."

The rain from the storm strengthened as Ford drove toward his parents' home. Barely able to see the road, he turned off Sycamore Lake Road to inch up the narrow Dock Road behind his parents' house. As he neared the barn, he felt his heart catch to see one of the huge sycamore trees on the property crashed on the ground near the front of the barn, its vast branches draped over the side of the structure.

Parking his car, he climbed the fence and headed toward the barn, calling. "Dad! Samantha!"

"Here!" he heard a voice he knew to be Samantha's. He followed it nearer the upper part of the tree, blocking the barn's door.

"In here," Samantha called again. "You'll need to climb over some of the tree."

He followed her voice to find her huddled over his father on the ground just inside the barn door. Panicked, he squatted beside her.

"Dang tree almost fell on me," his dad said, lying on his back. "I ran for the barn when I saw it falling. Just about made it." His dad grinned at Samantha. "Dang plucky girl pulled me out from that pile of limbs that knocked me out and had me pinned to the ground."

"Has he been unconscious?" Ford asked Samantha, automatically reaching for his dad's wrist to check his pulse.

She'd found a slicker in the house before she headed out but she was soaked. "He was unconscious when I found him," she answered. "Knocked out face down. It scared me. I worried the tree hit his head or back." She pushed a strand of wet hair behind her ear.

Ford leaned over to listen to his dad's breathing.

"I knew to check for breathing or pulse," Samantha continued. "When he started to wake, I knew it was okay then to roll him over face up, while continuing to check his airways and keep him warm." She pulled an old horse blanket she'd found in the barn higher over his dad's chest. "I think he's all right, but I called emergency."

"Are you hurting anywhere, Dad?" Ford asked.

"I ain't hurting much of anywhere except in my pride for being fool enough to get out in this storm. I was worried for the cows, wanting to get them in the barn if I could." He shook his head. "Of course, they'd all acted smart and headed for that open shed toward the back of the property. Smarter than me to seek shelter, to know the storm a bad one."

He paused. "I got bumped when the branches of that old tree whacked me in the back. Knocked me down and knocked the breath out of me for a bit. I'd say I've got some bruises, but I think I'm all right except for that."

Samantha smoothed a hand down his dad's arm. "A straight line storm blew though. I ran over here as soon as your mother called. I knew it wasn't like your dad not to answer a call from her." She lifted her eyes to his. "I heard the tree fall as I came up the road. Wind roared by me as I got closer, tore out some fence line, too. When I saw that huge tree across the field lying up by the barn, I started calling for your dad. It gave my heart a scare finding him just inside the barn, covered up with side branches and unconscious."

Ford looked around and could see where she'd used an old saw to cut away branches to get his father free. "You acted smart, Samantha. Dad and I are grateful."

His dad grinned. "Told you she was plucky. Stayed cool as a cucumber, talking to me, hunting up a saw and getting them limbs off me, moving me careful, covering me up. I didn't want her to call in emergency help but she did it anyway. Can't you just take me on home, Ford? Coralee will be worried and I don't want her left alone."

They heard the sound of the siren now.

"No, you need to get checked, Dad," he answered.

Emergency personnel came across the field through the rain, got their story, did their vital checks, loaded Burl carefully on a stretcher, covering him from the rain, and then readied to transport him to the ambulance.

"Ford, you go see about your mother before you follow over to the hospital. Take her to stay with Samantha and the kids. These boys will take care of me until you can get over to the hospital."

"He'll be all right." Samantha put a hand on Ford's arm as the emergency personnel carried Burl toward the ambulance.

Ford turned to Samantha after they pulled away. "You crazy woman. Why didn't you call me?"

"I saw the clouds earlier, knew there was a chance a widespread, straight line wind storm might move in. I heard it coming when your mother called, worried about your dad. A straight line storm sounds somewhat like a tornado." She looked out across the fallen limbs of the tree and into the rain still pouring down. "I know how dangerous those storms can be. I didn't think I should wait, knowing your dad might be outdoors in its path."

Ford put a hand on her wet face. "You put yourself in its path, too."

She shrugged. "I work with weather outside all the time."

He leaned over and kissed her forehead. "Thank you for acting smart and doing what you did for my father."

She looked up at him and grinned. "I think you can do better than that for a thank you."

Groaning, he gathered her up and kissed her with all the pent up emotion of the day and the last weeks.

After a few minutes, she said, "As good as this is, we need to go pick up your mother and I need to get back to the kids. They'll be scared and worried with both of us gone and all of this storm roaring around the area." She brushed her fingers through his wet hair. "You need to head to the hospital to see about your dad, too. They'll probably do some tests, check him over, but I really think he's okay. I doubt they'll keep him overnight."

"You make me forget everything," he said, framing her face in his hands, kissing her one more time.

"Storms will do that," she said with a grin. "They're pesky, distracting little things."

He laughed, despite himself, and then headed out into the rain with her toward his car.

CHAPTER 15

After emerging as a bit of a hero following the storm, it took little persuasion for Samantha to talk Ford into giving her two days off a week later. Burl was well-recovered, so he and Coralee could help with the kids, and Samantha needed to drive to Atlanta to check on her apartment, keep a doctor's appointment, and attend a work related meeting. The reasons for her visit to Atlanta were all valid, but her trip also involved a little more than she felt willing to discuss with anyone at this point.

After packing an overnight bag and saying goodbye to Dixie after breakfast, Samantha first headed toward Knoxville. Promptly at nine, she walked into the communications department at the University of Tennessee for a meeting with Matt Glenn, her friend from Weather First.

"Come on in Samantha," Matt said, spotting her in the hall outside his office. He gestured to a seat across from his desk. "Want some coffee?"

"No." She settled into her seat. "Thanks for your call the other day."

He studied her for a moment. "I wasn't sure if you might be interested in a new opportunity, but I couldn't help thinking about you when Ron Mitchell, the producer at WKSE called to ask if I knew anyone to recommend for a weather anchor position coming up."

Samantha shifted the briefcase in her lap to the floor beside her chair. "What made you think of me?" she asked.

"Frankly, I followed a hunch in calling you. I knew a position as weather anchor for a local station a comedown from your celebrity status with Weather First, but I remembered that I changed jobs in my late thirties after getting hurt out in the field."

"I didn't know that."

"Most of my time wasn't spent in the field like you, but I pitched in to cover severe weather situations locally when needed. I slid and fell while covering a snowstorm. Broke my leg." He shrugged. "You know in many of those storms you sometimes can't see your own hand in front of your face."

"You seem okay now."

"I am, but that time served as a wake-up call for me. It could have been worse." He shuffled some papers on his desk and then smiled. "In Atlanta, I really enjoyed going out to schools, talking to kids about weather, and teaching a class or two at a nearby college. I started looking around to see if I could find a full-time college teaching position. I put in applications at several schools, and I liked UT when I visited and the courses they wanted me to teach. It's been a good change."

"You mentioned to me that I could possibly do some teaching here."

"I did." He sipped on his coffee. "I liked the kids you brought to visit and how you worked with them. I thought if you were interested I might be able to pull some strings, but then the call from Ron came. One of their anchors is moving on to greener pastures. Ron often calls me when the station gets a position opening. He knows I have contacts. He networks for applicants along with posting the positions formally."

She fidgeted in her seat. "You know I already have a great job, Matt. Why would I be interested in a meteorologist forecasting position? I worked earlier as a morning anchor at Weather First."

Matt looked over the top of his glasses at her. "And yet you're here."

She frowned. "Did you think because I got hurt I wouldn't want to go back into the field full time? That I'm afraid?"

"No. I just followed a gut feeling that you might be open to talk to Ron. People change in what they want over time, in what's important to them. You have family here. The oldest girl you brought with you, the one interested in broadcasting, looks like you. Your niece, right?"

"Yes. Madison." She glanced toward the window at a thin line of cirrus clouds in the blue sky. "Three of the children with me that day are my sister's children. She and her husband were killed a number of years ago in a wreck. I've tried to spend time with the kids while on leave."

"Family can be important." He glanced toward a group of family photos on a nearby shelf.

Samantha found herself getting impatient with this meeting. "I'd prefer it if you were more direct, Matt. If you have something to say, just say it."

He bit back a smile. "When you visited, you might remember we took a tour around the building. You stepped into the restroom along the way and the kids quizzed me about the faculty teaching comment I'd made. It was obvious they want you to stay around the area. I found myself wondering if you might feel the same."

She took a deep breath and decided to be honest in return. "It's one of the reasons I'm here."

"And?" He waited, watching her.

She glanced out the window again, not answering.

"Ron Mitchell will ask you these things, too, Samantha. He will want to know why you would consider a local station opportunity after working for Weather First. If you get prickly with him, it won't help you to be seriously considered—if you want to be considered."

She rubbed her arm. "It's complicated."

He laughed. "Life's that way, but you well know a forecaster needs to be focused, even under pressure, and able to ad lib effortlessly. You seem to be failing at that today."

She closed her eyes for a minute and then glanced toward his family photos. "When did you meet your wife?"

He smiled. "In Atlanta. I chased after her until she said yes. I love her as much today as I did then and we have three great kids." Matt glanced at her hands clenched in her lap. "It isn't unprofessional to fall in love, Samantha. Is that a part of this?"

She sighed. "There's a vet in Dandridge…" She tried to think what else to say.

"You don't need to tell me more," Matt interrupted. "But when Ron asks you why you're considering a change, you give him that charming smile of yours, that you're famous for, and tell him you've met a man. And then laugh."

"He isn't the only reason I'm considering the job and I don't want to sound like a foolish girl."

"You won't. Ron Mitchell is a happily married man. I happen to know he left a larger station he really loved in Texas to move to Tennessee to work because his wife grew up here. She wanted to come home to live near her family. His family lives close by in Kentucky, too." He paused. "Family is an important part of life, Samantha. Ron won't fault you for putting family first."

"I suppose I assumed everyone would think me an idiot to consider changing jobs, moving from a big position to such a smaller one."

"As long as you think it's an idiotic thing to consider, that viewpoint will come across in any interview you have."

"You're right." She shook her head. "And thanks for being candid with me. I needed that. I don't know what's wrong with me lately. I've always been so focused, so sure in my goals, so confident."

He chuckled. "Love will mess you up. If you didn't know that, it's a new learning experience for you."

She looked out the window again, thinking about his words.

"Look, Samantha. I've told Ron about you, that you're here recuperating and might be open to a change because of family. He's excited about the opportunity of talking with you. I told him I was meeting with you this morning. He said to tell you his calendar was flexible today and that if you could come over after leaving here, he'd show you around the station, introduce you to people, and take you to lunch to talk. You know it would be a plum to the station to pick up an anchor with your celebrity status."

She twisted a ring on her finger. "I would like to talk with him but I don't want Weather First to know I'm considering another job."

"He knows that. This meeting is simply a chance to talk, an informal interview." He glanced toward her briefcase on the floor. "I assume you brought a resume and other materials he'll want to see? I doubt he'll need to see film of your work."

Samantha looked across at Matt then. "Do you think I'm making a huge mistake to consider this change? Be honest with me."

"A storm chaser's life is exciting but hard. It's physically demanding and, as you well know, it's dangerous. As you also well know, it offers little time for family and any kind of quality outside life. We both saw the divorces rack up with those prominently involved with storm team coverage." He paused. "Eventually in time, the demands of the job will pull you out of the field. You'll need to make a change at some future point—you know that—or if a more serious injury occurs. I don't want to be negative but it can happen. I talk about these things in my classes."

She waited.

"Listen, Samantha. I can't make your decision or know what's right for you. Only you can do that." He flexed his fingers. "Talk to Ron Mitchell. Give the opportunity thought if it seems a good fit and you like the network staff. Changes are not always easy to make but can turn out to be positive. I'm confident you will give thought to it all and know what you should do. If you are a person of faith, you might pray about it, too."

His last comment surprised her. "Thanks, Matt."

"You're welcome." He glanced at his watch. "Do you want me to call Ron to let him know you're on your way over?"

She nodded. "Yes, I'd appreciate that." Samantha glanced over the neat black slacks she wore with a short jacket, wondering if she should have dressed more formally.

"You look good, Samantha," Matt offered, catching her glance.

"More beautiful in person than on television. Ron will be wowed."

She laughed.

"There!" He laughed back with her. "That's the Samantha King I know so well. Put that joy and confidence on and go check out this opportunity. The hiring process for any major position at a network station takes time. You won't need to make an immediate decision. Ron won't offer anyone the position until he's completed a full search and interviewed a lot of candidates. You should remember that. Quit being so uptight. Think of this as an adventure. Enjoy looking around the station, meeting some great people who do the same kind of work you do. Have fun."

"I'll do that," she said, feeling more comfortable.

It didn't take long to drive over to the television broadcasting station in Knoxville. It had taken her thirty minutes to drive to the university from Dandridge; it wouldn't take her any longer to drive directly to the station.

Are you crazy doing this? she asked herself as she made her way from the parking lot to the building. Half the forecasters you know would give anything for the job you have with Weather First.

Stopping at the front door, she paused and closed her eyes. "God, if this is a really bad idea, please let me know somehow," she muttered. Then taking a deep breath, she put on a bright smile and her best television personality and opened the door to head into the station.

Ron Mitchell came out to greet Samantha with a firm handshake and soon made her feel totally comfortable, even making her laugh with stories from his early broadcast days. An attractive man in his fifties, he exuded an easy confidence, talking casually as they settled into comfortable seats in his office. She liked how he worked to make her feel relaxed before pursuing a more serious interview.

"You must know I'm thrilled to consider the idea you might join our network staff, Samantha," he said after a time. "You hold name recognition that would draw viewers. But I have to ask why you're looking at an anchor position at WKSE. You could easily reach higher, certainly command a bigger salary at a network in a larger city if you wanted to return to local forecasting. In fact, I'm sure Weather First would move you to a forecasting position if you wanted a change." He glanced down at her resume. "You spent five years doing morning broadcasts for them before starting to work on the storm team."

She remembered Matt's counsel. Smiling at Ron, she said, "I've met a man." She laughed, finally seeing the humor in it herself. "He's a vet with an established practice, part owner in an old family resort. I came home to Dandridge to recuperate, but got blindsided with this new situation."

Ron laughed, too. "If this works out remind me to shake the man's hand one day. And thank you for being honest in your answer. Is there anything else I should know? I know you were injured. Any continuing health problems?"

"None, and I can provide medical reports to confirm that. In fact, based on the most recent report Weather First decided to schedule me to come back sooner, in late August."

"You look fit and well. Will they put you directly back in the field?"

She nodded.

"Here at WKSE you'd have opportunities to cover severe weather situations and get out in the field—and we'd certainly draw on your expertise for that—but most of your work would be indoors. Would that be a problem? You're used to a very active, outdoor life."

She smiled. "I've had over ten years in the field. Frankly, I wouldn't mind a little softer life about now. Additionally, I've found life has other thrills I'd like to explore more." She wiggled her eyebrows, making Ron laugh again.

"Is he pushing this change, your vet?" Ron asked.

"No, not in the way you suggest. He has no idea I am checking out local possibilities." She paused. "I'd like to keep it that way."

"Will he be on board with you continuing to work?"

"Yes, and I know it's illegal to ask, and inappropriate as well, but he has family, including custody of my sister's children. I won't be stepping out of work to start a family. Eight is quite enough."

"Eight?" His eyebrows widened in surprise.

She laughed again. "Who would have thought a single, career-oriented storm chaser would become involved in a situation like this? But as Matt Glenn said earlier, life happens. Be assured the vet has a housekeeper and adequate help. He's managed on his own for years and won't have a problem managing the idea of me working. "

"You're being very candid."

"I thought it best. I love my work. I'm good at it, but I've also realized I want family in my life. When Matt called to tell me this anchor position was open, I decided I wanted to talk with you."

Ron tapped a pencil on the table. "As I see it, a fortuitous set of circumstances have come together that might allow WKSE to get an extraordinary anchor to fill our station's slot. If you'd been less candid with me, Samantha, I'd have questioned your reasons for a change, wondered if you'd stay with us if we hired you."

"I like to be direct," Samantha said. "It saves on confusion and misunderstandings."

"It does and I like honesty and good communications with my staff." He stood. "Let me go take you around to meet some of our people. Most of the morning show anchors are still here, the evening anchors beginning to come in. I think the main people you'd like to meet are here and I can show you around the studio. You know this position is for our main six o'clock evening broadcast, the most viewed in our day. You did the morning forecast at Weather First before. Is that slot your preference?"

"No, I loved the work, but I won't miss getting up at four in the morning to come in and prepare for it."

He laughed again. "I hear you."

Samantha glanced into the broadcast room with the familiar green screen as Ron walked her around the studio. He popped into different offices and work areas to introduce her to staff. The station's morning weather forecaster, Rita Dow, was older than Samantha, dark-haired, with an easy warmth, and Samantha liked the main evening newscaster Sam Bowling and the sports anchor Hank Mason. The names of some of the other staff began to blend together after a time, but the atmosphere was professional, efficient, and vibrant, as stations often are—with breaking news ongoing all the time. She found the environment relaxed, too, without undue strain or tension.

Ron did take her out to lunch later, where they shared stories from the field, talked more about the job and about their personal lives. She knew she would have no problem working with Ron Mitchell. Samantha also liked his associate producer Colin Varner, who Ron said was a computer whiz that worked closely with their digital platforms, social media manager, and other technical staff.

"What do you think?" Ron asked her as they shook hands before she left.

"It's a great station, well-run with good camaraderie from all I can see."

"You made good impressions with everyone," he told her. "And with me. You have all the attributes we look for—a passion for the field, intelligence, exceptional on-camera skills, a good fun-loving personality, a strong education, and experience beyond our job requirements. I want to put you into our pool of prospective applicants. Will you let me know if you have a change of mind about your application?"

"I will. I felt more comfortable here than I expected to." She wrinkled her nose and then grinned at him. "As a girl, my big dream was to be a forecaster for this station. One of your meteorologists visited our school; I watched her every evening after that, envying her job. Dreaming big dreams."

He smiled with warmth. "I like to hear stories like that. We still send our news and weather anchors out into the schools to talk to students. I'm glad to know those visits impact young people so positively." He held the door open for her. "I look forward to seeing you again, Samantha King."

After she left the station, she headed back to pick up the freeway to start south toward Atlanta. In truth, she did need to check on her apartment and she had a doctor's appointment in the morning with the surgeon who handled the bulk of her injuries. It would close out her record, give her that final clean bill of health for work.

Later, settled into her apartment and watching Weather First storm coverage of a hurricane developing at sea and heading toward the Florida coast, Samantha wondered if she'd miss the excitement and rush of covering major storms and severe weather. Many moments were thrilling and exciting but in other ways the job proved intense and hard month after month with dead times and set up times for new coverage between. Lonely times on the road, too, always traveling, staying in motels.

She looked around her apartment remembering how few people had come to see her after her injury, here or in the hospital. Her main friends were work colleagues, still on the job covering the hurricane or off to the next storm. Somehow now, she found she wanted more. Yet at the same time she felt conflicted, worrying she would miss the rush of facing down storms and inclement weather. The excitement, the action, the publicity. She wished she knew exactly what she should do.

CHAPTER 16

Ford missed seeing Samantha popping into the kitchen on the morning she left for her trip to Atlanta. Funny how quickly he'd gotten used to her smiles, her laugh, her chatter with the kids, her warmth—the way her presence filled up a room. The kids were quieter, too, that morning.

Later, his mother helped to supervise making chicken burritos for dinner with rice, black beans, and a tomato and avocado salad before she and Burl went home. A nice meal and a favorite of the children's. She'd also brought an applesauce nut cake for dessert that she'd baked the day before with her housekeeper's help. Yet Ford still noticed the children too quiet during dinner, their conversation stilted.

"I miss Aunt Samantha," Tamela said, breaking a lengthy silence as they finished dessert.

"She would have gone home by now anyway to eat with Dixie," Ford replied practically.

"That's not what she meant," Natalie put in.

Ford saw her exchange looks with the other children and then at Clay.

"Dad," Clay said then. "We'd like to talk to you." He sat up straighter, trying to look very adult for a ten-year old.

"Okay." Ford waited.

"We all really like Samantha," he said. "She's smart and fun to be with and really pretty, too, don't you think?"

"I agree," Ford replied, wary as to where this was leading.

Gareth leaned forward then. "We're wondering if maybe you could marry her so she would stay," he blurted out.

"Marriage is a very serious thing between two people," Ford answered, hoping to bring an end to this conversation. "A man doesn't propose marriage to a woman because he wants a full time sitter for his kids."

"But she would be our mommy, and we don't have one," Rebecca put in. "We'd like Samantha to be our mommy."

"Don't you like her at all, you know, sort of like a woman?" Clay asked, blushing a little.

Ford tried to hide a smirk. "That's pretty personal, Clay."

Natalie leaned forward to get his attention then. "I heard Grandma and Granddaddy talking today. Grandma said everybody could tell you were foolish about Samantha and no one understood why you hadn't realized it. Granddaddy said he thought you did know, that he'd seen you watching her like a lovesick cow."

Ford took a breath. "Did your grandparents know you were listening in on this conversation, Natalie?"

"No." She looked away from him. "But I didn't listen on purpose. I came in from outside to get a drink of water in the kitchen and I could hear them."

He looked around. "And did you tell the other children about this? You know it's gossiping to repeat things like that, especially things you weren't intended to hear."

"Everybody knows you like her," Gareth blurted out.

"Is that so?" He looked around the table, noticing for the first time that all the Bradley children were being unusually quiet during this quizzing.

His eyes passed over them. "You Bradley children are being rather quiet about this subject." He stopped to look at Wesley, eyes wide above his freckled eight-year old face. "Why do you think that is, Wesley?"

Ford watched his eyes race to Clay and Natalie's, wondering whether to answer.

Andrew rescued him. "When we were at the lake on the Fourth

of July, Ben Larsen told Vance Howard he hoped you'd wake up and go after Samantha before she left. So it isn't just us who think you like her. Don't be mad at Natalie."

"I assume Ben and Vance didn't include you in this conversation?"

Andrew rubbed his arm. "Me and Clay were playing in the water near the dock after riding on the tube. I don't think they saw us but we weren't eavesdropping or being sneaky to hear them."

"Sounds like a lot of people are trying to plan my life. Don't you think any decisions about my life should be my own?"

"Maybe you don't realize how you really feel," Natalie put in. "I read books like that all the time where it's obvious to everyone but not to the man in love."

"So now you've decided I'm in love."

She blushed.

"Are you in love?" Madison asked. "If you are you should do something about it. Aunt Samantha is going back to Atlanta soon. Maybe she doesn't even know you like her."

Natalie sent him one of her serious twelve-year old looks. "We simply wanted to let you know that if you were worried about how we'd feel about Samantha being our new mother, that we would all love it."

"I asked Dwayne if he thought you really liked Samantha and if you might ask her to get married," Clay said, getting in to the conversation again. "Dwayne said you always wanted to put us first in any decision you made. So, like Natalie said, we decided to talk to you tonight to tell you."

Great, Ford thought. Obviously everyone was discussing his love life. Or lack of it.

"Me and Tamela really want a mommy," Rebecca said, sniffing as if she might cry. "We don't hardly remember our mommies, even with pictures and stories. We want a real mommy."

"If you really like her, Dad, you should go for it," Gareth added, grinning. Ford felt sure, knowing Gareth, that he would certainly have gone for it himself, even at eight, which was a worrisome thought to consider.

"Look," Ford said after a few minutes, looking around the table at his children. "I appreciate your concern about me and my happiness. I also am glad to know how fond all of you are of Samantha. However, even if I had strong feelings about Samantha as a man, she is a very smart, independent, career woman. She loves her job at Weather First and has worked hard to climb to that position and status. You've all seen her on television. Can't you imagine she would miss her work? Do you think she'd be happy to walk away from it even if she loved all of us? It would be a hard thing for her to do."

"Mr. Glenn at the university said she could teach some courses there," Natalie said. "Samantha could find another job."

"She could keep her job at Weather First and just come home to us when she could, too," Wesley suggested.

Madison frowned at him. "Which would be practically never, Wesley. You know how often we've seen her over the years. Hardly ever."

"That might not be very nice for Dad, either," Clay added, blushing again. "Married people ..."

"I think we get the idea, Clay," Ford interrupted. "Couples generally need to live together for marriages to work well."

Natalie sighed. "Isn't there any answer, Dad? We don't want Samantha to leave. Do you?"

"We'll all miss her. And I admit I'll miss her. But we'll all be okay." He smiled around at them. "Why don't we clean up here and then go bike together around the lake? The days are long now; it won't be dark until nearly nine. And it's nice out."

With that thought in mind, they started cleaning up from dinner.

Later that evening when the children were settled down for bed, Ford couldn't get their earlier conversation off his mind. Evidently everyone was speculating about his love life but few knew his own personal agony.

On impulse, he pulled his cell phone out of his back pocket and dialed Ben Larsen. "Hey, Ben," he said when his friend answered. "What are you doing?"

"Watching an old movie *Murder on the Orient Express* with Vickie. How about you?"

He took a deep breath. "I could use a friend to talk to if you think Vickie could do without you for a little while."

"Sure, I've seen this movie before. I already know how it's going to turn out. I'll be over in about ten minutes."

"I'll be out on the terrace," Ford said, hanging up.

Ben Larsen walked up the back walk to the terrace porch a short time later. "I brought a six-pack of Saint Arnold's root beer. You know it's the best. Cold and chilled from the back of the refrigerator by the dock."

Ford smiled. He and Ben had always liked root beer ever since they were both kids.

Ben sat down in the chair by his, popped the top of two bottles of root beer and handed Ford one. "Beverages made of sassafras root were made by Indians for medicinal reasons. Did you know that? The point is that sassafras root is good for you. Dad said our grandpa used to make hot sassafras tea in a big pot over the fire. He said it boosted immune health and improved circulation. Fine stuff, I hear."

"Thanks for coming over, Ben." Ford studied his old friend, nearly bald now, a little heavier than in their youth but with the same round face, easy smile and manner.

"What's up?" Ben asked after a few minutes.

"The kids had a talk with me at dinner about Samantha. They don't want her to go back to Atlanta, have gotten fond of her. Decided she'd make a good new mother. The boys told me I ought to put some moves on her."

Ben laughed.

"They repeated a lot of conversations they'd been overhearing from family and friends. Seems like it's no secret an attraction has whipped up between Samantha and me. The kids seem to think I'm a little clueless in the situation, slow. Missing my opportunities."

Ben didn't reply, looking out over the lake.

Eventually he said, "Anyone who knew you would need to be

blind not to notice there's something going on. You acted on it yet?"

"Yeah. Some. And I hate myself every time for going there. Any time with Samantha is like getting a hit on a drug. You know you shouldn't do it. Know it's addictive, that you should stay away."

"You don't think it can go anywhere?"

"I've made enough comments in heated moments to let her know how I feel, that I'm holding back because I want more. With the kids in my life, I'm not looking for a fling. And especially with the Bradley kids' aunt."

Ben thought over his words for a few minutes. "You don't think if you went after her that you could change her mind about leaving? Especially if there's something there."

"You know her life, Ben, who she is, what she does. Beautiful, successful, in the spotlight, traveling around the country." Ford reached down to pet Jefferson, the family's black lab that had ambled up on the terrace to lay his head on Ford's feet. "Why would she want to link up with a small town vet when she has all that?"

"Don't sell yourself short. Just because she's known success, had some acclaim, doesn't mean she might not be open for a change in life. We can all see she loves the kids. She's good with them." He hesitated. "We've seen times when you two look at each other, too. There's really something there. It about fries the air sometimes. Must drive you crazy."

Ford leaned his head back to close his eyes. "As I said, I've put some words out there to let her know how I felt, what I wanted. Then sort of left it in her court. From all I've seen she's continuing to make plans to head back to Atlanta. She went down to spend the night for some meetings scheduled tomorrow."

"Dang." Ben reached for two more bottles of root beer. "I think this may call for snacks, too. Got anything in the house?"

Ford grinned. "Big can of peanuts, bag of pretzels."

"I'll go get them. No need to disturb Jefferson and you've got the cat on your lap now, too."

The big yellow tabby, Marmalade, had jumped up on his lap. Marmalade wasn't much of a lap cat except with Ford who'd saved his life.

"Look in the cabinet over the refrigerator."

Ben came back in a few minutes with nuts and pretzels, opening both of them to sit on the table between them.

They munched in silence for a few minutes. "Well, I figure you gotta give it a shot before she leaves, Ford. You'll hate yourself otherwise, wondering if you'd tried once more, talked to her again, to see if you could change her mind. Women wait for men to make the first move most of the time. Leaves us in a heck of a spot where we always have to be the one to make a fool of ourselves not knowing how the wind blows."

Ford laughed over his words. "I've already walked that road once or twice. But I suppose you're right. Even Gareth said I should go for it and he's only eight."

Ben grinned at that. "We're gonna need to keep an eye on that one later on. He's going to be a force to reckon with."

"He already is."

"When does Samantha leave?"

"School starts next week with August almost here. Juanita will be coming back to work part-time. Samantha will be around less, but I know she'll still stop over for time with the kids before she leaves. She goes back mid month sometime."

Ben ate a handful of peanuts, thinking. "Well, let's organize a little back to school party next Friday night—maybe at the pavilion down by the swim beach. The kids can be in on that. We'll invite the Howards, all bring food and share a pot luck dinner. I've been wishing for an excuse to get that old jukebox out. It'll be fun."

Ford reached down to pet Gracie, the family's other lab that had come up to join them. "All the kids would like that, assuming the weather is good."

"We can change the day to Saturday if we need to if bad weather kicks in." Ben finished off his root beer. "I'll tell Vickie we'll keep a closer watch on your kids than normal so maybe you can get

Samantha off by herself. Maybe you can plan a date with her, too. Vickie and I will keep the kids. Put your best romance shoes on and see what you can do."

"I'm really out of practice in that area." Ford shook his head.

"It will come back, boy." Ben laughed. "From what I've seen around you and Samantha King, there doesn't seem to be anything wrong with your libido."

"What if none of this works? What if she leaves and goes on back to work?" Ford gave Ben an agonized look.

Ben stood up and put a hand on Ford's shoulder. "You'll get by and you'll move on. You're a strong, good man. If this isn't the woman God has for you, He'll bring another in the right time. You know God's seen you through loss before. And you have good friends. Loving family."

"I do. Thanks for coming over," Ford said.

"Any time. That's what friends are for." As he started off the terrace, Ben turned. "You might want to start offering up some prayers for a little extra help from upstairs, too."

"I'll do that," Ford said, finding another spot for Oscar beside Marmalade on his lap after Ben left. Funny how the animals always seemed to know when he needed a little comfort and friendship. The small dogs were inside with the children, but the labs and all four cats had settled either on his lap or near him on the terrace. And Willodeen had bathed his hand with her rough tongue.

CHAPTER 17

The summer was waning and knowing the children would start school next week, Samantha decided to take them on a final field trip. She'd be heading to Atlanta soon as Weather First expected her back to work mid month. Her producer and several others on her team had already sent email notes saying they looked forward to seeing her again. In addition, her meetings at the main office while in Atlanta had been only positive.

A follow-up email from Ron Mitchell at WKSE expressed his pleasure in talking with her but confirmed they wouldn't be making a hiring decision until late August or early September. She'd be back in the field by then, and she wondered if she would even want to consider the position by that time. She'd promised the kids and Aunt Dixie return visits to Dandridge at Thanksgiving and at the Christmas holidays, assuming the weather cooperated and she wasn't called in.

In the sunny kitchen this morning at the Dandridge Inn, Samantha sat finishing breakfast and talking with Dixie before she headed over to the resort to stay with the children. Dixie always got up early at the inn. Many of her overnight guests left early, too, traveling on to other destinations, like the two couples that stayed with them last night, already on their way to Ohio.

"This will be my last field trip with the kids before they start school," Samantha said, finishing the last of her omelet.

"I hate how children's summer vacations have grown shorter and shorter." Dixie sat back in her chair. "It only gives children two months of summer instead of three. Even I have read that pushing children into more school days has not improved learning or educational scores. Besides, children need the creative, informal time that summer provides. Doesn't everyone know that play is children's work, like Maria Montessori always maintained, and that children need it for healthy development?"

Samantha smiled, remembering Aunt Dixie had sent her and Andrea to a Montessori preschool in the area when small. Her aunt had picked up an understanding of Montessori's educational concepts then.

"Shorter summer vacation time has never seemed right to me either," Samantha agreed. "It's hurt summer camps, too, pushing them to cram their sessions into a shorter block of time and making summer vacation sites more crowded." She got up to pour another cup of coffee. "Ford took the children camping in early June, when I went along, and he plans another weekend trip before August ends when campgrounds are less crowded. But he avoids July trips because of the summer crowds."

Dixie reached for one of the fresh blueberry muffins she'd made and began to spread butter and blueberry jam on it. "Are you still leaving at mid month to go back to work?"

"Yes. I'm expected then." Samantha avoided looking at Dixie, busying herself with stirring milk and sweetener into her coffee.

Dixie grew quiet for a few minutes.

Changing the subject, Samantha smiled at her as she came back to sit down at the table. "Are you sure it's okay with you to host the children for lunch today as part of their field trip with me?'

Her aunt's face brightened. "Oh, I'm looking forward to it. I've planned a lunch I think they will like—a fun Chopstick Tuna casserole, Pizza Biscuits with pepperoni and cheese, and a marvelous Frozen Sundae Pie with wafer cookies on the bottom and vanilla ice cream on top. It's already in the freezer. Right before serving I drizzle fudge topping over it, add sliced bananas, drizzle it with caramel topping, and then sprinkle peanuts all over."

Samantha laughed. "I've gained three pounds hearing about it!"

"Do you think you'll still get here for lunch about one o'clock?"

"I do. We're taking a history walking tour around Dandridge this morning. In some of our talks earlier this summer I was surprised at how little the kids knew of their own town's history. We've worked on reading and learning about that since and now I want them to see some of the places they've read about in person." She looked across at Aunt Dixie. "Lucy has promised free colas for a mid morning break at her store and then later, when we finish our tour, we'll come here for lunch. Afterward, we're driving over to the A. J. Bush and Company in Chestnut Hill to learn how they make their famous baked beans and other products. I want the children to take the tour at Bush's, see the free film and the displays. I haven't been there in years but I remember it's fun and interesting."

"It sounds like you've planned a fine day." Dixie finished off her muffin and then gave Samantha a thoughtful look. "Are the children ready for school? Do they have all the clothes they need?"

"Yes, I think they do," she answered. "So many people in their church, in the community, friends and clients of Ford's, bring the kids bags of hand-me-downs. Evidently, they've been doing this for years, ever since Ford and Laura took in Andrea's children. They bring nice clothes, too—pants, jeans, shirts, coats, jackets, dresses for the girls, even shoes. I've helped them sort through the bags."

"Well, that's nice." Dixie got up to carry their dishes over to rinse them and put them in the dishwasher.

"I've learned, too, that Coralee and Burl make runs to the thrift stores in the area looking for things the children can use. I was amazed at some of the great clothes and shoes they find. Coralee enjoys getting out and doing that. So does Burl. They find items to use for the cabins at the resort, too." She grinned. "One day the children and I took a thrift store scavenger hunt to look for things they needed. We had a good time."

"Well everyone in Dandridge admires Ford for taking in Andrea and Adam's children. You may not know it but he gives a lot of free veterinary help at different times of the year to help charities. They, in turn, help him."

"You help, too," she said as Dixie came to sit back down with her. "I didn't know before that you buy the children's school supplies every year—not only for Andrea's children but for Ford's, too."

Her aunt straightened a row of colorful bracelets on her wrist. "It's the least I can do, and besides it's not hard. The children get a list of their school needs when they begin school and Ford takes them on a run to pick up what they need; then I have them over to dinner so they can show me everything." She smiled. "It reminds me of how excited you and Andrea used to get buying new crayons, notebooks, and supplies in your school days."

Aunt Dixie leveled a studied gaze in her direction. "I also know you send money every year to help Ford with the children."

She looked away. "It's not much, considering all he's done."

"It helps. Ford is comfortable financially but raising eight children is expensive." She paused. "You might be interested to know your father also sends money."

"Dad?" Samantha knew she sounded shocked.

"Yes. He has sent monthly checks ever since Andrea and Adam were killed. He paid for their funeral service and the gravestones in our family cemetery section at the church, too." She frowned at Samantha. "Although your father gave little of his personal time to his family, he's always given financial support. He isn't all bad."

"I've begun to see that a little."

"I hope so. Sometimes we tend to focus only on the negatives with people." She gave Samantha a thoughtful look. "Speaking of which, how are you getting along with Juanita?"

Samantha shook her head in frustration. "Not much better. She came by the other day and was as huffy and unpleasant as any other time. Honestly, I don't know what else to do to bring her around. I sent flowers when her mother was injured. Several times the children and I baked extra cookies, and I sent some of the children to deliver them. One day Maria called to ask me if I would watch her two children Ana Sophia and Dylan while Juanita took her mother to the doctor. I did. They acted leery around me at first, as if they'd heard I was an evil witch or something, but then they came around, and we all had a good time. They're sweet kids; Ana Sophia is seven, Dylan five."

"Did Juanita thank you for any of these gestures?"

"No, and she made it clear when she came by the other day that she would be glad to see the last of me."

Dixie looked shocked. "Surely she didn't say that to you?"

"No, but she told me Ford asked her to be congenial when I came by to see the children for visits. She also, not very subtly, suggested it would be best if I visited after supper, with the days so long. Both of us well know she has left by then."

Dixie shook her head. "Well, I certainly don't know the answer to that problem. The woman has always been relatively cordial to me. Somewhat businesslike, as is her way, but cordial."

Samantha laughed. "I'd settle for cordial." She glanced at her watch. "I'd better head over to Ford's. It's time for him to go to the clinic."

When she arrived at the house though, it was to find Ford already gone.

"Daddy Ford got called in with an emergency. He only left a few minutes ago," Madison told her. "He said he knew you were on your way. I'll text him that you're here. He wants me to text when we leave for our field trip, too."

Their tour around Dandridge proved to be a lot of fun. The fact that the children had already read about the history of downtown spots and famous people helped. Samantha didn't need to give history lessons as they toured.

They stopped first at the Dandridge Visitor Center on East Main to pick up several walking tour brochures, and the children enjoyed following the marked route. Not far from the visitor center, Andrew got excited spotting the dike that the town built to save Dandridge from being flooded when Douglas Dam was built.

"This whole town might be gone without this dike and all covered up with water," he said, as they climbed the hillside to a sidewalk along the lake.

"Can they really flood whole towns and all the people?" asked

Tamela, shocked.

"They get the people out first, whether they want to go or not, and then they let the water through and it floods everything, making a lake."

"What if the people don't want to go?" Tamela asked.

"They make them go anyway," Clay answered. "Lots of people around East Tennessee lost their homes and farms, and some cities were covered up, when TVA built dams and lakes. Remember Aunt Samantha told us about it."

"How long is our dike?" Wesley asked, as they climbed back down the hill to the street again.

"About a thousand feet long," Andrew answered.

Questions and observations like this were common throughout their tour around the city. It was interesting to Samantha the things the children spotted that even adults might overlook, like the stepping blocks in front of the old Shepard Inn that helped the ladies of the past, with their big skirts, to get into their carriages more easily. They remembered, too, when she'd forgotten, that the first grave in the old Harris Family Cemetery, dating back to 1858, was a thirteen-year old girl and they went hunting for her gravesite.

They all wanted to visit the old Hynds house, now a store called the Maxwell House, where Bert Vincent once lived.

"Grandaddy Burl has some of his books," Natalie said. "He reads the stories in them sometimes to us. Bert Vincent wrote for the newspapers and he wrote a lot of articles about the people and the history of this area that got put into books. They keep his books at the library, too."

The children leaned over the rail to see the old spring and creek by the house but their biggest fascination came in finding one of the owners of the store sitting on a bench in a back room coloring pictures in a coloring book.

"I didn't think grown up men colored pictures," Rebecca said to him with candor, making Samantha wince with embarrassment.

The older gentleman looked up with a smile. "Well, I find coloring very relaxing." He laid aside his coloring book to tell them stories about the Hynds-Maxwell house and its history and about their home nearby they'd restored.

The children left the store, still more interested in finding one of the owners coloring pictures than recalling the house's history.

Gareth wrinkled his nose. "Do other men color pictures like that?"

"Stores sell lots of adult coloring books now," Madison chided as they left. "Anybody can color if they want to, no matter what age."

Clay raised an eyebrow. "But he had a color book like one of Rebecca or Tamela's, not an adult book."

"Maybe he doesn't have an adult book," Madison said, not wanting to give up her logic. "I have one I haven't colored a single picture in yet. I think I'll bring it to him the next time we come downtown."

"That would be nice," Samantha added. "It would be a good way to say thank you for the things he told us about the house's past, too."

While exploring inside the historic store, called Tinsley Bible Drug, Gareth came running around a corner to find them, laughing. "Come see the funny sign Wesley and I found."

Curious, they all followed him around the corner to the cafe booths. Wesley and Gareth, still laughing, pointed to a sign above one of the booths that read: *Beware of Attack Waitress* with a hissy cat picture below it. The children giggled over it until one of the employees gave them a frown, causing Samantha to hustle them out to the street.

"We need to show that sign to Dad the next time we come to town," Gareth said, still laughing. "He'll think it's cool. He likes signs."

Samantha looked away for a minute, remembering the old sign *What Happens At the Lake Stays at the Lake* that caused her to impulsively kiss Ford the first time. She sighed, realizing all these lake memories would soon be simply that: only memories.

They walked on, pointing out historic houses, churches,

cemeteries, and other interesting sites along Dandridge's quaint downtown streets. They stopped at the courthouse and the old jail, which intrigued the boys. And they looked at art and antiques in the old Roper Mansion, probably making the owners nervous with so many children wandering around in the tightly packed rooms. Finishing with their tour, Samantha let the children go into the Dandridge Mercantile, once an old general store, to look at all the store's items for sale—local arts and crafts, handmade items, candles, books, and toys.

Across the street on another non-historic note, they loved going into the Appalachian Yarn Company, walking upstairs to see the looms and spinning wheels, and learning that the owner had a farm with alpacas that supplied the fiber for many of the items woven in the store.

"Can we come to your farm to see your alpacas?" Rebecca asked with wide eyes, snuggling a sweet woven sheep toy she'd found in a big basket.

"What does an alpaca look like?" Wesley asked.

The owner Brenda Hane and her sister Wanda showed the children pictures then, telling them about the animals, a little smaller than a llama.

"I read alpacas will spit at you," Clay said.

Samantha saw the children's eyes widen.

"It's rare they do that." Brenda laughed. "But they can hum sometimes. Did you know that? Alpacas are interesting animals."

Samantha finally dragged them out of the shop, still talking about alpacas and what they had learned. They climbed up the hill behind the yarn store then, turning by the library on Circle Drive to walk down the street to the Dandridge Inn where Samantha had left their van when they arrived.

After lunching with Aunt Dixie, they loaded into the van and drove across the bridge over Douglas Lake to travel the eight miles to the Bush Brothers Visitor Center. It was fun to step back in time to learn about the history of the old company, known nationwide, but located right in their own back yard. They enjoyed the free film, museum, and interactive displays. In one fun exhibit downstairs they all laughed watching white balls pass through a "secret recipe stage" that changed them to brown balls, the color of beans.

"That's cool," Gareth pronounced.

The kids especially liked walking into a huge replica of a can of beans to see pictures of Bush's history and they loved looking around in the old-fashioned general store.

"Where's Duke?" Wesley asked looking around for the big red setter, the dog who knew the secret recipe for Bush's beans, made famous in the Bush Brothers' commercials.

"Well, Duke's not here today," their guide told them, leading to a little grumbling by the smaller children.

"There are Duke stuffed toys, though." Natalie pointed to a basket full of them, but this hardly satisfied the children.

"Duke is a commercial dog," Samantha tried to explain. "He lives with his trainers but he became famous as Bush's mascot dog. I know everyone here at Bush Brothers knows and loves Duke even if he doesn't live here."

"He doesn't live here?" Rebecca asked with surprise.

"No, and the real Duke is dead," Clay announced, making all their eyes pop wide. "Dad told me. He had cancer and died about a year or so ago. But he used to come up here from his home to do appearances. Dad saw him once."

Tamela turned to the guide with shocked eyes. "Is Duke really dead?"

"We have another dog acting as Duke now," their guide explained, trying to soften the blow. Then he smiled. "It's like the University of Tennessee's Smokey dog. There have been several Smokey dogs over the years."

Rebecca looked shocked. "Is Smokey dead, too?"

Clay frowned at her. "Different dog actors play Duke and Smokey. They even play Lassie like in the old movies and TV shows we watch. Dogs can't live forever. They only live about ten to thirteen years average."

Tamela stuck her lip out. "Well, it's still sad that Duke is dead."

She looked at their guide. "Is your new Duke dog here?"

"No, but I can show you some pictures," he said, hoping to cheer her up.

Fortunately, the children were soon distracted by the scales that would give their weight in beans, which made them all laugh as they tried it out.

After a full day, the kids were tired as Samantha drove them back home.

As a treat for supper, she'd called ahead and ordered four large pizzas of different types to take home for their supper from a local pizza restaurant. She knew there were salad makings at the house and the other half of a chocolate sheet cake she'd made with the boys last night. It would be enough after a long day.

She saw Ford's car already at the house as she pulled up. Madison had texted him ahead they were bringing home pizza.

He walked out to meet them as the van pulled up, reaching in to get the pizza boxes. "Stay and eat with us," he said to Samantha, giving her one of those looks that made it hard to say no.

"Okay, I'll call Dixie," she replied, climbing out of the van.

At Ford's suggestion, they decided to take their pizza outside to eat it on a couple of picnic tables pushed together on the back patio. The patio sprawled behind the wide glass doors and windows behind the lodge, offering a constant view of the lake in all seasons.

Samantha, with Gareth, Wesley, and Ford's help, quickly whipped up a big bowl of salad, and found plastic glasses, paper plates, and throw away forks to use.

"Let's keep it simple tonight," Ford said, loading the salad and a couple of bottles of salad dressing on a tray and sending the boys out with the rest.

Over dinner the children babbled away, talking and laughing and telling their father about their day, but Samantha kept noticing Ford watched her quietly while they talked. She caught his eyes on her every once in a while with the kind of lingering look that made her skin tingle.

After dinner, the kids played outdoors, the younger ones swinging in the big swing sets on the hillside and playing on the slide and seesaw. Samantha and Ford could see them from the patio, where they'd moved to sit in a couple of more comfortable outdoor Adirondack chairs.

The older girls were talking down in the gazebo and Andrew and Clay were fishing out on the walk-bridge that crossed the narrow neck of the lake. Across the bridge were the resort's pavilion, cabins, campground, and the loop road that led to the event center, chapel and a pavilion used for events.

"Want to take a walk by the lake?" Ford asked. "We can walk along the path to the swim beach, keeping the children in sight."

"Sure," she said, tired from the day but not wanting to miss this chance to share quiet time alone with him. It didn't happen often.

As they strolled along, looking out over the lake as twilight began to fall, she found his eyes seeking hers out often, felt him lean against her a time or two, brush his hand over hers, or find a way to touch her. He couldn't hold her hand with the children in sight, but he was certainly finding ways to connect with her, to let her know where his thoughts were traveling.

Gosh, he was charming and irresistible when he acted like this, she thought. What was he doing? Why was he acting like this?

He smiled at her as if sensing her thoughts.

She smiled back, feeling that rush building in the air now.

"This is nice, isn't it?" he said in a soft and sultry voice she'd heard only a time or two when he'd broken down and kissed her.

Mercy, she wished he would do that now, wished they were off alone somewhere and not here in plain sight of the children. Samantha wet her lips at the thought of it and saw his eyes darken.

"Dad!" A voice called out, interrupting her thoughts. "Dad, something's wrong with Gracie."

They turned toward the sound to see Clay waving frantically from the bridge. Focused now, they could hear Gracie barking. An agitated, upset bark. Even Samantha could tell that.

Ford started back toward the bridge now, walking rapidly,

Samantha keeping pace with him.

Clay hollered again. "Gracie keeps barking and running back across the bridge to the bank on the other side and then back to me again."

"I think she wants us to follow her," Andrew called out as they drew closer to the scene. "She never acts like this."

"Where's Jefferson?" Ford asked as they reached the bridge.

"I don't know," Andrew said, looking around for the other dog. "It's only Gracie."

Samantha watched the big white lab chase back across the bridge toward the other side, barking frantically.

"Gracie! Come!" Ford called.

The dog heard him and whined, knowing the command, but she didn't come, looking up the hillside and barking again.

"Something is definitely wrong," Ford said. He turned to Samantha. "The boys and I are going to follow her. Will you stay here with the girls and the younger children until I get back?"

"Of course." Samantha heard Gracie whine and bark again, running toward Ford again but then dashing away in the other direction.

"What in the world is wrong with Gracie?" Madison asked, as she and Natalie walked over from the gazebo, hearing the dog barking.

"We don't know, but she's upset about something," Samantha answered. "Your dad and the boys are going to follow her."

"Labs are retrievers," Natalie noted, watching the dog. "Sometimes they get excited about game. Maybe she saw something."

"You could be right," Samantha said, watching Ford, Gracie, and the boys disappear from sight past the pavilion across the lake.

She glanced toward the playground then. "It's getting dark. Let's go find the younger kids and head to the house. Ford asked me to stay until they get back. Rebecca and Tamela can get their baths started."

Madison glanced back toward the bridge. "I hope everything's all right."

"Me, too," Samantha said.

CHAPTER 18

$\mathbf{F}$ord hated his moment with Samantha had been interrupted, but he had no doubt something was wrong with Gracie. As he, Clay, and Andrew followed the white lab up the hill on the other side of the lake, Clay asked, "Why do you think Gracie is acting like this, Dad?"

"I don't know. We've trained Gracie and Jefferson not to chase the geese and ducks that stop by the lake migrating, but they might have run across some other kind of bird, like a grouse, or even a rabbit and gotten whipped up. They could have chased something into a nest or a hole or up a tree, too. Jefferson may still be there."

Gracie slowed to turn and whine, to see if they followed, and then ran on, starting down the road in front of the cabins.

"She's really acting weird," Andrew added as they ran along to keep the dog in sight.

Gracie raced up Cove Loop road past the cabins, heading toward the end of the road where the event lodge, chapel and a big outdoor pavilion stood on the backside of the lake.

Huffing from their run now, Clay said, "I hope she doesn't head up Highpoint Trail into the woods. It will be hard to keep up with her there."

However, Gracie passed the wooden entrance sign to the trail, cutting right off the loop road and dashing down toward the long boat dock that jutted out in the lake.

"She's going toward the lake now," Clay called, as they scrambled down the pathway from the pavilion to follow the dog to the long wooden dock.

Barking and whining, they saw Gracie scramble down the bank by the dock toward the water.

Ford slowed to make his way down the steep bank and then put out a hand to hold the boys back. "Stop. It's Jefferson," he cautioned. "There by the bank. It looks like he's been hurt. Stay back and let me check."

He climbed down to kneel by the dog, lying on the bank with his back legs in the water. "What's the matter, boy?" he crooned to the dog, as Gracie circled around them whining.

"Is he okay, Dad?" Clay asked, edging down the bank to get closer.

Ford saw the blood then and, as his eyes moved over the dog, he saw a gunshot wound in the dog's shoulder.

"She's been shot." He looked up at the boys. Spotting a plastic water bottle someone had tossed into the edge of the lake, he added, "Clay, get that bottle someone threw in the lake. I see clean water still in it."

Clay scrambled into the weeds to get it and brought it back, kneeling down beside the dog. "Is he gonna die, Dad?"

"I don't know yet." He looked up to see Andrew standing, anxious, nearby. "Walk back up the path to the dock, Andrew, and keep anyone from coming down while I see to Jefferson."

Andrew nodded, glad for a task to do.

Ford took his cell phone out of his pocket and dialed Maria. Knowing he seldom called except in an emergency, she answered.

"Maria, our dog Jefferson has been shot." He glanced over to the dog. "Looks like he's been hit in the shoulder. I need meds and more to stabilize and move him. Can you go down to the clinic to get what I need and bring it to the dock at Sycamore Point at the back of the resort? Or call Dwayne to bring it? Gunshot wounds hurt as you've seen. I'll need to anesthetize the dog to examine the wound and move him."

"I'm leaving right now. I will be there soon," she said, ending their call.

Ford called out to Andrew to watch for her and then turned to Clay. "I'll need you to help me here, son."

"What can I do, Dad?"

Jefferson whined under Ford's hand as he stroked the dog's head to calm him. "Take your T-shirt off and donate it to a good cause. I'm going to tear a strip to make a muzzle, put that on Jefferson, and then let you hold his head down so I can rinse this gunshot wound and see how bad it is."

"Okay." Clay peeled out of his shirt.

Ford studied the dog. "If I can get the blood cleaned off, I can tell more about the wound, stanch it with some of your shirt, and wrap the shoulder until we can transport. I can do the rest at the clinic."

He tore off a strip of the shirt, preparing to muzzle the dog.

"Dad! Dad!" Andrew called in an alarmed voice, interrupting.

Ford looked up at him standing on the dock. "What is it?"

"There's a body in the lake on the other side of the dock," Andrew replied, his eyes wide. "No kidding. Some woman face down and sort of floating. Should I go check it?"

"No, I'll call for help." Ford groaned and pulled out his cell phone again. He called his dad this time. "Dad, I'm at the dock at Sycamore Point. Jefferson has been shot. I'm with the dog, seeing what I can do. Maria is on the way from the clinic with what I need but Andrew has just spotted a body in the lake. Can you and Maury get up here to help with this situation?"

"I'm heading out the door now," his dad answered but then hesitated. "Is this an injury or worse?"

Ford got up to walk closer to the dock so he could see under it to the body on the other side. He winced. "I'd say worse from what I can see."

"Then I think I should call the police, too."

"Yeah, I'd say so. I'll send Andrew up to the road to direct anybody coming to us and he can keep the curious away, as well."

"Andrew!" Ford called out, scrambling back over to Jefferson. "Go up to the road and direct Maria and your Granddad down to us. The police will be coming, too. When people hear the sirens, they may try to come over to see what's going on. Keep any curious people away if you can."

"I'll do that, Dad," Andrew said, starting up the hill at a run. Probably glad to get away from the sight of the body. It wasn't pretty.

"Is that person dead?" Clay asked with wide eyes.

"Looks that way. There's nothing we can do about that from what I can tell. I saw blood, so the police wouldn't thank me for tramping around a crime scene." He looked down at the dog. "But we can do something to help Jefferson."

Ford tied the muzzle on the dog, let Clay hold his head and talk to him while he poured water over the dog's shoulder. Jefferson whined and struggled, but Clay held him steady.

With the blood washed away, Ford could see the wound site in the shoulder. To his relief, as he carefully moved the dog to examine the situation further, he could see the exit wound, too.

"Looks like the bullet went through his shoulder muscle and out here." He pointed out the wounds to Clay.

"That means you won't have to dig the bullet out," Clay said, holding the dog while Ford wiped the wounds and put pads over them. Then he wrapped the long strip of the shirt he'd created, tying two pieces together, around Jefferson's body to hold the pads in place.

A time or two Jefferson tried to struggle to his feet, but Clay and Ford did their best to keep him still. Maria arrived a short time later, bringing the anesthetic Ford needed and a crate to transport the dog to the clinic.

Burl and the police arrived as they began to carry the crate up the bank, Jefferson now safely inside it. Gracie followed, whining and worried.

"He's going to be okay, girl," Clay told her, petting the big white dog. "Dad says it's not a bad wound."

Ford hoped his son's words right. Any gunshot wound for a dog was dangerous. And he wouldn't know the extent of the damage until he got the dog into the clinic.

Ford's dad met him at the top of the hill as he began to load the dog's crate into Maria's van, the sirens of police cars right behind.

Police Chief Ben Barclay pulled up with another officer. A second car with two other officers pulled in right behind.

"Is it another murder?" Ben asked, walking over to them.

"It looks that way," Ford answered. "I didn't wade in to examine the body and I didn't want to contaminate the bank around the area with more footprints."

An officer Ben had sent down the bank looked up to shake his head.

Ben scowled. "Looks like another murder and, dad blast it, we haven't even gotten a lead on the first."

"I hate this is happening at our resort," Burl said, looking down the bank to the dock with a frown.

"Believe me, I am, too," Ben said.

"My dog has been shot—probably trying to intervene," Ford put in. "Labs are protective about their people and property. From what I can tell the bullet passed straight through the shoulder, but you might want to search for a bullet around the bank where we found him." Ford gestured to point out the site where Jefferson had been.

"Did you and the boys hear anything? Did anybody see anything?" the chief asked.

"We didn't hear or see anything but Gracie did," Clay answered. "She came to get us barking and barking to bring us to Jefferson."

"Sure wish that dog could talk." Ben's eyes moved to study the dog. "But we'll do what we can do. A medical unit is on the way along with our homicide detective Jim Culver."

"Whoever needs me for questions will find me at the clinic. I need to get the dog there now." Ford climbed into the van with Maria.

"Can I go, too, Dad?" Clay asked.

Ford nodded. "Yes. I suppose if you want to be a vet you need to be learning about these things. Climb on in the back. You can talk to Jefferson on the ride. He'll feel every bump in the road until that anesthetic fully kicks in."

Seeing Andrew standing nearby, Ford called to him. "Andrew, thanks for your good observation and all your help. Clay's going to the clinic with me, but it would be a fine help if you'd walk Gracie back over to the house and tell Samantha what's going on. She and the other children will have heard the sirens. They'll be worrying."

"I'll do that," he said, proud again to be doing something important to help. He pulled off his T-shirt. "Here, Clay, you can have my shirt. I'll get another one at the house."

Ford smiled at the boy. "Thank you, Andrew, and I'm proud of you and Clay for your help today. You're both growing up to be fine young men."

With that he closed the van door and let Maria head back to the clinic.

He noticed Maria's face, white with shock. "Do you want me to drive?"

"No, but *Dios mio.*" Her voice rose. "It is horrible to imagine our quiet resort a place for murderers. Shooting people. Shooting innocent dogs." She clenched the steering wheel. "What are these police doing about it, too? Very little. Look how long it's been since that other innocent woman was found in the cabin. And now this." She waved a hand. "I saw them turning that body over down at the lake. It was another woman. I could see it was."

Ford tried not to smile. When Maria got upset, she made him think so much of her mother Juanita in her reactions. Very dramatic.

"The situation is grievous, Maria," he offered in comfort. "I'm sure the police will increase their efforts to find the murderer now. However, we don't know this murder was even committed by the same person."

"And should that comfort me, thinking there may be two crazy people like that?" She put a hand to her heart.

"I wonder if this woman was killed the same way?" Clay asked.

"I don't know, son, but I imagine we'll have answers to many of these questions before the day is over," he answered.

Ford turned to smile at his son. "We can do little to solve these murders but we can do much to help Jefferson."

Dwayne met them at the clinic door. "Maria called me. I thought you might need a little help." He moved to help Ford unload the dog from the van.

"You didn't need to come in to the clinic, Dwayne, but I'm glad for your help today. It's hard when it's your own pet." He turned to Maria. "Why don't you go on home since Dwayne is here. He can assist. Your children and your family will have heard the sirens. They will be worried."

She hesitated. "Are you sure you won't need me here?"

"If I do, we'll call." Ford helped her back into the van. "Thank you for dropping everything to come and help as you did."

"I hope Jefferson will be all right." She looked toward the open door as Dwayne walked through with Jefferson in the crate. Reaching out to put a hand on Ford's shoulder before she left, she said, "We will pray for you. *Que Dios te acompane.* God be with you."

The next hour was a busy one. They put Jefferson more fully to sleep so they could do X-rays and blood work, treat the wound, remove blood, hair, and debris from around the site, and check for internal damage or broken bones.

"He's lucky that bullet didn't hit a bone or shatter his shoulder," Dwayne said, as he put sutures over the entry wound now, while Ford watched him. Ford's own hands felt shaky after the events of the day with his adrenalin beginning to wear off, and he was glad to give this job to Dwayne.

Clay sat on a stool in the corner of the exam room. He watched everything they did, asking a few questions but not getting in their way.

"Can you tell what kind of gun he was shot with?" Clay asked.

"Probably a small handgun," Dwayne answered. "Looks like he was hit with one bullet, not too large. Moved right through the muscle real fast and out here." He pointed at the exit wound. "We can count our blessings it wasn't buckshot. Would have made a worse mess."

"Jefferson is going to be okay now, isn't he?" Clay asked.

"I hope so," Ford answered honestly. "He lost some blood but Dwayne and I don't see any tendon or ligament damage and I hope there's no tissue or nerve damage. We cleaned the wound well; we administered antibiotics but there's always the possibility of shock from the injury, infection of the wound, collateral damage from the blood loss. We'll know more by in the morning."

When Dwayne finished with his work, Clay got up to stroke the big dog, still out from the anesthetic. "Poor guy. When can we bring him home?"

"Tomorrow or the next day if all goes well. He'll need to stay here at least tonight." Ford rubbed a hand across his own neck, tired now. "I'll stay another hour or so here at the clinic where I can check on him often."

"Ford, I can do that, so you can go home to the children," Dwayne said. "And so Samantha can go home."

Ford shook his head, suddenly realizing Samantha was probably still at the house.

"I'll call the house. Dad and Mother may have come over. It's late." He glanced at the clock.

"We only have two other dogs in our motel tonight." Dwayne grinned at his terminology. "The Gilbert's little terrier Skeeter that cut his foot on that nasty broken glass. He's doing good; just hobbling around. But we wanted to pump him with some more antibiotics and check him tomorrow before sending him home. And we have the Wilkerson's cocker spaniel Molly you spayed this afternoon. Since we didn't get her early this morning, you wanted to keep her overnight."

Dwayne started cleaning up the exam room. "The only cat we have staying in the cat ward is Delilah, the Peterson's cat."

"I know the Petersons," Clay said. "What's wrong with Delilah?"

Ford smiled at him. "She made the mistake of getting a tapeworm from a rat she caught."

"Ewww!"

Ford laughed. "It wasn't a pretty sight when she passed it—

looked like a long, thin, white ribbon. Tapeworms are nasty little parasites but Delilah's going to be fine. We gave her the needed medication by injection to pass the tapeworm, but she'll need to come back in two to three weeks to get a second dose to kill any larva that might be left behind."

Dwayne stroked his hand down Jefferson's back. "Clay, did you know fleas can carry worms, too? A little ole' flea can jump thirteen inches to get on a dog or cat. Crafty little boogers."

Ford walked out of the exam room while they talked to call the house. Samantha answered.

"I thought you would have gone home," he said.

"No. Your dad offered, but I told him I'd be fine. How's Jefferson?"

"Good for now." Ford filled her in. "How's the situation there?"

"That detective and another officer came by to talk to Andrew, since he was the first to see the body." He heard her sigh. "They said it was another woman, killed the same way as the first with a wire and then dumped in the lake off the dock."

"We'll need to bump up security at the resort again, maybe hire extra help another time like we did before."

"Your dad said to tell you he and Maury were already at work setting that up. Several campers checked out, too. I guess they were scared."

He laughed softly. "In all honesty, if I'd been camping at the resort with my kids, I'd have loaded them up and headed home as well. Not many people like the idea of closing their eyes to sleep in a tent, RV, or cabin knowing there might be a murderer on the loose nearby."

"Well, this is turning into a scary situation."

"That it is." He hesitated. "Look, I need to hang around here for a while until Jefferson comes out from the anesthesia. I want to make sure he's all right, resting comfortably before I come home. I can call to see if Juanita can come to sleep over or maybe Dad."

"I'll stay until you get back," she said. "Your dad has enough on his mind and needs to be with Coralee. Juanita has her mother to tend to, not very mobile from what I hear and still needing help."

"Thanks."

He heard her laugh. "We storm chasers are used to crises and long hours, Ford. I'll be fine and I've talked to the children, calmed down some of their worries. Troubles pass. People move on through harder things than this."

"You're a comfort, even to me. I'll see you later." He hung up and walked back into the exam room.

"Jefferson's starting to wake up a little and I took the IV off," Dwayne told him as he came back in the room. "We can crate him and put him in the ward now. You know he'll probably be groggy for about twelve to twenty-four hours. He should sleep fine through the night though, if you want to head on home. I can stay longer if you want."

"No. I'll hang around for a while to check him a few more times, but maybe you can take Clay up to the house."

Clay looked up from where he sat on a stool by the dog. "I'd like to stay and go home with you, Dad."

Dwayne grinned. "He's turning into a vet already."

Ford smiled. "Okay, son."

Dwayne finished putting the last of the now clean instruments away and gathered up the trash to take out with him. "If you guys want a snack, there's some microwave popcorn in the kitchen and colas in the 'frig."

A little later, he and Clay sat on the floor of the hallway, in front of the dog ward, where they could see Jefferson's crate. Clay had wanted to stay nearby to watch the dog for a time. Between them was a bowl of popcorn they were munching on between sips from two bottled colas.

Ford had checked the dog a few minutes ago and found him resting easily, breathing well. "He's doing good, son."

"I'm glad. I'll bet Gracie is missing him."

Ford smiled. "We'll bring her down here tomorrow to see Jefferson in the ward, to see that he's doing okay. He'll be up and around some then. If there's no sign of infection, no problems, I might be able to bring him home with me tomorrow at the end of the day."

"Do dogs die from gunshot wounds?"

"Sadly, a lot do. If the bullet hits vertebrae or the abdominal area or if there's too much bleeding, it can be difficult for a dog. I didn't know how long Jefferson lay in the mud by the bank before we came. I couldn't know how much blood he'd lost, if dirt or other debris had gotten in the wound. Jefferson couldn't tell us if he was shot by the bank, or ran to that point and fell, not able to go further."

They munched popcorn for a minute or two, listening to the silence. "I wish Gracie could talk to tell us all that. She probably saw the murderer, too." Clay looked across at Ford. "Do you think Jefferson tried to stop him from killing that woman?"

"I don't know, but I think it's probable he and Gracie started barking over the murderer trying to dump someone in the lake."

Clay nodded. "That person probably shot at them to shut them up and hit Jefferson."

"Maybe in time we'll know for sure what happened when the police find who's been committing these crimes." He took a long drink from his cola. "I hope that's soon. It isn't helping the reputation of the resort and I don't like the idea of someone demented like that around our property. You children will need to be watchful until all this is resolved, stay close to the house, don't go off by yourself."

"We'll be in school most of the time now." He grew quiet after that last comment. "Dad, do you like Samantha?"

"Son, I think we've had this conversation. You know I like Samantha but she needs to go back to the work she loves. It's important to her, just like my work here is to me."

"Do you like her enough to sleep with her?"

Ford looked across at his son, shocked. "That's a pretty adult question for a ten-year old to ask."

Clay shrugged. "I watch TV and movies and the guys at school talk."

Ford tried to think what to say. Deciding to be honest, he said, "I'm very attracted to Samantha in every way. I admit I wish things were different and I could act on that, but I'd act on my feelings honorably by asking her to marry me. The desire to mate is a biological urge. Animals just follow it, as you know, but for people it's better with commitment, with deep feelings of love and with marriage."

He considered what else to add. "You know God made Eve for Adam to be a helpmeet, from his rib, to be a part of him, protected and loved by him. Don't ever be a man to take a girl's innocence just for an urge or a thrill. I know guys talk about it that way, but it's never something to be proud of doing, a thing to brag about to other guys. It's disrespectful of the union between a man and woman that's meant to be sweet, strong, and personal."

"Like you had with mom."

"Yes." He ate another handful of popcorn. "A lot of people sleep around. A lot of people do a lot of things that aren't right—cheat at school, lie, steal, drink, do drugs. Each time sears the conscience. A person starts justifying what they do that's not morally right. They find ways to see it as right. But no matter what people say or how they justify it, it's still wrong. Not that we can't be forgiven for wrongs, just that we shouldn't seek them out."

Clay grew quiet for a few minutes. "I'd like it if you married Samantha. We all would. Gareth says maybe you should try to talk her into it." He grinned at his dad. "He says you should put some moves on her to make her want to stay here and not leave."

Ford decided not to tell Clay about the times he'd tried exactly that. "Well, I'll keep that in mind," he said instead, chuckling.

Pushing up off the floor then, he said, "I think Jefferson is doing well, sleeping good, and that you and I can go back to the house now to get some sleep ourselves. I won't be much good in the clinic tomorrow if I don't get some rest. And Samantha needs to go home. It's after eleven."

"Okay. I'll put these bottles in the trash and take the bowl to the kitchen. I know you'll want to check all the dogs and the little cat before we leave."

After locking up the clinic, the two walked up the road to the lodge. With the moon full in the sky and shining amid a myriad of stars in the clear night sky, it was hard to believe bodies had been found here at this quiet resort.

Letting themselves into the kitchen, Ford sent Clay up the back stairs to his room to go to bed, Gracie following him tonight, needing extra comfort. Then Ford went into the living room to look for Samantha to tell her she could head home.

He found her lying asleep on the sofa, an old afghan pulled over her legs.

Walking quietly around the sofa, he sat on the chair across from her to look at her, wishing this could be his life, to come home and find her waiting for him when he'd had a long, hard day. That he could curl up with her here, bury his face in her neck and hair.

"Don't leave me Samantha," he whispered.

She opened her eyes, blinking, to look across at him. "Oh, you're home." She started to push herself up, but he stopped her, moving to sit beside her on the sofa and leaning over to kiss her.

"You tempted me too much to resist that," he said, kissing her neck near her ear. "I loved coming in, finding you sleeping on my sofa. I hope you know how hard it's going to be for me to let you go."

She traced her fingers down his face. "For me, too," she whispered back, leaning in to kiss him again and wrapping her arms around him.

After a time of pleasure like this, probably too much time, Ford sat up at last. "I need to let you go while I can. It's late."

He stood and helped her to her feet, trying not to pull her into his arms again. To keep some restraint and respect, like he'd preached to Clay.

"How's Jefferson?" she asked, slipping on her shoes and starting toward the kitchen and the back door, looking for her purse.

"Doing well. We were lucky—or blessed. The bullet only grazed through the muscle on Jefferson's shoulder. No other internal problems, no bones hit." Ford paused. "How have the kids been doing?"

"I told you. They're fine. Go get some sleep now, Ford." She leaned closer to give him a quick kiss before she started out the back door. "And sweet dreams." She wiggled her eyebrows at him.

CHAPTER 19

On Monday, the children started back to school for their first half day. Juanita returned to take care of the house and the family at Ford's home. Samantha had promised the children she would come over to the resort, after they came home from school, to enjoy a final afternoon on the lake with them. Despite the disfavor she knew she'd face with Juanita, Samantha was determined to keep that promise.

Arriving at the house, she quickly hit Juanita's disapproval.

"The children have afternoon chores to do," she told Samantha. "Ford likes his schedule kept."

Samantha leaned against the counter in the kitchen where Juanita worked. "Listen, Juanita. Like it or not, four of these children are my family and the other four feel like family to me now. I've kept them all summer. I'm leaving later this week to go back to Atlanta and I promised these children I'd come over and spend the afternoon with them on the lake. Ford gave his okay for that. Feel free to call him."

"Very well," she said with resignation. "My grandchildren are also here today. Ford gave his approval for that, too."

"Fine. They're welcome to come down to the lake to swim with us. Just let me know their swimming skills and abilities."

"There are murderers about." She lifted her chin. "I will keep them here with me safe until I can come down to watch them. I have work to do first to finish some things in the house and the kitchen. I have pies in the oven, too."

Samantha saw no point in arguing. She felt bad for Ana Sophia and Dylan, but she left the issue alone. They were Juanita's grandchildren.

The other children began to wander into the kitchen, hearing her voice, already in their swimsuits ready for a fun afternoon.

Ana Sophia and Dylan followed, looking disappointed when told by Juanita they couldn't go.

"I have another swimsuit Ana Sophia can wear," Tamela offered.

Wesley perked up at her suggestion. "Dylan can wear one of mine, too. One of my suits is too tight anyway."

Both children, excited now, looked to their grandmother.

She paused, her face softening, and for once Samantha realized she hated to disappoint them. But then, glancing at Samantha, her face grew hard again. "Leave the suits out. I will bring Ana Sophia and Dylan down after I finish here."

Dejected, the children's faces wilted.

"You'll get to come down soon." Samantha smiled at them as she left with the other children a short time later.

"Juanita can be mean sometimes," Madison said to her as they walked down the path toward the swim beach.

Natalie glanced back toward the house. "Juanita is a really good woman, but she has a lot of fears. Sometimes she can be stubborn about things, too."

"Is she good to all of you?" Samantha asked.

"She really is," Natalie said.

"I don't know why she acts so ugly to you sometimes. You've always been nice to her." Madison wrinkled her nose.

Clay, walking with them, added, "I heard Daddy say to Ben that she feels competitive about you, worries you might take her place."

Deciding to change the subject, Samantha asked, "How is Jefferson doing?"

Clay brightened. "He's doing great. He's whining to go outside, but Dad is only letting us take him out on a leash until his shoulder heals up."

Madison looked across the lake. "It's creepy to think they've found dead people in our lake and in one of our cabins."

Andrew, also walking near them, said, "That detective came by yesterday afternoon to give Dad and Granddad a progress report. The police really haven't found any good clues to help them find out who brought the bodies here."

Samantha kept her eye on the four younger children racing ahead of them toward the swim beach. "Don't go into the water until I get there," she called after them.

Gareth turned, waving back that he'd heard. Usually all the children raced to the lake, but today the older ones hung closer to Samantha, as if wanting time with her before she left.

Andrew continued with his earlier conversation. "The police do know now that both murders happened somewhere else and that whoever did it brought the bodies here."

Clay snorted. "So Juanita doesn't really need to worry about murderers maybe grabbing us and killing us every time we go out the door."

"It is important to be watchful though, Clay," Samantha said. "You children shouldn't go off alone or too far from the house until any criminals involved in this are caught. It isn't pleasant to find a dead body, as you should well know, and it would be dangerous to run into these people."

"Yeah, we know," Andrew added. "Jefferson got shot for it."

"That's my point," Samantha said but then laughed. "However, I can't imagine any criminal in their right mind showing up on a sunny day at the lake with eight children hooting and hollering and having a good time." She grinned at them. "And that's what we'll be doing."

At the lake, Samantha went over their safety rules—the buddy system, the restrictions based on swimming ability, age, and more. The children then raced off into the water, while Samantha settled into a chair by the lake to relax and watch them for a time.

The older four, all strong swimmers, tended to play near the swim raft further out in the lake, while the younger ones played nearer the bank, creating games, digging in the sand, playing on floats and water toys. For safety the youngest girls still wore their swim bubbles around their waists, providing extra protection until their swimming skills increased. Samantha insisted that all the younger children put on float belts or took swim noodles, tubes, or paddleboards with them when they swam out to the raft. She usually went with them into deeper water, too. All the children swam well, but water could always be dangerous, whether quiet water in a lake or roaring waves in a hurricane.

With the afternoon warm, Samantha soon swam out to the raft to join the older children. The younger kids wanted to jump from the raft, too, so Samantha let them come but insisted they all put on swim float belts.

"I'll need to watch all eight of you in deep water out there," Samantha insisted when the older boys grumbled. "You'll be wanting to jump off the raft and horse around. With swim belts on, I know you'll be safe out there if I don't keep my eye on you every second. I want to swim some, too."

Out on the raft they all played and enjoyed the hot summer afternoon. She'd carried sun cream out with her and made everyone lotion up while they sat around on the raft talking, the kids telling her about their school day and new teachers.

"Are you really going back to Atlanta later this week?" Tamela asked.

"I am, but I promise I'll write and come back soon." Samantha pushed a strand of wet hair behind her ear and then tightened the band that held her long hair back in a ponytail today.

"Seeing you on the TV isn't the same as you being here." Wesley said, frowning.

"No, but that's my work," Samantha answered.

"I wanted you to go camping with us at the end of August," Rebecca said. She looked toward Natalie. "Where are we going? I forgot."

Natalie smiled. "We're going to the Elkmont Campground between Gatlinburg and Cades Cove. It's a real pretty campground but we haven't visited there in a long time."

"It's going to be cool," Gareth added. "You can tube in the creeks, there are good trails, and Gatlinburg isn't far."

"I'm sure you'll have a great time," she said.

Glancing toward the shore, she saw Juanita coming down toward the swim beach, her two grandchildren dancing alongside her and waving at the other children.

"There's Juanita," Samantha said. "I need to swim back now." She looked at the younger children. "You guys need to come back with me."

"Okay," said Rebecca and Tamela, both ready to play again on the beach.

"Can we stay a little longer?" Gareth begged. "Wesley and I will keep our float belts on."

"And we won't do anything stupid," Wesley added.

Samantha considered their request. "What about Dylan? Won't he want to play with you?"

"He's only five," Gareth said. "He mostly plays with Rebecca and Tamela."

"We'll come back in a little while to play with him," Wesley said with kindness. "I'll show him how to use a paddleboard."

"All right," she agreed, climbing into the water. Then she followed the girls closely as they swam back to the shore.

Juanita, still dressed in the slacks and shirt she'd worn earlier, settled into a chair in the shade under a big tree.

Samantha toweled off and then sat in a chair nearby. "It's a great day for the kids to be outdoors."

She saw Juanita glance over her wet hair and swimsuit as if in disapproval. Samantha felt glad she hadn't worn her bikini. That probably would have brought her a real sneer.

When Juanita made no further efforts at conversation, Samantha asked about Juanita's mother and then told one of the school stories the children had shared with her, netting only a few comments from Juanita.

Finally, annoyed, she said, "Juanita, I wish we could have become friends this summer. I wanted that in case you don't know. I admire so much how you came to help Ford after Laura died, taking care of him and all the kids. They all tell me what a great cook you are and about how well you care for them. I know they love you."

Juanita glanced at her, surprised.

"You made it clear to me at the beginning of summer that you disapproved of me because I didn't put family ahead of my career and come home to raise my sister's children when she and Adam were killed."

"You seldom came home later to visit, either."

"I was wrong in that. Being with the children this summer has taught me how much family means. I see that more now."

Juanita looked across at her. "And yet you are walking away again."

Exasperated, she threw up her hands. "What do you expect me to do?"

Juanita looked out to where the children played in the water near the sand beach before replying. "I thought you might realize you could fill a place in a lonely man's life," she said, surprising Samantha. "Everyone has seen how he looks at you. He has been hurt so much, suffered so much loss, when he is such a fine, good man. I know he will hurt again when you leave. Have you even thought of that? Do you have no feeling toward him?"

Samantha took a breath. "Those are very personal questions, Juanita. Perhaps ones I struggle with in my own way."

She sent Samantha a hard look. "I know that man now as if he was one of my own sons. I know if he cared for you he would have offered for you. He is honorable that way. And since you are leaving, I know you have said no. Forgive me if I feel hard toward you, but I will be one of those left behind to try to help him with grief again, to help those children with their grief, too. You know they have come to love you. Every day already I see their sad faces knowing you are going away soon."

"I guess you don't understand much about women having careers," Samantha said in what she knew a testy tone.

Juanita laughed then. "Do you think I have sat home all this life?

No. I worked in the restaurant until it grew larger. I helped to put my children through school so they could have a better life here in this country. I took in my parents when they came to America. In my time, I've cleaned houses, cooked for others, ironed, taken care of children, whatever I needed to do. Perhaps my work has not been as celebrated as yours, but you may be assured I understand work and the necessity of it." She paused. "Furthermore, I understand the need for useful work. We are not meant to have idle hands in this world. Honest hard work is something the good Lord expects from all of us. We are not meant to be sluggards."

Samantha found herself tempted to tell Juanita she'd been seeking work here so she might possibly stay, but then checked herself. Instead she stood.

"I think I'll walk up to the restroom at the pavilion on the hill for a minute," she said. "The children know their rules about what to do at the lake, and I'll be right back."

Walking up the hill helped to clear her mind from Juanita's words. Unless something changed in her life, it seemed unlikely she'd ever rise to the A-list in Juanita's mind. That was for sure. But she felt rather glad she'd talked to the woman anyway. Cleared the air somewhat.

Starting down the hill back to the beach, she heard Madison's voice streak across the air, shrill and panicked. "Aunt Samantha, something's wrong with Dylan."

She looked where Madison pointed, halfway between the dock and the beach where the small boy floundered in the water.

On the bank, Juanita stood, beginning to wail and cry out.

Running now, Samantha reached the beach, kicked off her shoes and swam as hard as she could out to the small five-year old boy. Who let him go out into that deep water? she wondered, her heart hammering. Didn't Juanita know better than to let that child swim out into the lake? Samantha had sorrowfully seen many small children drown over her lifetime in the field. Boys, especially, reckless and foolhardy, feeling invincible about incoming storms and towering waves. Seeing it all as exciting.

Drawing near the boy now, she felt panic rise in her heart to see the child attempting to swim but making no forward progress, his body nearly vertical in the water with little or no leg movement, his head too low, dipping below the surface now. She would have preferred to see him coughing, sputtering, flailing his arms and hollering.

Reaching him, she wrapped her arm around the small boy and turned him to his back, supporting his head on her shoulder and beginning to swim back to shore keeping his head out of the water.

At the shore, she had to rebuke a panicked and distraught Juanita to keep her out of the way while she laid Dylan on the sand and started CPR, tilting his head back. Staying calm, she alternated breathing with chest compressions every fifteen seconds, and to her great relief, after a moment Dylan coughed. Samantha turned him to his side and he vomited water, soon beginning to cry, too.

"*Dios mio*," Juanita cried, falling to her knees in the sand beside them. "I only took my eye from him for a moment and then saw him walking out into the deeper water, calling to the boys. Then suddenly he was flailing and struggling ..."

Samantha tried to calm her breathing. "There's a deep drop off there in the lake. Does he not swim?"

"*Un poco*. A little bit," she replied, holding the crying boy to her now, wiping his face and kissing him.

Ana Sophia ran over, weeping, to stand nearby. "Is he going to be okay?" She sobbed. "I didn't know what to do."

Rebecca and Tamela came over, both crying, too.

"We told him not to go out to the raft, but he said he could swim," Rebecca said.

Tamela sniffed. "Me and Rebecca tried to get him to put on a waist float or to get a noodle or something, but he wouldn't listen."

"It's not your fault," Samantha said to the girls in a soothing voice.

"No, it is mine," Juanita said, still cuddling Dylan. "I was the adult in charge. I should have kept better watch."

Samantha watched Dylan carefully as they talked. He seemed to be breathing well but he leaned over then to spit out more water.

"Why is he sick?" Juanita asked her.

"When children panic in the water, they often swallow a lot of water and it goes into the esophagus and down through the digestive tract," Samantha explained. "What is needed, when you get them out of the water is to open up the blocked airways. Most vomit then, to get the water out."

She didn't add that if a child swallowed too much water, that if the water went into the lungs, and if the child wasn't pulled from the water soon enough that the lack of oxygen could cause damage to the body's organs, brain and heart. Even a little water could cause serious problems. Recovery often depended on how long a child was in the water before being retrieved, too.

The older children had come in from the raft now, and Samantha turned to Madison. "How long had Dylan struggled before you called me?"

"Only a few minutes Aunt Samantha," she said with wide eyes. "We saw him walking out from the beach, like he wanted to come to the raft, but we thought he would stop in a minute. That he knew the rules."

"Then he stepped off that deep spot." Clay jumped into the story. "He panicked, I guess, and started flailing around, taking himself out deeper instead of swimming back. And he kept going under."

Samantha took a deep breath. "This is a good lesson to all of you that water can always be dangerous." She turned to Juanita. "I would like you to take Dylan to see Dr. Ben Larsen. I'll call him on my cell. He'll look Dylan over to see that all is well."

"We know the Larsens and Dylan knows Ben." She looked at the boy. "Doctor Ben will look at you to be sure you are fine," she told him.

Samantha didn't add that Ben would probably send Dylan on to the ER for further tests. Both Juanita and Dylan were panicked enough already.

She got up to go get her phone from her bag on the table and stepped away from hearing to make her call.

Reaching Ben, she told him quickly what had happened and that she wanted Juanita to bring the boy over to be checked. "If I tell her now that Dylan may also need to go to the hospital, I think they both might freak out. You know how five-year old boys are about hearing the word hospital."

Ben chuckled. "Send them over; I'll make space to see the boy as soon as they get here." He paused. "You acted fast, Samantha. You know if you hadn't gotten that boy in when you did, he probably would have drowned. It doesn't take long, and accidental drowning is the second cause of death among young children. I see it often enough to my sorrow. Why did Juanita let him head out into that deep water?"

"I don't know," Samantha answered. "I heard she doesn't swim, so she probably doesn't know much about water safety."

"For Pete's sake, the woman and her family live on a lake." Ben sounded annoyed. "You can be sure I'll have a talk with her, and with Maria, about seeing to it that all her family learn more about staying safe around the water. Everyone in that family needs to learn to swim, too, including Juanita. If I need to teach them myself, I'll see to it they learn."

"I'll send them on," Samantha said.

Getting off the phone to Ben, she called Ford next. He could talk to Maria. Samantha felt sure she would want to leave the office to go with her mother and son to Ben's office. Finishing her calls, she turned back to Juanita.

"Maria is coming over from the clinic to drive you and Dylan to Ben's office," she told her. "Let me carry Dylan back up to the house to meet her there. You can help him into some clean clothes and get your purse."

Turning to the kids, she said, "All of you dry off, get your things and follow us to the house." Looking at Madison, she added, "Bring my bag with my purse and towel in it, too, okay?"

"I'll get it right now," she said, happy to do something to help.

Samantha picked up Dylan gently. "You're shaky from your time in the water Dylan, so I'm going to carry you up to the house. Okay? Your mom is on her way."

He started to cry. "I almost drowned."

"But you didn't." She smiled at him as she started up the path to the house. "And you're fine now."

When Juanita started to scold him, Samantha shook her head at her. "There's time for that later," she said quietly.

Back at the house Juanita fluttered about, worrying over what to do about the unfinished supper.

"The kids and I will take care of supper," Samantha assured her. "You go with Maria to see about Dylan. If he isn't better tomorrow, let me know. I can come over to stay with the children after school."

"For now," Juanita couldn't resist adding as she headed out the back door.

After they left, the other children needed some calming from the scary incident that had taken place. Samantha talked with them for a time, teaching them some understandings about water safety. They could probably see the need for her words better now than at some other time.

Then she sent them upstairs to change clothes and to hang wet towels and swimsuits on the old clothesline outside when finished.

Samantha called Dixie while the children changed clothes to fill her in on the situation. "I'll hang around here and help with supper until Ford gets home," she told her.

"Do you think that boy will be all right?"

"I think so. I got to him fast." She hesitated. "He wasn't breathing much or maybe not at all when I got to him in the water. But I got him back to the beach quickly and started CPR."

"You know very well you saved that child's life."

"It was a touchy situation," she replied. "I admit I felt scared."

"Jackson used to say bravery isn't about not being scared but about doing what you need to with courage anyway."

She smiled at the compliment. "I'll see you later, Aunt Dixie."

CHAPTER 20

Ford walked into the back door of his home on Friday afternoon tired and battling with what his grandmother used to call "the melancholies," an overload of sad thoughts. He hated himself for letting personal feelings affect his mood and his daily life. He had a good life, a great veterinary practice, a wonderful family, and many more blessings he could count and name. But his heart was still heavy that Samantha was leaving this weekend to go back to Atlanta.

He found Juanita in the kitchen and stopped to snag a fresh cookie she'd just pulled from the oven.

She shook a finger at him. "Those are for the potluck dinner and party at the lake tonight. Don't let the children see you sneaking one or they will all want one, too." She smiled at him. "Did you have a hard day?"

"We lost a little cat with a gastrointestinal infection. Her people simply didn't bring her in quickly enough. Poor little thing was full of infection, dehydrated, too weak from vomiting and diarrhea to recover. We tried our best but it wasn't enough."

"Maria says those times when people don't care for their animals or when abused animals are brought in are the hardest."

"That's true." He smiled at her. "Maria has taken her share of animals, literally left in a box on our front porch, home with her and fostered them until homes could be found. I appreciate that."

Juanita turned back to pull out another tray of cookies from the oven. "I made a potato salad for the potluck dinner tonight as well as cookies. You told me the Larsens were bringing ham and baked beans and the Newmans a broccoli salad and watermelon. And I know you picked up the drinks at lunch."

"We'll have a feast and everyone is looking forward to the evening." Glancing around to see none of the children nearby, he snagged another cookie. "How is Dylan?" he asked, sitting down on a kitchen stool.

"Very well and fully recovered." She pulled a bottle of water from the refrigerator and passed it to him. "Tell Ben again we are grateful for his care of Dylan. All his tests at the hospital were good, no need for him to stay."

She sat down on a stool opposite him. "I know Samantha saved the child's life. Be assured I am grateful. I provoked her with some direct talk that day, causing her, I know, to head up the hill to the restrooms at the pavilion probably just to escape from me. If she'd stayed, she would have seen Dylan moving into danger as he waded out into the deeper water. She'd have called him back. I didn't. I was looking at a magazine, lost in my thoughts. By the time I saw the trouble, heard him call out, I panicked. I didn't know what to do." She looked down at her hands in her lap. "I can't swim and I am afraid of the water."

Ford waited.

"Ben Larsen gave Maria and me a stern lecture insisting we all learn more water safety living on the lake as we do at Willow Point. Maria and Carlos are taking the children to swim classes and reading books about water safety that Ben gave us." She blushed. "They are working to teach me to swim, too."

"I'm glad to hear that." Ford thought over her words. "I hope you shared your gratitude with Samantha as you did with me."

"I have done so and with humility. I have not been kind to Samantha and yet she has shown only kindness to me, and she did not hesitate to risk her own life to save the life of my grandchild. I am indebted to her. In my family, in the culture I grew up in, we hold strong loyalty to any who risk their lives for us, who give beyond the call of duty. I honor her now."

With surprise at the intensity of her words, Ford nodded. "Well, that's good." He tried to think what else to say. "I am sorry Samantha was injured in the hurricane but in many ways I am grateful she had this time to get to know the children better this summer. They will miss her."

"As will you." She gave him a direct look. "Trust your heart and fight for what your heart speaks to you. Even if your heart is on your left side, it is always right." She smiled at her last words.

He sighed. "I wish it was as simple as you suggest."

"Then we pray. I have always believed the Good Lord a God of second chances. He can work miracles we sometimes cannot see for ourselves."

Several of the children ran into the kitchen then, excited about the evening to come.

After Juanita left, Ford went back to his own room to shower and change for the evening. On the dresser, as he finished getting into clean clothes, his eyes moved to the photo of Laura sitting on his bedside table.

He picked it up, looking at her smiling face, short pixie-cut hair, happy brown eyes. How sad that her life was cut short. Ford had talked with her about his growing feelings for Samantha. He believed those who'd gone on to heaven continued to watch over the lives of those they loved—checked in, listened in, wanting their continuing happiness. He knew he would.

Ford sat her photo back on the table and looked across to a recent shot of all the children taken down at the lake, a photo with Samantha laughing in the midst of them. "Lord, I would be grateful for your help and favor with this situation," he prayed. "I have seen you to be a God of second chances and you know my heart wishes I could make a second marriage, a second life with this vibrant, fresh woman. The minister said last Sunday that many times we forget that you want us to ask in order to receive and to not just assume you know our heart and thoughts and desires. So I'm asking, Lord. I don't know the answer to all the obstacles here but you do. So I'm asking you to make a way where there is no way.

You're good at that."

Resolved that he'd laid his problems in competent hands, Ford called for the children and with their help began to load up the food, coolers, chairs, and picnic items they'd need tonight into his SUV. The children could walk over but they had too many other things that needed transport to the big picnic pavilion above the swim beach.

As he was finishing unloading at the pavilion a little later, Samantha pulled up in her small Acura. He watched her climbing out of the car, calling out to the children, smiling and happy, her nose crinkling as she laughed, the afternoon sun shining on her long, wavy red hair, loose and free around her shoulders. She wore sunny yellow tonight, a perfect color for her, and as she walked toward him her green eyes sent him a personal welcome he didn't miss.

"I came early to help you set up," she said. "What can I do?"

"Mother reminded me we had a stack of blue-checked tablecloths in the storage room from past events at the resort. I pulled them out and Juanita insisted on ironing them." He pointed to the stack. "I thought we might put them on the tables, make things a little more festive."

"I love them," she said, going over to check them out. "Oh, and you got blue plastic party plates and cups to match. And there are even blue-checked napkins to match the tablecloths."

"Mom remembered those, too." He opened a cardboard box. "She sent over this box of candles in Mason jars, too. Thought they'd be festive. She tied the blue ribbons around them, not me."

"Your mother has such lovely creative skills. That gift totally bypassed me." She began taking the candles out of the box. "We can make everything pretty and decorative with these."

As they began to set up, a red van pulled up. Paulette Everett got out and waved to them.

"Hey, you two," she called as she walked over to join them. "Ford said earlier today I could drop by here to get the keys for the event center. I'm setting up for the Hickman's fiftieth anniversary party tomorrow night. They're having a dinner catered, a band, and dancing. I think they even plan to renew their vows in the chapel." She laughed. "It seems to me that making it to fifty years is commitment enough."

Ford pulled the keys, on a labeled key ring, out of his back pocket.

"Everything looks pretty here," Paulette said, looking around.

"I take no credit," Samantha said, grinning at her. "Coralee's artistry is behind all you see."

Handing Paulette the keys, Ford asked, "Are the Hickmans not concerned about the body found at Sycamore Point at the dock?"

Paulette propped against a picnic table. "No, they didn't seem to be, Ford. They live local, have kept up with the news and know the murder victims both were brought to the resort and weren't killed here." She shivered. "It is gruesome to think about that though, and I'm sorry the resort is involved."

"It hasn't helped business," Ford replied.

"I knew both the women killed," Paulette told them. "My mother lives over near the Cross Corner Market and gas station. I often stop in at the café to eat when I go to Mama's. They have good blue plate lunches. I got to know Norma there. Nice woman."

She shook her head. "I was there just the other day. Earl and Calvin are both really torn up over this, especially with the police not finding the murderer. You know Earl's really turned around and he's started to work hard in the business now, cooking and everything. Norma would have loved that. Earl kept trying to get back together with her. If he'd shown her the change I'm seeing now, she might have relented and taken him back."

"Who was the other woman killed?" Samantha asked. "You said you knew her, too."

"That was Shirley Crawford, pretty little school teacher with blond curly hair. She taught English at the high school. She lives up near Mama, too, toward Grants Chapel. I run into her every now and then at the café. We went to school together as girls so we always talk a little to catch up."

"I think I know her husband Wes," Ford put in. "He likes to hunt and keeps some bird dogs that I treat at the clinic."

Paulette made a face. "Well, he cheated on her just like Jimmy did me. They separated. Men seem to think women should forgive easily when they stray and Shirley told me Wes has tried hard to get her to forgive him. Jimmy is still trying to convince me I should give him another chance, too."

"Sometimes second chances can be good," Ford replied, glancing over to catch Samantha's eyes as he said the words.

"Easy words to say but it's hard when trust is broken," Paulette replied.

"I'm sure it is," Samantha said with kindness.

Paulette glanced at her watch. "I need to run. I'm going to zip over to the event center, check things out, remind myself what I need to bring in the morning. It will take me most all day tomorrow to decorate and then the caterers will come in with the food nearer supper. Their shindig starts at five."

"It was good to see you again, Paulette," Samantha said.

"Aunt Dixie said you're heading back to Atlanta soon. You have a safe trip and don't be a stranger. Come on back when you can."

"I will." Samantha waved at Paulette as she got in her car.

Ford stood looking after her. "I didn't mean to make light of Jimmy cheating on Paulette. He knows he made a fool of himself getting involved with that younger woman. He's real sorry, too."

She turned back to finish setting up the tables. "Maybe they'll work something out, and I really hope the police find some leads to help arrest whoever killed those women. Thinking of those wires they were strangled with is creepy."

"Jim Culver, the detective working on the case, said in both murders they found evidence that the women had been tied up before being murdered. They're following up every lead they can. I'm sure they'll get a break eventually."

"I hope so," Samantha added. "I read that about forty percent of murders are never solved by the police. That isn't a comforting thought."

Ford looked over to the big playground where all the children played on the tall swings, slide, jungle gym, and seesaw. "I admit I'll feel more peaceful if these murders are resolved and if the police learn why the murderer brought the bodies here to our resort."

"Me, too." She moved closer to him, reaching up to touch his face. "I'll miss you, Ford McDaniel."

He sighed. "If I didn't have eight children watching us, I'd show you how much I'll miss you, too, Samantha King. If I knew anything to say to convince you how much I want you to stay here with me, I would say it, on my knees if I needed to."

"That's a pretty picture," she said in a teasing tone.

He put a hand to her hair, smoothing a strand behind her ear. "If your heart calls you back, listen to it. I'm praying God will find some way for this to work out even though it seems impossible."

"Do you know, we have never even had a date? I don't think I've ever had a man basically propose marriage to me without a date." She grinned.

"I'll pick you up tomorrow night at six, take you to Angelos on the Point for dinner. We can sit at a table on the patio and look out across the lake while we eat." He hesitated. "Ben said he and Vickie would keep the kids so we can go to dinner before you leave."

She smiled at him. "I'd like that. It would be a sweet memory to take away with me."

Their conversation was interrupted by the arrival of their friends—Vance and Lucy with their two children, Claudia and Mackie, and Ben and Vickie, with their three, Courtney, Jake, and Emmylou. Ben, in his typical, jovial style, soon had everyone laughing, and Ford, eager for some fun after a hard week, laid aside his gloomy thoughts to enjoy a good time on a warm, sunny Friday evening at the lake.

With the tables decorated and ready, everyone soon began to fill up their plates with all the food everyone brought. Ford had plugged up the icemaker inside the snack bar earlier that morning so they'd have all the ice they would need for drinks, and he and Maury had even pulled out the old jukebox for entertainment and dancing later.

The children segregated off by gender to eat, the seven girls at one table, the six boys at another. Samantha had pulled a table for the adults over to one side so they could eat with a little quiet, and Ford enjoyed not being the lone man among two happy couples tonight.

"What will you do when you go back, Samantha?" Lucy asked.

"I'll probably spend the rest of the month in the office in Atlanta, getting back into the swing of things, catching up, doing whatever is needed locally. I should be out in the field again in September, unless a big weather situation develops before then." She smiled. "One of the girls on my team, Margie Benson, has been staying in my apartment. Her marriage broke up and she needed a place to stay for a time. It's kept my place from being empty all summer. I don't really mind her staying on longer if she wants. We're both gone so much out in the field and my place has two bedrooms."

"How soon does your team head to an area when a fire, hurricane, tornado, or weather problem occurs?' Vance asked.

"Many weather situations develop unexpectedly, even violently, like an earthquake without warning. We move into an area immediately with a situation like that." She smiled, as if thinking back. "Other times, like when the station is tracking a big storm at sea and Weather First knows approximately where the storm will hit land, our teams are sent into those areas to set up and get ready for coverage. We often get there a week ahead of any weather."

She grinned. "You'd never know in those early days in a beach town that a storm was heading in. The sky is deceptively blue and often cloudless with no hint a walloping hurricane is developing that could come roaring in and tear down buildings, flood streets, take out power lines, and threaten lives. Around giving a few early coverage reports, getting in supplies and setting up the week ahead of a storm, we sometimes get some down time to sit out at the beach or around the pool."

"Tough life," Ben teased.

"It is tough when the storm begins to move in," Samantha replied. "Then you're staying while others are evacuating for safety.

You know you're at risk, even if your team has found the safest hotel to stay in. And, of course, you continue getting out into the incoming storm to keep the audience informed of the situation."

"That sounds hard," Vickie commented.

"It can be." She paused. "How challenging depends on the severity of the storm and many other factors. Seeing a tornado whirling directly toward your area or covering severe floods, big earthquakes, harsh blizzards, and out-of-control wildfires can prove to be difficult."

"It's a dangerous life," Lucy said, saying the words Ford was thinking. "I'm scared for you sometimes when I see you in those situations."

"What is something about your job most people watching you don't know?" Ben asked.

Samantha laughed. "How we're wired and dressed to be out in that weather. Oftentimes I have to strap my microphone pack into my bra or onto my calves or thighs to get it out of sight and keep it protected from the weather. If we're going to be in wet weather or storms, we often wear a wet suit under our clothes or when its vicious cold we stick heat wraps all over our body to try to stay warm."

"Do you ever inflate or exaggerate what you're seeing to make the coverage more exciting for your viewers?" Ben asked. "I've read that."

"It's a big responsibility covering the weather." Samantha looked thoughtful. "You know people are watching and depending on your guidance for how to plan, what to do. You know, too, that people are often reluctant to listen to the advice and warnings they should heed to be safe. If we do a little psychological maneuvering to help people keep safe, I don't feel guilt about that. I'd rather people be safe than sorry any day with severe weather moving in. Weather is so unpredictable; it can turn and change on a dime."

"How accurate can you be in your predictions?" Ford asked.

"The closer to the forecast date, the better. If we're predicting two or three days out or less, meteorologists are about ninety percent accurate. When the time lengthens toward a week, that percentage decreases." She shrugged. "Beyond seven days, it's always sort of a toss up."

"It must be an interesting job, even if dangerous sometimes," Vickie said.

"Life was less dangerous when I did daily forecasting, mostly in the station. I did that for my first five years, coming in and briefing myself on the national weather, analyzing observations, radar, and poring over incoming situations, getting my broadcast together. That's the science aspect of the job I like almost as much as broadcasting. I love making weather understandable to people. I like going out into schools to talk with kids, too, when my schedule permits."

"What did you like least about daily forecasting versus working on the storm team?" Vickie asked.

Samantha laughed that deep throaty laugh of hers. "Wearing a dress everyday and a very particular kind of dress, too, usually solid, and getting slathered with makeup to go on camera. I had a whole wardrobe of appropriate solid dresses, good for the camera." She looked around at them. "Did you know a forecaster can never wear green? When you're up against the green screen, the color disappears."

Lucy laughed. "Oh, I didn't know that."

"I love all these insights you've shared. I'll be aware of things I never noticed before now," Ben said.

They talked congenially about other things then and after cleaning up from dinner, Ben began to punch numbers into the jukebox so they could dance. The adults danced and laughed over the oldies on the resort's jukebox and so did the children. Ben especially loved teaching the kids old dances from the past like The Twist and The Pony, which had them all giggling.

After everyone danced and sang along with a Motown song by the Temptations called "Ain't Too Proud To Beg," Ford was glad that a slower number followed. He moved closer to sweep Samantha into a slow dance around the floor.

Against her ear he murmured, "Like the song says I'm not too proud to beg you to stay, Samantha, if I thought it would do any good."

"It's my life that would change the most, Ford," she answered him. "You've got to let me make my own decision. Maybe I need to go back to know if I should have stayed."

He thought about her words as they danced slowly around the floor of the old pavilion in the dark. "Well, I'll keep my heart and my door open," he decided to say at last.

CHAPTER 21

On Saturday morning after most of Dixie's weekend guests had left on their travels, or gone exploring around the lake or in the Great Smoky Mountains, Samantha sat in the kitchen visiting with her aunt. As they chatted, Dixie worked preparing a sweet bread she planned to serve with her Sunday morning breakfast.

"Carver's Orchard had some wonderful Ginger Golds when I stopped by there on Friday," Dixie said as she worked peeling and cutting up a pile of crisp green-skinned apples. "They are so good in tarts and pies, so I decided to make some loaves of my Cinnamon Apple Bread. My guests always love it."

Samantha reached over to snatch a couple of pieces of chopped apple. "Ummm. These are good."

"They are good, and this recipe makes a moist breakfast bread with a marvelous brown sugar and cinnamon topping. After I pour the batter into the loaf pans I push some of the sugar-cinnamon mixture down into the batter, too." She turned to smile at Samantha. "I'll send an extra loaf home with you in the morning when you leave."

Samantha frowned, gazing out the kitchen window.

"You're conflicted over leaving aren't you, darling?"

"I am. It seems like two lives are calling to me, pulling me in different directions."

Dixie gave her a fond look. "It's hard sometimes to know exactly what to do in life, especially when the road divides and two alluring paths appear." She chuckled. "I must say alluring is a nice word to describe Ford McDaniel."

Samantha giggled, despite her mood.

"Are you still going out to dinner with him tonight?"

"I am. I hope you don't mind." She reached across to grab another bite of apple. "I teased him the other night that we'd never had a real date, so he suggested we go out before I leave."

Dixie was quiet for a minute, using her electric mixer to beat ingredients into the batter. "Knowing Ford as I do," she said after a moment, "I imagine with the interest he's shown toward you, that he's found a way to act on those feelings here and there, and that he's probably suggested a more permanent relationship. Am I right?"

Samantha shrugged. "Even if he has, it's complicated."

"I was watching one of those television preachers one night and he used a scripture I looked up later. I liked it so much." She paused, thinking. "It said that as we walk God will show us the direction or way to go, to the right or to the left. I think it was in Isaiah somewhere. I find that comforting that as we walk along, following the best path we know to follow, that God will let us know if we're going the right way or not. I think far too often we believe we have to know it all out front and we beat ourselves up over it when we don't."

"That is true, Aunt Dixie, and thanks."

"You're welcome, darling, and I'm glad we can talk about spiritual things together more now." She smiled across at Samantha. "I feel sure you'll find your right direction and I'll be praying God helps you with that."

The inn's main phone rang then, an old landline hanging on the kitchen wall.

Dixie glanced toward it and frowned. "Honey, pick up that phone and answer it. I don't want to miss a possible reservation and I've got batter all over my fingers."

Samantha reached across the counter to pick up the receiver. "Dandridge Inn, can I help you?"

"Hey, Samantha, this is Paulette," her voice came in a rush. "I'm out at the event lodge at Sycamore Point in the resort, setting up for the Hickman anniversary party tonight." Her voice dropped. "Listen, I tried to call Ford but couldn't get him. I tried to call Jimmy, too. I left both a message but haven't heard back. I think someone is skulking around here and I've had the odd sense someone is watching me. Would you try to reach Ford and ask him to run up here? It's probably nothing but…."

Samantha heard a sound.

In a rush, Paulette said, "I think I see someone at the door; I need to go." And the connection clicked out.

"Well, that was odd." Samantha stared at the receiver.

Dixie sent her a questioning look.

Samantha briefed Dixie on the conversation as she hung up and then watched her aunt's face grow concerned.

"It's probably only one of the campers at the resort looking around, but I think I'll run over there to check on her," Samantha said.

Dixie nodded. "I think everyone is a little spooked over those murders. You do that, honey. I'll call Ford again and ask him to meet you up there." She smiled. "You were planning to run over to the resort for a little while anyway to see the kids again since you're leaving in the morning."

"Yes, I was." Samantha tried to smile back and act nonchalant as she gathered up her purse to leave, but she felt a sense of itchy worry. Paulette Everett wasn't the sort to imagine problems, and Samantha hadn't liked the panicked edge to her voice.

Backing her silver Acura out of the inn's garage, she headed down the familiar route to the Sycamore Lake Resort on the highway. En route, she put in another call to Ford herself and left him a message of her own as to where she was going. "Ford, I'm on my way over to the resort to check on Paulette at the event lodge. She called and said she thought someone was hanging around there. It made her nervous. Come up to the lodge as soon as you get this message. It's probably nothing but…" She looked at her watch. "It's about eleven thirty now."

Passing Ford's house, she noticed the garage door up and Ford's van gone. Evidently he was out somewhere with the kids.

Drawing on years of emergency training, Samantha slowed her car in caution as she came to the last cabin on the backside of the resort. Instead of driving on around the loop road to the event lodge and chapel, she decided to pull her car to the side of the road and walk in, too. Before locking her car, she snagged a small canister of OC pepper spray from her glove compartment and tucked it in her back pocket. Working alone so often, she knew it a strong defense if ever needed.

She edged her way along a side path to the point, versus walking directly in on the road. As she drew closer, she saw only Paulette's red Toyota parked by the big rustic event lodge.

Still feeling edgy, Samantha circled below the pavilion and walked up to the backside of the lodge. Moving closer, she peeked in to the large lodge room, being careful that her face wasn't visible to anyone inside.

Scanning the room, she saw all the evidence of Paulette's decorating in progress, with open boxes around on many tables. But no Paulette. As she inched on around the side of the building, to check the kitchen windows, a snort surprised her, stopping her in her tracks and making her catch her breath in surprise. A horse was tied up next to the back door.

What in the heck was a horse doing here? she asked herself. Feeling even more edgy now, she crept quietly to a window looking into the kitchen and froze at the sight there. A man had Paulette tied up to a kitchen chair and gagged, and he was pacing the kitchen floor talking to her. The man was older, grizzle-faced with a shock of white-gray hair, dressed in work boots, old gray slacks and a faded blue sweatshirt. And he was obviously upset.

Edging closer, Samantha could hear his voice. "A woman ought to love her husband and be true to him, not haul off and leave him just because things don't go so well. Your man, even if he made himself some mistakes, was still your man. Your husband you vowed to stand by."

The man paced, agitated and angry. "I've talked to you before. I told you that you ought to forgive your man, take him back. But you're stubborn and hard, just like she was. She wouldn't listen to reason either. Determined to do what was wrong. Things happen to people who don't do right."

Samantha saw him walk over to a nearby table to finger a length of wire and her heartbeat kicked up at the sight. "There's a punishment in this life fer a wrong. My Faye wouldn't stay with me. She wouldn't listen to reason neither. That's why her life had to end. It was all her fault, not mine."

His whiny voice now let Samantha know clearly the man was demented and she could see Paulette's eyes widen with fear.

The man walked closer to Paulette. "Your hair's purty, blond and curly like Faye's was." The man reached over to touch Paulette's hair, making her cringe and pull back.

Samantha looked around, trying to decide what to do. It was obviously too late to call anyone for help, and the man's revolver, also on the kitchen table, let her know she had to act wisely and quickly no matter what she did.

Samantha listened to the man babble on for a minute while planning her strategy, and then when he walked a distance away from Paulette, the table, and his weapon, she wrenched open the door—praying it wouldn't be locked as she did—sprang into the room and sprayed the man with pepper spray as he turned, startled, lurching towards her.

"Ahgggg!" he cried, holding his eyes and bending over, trying desperately to breath.

With the man immobilized, Samantha grabbed the gun on the table and pushed the struggling man into the kitchen closet behind him. She wedged a chair against the door to secure it and then grabbed her phone out of her back pocket and dialed 911 to call the police to the scene.

Keeping the gun poised on the door in case the man tried to break out, Samantha then used her other hand to get the gag off Paulette's mouth and untie her from the chair.

"Gracious heavens, I'm glad to see you," Paulette said, helping her with the rope ties. "That crazy man was going to kill me!"

"Let's get some more weight in front of that door until the police get here," Samantha said, looking around. "That pepper spray will take the man out for fifteen or more minutes, with burning and temporary blindness, spasms, coughing, and difficulty breathing, but I'd rather he didn't get out of that closet for any reason."

The two women began pushing whatever they could find of weight into a blockade around the door.

"Do you know who that man is?" Samantha asked.

"His name's Yancey Keaton. He lives on a back road somewhere off Green Hill Drive. I'm not sure exactly where. He hangs out a lot at the Cross Corner Market diner."

"Who was this Faye he talked about?"

She frowned. "His wife, I think. I seem to remember she got killed accidently a year or so ago." Paulette limped over to a chair. "Let me sit down. I'm starting to shake all over."

"Me, too," Samantha said, leaning against the kitchen table, but still keeping the gun in her hand.

Both heard the sirens wailing then.

"Looks like help is on the way." Paulette tried to smile. "Honey, I sure am glad you came. I tried calling Ford and even Jimmy when I thought I heard someone creeping around outside, but when the man knocked on the door, I figured he was only a visitor to the resort or something, looking for someone." She shook her head, closing her eyes. "I sure was wrong."

Samantha walked over to the kitchen door to open it as she heard the police heading into the front of the lodge. "We're back here in the kitchen," she called, spotting two officers heading in with guns drawn. "We're okay."

She and Paulette then told enough of the story to direct the officers to get Yancey out of the closet to take him into custody. Still staggering and struggling for breath, it wasn't much of a challenge to cuff him and take him outside to one of the police cruisers.

"Pepper spray?" one of the officers asked.

Samantha nodded.

He glanced at the gun she'd laid on the kitchen table beside the coil of wire. "Looks like you had good cause."

Paulette put a hand to her heart. "If Samantha hadn't acted fast, I'd be a dead woman now." She went over to hug her. "Thank you, honey. You truly saved my life."

One of the officers came forward. "I'm Police Chief Ben Barclay. Do you think you women could sit down and tell me what happened here?"

"Yes, but could we do that in the lodge room at one of the tables?" Samantha asked. "I think Paulette might like a change of scene and I wouldn't mind one, either."

As they headed into the open lodge room Ford burst through the front door, followed by Jimmy Everett, Paulette's ex-husband.

Jimmy's face looked white. "One of those officers out there said someone tried to kill you in here, Paulette. I was on my way here, after finding your message, and I heard all the sirens. Sweetheart, are you all right?" Heedless of the officers he ran over and grabbed Paulette into his arms and hugged her tight.

"I'm all right, Jimmy," she said, but then she burst into tears and let him hold and pat her again.

As Samantha watched, Ford walked over to reach an arm around her to pull her against his side discreetly. "Are you all right, too, Samantha?" he asked quietly.

She grinned up at him. "I've had better days, even in the middle of a tornado."

He smiled. "Storms do tend to find you or you find them."

The chief cleared his throat, interrupting the scene. "Ladies, I'm sorry to interrupt, but I need to get enough facts of this story to know why we have that man in the back of our vehicle waiting to transport to the jail."

They all settled around in a group of chairs at the end of one of the big tables in the lodge room then.

Paulette jumped up suddenly as they began to get comfortable.

"Let me pull back this white table cloth," she said. "I've got an event here later and I don't want things getting dirty." She moved decorations away from their end of the table and folded back the long white cloth carefully.

Jimmy grinned. "I think she's starting to feel more like herself."

Paulette punched at his arm. "Funny guy. Why don't you go in the kitchen to the refrigerator and get some of those bottles of cold water in there? I'd like to wash down the taste of that nasty gag I had in my mouth."

While Jimmy went after the water, Ford looked across at Samantha and Paulette. "I'd taken the kids over to get some things they needed for school at the dollar store," he said. "I left my cell phone at the house. When we got back, I'd just started to listen to my messages, when I heard the sirens. I'm sorry I didn't get here sooner to help."

As Jimmy came back in the room with their water, he said, "I was helping Tom Howard with a problem at the marina and I left my phone in the houseboat while I did. I still can't get used to carrying them blamed things around with me everywhere, but I can see I need to."

The chief nodded, introducing them to another man who'd just arrived. "This is Jim Culver, homicide detective working on this case. I alerted him as soon as your emergency call came in, Samantha. Now tell us what happened here."

Paulette began, telling her part of the story first. "I'm Paulette Everett. I was working here to set up for a big reunion event I'm catering tonight. While working, I started to feel like someone was watching me. Just a feeling. But then I started hearing some noises outside. Made me nervous, being alone out here at the point." She paused to take a long drink of her water. "I called Ford, didn't find him, and left a message. Then after hearing a little more rustling around behind the kitchen area, I called Jimmy. I didn't find him either. Then I called Dixie."

She shook her head. "The world's gotten to be a funny place where no one answers their dang phones anymore. You just have to leave a message and you never know when or if they'll get back to you. Fortunately, Samantha answered at Dixie's. I've found people with landlines still tend to actually answer their phones when you call. Lucky for me."

Samantha saw Ford and Jimmy exchange a guilty look.

"Why didn't you call the police?" Jim Culver asked.

She put both hands on her hips to give him an exasperated look. "Now surely you can imagine what you'd have said if I called to say I thought I heard something and had a creepy feeling about it?"

Jimmy sniggered.

Ben Barclay cleared his throat. "So tell us what happened after you made the calls."

Paulette continued her story. "While I was talking with Samantha, I saw a man knock on the door. I thought then, seeing an older man, it was probably just a visitor at the resort, maybe someone staying at the campground or one of the cabins, looking for someone. But when I went to open the door, he pulled a gun on me."

"You'd locked the doors?" he asked.

"I locked the front door after I finished unloading and started decorating, but I left the back door to the kitchen open so I could take things out to the trashcans as I needed to."

Samantha noticed Jim Culver taking notes as they talked.

Paulette sighed. "Fear hit me real hard when I saw the gun. I guess I wasn't thinking so much of the past murders as maybe of getting raped." She dropped her eyes to her hands. "He was babbling and talking while he made me go in the kitchen where he tied me up to one of those old chairs with arms. I didn't nearly wet my pants, though, until I saw him get a big coil of wire out of his side pocket and put it on the table."

"Did you know the man?" Jim Culver asked.

"Not at first, but then I remembered I'd seen him now and again at the Cross Corner Market. His name is Yancey Keaton I think. Norma mentioned it once. Evidently he was one of the café's regulars. Didn't live far away."

Ben Barclay looked at Jim Culver. "I thought I recognized the man. We got called out to his house about a year and a half ago when his wife Faye accidently fell down the stairs."

Paulette snorted. "You might want to look at that case a little more closely. I'd guess that crazy man killed his wife. He kept talking about someone named Faye that deserved to die."

Samantha saw Ben Barclay wince.

"What other things did the man say while he had you tied up that might help us link these murders?" Jim Culver asked. "Did he mention any other names? Did he say anything more about his wife?"

Paulette closed her eyes. "He said his wife wanted to leave him, that he tried to talk her out of it. Said it was wrong for a woman to leave a man. He started ranting on about how women should forgive men for their wrongs, not leave them, take them back." She looked toward Jimmy, her face flushing. "He said I should forgive my husband and take him back. Said women who didn't forgive their husbands and take them back had to pay."

Jim Culver's eyebrows lifted and he passed a look to Chief Barclay.

Paulette frowned. "He also said I had pretty blond curly hair like his wife Faye's." Paulette's eyes widened and she leaned forward with a little gasp. "Oh, my gosh. Shirley Crawford had short blond curly hair, too. That creepy man even patted and played with my hair. It gave me the creeps."

"I saw that," Samantha added.

"Is that all?" Ben asked Paulette.

She put her hands to her face. "I think so. While he was ranting and talking crazy, Samantha crashed in through the kitchen door, sprayed him with pepper spray and grabbed the gun. I was scared then he'd try to kill her, but that spray really messed him up. He was screaming, clawing his face and he could hardly breathe. Samantha opened that big closet behind him and pushed him in it. I saw him fall to the floor in there before she slammed the door shut."

Paulette looked toward Samantha beside her. "That was real smart thinking, honey."

She turned back to the officers. "Samantha called you then—called 911. She pushed a chair up against the closet door, and then got me out of that gag and untied me from the chair. Then we barricaded the closet door with some more pieces of furniture." She rubbed her arms, wincing. "I'm sure going to have some rope burns from that rough old rope."

Ben turned to Samantha. "What made you come over to the lodge and decide to take this criminal on by yourself?"

Samantha felt annoyed at the wording of his question. "Although you make it sound as if I knew I'd run into a murderer here, that wasn't exactly how it happened. Paulette sounded upset when she called. I knew she wasn't the squeamish sort ordinarily. I've known her since I was a girl. I told Aunt Dixie I'd come over to check on her. She felt worried, too. The world has a lot of creepy, odd people in it. I thought maybe some guy was hanging around the lodge peeping in at Paulette or that one of the campers, staying at the resort, had wandered over. It could have been something or nothing."

Samantha drank some of the water. "I phoned Ford again as I drove into the resort. I noted, too, that his van was gone as I passed by his house." She hesitated. "I work in some pretty serious weather conditions on the road. I've learned to be prepared for difficulties and for difficult people. So as I drew closer to the event lodge, I parked my car, put my spray in my back pocket and walked in. I walked around to the back of the lodge, too. I didn't see anyone inside, only the beginnings of Paulette's decorations." She gestured around.

"It wasn't until I went around toward the kitchen that I met my surprises." She smiled at the officers. "There is a horse tied up behind the kitchen in case your officers haven't found him yet. It seems very likely Yancey Keaton rode in to the resort." Samantha grinned to see both Ben and Jim Culver's eyes widen.

Ben gestured to an officer at the door, who came over for a quick consultation and then left.

Samantha turned to Ford. "Where does the Highpoint Trail behind the loop road lead?"

"Up and over the ridge to the back fence line of the resort property. From there the trail loops and returns to where it started," he answered. "As a boy I used to cut over the fence at the back of our property line, though, and hike down through the woods to come out on a back road off Green Hill Road where one of my friends lived. I'm sure there are other trails through the woods I haven't explored, as well."

Ben nodded at his words. "Seems like I remember Yancey's place was back there somewhere."

"He could have ridden in, bringing victims tied over his horse," Jim Culver proposed. "It could explain how they got here and perhaps why. If he took the other women to his home and killed them there, he could have loaded them on the horse and brought them here to the resort so they wouldn't be found near his house."

"Remember, too, that Norma, Shirley, and Paulette all had blond curly hair like Yancey's wife," Samantha couldn't help adding. "I think that man isn't right in his mind and focused his attention in some way on those three women in particular because they reminded him of Faye."

Paulette nodded. "And maybe because all three of us were separated or divorced women, too." She glanced at Jimmy. "Norma's, Shirley's, and my husband all wanted us to get back with them, too."

Ben scratched his head. "I think I remember Yancey spent a long time in the military in past. I'll need to check on that. We'll study into all this."

Jim Culver closed the small notebook he'd been writing in. "I think we've asked all the questions we need to for now. As we investigate this further, I'm sure we'll have more questions to ask you, though."

Samantha started to say they'd better ask any questions of her soon as she'd be leaving in the morning, but decided better of it. If they didn't suggest she stay in the area, she had no reason not to leave tomorrow as planned. If they called Dixie to question her later, Dixie could give them her Atlanta number. She could answer their questions in Atlanta as well as here.

As the men stood, Paulette said, "Excuse me, but I think you men owe Samantha King a big thank you, don't you? If she hadn't come over here when she did you'd have another dead body on your hands right now. In addition, she used her head, thought smart, and acted fast. She not only saved my life but incapacitated your criminal for you."

"Be assured the police are always grateful for help," Ben said, not willing to say more. He looked around then. "Do any of you need transport back to your homes?"

"We all have cars," Ford answered. "And thank you for arriving so quickly," he added, trying to soothe Paulette's criticism.

Samantha hid her smile as she and Pauline stood to say goodbye.

As the officers left, Jimmy moved closer to Paulette. "My heart would have died if anything happened to you Paulie." He wrapped her in another big hug again. "You keep thinking on my apologies for being such a danged fool. I must have eaten a crazy bean to get involved with that woman like I did. I promise you if you'll consider taking me back you can be sure I'll never stray again. I love you, sweetheart. Today showed me that even more. Don't let my one foolish lapse ruin all the love and years we've shared together." He paused. "What can I do to show you that I'm sincere?"

Samantha saw Paulette's eyes soften. "For today, you can help me get this lodge set up and decorated and that pavilion fixed up. I need lights all around that little pavilion outside and you can help me with that." She glanced at her watch. "I'm way behind with all this craziness happening today."

"I'll get right on it and tomorrow after your event's over, I'll take you to dinner at the Chop House in Kodak. You like it there."

"We'll see," she said, but Samantha saw her smile.

Samantha looked at Ford. "Is there anything else you need to do here before we leave?"

"I guess not." He smiled at the scene of Paulette beginning to direct Jimmy to the box of lights not yet unpacked.

Samantha gave Paulette a little wave and then started out the front door.

As they walked outside, they saw an officer leading the horse around from behind the lodge to load him into a horse trailer.

"I'll walk you down to your car," Ford said, moving into stride beside her as they started down the road.

The truck pulling the horse trailer soon traveled past them.

Samantha laughed. "I'll bet that horse could tell some tales. Wonder what he thought about carrying dead women over the mountain on his back?"

Ford paused and then yanked her over to the side of the road under a big sycamore tree to grab her and kiss her. "You crazy woman," he said against her lips after a while. "You could have gotten yourself killed. What if you'd missed with that spray, tripped, or he'd gotten to that gun before you?"

She put her hands to his face. "Then he would have killed Paulette. I had to try to save her, Ford. There wasn't time to call for help or to wait."

He kissed her again. "Do you know how much I love you? I totally lost it when I came in and got all those upset messages from Paulette, from Dixie, and then from you. I left the kids alone, tore out to my car and then heard those sirens. The last two times I heard them, I got to view dead women. I can't tell you how I felt driving up here and then the relief in my heart to come in behind the police to see you were all right." He ran his hands down her arms and back as if confirming her okay even now.

She leaned into him, enjoying the mannish scent and feel of him, locking the memory in her senses to take with her. "I'm fine, Ford. Really I am."

"And you're so calm. Even making jokes."

She chuckled a little. "I'm used to pressured, tense situations. And you weren't around when I looked in that window and saw Paulette tied up and gagged with that crazy man walking around babbling. That's when I had my moments and especially when I saw that coil of wire on the table. I knew then I'd run into the murderer and I knew what he could do." She looked into Ford's dark, concerned eyes. "You may be sure I was scared then, too, Ford. I knew, though, that I was the only one who could save Paulette. I had to try. You would have done the same thing."

He closed his eyes and sighed. "I'm sure I would have." He smiled a little then. "But I think I might have wanted to hurt him worse than you did, belt him a few times before throwing him in the closet."

She pushed her hair back. "Believe me, if you've never been blasted with pepper spray, he probably suffered enough."

"Listen, Samantha, if you don't feel like going back to see the kids, they'll understand. You've been through a lot already." He made a face. "And you know they'll ask a million questions."

"It will calm me to talk to them, make me feel normal again." She ran a hand down his face. "Being with you calms me, too."

He ran a hand over her face and lips. "Being with you calms me sometimes, but other times being with you drives me nearly out of my mind, excites me, paints wild and crazy pictures in my head."

"I like the idea that I ruffle your feathers when you're usually such a calm, sensible, and controlled man."

"I can assure you that you definitely ruffle my feathers." He kissed her again.

She pulled back at last. "We need to go. The kids will be wondering where you are; they will have heard the sirens."

"Dad and mom are with them. I called them on the way up here."

"Then they'll be wondering what happened, too."

They walked toward Samantha's car parked around the corner.

"Do you still want to go to dinner tonight at Angelos?" he asked. "It might be too much for you after a day like this."

She grinned at him. "What did Paulette do after the police left? Faint away, whine, and go home to lie down?"

He laughed. "No, she's a trooper like you." He stopped to lean over to pick up a pinecone on the ground. "I kind of hope she and Jimmy will get back together now. I think he's really sorry for being unfaithful. They shared a long, rich life together. Maybe she'll consider that and forgive him."

"Dixie told me that God's a God of second chances. So maybe Pauline will decide it's right to try again."

He fell quiet for a few minutes. "Being someone's first love is sweet, finding the person you think you can live all your days with, want to share your hours and life with, but to find a second love can be even sweeter. "

She fixed her gaze on him. "So you think love is sweeter the second time around, like the old song?"

"I might not have thought so once, but I know so now."

CHAPTER 22

Later that evening, Ford dropped off all eight of his children at Ben and Vickie's house before driving to pick up Samantha for their dinner date. It was rare for him to get an evening out on his own and he couldn't remember one time he'd had an actual date since Laura died.

"Are you sure you don't mind keeping all these kids for me?" he asked Ben.

"Nah, go have a good time, buddy. You're due," Ben answered, grinning and slapping him on the back.

Hating to pick up Samantha in the huge family van, Ford drove it back to the resort to trade it for his smaller SUV. Out of sight of the kids now, he sprinted into the house to check himself in the mirror one more time, studying his neat gray pinstriped shirt and dark gray slacks. Did he look all right? Dressed up but not too much?

"I'm too out of practice with this dating stuff," he said to himself, adding cologne and checking to make sure his socks matched. Then he locked up and headed over to the Dandridge Inn.

"Samantha honey, Ford is here," Dixie called as she let him in the front door of the inn a short time later and then led him to the drawing room in the middle of the house.

"We'll just sit down here for a minute to wait for her." Dixie settled into one of the comfortable old chairs in the family room, gesturing to another nearby for him.

He settled across from her, trying to think of something to say, feeling as nervous and awkward as a high school boy picking up his date on a Saturday night. If Dixie noticed his awkwardness though, she didn't comment on it, but simply chatted away in her usual amiable way until Samantha came around the corner to stop in the doorway, smiling at him.

Ford felt his breath catch in his throat as he looked up at her. She was wearing a dress. His eyes swept over the soft yellow dress, floating below her knees. He rarely saw her in a dress.

"You look really nice," he said, standing up after realizing he'd sat there too long staring at her like a lovesick cow.

"Thank you. So do you." Her eyes drifted over his neat shirt and slacks.

"Well, you two enjoy a nice time," Dixie said, standing herself. "The Fergusons and the Jordans are staying here tonight, two couples I know that have stayed with me before. They drove down the highway to eat at Cowboy's on the lake, but I'll be busy entertaining them when they come back. They love to play rummy. So you two stay out as long as you like."

"Thanks, but we won't be late," Ford answered politely, still feeling awkward as he led Samantha out the front door.

Samantha winked at him as he tucked her into his car. "I felt like a kid again saying goodnight to Aunt Dixie before a date," she said, echoing his thoughts.

He laughed with her as he pulled out of the driveway, talking and feeling easier and more comfortable now. Ford drove over the bridge behind downtown Dandridge, and soon turned left on a side road to Angelo's at the Point, a nice local restaurant on Douglas Lake.

"Do you want to eat inside or out?" Ford asked Samantha as he helped her out of the car.

"Outside on the patio and in a quiet spot away from the bar if we can manage it."

They fortunately got their wish and soon settled into a table close to the lake, tucked away from the other diners. Since it was a special occasion, Ford ordered two glasses of the restaurant's house Riesling after asking Samantha's preference.

"Ah, this is nice," Samantha said, looking out across the lake with its silvery appearance in the early evening.

"Yes, and it's nice being here with you." Ford's eyes moved over her appreciatively. "That dress is really beautiful on you—soft and sunflower yellow. You know, the first time you stormed up to my vet clinic you were wearing that color. I've seen it on you often since. It suits you perfectly."

She blushed at his compliment. "You're acting very sweet tonight and I didn't realize you were so observant about what I wear."

"More so than you know," he replied. "I've been storing up memories to take out and look at in my mind later on."

"I think I like this new romantic side of you," she quipped to shift the mood. "What's in that bag you're carrying?"

He picked up a somewhat large gift bag from beside his chair to put it on the table in front of her. "The children sent you gifts to take home with you. They meant to give them to you this afternoon, but with all that was going on, we forgot."

"We all had a somewhat hectic day, that's for sure." She wiggled her eyebrows at him as she dug into the bag.

Wrapped in tissue at the top was an enlarged photo of Samantha with all the children sitting in a row on two picnic tables pushed together, the lake sparkling behind them.

"Oh, I love this," she said smiling and studying the children's happy faces.

"There's more," Ford said.

"I can see that," she replied, starting to unwrap what she quickly saw was another photo.

"That's one that Madison took of us together," Ford explained. "She and Natalie found the frame for it."

It was a sweet photo of them standing in the old gazebo, the sky colorful with a sunset behind them of pinks, blues, and golden yellow.

Samantha flushed over this one. "We look rather fond of each other in this shot, don't we?"

He chuckled. "That we do. I seem to recall that as one of those times we got caught up in one of those gathering storms no one else but us noticed."

"We do tend to experience those moments sometimes." She laughed. "What else is in here? Those children shouldn't have felt they needed to buy gifts for me."

"Don't worry. I donated a little money to the cause when they came up with the idea. I helped pick out the next two also."

"Then why am I not surprised it's one of your signs." She pulled out a rustic wooden sign labeled Lake Rules and began to read the different rule suggestions. "Sit in the sun; Take long walks; Relax and go fishing; Gather with family." She almost choked up over that particular one, but then recovered to read on. "Eat too much —that is so true!" She laughed. "Read a good book; Just breathe; Be grateful for this day." She hugged the sign to her. "I really love this, Ford."

"I'm glad," he said, watching her struggle with her emotions.

She dug into the bag to pull out the next gift.

"Another sign," she said, grinning. She read the words *The Lake Is My Happy Place*, sniffling now and brushing away a few tears, not the norm for her.

"These are perfect memories," she said looking across the table and smiling at him. "I'm going to make a decorative cluster of these signs and photos right inside the entry of my apartment. I know the perfect place."

"If our happy place here at the lake calls to your heart," Ford said softly, reaching over to brush away a tear. "Listen to it and come back any time."

She didn't answer, tucking her gifts back into the colorful bag and sitting it on the floor by her chair.

Their waiter arrived then to take their order. Ford ordered prime rib, one of Angelo's specialties, and Samantha decided on crab cakes.

"We'll have salads ahead, too," Ford directed. "Homemade blue cheese dressing for me, I think." He looked to Samantha.

"I'll have the honey mustard," she said, glad the waiter came when he did to break the intense moment developing. This was a sweet night but it wouldn't be an easy one to get through for either of them.

"Have you heard any more from the detective about the murders?" she asked to redirect their conversation.

"Jim Culver, the homicide detective, stopped by late this afternoon, not long before I came to get you. He drove out specifically to give Dad and me an update. Since our resort was so heavily involved in the murders, I asked him to let us know anything they learned as soon as they could."

"Did the police find more evidence?"

"They did; they've been working rapidly since earlier today." He took silverware out of his napkin as he talked and dropped his napkin over his lap. "First they learned while checking Yancey's military and medical records that he had PTSD and some mental health issues."

Samantha almost laughed. "Why does that not surprise me?"

"It shouldn't surprise any of us now," he replied. "Friends and other family, that Jim Culver talked to, said Faye planned to leave Yancey because of his instability and temper snaps. However, there's no evidence of Yancey killing Faye. According to the police records, she fell down the stairs at their home. In the report Yancey claimed he came home from work to find her dead. The police are still looking into that one."

Samantha offered a thank you to their waiter as he brought their salads.

Ford continued when he left. "At Yancey's home, they did find old blood stains that point to the other murders being committed at his home. I'm sure they'll analyze those more as the investigation moves on."

"There are still so many unanswered questions. I keep wondering how Yancey got those women to come to his house."

"Probably by force or gunpoint. The areas around Green Hill Road are rural, the drives and side roads have few homes on them."

"Did they find a way Yancey could have brought the women over to the resort from his house?"

"Yes. A rough trail winds through the woods behind his home and up over the ridge to a spot on the resort's back property line. Jim said the officers who investigated the trail said it looked like the barbed-wire fence had been cut and repaired more than once."

"So he probably brought the women over to the resort by that trail."

"It looks that way. Maury Beck said Yancey knew the resort well from all the times he's fished at the lake."

"It would be a way to move suspicion away from him to take the bodies to another place, too."

He nodded. "Jim Culver said photos of Yancey's wife Faye, found at the house, show that she greatly resembled Norma, Shirley, and Paulette in looks, like Paulette suggested. All were of a similar height and age and each with blond curly hair."

Samantha drummed her fingers on the table. "I'll bet Yancey had a part in Faye's death, and in some twisted way wanted to continue to punish her through the other women."

"I guess no one will know all those facts unless Yancey confesses more. Right now he isn't saying much." Ford stopped to eat more of his salad.

"Even if a little loony, Yancey acted smart in how he planned and executed his crimes," Samantha said. "He might know, too, that it's smart to stay as silent as possible at this point, or a savvy lawyer might have cautioned him to keep his counsel."

"You're probably right," Ford agreed.

The waiter stopped by to add a little wine to their glasses.

"Jim Culver went to talk to Paulette more, too," Ford told her. "Paulette said she remembered a time in the restaurant eating lunch with Shirley when Yancey was there. It's a small café. Paulette said he could easily have overhead the two of them talking about their marital situations, their husbands wanting to reconcile."

"I wondered how he knew so much about Shirley and Paulette's lives." Samantha paused, thinking. "It looks like, the same way he got angry at his wife for wanting to leave him, that he got angry at Norma, Shirley, and Paulette for the same reason. It's a sad, twisted story overall, isn't it?"

"It sure is," he agreed, finishing the last of his salad. "On a positive note, though, Paulette told me she and Jimmy are getting back together again."

"Oh, that's good to hear." Her eyes lit up at the news. 'I always liked Jimmy and I know Paulette misses him. I like to think of them back together."

Their dinner came and they changed their conversation to more casual topics. They talked about the weather, the children, and small happenings in their day.

"Did the Hickmans decide to still hold their anniversary party at the event lodge after learning Paulette was nearly killed there?" Samantha asked. "I know Paulette and Jimmy kept right on setting up, but I wondered if the event would cancel or be moved to a later time or place."

"The Hickmans didn't cancel. Dad said he stopped by to see Paulette later in the day, to make sure she was okay. Paulette told him she called the Hickmans to let them know what happened," Ford answered. "Bruce and Flora Hickman said they saw no reason not to hold their anniversary party at the resort if Paulette was okay with it. They said it would make great dinner conversation."

She laughed. "I imagine so."

"Dad and I were glad they didn't cancel; it sort of helps to take the stain off our resort."

"I know all of you are grateful this is past."

"I think that goes without saying," he agreed.

As they finished their meal, Ford talked her into dessert and coffee. While they waited for key lime cheesecake, Ford took a breath and then leaned forward. "I want to talk to you about something."

Samantha gave him a wary look. "Look, let's simply enjoy this time, Ford, and not talk about the future. Let's not put out any questions or issues we've already discussed."

Ford shifted in his seat. "Well, this is something different," he said. "But I feel it's important."

She waited, watching him hesitate. "Spit it out, Ford."

He sighed. "Okay. Laura loved babies, loved children, even loved being pregnant. She experienced easy births, seemed at her happiest when pregnant or carrying a baby around. She never seemed to mind all the sleepless nights that came with babies, the care, or the times of sickness. She was a cheerful woman with the children even at the worst of times, and handled all of them well."

Samantha listened, obviously wondering where this was going.

"I didn't fare so easily," he confided. "I admit I often suggested spreading out the births of our children more, limiting the numbers." He rubbed his neck. "I wasn't as eager and enthusiastic as Laura to take in four children when Andrea and Adam died either. The idea of eight small children under the age of ten overwhelmed my mind. Two were babies, two toddlers. You often suggested I was so good and generous to do all that, to take on that obligation we committed to with Andrea and Adam. But I have to tell you it never dawned on me in a million years they would die early like they did, that I actually might need to raise their children as well as ours. Anyway, my point is I wasn't as noble through all that time as you seem to think. It was probably because of that I harbored a little bitterness toward you. Before you left, I wanted to say I'm sorry for that and to tell you I now understand your decision better."

She smiled at him. "Well, thanks for that, although I think we sort of discussed this before."

He looked out over the lake, uncomfortable.

"Do you still feel guilty about those feelings?" she asked. "Or about not being as enthusiastic as Laura?"

"No." He took a deep breath. "But I feel guilty that I had an operation to ensure there wouldn't be more than eight children in our home. Laura had this tendency to be careless about birth control when eager for another child." He gave Samantha a pained look. "I never told Laura I had the operation. I meant to, but I never did. Then, of course, I couldn't."

"So now you're still beating yourself up over that?" she asked softly, reaching out to put a hand over his.

"Probably a little, but I worry more that this might cause a problem for you if things changed for us in the future."

"Ahhh," she said, realization dawning at last. "You think I might want to have a child."

"Women often bear children even into their upper thirties today, and you haven't been married before or known that experience. I thought you might want it."

The waiter came bringing coffee and dessert, and Samantha busied herself with it for a few minutes.

Finally after the waiter left she said, "You are a good, fine man, Ford McDaniel. I count myself fortunate to have met you. And since you've bared your soul here, I guess I need to bare mine."

"Listen, don't feel that you …"

Samantha held up a hand, when he started to argue and intervene. "No, let me have my turn, Ford." She stopped to think how to begin. "When I moved into broadcasting as a meteorologist, it was suggested to us, in a meeting at Weather First, that any new single women on staff consider getting on some type of birth control. They reminded us that a meteorologist's job is a highly public one with high visibility. A number of women experience problems with being stalked; a few attacked or raped."

She looked down at her lap. "As you know, television tends to select meteorologists who are not only well educated and well qualified but attractive. It was explained to us that this makes the young women even more a target. Additionally, meteorologists often work late nights out in the field or in office and sometimes work alone, walking into dark garages by themselves, tramping through alleyways covering weather, encountering a diverse population of people." She shrugged, hoping he got the idea.

"After considering my options, I decided on an IUD. I was one of those one in a zillion women where something went wrong with that. Perforation and infection. It left me with a bunch of problems that put childbearing out of the picture for me." Samantha, probably glad for the darkness, looked out over the lake, not wanting to meet Ford's eyes.

"This happened about the time Andrea was happily at home with a beautiful baby and expecting another," she continued. "I'll admit, that I selfishly avoided coming home much at that time. I hadn't actively wanted a child, or even a family, but the idea of all my choices regarding that taken away from me hurt. In a way I hadn't expected." She tried to send him a bright smile. "So you see even if you yearned for another child, I wouldn't be a good candidate for the job."

He reached over and took her hand before she could snatch it away. "I'm sorry Samantha."

"Well, don't pity me." She glared at him. "Unlike Andrea, I wanted a fulfilling career foremost and I wasn't certain if I ever wanted to take time from my career to bear children anyway. I have a great job, as you know, and a happy and satisfying life. I only shared this with you because you've been so candid with me."

"We all carry our secrets that others seldom know."

"That's true." She grinned at him. "Besides, as the sign in your home says so well, eight really is enough children for any home. I wouldn't worry that any woman you might want to align your life with would want more than that regardless of who she is."

He smirked. "That's good to know."

She pulled her cheesecake toward her, wanting to shift the topic of conversation again. "We should eat our dessert now before the waiter comes worrying we don't like it."

Ford picked up his fork and began to eat, not pushing her to talk about this subject more.

Both fell quiet for a time as they ate, thinking about what the other had shared.

Finally Ford said, "Thanks for sharing with me, Samantha, and for letting me share with you. I've carried around guilt and worry most of the summer that if I told you that I couldn't have more children your interest in me might change."

She gave him one of her saucy looks then. "My interest in you, Ford McDaniel—if you want to call it that—is based on my respect for you as a person and on the amazing attraction that flares between us. I'm sure you know what I mean about the latter."

He gave her a slow soft grin. "Yes, I do. I've known attraction in the past, but nothing like this before. Perhaps every relationship has its own special qualities, grows from its own unique artistry."

"Perhaps." A small smile twitched at her lips.

Ford could feel the air begin to sizzle between them as he looked in her eyes and his skin prickled as the awareness between them spread. "I want you to know this flare between us is like nothing I've ever known before. It's the sort of thing to keep a man awake at night imagining."

"You're not making this evening easier with talk like that," Samantha said on a whisper.

Ford reached a hand under the table to put it on her knee. "If you miss me, if you miss this storm—and this lightning—that brews between us, come back if you can find a way. If I thought I could say anything to cause you not to leave me, you know I would. I have fallen deeply in love with you. I want you in my life in a fierce protective way I can't explain to you."

"I know." She put her hand in his under the table and they sat there simply looking at each other for a time, enjoying the warmth, the knowing of affection, the surge of physical attraction passing between them.

Ford's cell phone rang then, interrupting the moment. He pulled it out, glanced down at the number and then answered.

"Daddy, I'm sorry to interrupt your date but Rebecca is throwing up and crying," Natalie said. "I heard Ben and Vickie say they hated to call you when they knew you and Samantha were having your dinner, but Rebecca is crying really hard. You know how she gets, almost hysterical. She's crying that she wants to go home, that she wants you, and she's getting a fever. Ben took her temperature."

Ford glanced at Samantha with regret. "You were right to call me, Natalie. Samantha and I just finished our dinner, and she has a long trip ahead of her tomorrow. I'll take her back to the inn, run by the lodge to get my van, and come get all of you." He glanced at his watch. "Tell Rebecca I'll be there soon."

He lifted his hand to flag the waiter as he hung up, explained that he needed to leave quickly and passed the young man a credit card.

"I'm sorry, Samantha," he said. "Ben and Vickie have all eight of my children at their house tonight. It was a lot to ask in the best of times." He shrugged. "And now Rebecca is throwing up, crying, and sick."

"Of course you need to go," she said, picking up her purse and gift bag as the waiter returned with a tab for Ford to sign. "I had a lovely time and you know it was time for us to say goodnight anyway."

Ford signed for their dinner and then put a hand to her back as they walked out to the car. In the darkness as he opened the door for her, he leaned in to kiss her, backing her against the car. "I had in mind more time to enjoy moments like this with you before we said goodnight," he murmured against her neck, closing his eyes to take in the warmth and sweetness of her.

Samantha kissed him back in the darkness, kicking up his heartbeat. She didn't stop him from kissing her again when he let her out at the inn.

Ford held her tight for a long time before pulling away at last. "I'll miss you more than I can say."

He took a deep breath as he walked around the car to let her out, trying to calm and collect himself. At the front door, with the bright porch lights blazing all around them, and Dixie probably listening for them, Ford didn't do more than hold her hand a little too long before he opened the door for her.

Driving away, he thought of how many times he'd said goodbye to people he loved—not wanting to say goodbye, hurting and in pain to do so. He'd stood as a boy at his grandparents' graves, not understanding why they had to die young and leave him. He'd grieved again when Andrea and Adam Bradley were senselessly killed in an auto wreck, leaving four small children alone and scared. Then only three years later, his heart barely healed, he'd buried Laura, snatched from him by a sudden death, giving him no warning, leaving him torn in two with grief and trying to comfort eight small children who'd loved her, too.

And now Samantha had left him. At least she hadn't died, he thought. He should comfort himself with that. He would see her again. Hold her again perhaps. But it would be small comfort tonight as he climbed into his bed alone, after he picked up the kids, and small comfort in the days ahead as he grieved her loss, missed her every day, and ached for her.

"God, you've helped me before. Help me again," he prayed. "She's woken me as if from a long sleep. This time won't be easy now that I'm alive again."

CHAPTER 23

Samantha's drive back to Atlanta proved uneventful. She settled back into her apartment by evening, raced out to the store to pick up groceries, and reported to work on Monday morning.

The next two weeks were hectic, filled with meetings, briefings and a jam-packed schedule with her filling in for a variety of jobs as needed for Weather First. Used to more casual dress in the field, she had to dig through her wardrobe for the dresses she needed for the forecasts she covered as asked, subbing for other broadcasters on vacation or out sick.

At home, on an off day mid week, Samantha sat sharing dinner with her roommate Margie Benson. They sat out on the patio deck of her apartment at a small table, both in shorts, old T-shirts, and flip-flops.

"Thanks for throwing dinner together," Margie said, propping her feet on the deck rail. "First my team was down in New Orleans covering Hurricane Barry in July, then in Oklahoma reporting on those tornadoes, and after that we flew to California to bounce around keeping up with those earthquakes." She turned to Samantha. "In truth, would you ever move out to California after all the quakes and fires we've covered there? Especially anywhere near that San Andreas Fault line?"

Samantha smiled at her. "It's not on the top of my list."

"Mine either." Margie babbled on while they ate.

Samantha loved Margie's dramatic nature and talkativeness. Her sunny, fun nature had helped to fill up some of the heartache and loneliness Samantha had battled since coming back home.

"I love this salad." Margie put a hand to her heart. "What's in it? You are such a good cook."

"This is an Avocado Shrimp Salad—simple ingredients and super easy to make. I sautéed shrimp with Cajun seasoning, garlic, and butter and then tossed it over romaine lettuce, chopped tomatoes, purple onion, cucumber, sliced avocadoes, and fresh corn left over from last night. The dressing is just olive oil with a little fresh lemon juice and chopped cilantro." She grinned at Margie. "You could make this."

"Is it one of your Aunt Dixie's recipes?"

"It is. If I have any cooking skills, Dixie gets the credit for it. Andrea and I were both taught to cook from the time we could stand on a stool in the kitchen."

Margie took another bite of the salad and made an appreciative face. "Well, this salad is fabulous and I am thrilled to benefit from your cooking expertise, which I've enjoyed ever since I got back. Be sure to thank Aunt Dixie for me."

"I will. She'll appreciate the compliment."

"While I've been on the road, how has your job been going?" Margie asked.

"Weather First has kept me busy in the studio, filling in shifts for forecasters on vacation, covering office duties, and sticking me out in the field for local storms and weather conditions. Like that flood outside Atlanta and the bridge that collapsed." She smirked. "I think Weather First decided I needed a couple of weeks of boot camp to see if I was really back up to speed after nearly a year out. They've given me grueling hours, an erratic, irregular schedule, lots of overtime, mornings up at four to do the early forecasts, night shifts and more."

"Well, I'm sure you passed with flying colors. When will you be back on the team and out in the field again?"

"Sometime in September."

Margie laughed. "Or as soon as the first big hurricane or disaster hits."

They ate their salads, listening to the sounds around the apartment complex—car doors slamming, laughter, muted conversation as people walked by. Everyday noises.

"I'm glad you're back." Margie sighed. "It's helped me to stay at your place, too. I still miss Evan many days, even if it didn't work out between us."

"How long were you married?"

"Not even two years."

"I liked Evan the one I time I met him," Samantha said, trying to picture him in her mind. "Steady, nice guy."

"That was Evan. He ran the family hardware store with his brother Tom. Good, dependable small town guy."

"How did you meet him?"

"In my hometown at Christmas one year. I'm from Starkville, Mississippi. I went to school with Evan." She picked up a last piece of avocado to stick in her mouth. "Looking back, I think I got nostalgic that Christmas, remembering the joys of growing up there. And Evan was so different from all the players, the high energy and high profile types of men we meet. You know." She shrugged.

"I do."

Margie brushed back her short dark hair and gave Samantha a regretful look. "I think I was a new change for Evan, too. Maybe an exciting change." She looked away. "He hadn't realized I'd be gone so much though. He thought I'd change, want to stay home, start a family. He didn't understand me at all."

She laughed with a tinge of regret. "Can you imagine me in an apron, cooking, pregnant with a toddler crawling around on the floor and a pile of laundry on the counter?"

"That's what Evan wanted?"

"Yes." She pushed the last of her salad around on her plate. "I learned after Evan asked for a divorce that he'd met someone else. A nice waitress at the restaurant next to the hardware store, who dreamed of the life I didn't want. They're married now." She looked away. "I hope I'm on location this Christmas. I sort of hate to go home."

A thought suddenly floated through Samantha's mind of someone else coming into Ford's life. Someone who only wanted to be a wife and a mom. Content and happy to look after Ford and the kids. The image hurt.

Wishing to avoid the scenes parading through her thoughts, Samantha said, "Let's go down to the pool and swim some laps. Cool off."

Margie brightened. "Yes, and check out the men." She winked at Samantha as she stood to gather up their supper dishes.

Pushing open the sliding door with one hand, Margie added, "I've loved living here with you at the apartment just to enjoy all the men. Plus your place is so close to the office at Weather First."

Samantha followed Margie inside, shutting the door.

"Do you mind me staying on a little longer?" Margie asked. "If you'd rather have your privacy back again, several other apartments are opening up nearby. I want to stay here in the complex though. Even if I moved I wouldn't be too far for us to hang out when we both get time off at the same time."

"Just stay for now," Samantha offered. "I have two bedrooms." She smiled at Margie. "I've enjoyed your company, too."

Margie carried their dishes into the kitchen. "I'll bet like me you were glad to get out of small town, U.S.A., and back to the city, even if your aunt owns that nice old inn on the river. I looked up Dandridge on the Internet. It's a really out-of-the-way place even if cute. I imagine you got bored trying to find something to do there while you recovered."

Samantha didn't comment, working to clean up the remains of dinner. She'd shared nothing of her private life with Margie or with any of her friends and colleagues at Weather First. In the highly public arena she worked in, she'd always kept her private life tight and close. This time was no exception. And with Margie here, she'd kept her photos of Ford and the children and her lake signs tucked in a box under her bed.

Two days later, with a major hurricane starting to brew in the

Caribbean and projected to head into the Atlantic to slam into the North Carolina coast by the weekend, Margie and Samantha were both directed to pack their bags to head to cover the incoming storm. Early projections showed the storm should hit land somewhere between Myrtle Beach and the Outer Banks, so the storm teams were split out to cover several areas, all preparing for possible impact. Margie's team was sent north to Topsail Beach above Wilmington, Samantha's to Creswell Beach on Oak Island below Southport. The other two teams went south to Myrtle Beach and north to Cape Hatteras for now. In the days to come they would know more clearly where the storm's eye would hit and how severe the storm would be as it approached land.

Arriving far in advance, Samantha's team took rooms at the far end of a group of secure rental villas across from Oak Island's golf course community. The villas had patios looking out directly on the beach for good coverage and if the storm surge began to encroach too closely, the station had arranged for accommodations in villas in the golf community across the road on higher ground. Samantha was working with familiar crew members and camera staff, along with storm team forecaster Alex Hart. As often the case, she was the only female member on the team.

"Glad to see you again," Alex said to her as they settled in for a preliminary meeting. "Looks like this hurricane might be a harsh one; it's a big storm already and gaining momentum."

"Yes. Hurricane Isadora." Samantha studied data coming in to them from the station. "The tracking shows Nassau and the Bahamas may get hit before it plows through the Atlantic toward our area."

"Winds are 130 miles an hour already."

A little later after another station briefing, Alex said, "You wanna go into Southport to pick up supplies with me and maybe get some dinner? We won't see any action here for a couple of days. Art and Tony are staying here to keep in touch with the station; the other guys are going to the Fish House on West Beach Drive to eat."

"Yeah, I'll go with you. It sounds good."

As Alex drove into Southport a short time later, he said, "You want me to drop you downtown to poke around in the girly shops while I run up the road to the Walmart to pick up supplies?" A married man, Alex understood some of the differences in men and women's interests a little more readily than the other men in the crew. "I'll need an hour or two to get everything and I might need to run by another shop if they don't have all we need."

"That sounds great, Alex. I remember a couple of cute stores I liked from a few years ago when we hunkered down in this area."

Alex glanced at his watch. "I want to eat at the Provision Company on the waterfront on Yacht Basin Drive. They have some of the best seafood in town. I'll meet you there at five. If I get to the restaurant a little early I'll hang out in the bar. Look for me there if you don't see me outside."

"Sure," she said, as he headed into downtown to drop her off.

She poked around in several local shops after Alex left, listening to the locals talk about the weather, stopping at one point to see what the area weather station was projecting. Southport, set back from the coastline, wouldn't get the impact the islands would get if the storm hit here directly, but they could get winds, power outs, and flooding. Already, people were worried, and she heard tourists making plans to head home early from their vacations.

Back working in the field now, she felt much the same as always but oddly different, too. She couldn't put her finger on the change in herself. It didn't feel painful like the break-ups with boyfriends she'd known in the past, sniffley, whiney times. But she felt oddly incomplete. Off in some way.

Inside a small arts and crafts gallery, Samantha found a local potter working at a wheel in the back of the store and she stopped to watch.

The woman had white hair pulled up in a bun. She glanced up at Samantha for a minute. "I'm pulling up the wall of this piece right now," she said. "Applying a little pressure with my fingers, adding water as I do. But it's important not to push your fingers too tightly inward as you pull the walls up." She smiled at Samantha as she paused for a moment. "Are you a potter?"

"No, ma'am, I'm a meteorologist here covering the storm moving in."

"Ah, Hurricane Isadora. The reports say she may be a big one." The woman looked up briefly from her work. "I'm Emily Brighton. And you?"

"Samantha King, Weather First."

"Pleased to meet you."

Samantha nodded. "Do you live here? Will you evacuate if the storm moves closer, gets more intense?" It always interested Samantha to learn who moved out quickly and who stayed, not heeding good advice to leave.

"I live inland in Charlotte. I'm only here as a visiting artist for a few days. I'll be heading home in the morning, long before Isadora pays a visit—if she does. This gallery sells my work." She gestured toward a shelf display of colorful, glazed and finished pieces.

"Your work is beautiful." Samantha moved closer to examine the pottery.

"As you can see I'm especially fond of bowls of all sizes. It seems like you can always use a pretty bowl for something in your home."

Samantha picked up a small, round, shiny one glazed in a deep cobalt blue.

"You like that one?"

"Yes, I do." Samantha glanced back toward Emily Brighton, watching her press down on the clay on her wheel, adding more water as she did. The wet clay changed shape as Samantha watched.

"It's amazing to think that round shape, so soft and wet, will become a bowl like this."

"It's more amazing to me that it started out as a hard lump of clay." She pointed to a stiff block of clay nearby. "The original hard piece is worked with water and with the hands of the potter into a chosen shape, fired, then glazed, and fired again until it becomes what the potter has envisioned."

"I think I remember a scripture that sounds like that," Samantha said without thinking.

Emily gave her a sweet smile. "Yes. 'Arise and go down to the potter's house…where you will find the Lord making something on the wheel…as it pleases Him, the master potter, to make.' That's in Jeremiah 18, my paraphrasing. It is one of my favorite scriptures. Do you know the Lord?"

"Yes, I do." It really felt good to say those words and to know that she did.

"I believe God has purpose and plan for each of us, that He is the master creator."

"Do you think God changes his mind in His plan for us?"

"No. But it's just a process, like we've been talking about."

Samantha turned the blue bowl in her hands. "I feel like I'm in an odd time, where I thought I was completed, looked complete, felt complete like this bowl and then suddenly I find myself uncomfortable with my shape, wondering if I shouldn't be something different."

"Remember God is always working and remaking. Taking us to a higher calling and a higher purpose. We will always be His workmanship but our end is not stagnant like this bowl." She laughed a little. "I was a corporate attorney earlier in life. A very successful attorney and a good one. Then along the way the nudging of God took me on an entirely new road."

"Did you find that transition easy?"

"Oh, my goodness no, not at first. It took me a little time to decide to surrender my neat little agenda in life to move into the new way God had in mind. But in odd ways I saw, too, how God had prepared me for this work through the work I did before. Not that it's easy to see the links, but God knew what He was doing. I've always liked shaping and controlling and even performing. Seeing things set right. Put in order." She smiled.

"Has it proved a happy change for you?"

"In more ways than I could ever have expected. I could share much more about that, but the important thing is to always trust that whatever way God is leading will work out best."

Another family walked up then to watch Emily work and

Samantha stepped back to let them talk to her. She browsed around the store for a few more minutes and then bought the blue bowl before she left.

Sitting at dinner later with Alex, looking out over the waterfront behind the restaurant, Samantha looked up to find Alex studying her. "You seem different, Samantha."

She tried to send back one of her saucy replies. "Different good or different bad?"

"Different good, I think." He paused. "Don't get mad and kick me under the table. But you seem softer, deeper, more womanly."

She laughed. "Was I manly before?"

"Ah, come on. You know that you turned eyes as you walked in the door tonight. I'm talking about something inward that slips out every now and then. Something I haven't seen before in you."

"Maybe it was that near death experience I faced at Mexico Beach." She cut into the fish she'd ordered.

"We face those experiences all the time. I've nearly been taken out several times."

Curious, Samantha asked, "How does your wife feel about that?"

"I'm sure it scares the crap out of her." He looked down at his seafood platter. "I'm thinking about moving into a more indoor position in storm coverage in the year to come. I haven't told anyone, though, so keep that tidbit of knowledge to yourself for now. Will you?"

"I will."

"Frankly I'd like to see a little more of my kids."

"You have two, don't you?"

"Two girls and a boy on the way." He grinned. "Rita has carried a lot of responsibility keeping the home front going on her own so much. The main reason it's worked is because she knows how much I love my job and because her family all live close around."

"Does she work?"

"She might like to, later. She was a teacher before we met and a good one. When the kids grow older I think she'll want to teach again." He studied Samantha for a moment again. "What about you? Don't you ever think about or want a family life?"

She smiled at him. "I'll let you know if I make any decision about that in the future."

He held up his glass to her. "Well, let me know if you do and invite me to the wedding."

Back on the island, she had a lot to think about from her day. But the old excitement and adrenalin bubbled within as word from the station showed the hurricane strengthening and now projected to hit the North Carolina coast. Tomorrow they'd start broadcasting and the next days after would be hectic ones.

CHAPTER 24

The weeks after Samantha left moved onward, as life always does. The stomach virus Rebecca caught swept through the family, keeping Ford busy with upset, sick children for more than a week. He cancelled their planned camping weekend to Elkmont in August because of it, but managed to reschedule the trip for the Labor Day weekend, thanks to a last minute cancellation at the campground.

He wanted to continue enjoying good times as much as possible with the children to offset their distress and hurt over Samantha leaving. They missed her just as he did. He knew they felt disappointed with him that he didn't find a way somehow to make Samantha stay. Children always expected that the adults in their lives could fix everything. He had heard his share of comments along that line over the last weeks.

Now, the children's minds were diverted for a weekend, at least, enjoying the out-of-doors camping. He'd closed the clinic for the whole Labor Day weekend, giving Dwayne and Maria a chance for time with their families, too. Any emergencies could go to the University of Tennessee clinic not far away and they'd left a message on their answering machine with that information.

Closing early on Friday, Ford and the children traveled to Elkmont to set up camp near the back end of the campground on the Little River and, fortunately, also near the restroom area. After setting up the tents, securing the camper, and unloading chairs and supplies, Ford led all the kids up the quiet road behind the campground to

Meigs Mountain Trail for a hike.

"Who lived in these cabins before?" Wesley asked. "And how come they're falling apart now? They look awful."

"They look sad," Rebecca said, slowing to study one, crumbling and derelict, its roof falling in.

Natalie frowned. "I read about Elkmont and I think its stupid how the park took back the houses and then let them all die like this."

Gareth looked around. "Man, they could have made money renting these. People would pay to stay here."

Ford tried not to laugh at Gareth's profit-oriented comment. "You do have a point Gareth," he admitted. "I think it's sort of an unfortunate story, too, what happened here." They walked along in a cluster on the old road, stopping every once in a while to look at the ramshackle ruins of another house that had once been a charming vacation home.

"What really happened here Dad?" Clay asked.

"You know the first settlers arrived in the mid 1800s and established farms and built cabins in this area. They called it the Little River community. Early families were Ownbys, Trenthams, and others. Life stayed simple here—although often harsh—until the early twentieth century when big logging companies moved into the area, bringing a railroad line, and changing the picture of Elkmont."

"That's when all these homes were built for the wealthy loggers' families for summer homes and for other rich people that started to discover the mountains," Madison put in.

"That's right. All these homes were built then, plus the Appalachian Clubhouse and the Wonderland Hotel. A whole resort community grew up. Then later as the national park came— established in 1934—the government took all this land, buying it through their power of eminent domain. However, they let the old owners continue to lease the homes for a long time after. When the leases expired, the plan was to remove the buildings and let the land return to wilderness."

"So how come these houses are still here?" Gareth asked.

Ford shrugged. "I suppose the park just never got around to removing the buildings and so, unoccupied, they began to run down."

"They look gross," Tamela added.

"And really sad," Rebecca repeated.

"Are they still going to take them all down?" Andrew asked. "It looks like they're fixing some up now. Why is that?"

"Well, in an odd twist, to my way of thinking, a group of these buildings, even in their rundown state, were determined eligible for the National Register of Historic Places for historic value. The next year the whole of Elkmont was put on the National Register as an important historic district," Ford explained. "Perhaps kind of in a spot now, with attention drawn to the history and significance of the area, the park decided to restore some of the cabins."

"How many?" Andrew asked.

"About eighteen, I think. Some buildings are already finished. When we hike the Little River Trail tomorrow, we'll stop by to look at the Spence Cabin that's been restored."

Gareth wrinkled his nose. "That doesn't make sense. So now the park is spending gabillions of dollars to fix up stuff they let run down. I bet they probably feel really dumb now for how they didn't save this whole place."

"Maybe." Ford smirked at Gareth's candor.

"Well, I guess we can be glad they're saving some of the homes," Natalie said. "But it's sad to think all these others will be lost. You can tell they were really pretty once."

After a half-mile up the road, they turned right at the trail sign for the Meigs Mountain Trail. The trail dropped steeply downhill at first to cross a long footbridge over Jakes Creek then wound gradually uphill on a narrower pathway. When hiking single file Ford always put the smallest children in the middle of their hiking line, the older ones at the end.

They talked as they walked. With young children and short legs they never hiked fast and they always stopped to look at trees, plants, insects, remnants of old settlers' homes, and stone foundations along the way. The kids liked rock hopping over the creeks and they chatted happily until they came to their destination, the King Branch Campsite, at 1.6 miles. It was a long enough hike for the kids this afternoon at just over three miles roundtrip. When they got back to camp they'd be ready for dinner, and Juanita had graciously made fried chicken, potato salad, and slaw for their supper tonight, plus one of her marble-swirl cakes, a favorite of the kids.

Coming back, they cut through a side path into the campground to reach their site again. As they drew closer Ford, to his shock, saw Samantha sitting in one of their outdoor chairs, her feet propped up casually on the bench of a picnic table. He almost stumbled at the sight at first, wondering if his mind had conjured up the picture for him.

But then the kids hollered, "Samantha!" and started running toward her, thrilled and excited to see her.

She stood up as they arrived, hugging each one of them as they launched themselves at her, laughing and smiling. Ford stopped to watch the sight, his heart overwhelmed. How could the mere sight of someone impact a man like this, causing him to fight himself not to race forward, too, to sweep her into his arms? Wanting so much to touch her.

He walked forward at last after the hugging session eased, holding out his hand to her. "It's a good surprise to see you," he said.

She shook her head at him, grinning. "Well, I can tell you flat out, a handshake isn't good enough, Ford McDaniel." She wrapped her arms around him to hug him, nestling her lips against his neck and then kissing him on the cheek.

He struggled to keep restraint, to not hug her back.

She pulled back to look at him with dancing eyes. "Don't you know you should always hug old friends when you see them?"

Ford tucked his hands in his pockets to keep them to himself.

"What are you doing here?" Wesley asked with typical candor. "And how did you find us?"

"Did you drive all the way from Atlanta?" Madison asked.

Samantha held up a hand to stop the questions. "I just got back from covering a big storm. I had the weekend off, and decided to drive up to see you. I told you I'd try to come more often when I could." She grinned at Madison. "You texted and told me where you were camping this weekend, too. Remember?"

Tamela's eyes grew wide. "Are you staying all weekend?"

"I am. I have to be back at work on Monday morning but I'm off through Sunday, so I thought I might stay a couple of nights if I'm invited to do so. I brought my own sleeping bag." She winked at Ford over the words.

"You can have our tent, Aunt Samantha," Wesley offered. "Me and Gareth can sleep with Clay and Andrew."

"No need for that," Ford put in. "Our extra tent is stored under the camper. Samantha can sleep inside the camper with Rebecca and Tamela, like she did before. I'll sleep out in the tent."

"Yeah!" Tamela yelled, Rebecca joining the chorus.

"We'll help you put the tent up, Dad," Clay offered. "Andrew and I can almost do it by ourselves now."

"That sounds good." Ford tried to settle his heartbeat, still hammering in his chest. "We'd be glad for you to stay, Samantha."

"Good. I'll get my stuff out of the car." As she walked by him, she looked up at him with dancing eyes. "Aren't you glad to see me, Ford?"

He clenched his fist to keep from grabbing her arm. "Don't tease me, Samantha. Even in front of eight children I'm hanging on the edge here."

She leaned a little closer, putting a hand on his chest. "Well, that's good to hear." Her voice softened. "I'm glad I'm not the only one."

She walked off, leaving Ford with a strong desire to dunk himself in the cold mountain creek by their campsite. "Get a grip, Ford," he mumbled under his breath as he headed to pull the tent out from under the camper and to set it up, glad for a new focus.

At nearly five o'clock now, the kids, hungry after their hike, started clamoring to eat, so the next hour was full with setting up the tent and getting dinner out. They ate around two picnic tables pushed together to accommodate their large group. And over dinner the children pummeled Samantha with questions about the hurricane she'd recently covered on the coast.

"We watched you on TV," Rebecca told her. "It looked scary with the wind blowing things around and those waves so big."

She smiled at Rebecca. "We were lucky the storm dissipated before it hit land. It earlier targeted the Southport to Wilmington area for a time but then, as hurricanes often do, it slipped north and pounded the Outer Banks. The eye hit a less populated area near Cedar Island and then rolled inward across the Pamlico Sound, plowing through areas near Swanquarter, doing some wind and flood damage there. It could have been much worse though."

"We looked up on the Internet where you were sent," Madison put in. "For a long time your station said the hurricane might hit right there."

"That's right, but this time my team ended up way south of where the worst of Isadora hit."

"I'm glad," Tamela said. "We didn't want you to get hurt again."

"That seldom happens, but thanks, sweetheart."

Natalie leaned forward. "We saw you on television, too, when that lady interviewed you after the storm passed," she said. "A reporter, I think."

Samantha nodded. "Yes, a reporter from the newspaper. She asked me how it felt to be back out in the field, if I'd missed the rush and excitement of storm coverage." She paused. "Did all of you see that little interview?"

She looked directly at Ford as she asked the question, watching his face. He tried to keep his expression neutral. Not easy, since he'd remembered that scene and her comments over and over in his mind this week. What had she said? He replayed the scene again in his mind, trying to recall the exact words.

Pushing a microphone toward Samantha, the reporter had asked, "Have you missed the rush and excitement of storm coverage?"

"Covering storms like this can definitely give you a rush," she'd answered, flashing a smile and turning toward the camera, "but many everyday experiences can be just as sizzling and exciting as standing in the face of a hurricane." She'd paused. "Just now I'm thinking of someone who taught me exactly that." Then she'd grinned and winked before walking off camera, leaving Ford sitting at home wondering if she could possibly mean him. Of course, those words could have meant anything. He knew that.

"I seem to recall you said something about everyday scenes also being exciting," Ford said, trying to sound casual.

"Yes, I think I did." She gave him a catbird smile, not saying more, and he wanted to shake her.

Ford never found a minute alone with Samantha during, or after dinner. The children, all so glad to see her, kept shooting her an ongoing barrage of questions and filling her in on their lives. All of them wanted to tell her about school, their new classes, and teachers, funny happenings, sports and activities they'd gotten involved in. As always, she sat rapt through their stories, genuinely interested in every little piece of their lives. Laughing at their silly jokes and tales. Acting amazed over everyday progress and accomplishments and especially over anything they'd learned.

"Always remember that being smart is the best thing you can be," she'd pop in when they were talking about school. Or if they were sharing about something at church, she'd say, "If you learn more about God and get close to Him, He will always help you find your way." She was always so positive and encouraging.

Ford took a back seat in the conversations of the evening, just enjoying watching her, soaking in the look and feel of her, listening to her deep throaty voice, her rich, easy laugh.

"What are you thinking?" she said to him quietly at one point as she walked by him after getting a cold drink from the cooler.

He looked up at her, letting his eyes roam over her face and hair. "I'm simply thinking how glad I am that you're here," he replied honestly.

"Me, too," she said, winking at him before she sat back down.

"Does anybody have any more news?" she asked after sitting down again. When the children didn't immediately reply, she said,

"Well, I have some news to share." She smiled around at them.

"What?" Wesley asked.

"I've had a new job offer."

Andrew leaned forward. "Are you going to chase storms with another TV channel?"

"No. I'm thinking of being a forecaster again. It's hard traveling and being on the road all the time." She smiled. "Sometimes, like Rebecca said, it's scary, too."

"So has Weather First offered you a forecaster job again?" Natalie asked.

"They might if I wanted one, but the offer I received is with a television station called WKSE. Do you know where that is?"

Ford dumped his cola over hearing the call letters.

Madison's mouth dropped open. "Oh my gosh, Aunt Samantha, that's the Knoxville news and weather station we watch all the time. Did you get an offer near us in Tennessee?"

"I did."

"Are you going to take it?" Wesley asked, pumping a hand in the air. "If you do, we could see you lots!"

"I thought of that," she said crossing a leg and leaning back in her chair. "But I thought I might need a little incentive to say yes. Something to sweeten the offer, to make it hard to say no to."

"Like more money?" Gareth asked.

"No. The pay is good for a weather anchor, although perhaps not as good as the money I make now. But good and more than adequate, Gareth."

Gareth wrinkled his brow. "Then what kind of incentive do you want?"

"Something more personal."

All the children sat looking around the campfire at each other, confused. Then several of their mouths dropped open, and they looked toward him and back to Samantha, their eyes widening.

"Are you talking about Daddy?" Natalie finally asked, saying what none of them had dared to.

"I bet that's it." Gareth almost shouted, leaning forward. "That's it, Dad. Go for it. What are you waiting for?"

Ford, sitting in a shocked stupor, looked across at Samantha. She sat there trying not to laugh, a twitch of a smile on her face.

He got up on wobbly legs somehow and walked over toward her, dropping to one knee in front of her. "Have you really received a job offer at WKSE in Knoxville as their news anchor?"

"I have. I got the call yesterday. I need to give them a definite answer by the first of the week."

"When did you interview for this job?"

She smiled at him. "Before I went back to Atlanta."

He closed his eyes. "Why didn't you tell me?"

"I didn't know if I'd get the offer and I wanted some time to be sure about some things."

Oblivious to the children, he asked, "Are you sure now?"

That smile twitched on her lips again. "Well, like I said, I could be easily persuaded with a little incentive."

He reached out to grab her hands then in front of a sea of wide eyes. "Samantha King, if this might be the right personal incentive, I'd like to say before you and these eight witnesses that I love you with all my heart, cherish having met you, respect and admire you, and would count myself the most blessed and fortunate of men if you might agree to marry me and spend your life with me and this astonished group of children. Could you possibly consider saying yes?"

"Yes, I could, and I definitely do say yes." She reached out to touch his face. "I think that was exactly the incentive I'd been hoping for."

Forgetting their audience, Ford pulled her to her feet and against him to kiss her, thrilled when she wrapped her arms around him to kiss him back.

"I think they've done this before," Gareth commented. "They look like they're pretty good at it."

"Yeah, we're working on it," Ford said, laughing and swinging Samantha around before kissing her soundly and more deeply once again.

"Gross," Wesley said after a minute. "This is like one of those mushy romance movies."

"Oh, hush," Natalie said on a sigh. "I think it's wonderful."

"Does this mean Samantha is going to be our mommy?" Rebecca asked.

"Yes, it does," Natalie answered; then she paused. "Daddy, do you want us to take a little walk or something for a while so you and Samantha can be private?"

Ford, looking around at the darkness deepening, pulled away from Samantha with reluctance. "No, we're good, Natalie. I just got caught off guard with Samantha's news."

Samantha, sitting down on a bench at the picnic table near them, pulled Ford to sit down beside her. Then she turned to the children. "Your dad has asked me to marry him, but I know marrying your dad is a package deal. Are you sure it would be all right with all of you children? I'll be a working mom, a different kind of mom than ones many of your friends have who stay home."

"Lots of our friends' moms work, Aunt Samantha. We don't mind if you work," Andrew said.

"No, and we've got Juanita, too," Clay added.

"She really likes you now," Madison said with a smirk.

"Yes, we are on better terms now," Samantha agreed, trying to hold back a laugh, her eyes twinkling.

"We all say yes to your question," Natalie put in. "A happy yes." She smiled around at her brothers and sisters, who added their enthusiastic agreement with more yeses, hoots, and excitement.

Tamela impulsively ran over to hug Samantha then. As if her gesture opened a floodgate, the other children jumped up, too, to hug both of them with noisy enthusiasm as if finally realizing what was happening.

"Our Daddy is getting married." Clay announced with big eyes. "That's way cool."

"So does that mean you're engaged now?" Andrew asked.

"Yes. Officially as of today." Ford smiled at Samantha.

Tamela scowled then. "Samantha doesn't have a ring."

"We'll have to work on that," Ford said, smiling. "And we'll need to do some other planning as well."

Samantha held up her left hand, studying it, and then looked at Ford with a grin. "You know, Ford, your mother Coralee still has your Grandmother McDaniel's lovely engagement ring. She was showing me, and the girls, some of her jewelry one day and commented she'd kept the ring, always liking it."

Madison's mouth dropped open. "You tried it on, too, and it fit perfect."

"I remember that. Pretty thing. It's stayed in my mind."

Natalie looked thoughtful. "Grandmother said that day she hoped if Daddy married again his wife might like it."

"I remember that, too," Samantha said, sending him another little smirk.

Ford had never thought of passing down a family engagement ring. "I can buy you a new ring, Samantha, whatever you'd love."

"Actually, I really liked that one," she replied, studying her hand again. "Coralee kept the matching wedding ring, too, and I thought maybe you could wear your grandfather's wedding ring. I know Coralee kept it. I remember your McDaniel grandparents well, Ford, and I envied their love and warmth for each other. It would be nice to honor that memory, to hopefully walk in their footsteps, continuing the resort."

"Well, we can talk about that more later," Ford said, liking the idea as he considered it and flattered Samantha thought of it.

"When are you going to get married?" Gareth asked, as all the children settled back down around the campfire.

"Ford and I haven't talked about it yet, but I have a plan."

Surprised again, but thrilled that she had been thinking so much abouit this, Ford squeezed her hand and said, "Let's hear it."

"I need to give two weeks notice to Weather First. Then my new job at WKSE starts the first Monday in October. I'll be busy settling in for the first month or two…"

Ford felt his spirits drop.

"So I thought we could get married before my new job starts.

Maybe in two weeks on Saturday."

He turned to her, shocked. "In two weeks?"

She gave him a sweet smile. "Is that a problem? Do you need more time to be sure?"

He shook his head, stunned. "No. It's just that most women want months and months to plan these things."

She shrugged. "Well, actually I only want something small, and I guarantee that my Aunt Dixie and Paulette can easily pull together a wedding at the Dandridge Inn in two weeks. That would be Saturday, September fourteenth." She smiled at him. "Could you get off the week after?"

"The week after?" Her question confused him.

"For a honeymoon." She leaned over to kiss him again. "I'm sure Wesley wouldn't want us to honeymoon around the house. Besides, I have the perfect place in mind."

"Where?" Madison asked, leaning forward.

Samantha turned to her. "I have tons and tons of frequent flier miles, so plane fare isn't a problem and while my team was on location one time in the Florida Keys I discovered this lovely private spot called Little Palm Island Resort. It has thatch roof bungalows and you can only get to the resort by plane or boat." She turned and smiled at Ford. "With our busy, public lives, I sort of like the idea of a quiet, delicious little getaway like that, don't you? It looks like Tahiti in the photos, quiet pools and private beaches, lovely food, roses scattered over the beds. What do you think?"

He almost swallowed his tongue at the visions in his mind. "It sounds beautiful. I think I can work something out. Dwayne can cover at the clinic and we can get a senior veterinary student to come over from the university to help. I'm sure Mother, Dad, and Juanita could manage the house for a week, too." He hesitated. "But are you sure two weeks wouldn't be too soon to get a wedding together?"

She looked at him smiling. "We need a bride and a groom. We've got that. We need a maid of honor and a best man. I'm sure Lucy and Ben will be excited to say yes to that.

She looked at the children then as if considering the idea. "I could use two junior bridesmaids. Natalie and Madison, do you two think you'd like to fill those positions?"

"Oh, yes ma'am," Madison said, eyes wide. Natalie nodded, too.

Seeing Rebecca's mouth starting to pout, she added, "And of course we'll need two junior flower girls. Maybe Rebecca and Tamela would like to do that?"

They all but clapped their hands with excitement.

Eyes wide, Rebecca said, "I've never ever been in a wedding."

"Well, we'll take care of that soon."

"I see no need to have ring bearers," she continued, "but I think four junior groomsmen would be nice to balance the four girls. Equal numbers make for lovely wedding pictures." She leaned toward the boys. "Do you boys think you could help out with that?"

"Sure," Clay said sitting up straight.

Wesley scowled. "Do we have to wear fancy suits?"

"I have a more casual idea about that you might like." She put a hand to her chin, thinking. "We need a pianist. Vicki can play the piano, and Aunt Dixie and Paulette have rolled the inn's piano out to the patio from the drawing room enough times before. We also need a minister. If the pastor of your church can't do the ceremony, Ford, I'm sure I could ask Dixie's pastor at the church I grew up in."

She spread her hands. "That's pretty much it, don't you think?"

"Well, yeah, I guess," Ford said, his mind whirling. "Except for wedding clothes and flowers and all that."

"Dixie and Paulette will take care of those things. And I already picked out clothes at a bridal shop and tuxedo store in Knoxville. Come look and see what you think." She got up to retrieve her purse and pulled out some photo copies.

"I knew we wouldn't have any WiFi here so I printed a few pictures to show you." She gestured to gather them all around her and then pointed to one of the photos. "I thought these nice charcoal gray suits perfect for the groom and best man. What do you think, Ford?"

He nodded.

She smiled at the boys. "I thought the boys could just wear charcoal gray slacks and vests. Will that work for you guys?"

"Cool red bow ties," Gareth said.

"Those are actually rose red, or what the website calls cerise, a perfect match to the two bridesmaid dresses." She showed them another photo of long, sweet deep rose-red dresses for the girls.

Natalie and Madison sighed audibly.

"Those are so pretty," Natalie said, putting a hand to her heart.

"The maid of honor's dress for Lucy is basically the same color." She looked at Rebecca and Tamela. "And of course flower girls wear white like the bride with flowers in their hair and flowers to toss out as they walk down the aisle. Don't you think these are pretty, Rebecca and Tamela?" She pointed to another picture.

"Oh, we'll look like princesses!" Tamela exclaimed.

While the children chattered with excitement, Ford looked at Samantha in amazement. "I can't believe you have all this planned out already."

"I hope you don't feel left out of the planning." She bit her lip.

"No. As long as you're happy, I am."

She took his hand and squeezed it. "I told you I just wanted something simple. Dixie and Paulette and your mother will take care of the rest, inviting close family and friends." She smiled a little wistfully then. "If I'm lucky my Dad will fly in to give me away, too."

Ford decided he would call her dad and push for that.

Samantha leaned against him. "You've done all this before, Ford, but this is my first time."

He ran a hand down her arm. "Everything you've picked looks beautiful. I'm sure everything will be lovely."

"Thanks." She bit her lip. "I didn't mean to take things over, Ford, but I wanted time for us to honeymoon and then two weeks back at home to settle in at the house before I head back to work." She blushed then, surprising him. "A lot of these things about being married you will need to teach me, since you're the expert there."

Not saying more with the children around, he winked at her instead. "I look forward to that, Samantha. Don't worry."

She wiggled her eyebrows at him. "We do seem to do well in that area, don't we?"

He laughed as she put the photo copies away.

With the children almost too excited to settle down, they all went for a walk in the dark around the Elkmont campground. They listened to the night sounds of cicadas and spotted lightning bugs flashing in the night.

"Lots of fireflies live in the Smokies, Aunt Samantha," Andrew told her. "In June, during the lightning bugs' mating season, you can come here and see the fireflies all flashing at the same time." He turned to Ford. "What's the big word for that?"

"It's synchronous fireflies," Ford answered. "I'm sure Samantha knows this is one of the few places in the world where the lightning bugs flash at the same time."

She grinned. "Yes, I've gotten to see that once in past. The males fly and flash their lights and the females, usually closer to the ground, answer with a flash back. It's a sight to see."

"It's hard to get a place to camp here when that happens now. But we came once when I was little," Andrew said. "A ranger gave a good talk about the fireflies, too."

Ford listened to their quiet talk, still hardly able to believe Samantha was coming back to live at Dandridge, taking a job he knew well below her current salary level and with less prestige. Would she be happy? Would she have regrets later? Would she wish she hadn't been lured to marry him when she settled into their day-to-day life, and had to deal with the first sweep of sickness to hit the kids?

"I can almost hear your worries," Samantha said, drawing him back a little from the children walking along and chattering. "Stop it. You hear? I gave this thought and prayer. I want to live my life with you. Stop questioning it. Be happy."

"I am happy, but still stunned."

"Life can have many happy changes in it. God is always working on us, recreating our lives for His purposes. A wise woman taught me that recently."

He ran a hand over her hair. "It just seems so unbelievable that you've come into my life, that I've been given a second chance for love and joy."

"Don't you think you deserve a second chance for joy?"

Ford leaned over to kiss her forehead. "Well, evidently I do. I'll try to make you happy, Samantha."

She paused, giving him a serious look then. "Happiness is from within, Ford. I am already a happy person but I expect to know more joy sharing life with you. Don't expect too much from yourself or from me; you can't make someone else happy." She frowned. "I've seen sorrows and disappointments when people marry expecting the person they marry to make them happy. So here's my advice: You simply continue being your best self, rising to your personal best, and you'll be happy. I expect to do exactly the same."

"That's good counsel. You're a wiser woman than I once thought."

"You just wait, honey," she said. "We storm chasers are full of surprises. You better get ready for a fun ride."

Her laughter rolled over him softly, and the wonder of finding this incredible, vivacious woman rolled over him once again.

EIGHT AT THE LAKE

Lin Stepp

About This Guide

The questions on the following pages are included
to enhance your group's reading of
Lin Stepp's *Eight At The Lake*

DISCUSSION QUESTIONS

1. This book begins in the midst of Hurricane Michael, an actual hurricane that hit Mexico Beach, Florida, in October of 2018. It was an unprecedented Category 5 hurricane in the Panhandle region and caused catastrophic damage. Do you remember reading or hearing about that storm on the news? Do you know anyone who was impacted by that severe hurricane or have you ever been in a hurricane yourself?

2. What job does Samantha King have as the book begins? What was she doing at Mexico Beach, Florida? What happens to her as the hurricane hits? What were her injuries? When she wakes from a nightmare remembering the hurricane, where is she? Why is she at her Aunt Dixie's inn at this time? How does she feel about being forced to take a break for her health to strengthen?

3. Dixie, Samantha King's aunt, owns the historic Dandridge Inn in the small town of Dandridge, Tennessee, on Douglas Lake. Have you ever been to Dandridge? What do you remember about it? What did you learn about Aunt Dixie's inn and its history? What part did Dixie, and the inn, play in Samantha's life growing up? When did Samantha and her sister Andrea come to live with Aunt Dixie and why? What did you learn about Samantha's sister Andrea and her family? And about Aunt Dixie's husband Jackson?

4. Knowing that Samantha will be staying for a time in Dandridge to recuperate, Aunt Dixie encourages her to spend time with her sister Andrea's children to get to know them better. How does Samantha first react to that idea and how did Dixie respond? What do you learn about the children and about Aunt Dixie's role

in their lives? How many children did Andrea and her husband Adam Bradley have?

5. Samantha's nieces and nephews, Madison, Andrew, Wesley, and Tamela Bradley, all live with Ford McDaniel, a local Dandridge veterinarian and part owner of the Sycamore Lake Resort. How did Ford and his wife Laura end up taking in Andrea and Adam's children? How many children did they have of their own at that time? What do you remember about the McDaniel children, Natalie, Clay, Gareth, and Rebecca? What happened to Ford's wife Laura three years after taking in the Bradley children? How has Ford managed in this difficult situation, as a working parent with eight children?

6. How did Juanita Helton become a needed help to Ford after he lost his wife? How does Juanita act toward Samantha when they first meet? Why does she act this way? Did you think Juanita's views about Samantha were justified? Does their relationship improve over time? What event much later in the book turns the tide, at least somewhat, in Juanita and Samantha's relationship?

7. In the early chapters of the book, what do you learn about Ford's veterinary clinic, his associates, and the Sycamore Lake Resort where he, the children, and his parents live? What do you think of Ford? Is he the kind of vet you'd like to take your pet to? As you see him interacting with the children later, do you think he's a good parent? How do Ford and Samantha meet in the book? Why does Samantha come to Ford's veterinary clinic, mad and upset? Does Ford recognize her? When had he last seen Samantha? Why has Ford felt somewhat resentful toward Samantha over the years?

8. Even though Ford and Juanita, and even Ford's parents, Burl and Coralee McDaniel, have mixed views about Samantha, all

the children seem to take to her and like her right away. Why do you think that is? What characteristics does Samantha have that attract the children?

9. Who is Lucy Newberry Howard? How long have she and Samantha been friends and where does Lucy live now? What is her business called in downtown Dandridge? What do you learn about their friendship as they visit and catch up? What does Lucy tell Samantha about her niece Madison that troubles her? How does Samantha get involved later with this situation between Madison and Michael Denby? Did you think she handled the situation well when Madison went missing?

10. On the way back from her visit with Lucy, Samantha also runs into another old friend Paulette Everett. How does Samantha know Paulette? What has happened between Paulette and her husband Jimmy? How does Paulette later play into an ongoing series of criminal mysteries going on in Dandridge, related to the Sycamore Lake Resort?

11. Early in the book, when Juanita's mother has an accident, leaving Ford in the lurch for someone to take care of the kids and his home, what does Samantha offer? Why does Ford hesitate to say yes? What new feelings are going on at this point between Ford and Samantha? Dwayne, who works with Ford, is one of the first to notice Ford's interest but others soon notice, including Samantha. When does this new "interest" between Samantha and Ford first erupt into a romantic scene? What part does one of Ford's signs *What Happens at the Lake Stays at the Lake* play into this scene? How did one of Ford's signs also inspire the book's title?

12. Friends are a blessing in many ways. Vickie and Ben Larsen are two of Ford's best friends, and Vickie becomes a good friend

to Samantha. What does Vickie share about her life and her faith that makes Samantha think more about her own faith? What does Vickie also tell her about Ford's faith? Do you think Ford's faith helped him with the problems and losses he faced in his life? Do you think a strong, rich faith can change how a person sees their life and lives it?

13. As Samantha gets to know the children and begins to build love and affection toward them, you—as a reader—probably do, too. What are some of the memories you have about the individual children and their characteristics? How are they different and unique? Which child do you remember most fondly? What system has Ford used with the children that helps with the challenges of raising eight children? Do you like how he handles problems with them? Have you ever used any of his child-rearing rules in your family?

14. About midway through the book, Ford's father pounds on Ford's door one afternoon to to tell him one of their employees, Maury Beck, has found a dead woman in one of their resort cabins. What happened to her? How do Ford's dogs Gracie and Jefferson get involved in another murder scene at the resort? What happened to Jefferson in that situation? Even after two murders, the police still can't seem to find any leads, leaving everyone anxious over the situation. When Paulette Everett calls Dixie and Samantha, worried someone might be hanging around the event lodge where she's setting up for a party, what does Samantha do? When she gets to the lodge, what does she find and what action does she take? Later, what do you learn is the link between the murdered women?

15. Samantha's work as a weather chaser has trained her to act quickly in emergency situations. How does Samantha's quick thinking later in the book help to save Ford's father Burl in a

storm? How, also, do Samantha's quick actions save Juanita's grandson from drowning at the lake? Do you admire this attribute in her? In what ways was Samantha even somewhat impulsive in romantic situations? Would you describe yourself as more impulsive or cautious in nature? How can both attributes be good?

16. A favorite pastime for Ford and the children is camping. Ford invites Samantha to go camping with them to the Cosby Campground. Have you ever been camping and do you and your family still like to camp? How does Samantha help to entertain the children on that trip? Spending so much time together brings Ford and Samantha's feelings for each other more to the forefront. What happens? Why does Ford tell Samantha that despite his attraction for her, that he will work hard not to let their relationship develop further?

17. As Samantha finds her own feelings for Ford deepening, she finds herself in a dilemma between her work and her draw to Ford. Why is this especially a problem and a challenge for her? What scene with her own father, Robert King, helps her emotionally to see her way clearer? How does an old friend, Matt Glenn, at the University of Tennessee, also help her with this problem by opening a possible door for another position later? Why does Samantha not tell anyone she is even considering a change even when the possibility of a new job is there? Back on the job with Weather First later, preparing to cover an incoming storm, how does yet another friend and associate, and a potter she meets in a shop in Southport, North Carolina, help Samantha see what she really needs to do?

18. Ford is devastated when Samantha returns to work. With her, he'd gotten a taste of love and happiness again, only to experience another loss. The children are grieving, too. When

he takes them camping at Elkmont as a good diversion for them all, who shows up unexpectedly? How do Ford and the children react? When Samantha shares her news about a possible job she might take nearby – and that she's hoping for an incentive to say yes – who first picks up on what she's hinting at? Then what does Ford do and what happens afterward?

About The Author
Lin Stepp

Lin Stepp is a native Tennessean, businesswoman and educator. A *New York Times, USA Today, Publishers Weekly,* and Amazon best-selling international author, Lin has twenty published novels out now, including her twelve beloved Smoky Mountain novels, all set in different Tennessee and North Carolina locations, three Mountain Home books, a novella in one of Kensington's Christmas anthologies, and four South Carolina coastal novels, including her three Edisto Trilogy books and her first release in the new Lighthouse Sisters series.

Lin and her husband J.L. also write regional guidebooks, including a published Smoky Mountain hiking guide and a TN and a SC state parks guidebook, all filled with hundreds of color photos. Writing and adventuring are her joys and more novels set in the Smokies and at the beach are on the way, as well as more colorful regional guidebooks. Lin's title *Claire At Edisto* was the *2019 Best Book Award Winner in Fiction: Romance*, sponsored by American Book Fest and her novel *Welcome Back* a finalist in the 2017 Selah Awards. Lin enjoys speaking for events, festivals, libraries, and book clubs. And she loves reading, hiking, exploring out of doors, and keeping up with her readers. Look for her pages on Facebook and Twitter and follow her monthly blog and newsletter, too, that you will find on her website at: *www.linstepp.com.*

www.ingramcontent.com/pod-product-compliance
Lightning Source LLC
Chambersburg PA
CBHW051217130726
47988CB00001B/125